The
LATECOMER

Also by Jean Hanff Korelitz

The Plot

The Devil and Webster

You Should Have Known

Admission

The White Rose

The Sabbathday River

A Jury of Her Peers

MIDDLE GRADE FICTION

Interference Powder

DRAMA

The Dead, 1904 (with Paul Muldoon)

POETRY

The Properties of Breath

The LATECOMER

Jean Hanff Korelitz

This is a work of fiction. All of the characters, organizations, and events portrayed in this novel are either products of the author's imagination or are used fictitiously.

Printed in the United States of America. For information, address Celadon Books, a Division of Macmillan Publishers, 120 Broadway, New York, NY 10271.

www.celadonbooks.com

Library of Congress Cataloging-in-Publication Data

Names: Korelitz, Jean Hanff, 1961– author.
Title: The latecomer / Jean Hanff Korelitz.
Description: First U.S. Edition. | New York : Celadon Books, 2022.
Identifiers: LCCN 2021059413 | ISBN 9781250790798 (hardcover) | ISBN 9781250865571 (international) | ISBN 9781250790774 (ebook)
Classification: LCC PS3561.O6568 L38 2022 | DDC 813/.54—dc23
LC record available at https://lccn.loc.gov/2021059413

Our books may be purchased in bulk for promotional, educational, or business use. Please contact your local bookseller or the Macmillan Corporate and Premium Sales Department at 800-221-7945, extension 5442, or by email at MacmillanSpecialMarkets@macmillan.com.

First U.S. Edition: 2022
First International Edition: 2022

10 9 8 7 6 5 4 3 2 1

For Leslie Vought Kuenne,
in memoriam

I caught him with an unseen hook and an invisible line which is long enough to let him wander to the ends of the world and still bring him back with a twitch upon the thread.

—C. K. Chesterton, via Evelyn Waugh

Foreword

The Oppenheimer triplets—who were thought of by not a single person who knew them as "the Oppenheimer triplets"—had been in full flight from one another as far back as their ancestral petri dish. Not one of the three—Harrison (the smart one), Lewyn (the weird one), or Sally (the girl)—had a speck of genuine affection for either of the others, or had ever once thought of a sister or a brother with anything resembling a sibling bond, let alone as counterparts in a tender and eternal family relationship.

And this despite the years of all-consuming effort from at least one of their parents, to say nothing of the staggering advantages they had enjoyed, beginning with the not-inconsiderable price tag of their making! No, a lingering discontent overhung each of those three, and had since they were old enough to glean their shared origin story, judge their parents, and basically make up their minds about the other two. For eighteen years they'd been together, from that petri dish to their crowded maternal womb to their shared home on the Brooklyn Esplanade (and their shared summer cottage—not really a cottage—on the Vineyard) and their shared education (or indoctrination, in

Harrison's view) at the lauded Walden School of Brooklyn Heights, where a frankly socialist ethos stood in bald contrast to soaring tuition . . . and at no point did they ever grow closer, not even slightly, not even out of pity for their mother, who had wanted that so badly.

And then they were eighteen, and not just leaving home but desperate to begin three permanently separate adult lives, which is exactly what would have happened if the Oppenheimer family hadn't taken a turn for the strange and quite possibly unprecedented. But it did—we did—and that has made all the difference.

PART ONE

The Parents

1972–2001

Chapter One

The Horror of It All

In which Salo Oppenheimer meets a rock in the road

Mom had a way of obfuscating when anyone asked how she and our father first met. Mainly she said it was at a wedding in Oak Bluffs, to which she'd been brought as a date by the closeted brother of the groom, and there was her future husband, an usher for one of his fraternity brothers. Both factoids were perfectly true, though the broader assertion was also utterly false. Our parents had met once before, under frankly terrible circumstances, and this is why we all, eventually, understood how impossible it was for her to be truthful. It's supposed to be a happy question—*Where did you two meet?*—with a happy answer, opening out to a lifetime of companionship, consequence, and progeny (in our case, lots of progeny). But when that moment dovetails with the very worst event in a young person's life? Who wouldn't wish to spare him, and the person innocently asking the question, and, as it happened, our mother herself? The shock. The glare of disapproval. The horror of it all.

The bald fact was that our parents met in central New Jersey, in a conservative synagogue that looked like a brutalist government building somewhere in the Eastern Bloc. The synagogue was Beth Jacob of Hamilton Township, and the terrible occasion was the funeral of a nineteen-year-old girl named Mandy Bernstein, who had died four days earlier in a car driven by her boyfriend, our father, Salo Oppenheimer. Mandy was, by every account, a vibrant young person with a glowing white smile and long dark hair, the eldest child and pride of her family (the Bernsteins of Lawrenceville, New Jersey, and Newton, Massachusetts), a Cornell sophomore and likely psychology major, and (as far as she herself was concerned) the joyfully intended future life partner of Salo Oppenheimer. Mandy Bernstein was one of two Cornell students who'd perished in the accident, the other being Salo's friend and fraternity brother, Daniel Abraham, a kind boy who was on a first or possibly second date with the other person in the back seat. That person was still hospitalized in Ithaca. Salo alone had walked away from the wreck.

Even then, nobody blamed him. Nobody! Even in those early days, in the grief and rage of the Abraham and Bernstein families and the many friends of the two young people who were suddenly, horribly, not there, it was somehow held by all present in the synagogue (and, the following week, at the E. Bernheim and Sons Funeral Chapel in Newark, New Jersey, where Daniel Abraham would be memorialized) that Salo Oppenheimer's brand-new Laredo had been traveling at an eminently reasonable speed down a perfectly respectable road when it hit a loose rock and—abruptly, incomprehensibly—*flipped,* landing on its roof, half on and half off the road. It was, in other words, at least in those houses of God, as if the *hand of God itself* had picked up that vehicle and dropped it back to earth. Who could explain the mystery? Who could make comprehensible the loss?

Not Salo, that was certain. He sat in the second row at his girlfriend's funeral service, four stitches in his scalp and an Ace bandage (not even a cast!) on his left wrist, out of his mind with shock and guilt, barely taking in the stream of Mandy's cousins and high school friends and the contingent of Bernsteins who'd made aliyah a few years earlier but were now, appallingly, here in Hamilton Township, weeping and looking at him but still: *not blaming* him. At least to Salo's face, everyone seemed to be blaming . . . the Jeep.

Why the Jeep? *Why, why,* the Jeep? He'd had his choice of cars, and in fact had been on the point of purchasing a sparkling gray 300-D from

Mercedes-Benz of Manhattan when his grandmother phoned his mother to say that it was a disgrace for any Jew to drive a Mercedes, and was Salo so removed from his own Jewishness, from the fact and fate of his own martyred ancestor Joseph Oppenheimer (Goebbels's own *Jud Süss!*) that he did not understand the company had used concentration camp labor to build armaments and airplane engines? In fact, the answer to that was: yes, as Salo's Jewishness was not particularly acute, either in the religious or, at the age of nineteen, all that much in the historical sense. Certainly he was well aware of the mythic Jud Süss—"court Jew" to the Duke of Wurttemberg in the 1730s, convicted of a bouquet of fictional crimes when his boss died suddenly, and executed, his corpse hung in a gibbet for six years outside of Stuttgart—but that all felt so very eighteenth century, and Salo was a young man fresh out of the 1960s, when the entire culture had coalesced around his own generation's youth and vigor and renunciation of the past. Besides, he'd really, really liked that Benz a lot, its sleek shape and leather seats, the vaguely European sophistication he'd felt sitting behind the wheel. After that phone call, though, it was a moot issue, and some instinct had sent him in the opposite direction: from the Nazi Mercedes-Benz company to that perfectly all-American anti-Semite Henry Ford.

Later, the instability of those 1970s Jeeps would become something of a cliché, but at that time the notion of a rugged, gritty 4x4 driving machine, suggestive of the Manifest Destiny frontier, was one of capability, not compromise. And if Salo Oppenheimer, in the market for his very first car, was willing to forgo the interior luxuries of, say, an uber-German automobile with a long company tradition of sophisticated design (alongside the slave labor), then surely it would only be for the enhanced ability to drive the wild roads surrounding Ithaca, his college town, even in its insane winter months. A Jeep for gorges and icy highways! A Jeep for the back roads of upstate New York! A Jeep for weekend jaunts with buddies and girlfriends, who didn't even, that fateful Saturday morning, have a precise destination in mind.

In the aftermath, he had no recollection of the rock in the road, or the sickening arc through the air, bright winter sun streaming directly into his eyes. His only impressions would be the shriek of crushing metal—that absurd sardine-tin roof, crumpling on impact—and the open-mouthed surprise of Mandy Bernstein, whose sweet, freckle-dusted nose he had thought adorable, instantly, the first time he saw her at a reception for new Jewish freshmen. Mandy was made of joy, perpetually on the verge of laughter, close to her parents and younger sisters back in New Jersey (if she wasn't in her room, she was likely in the phone booth down the corridor in Balch Hall, coaxing Lisa or Cynthia through some high school social maze or perceived parental injustice) and to her cousins in Newton, the mother ship of the Bernstein family. She liked to wear her hair in a high ponytail, sometimes with a red bandana wrapped around it (a fashion she'd picked up on a kibbutz she'd visited one summer during high school), and she rotated three pairs of well-loved bell bottoms that she was perpetually embroidering: butterflies, rainbows, a rendering of the family poodle, Poochkin, in lavender. By December of their freshman year they were "dating," which basically meant that Salo took her out to football games and walked her home to her dorm when the library closed. They sampled the brand-new and exotic Moosewood restaurant downtown for something called "tofu" and went for numerous Hot Truck runs on the way back to their North Campus dorms. Mandy was fond of the pizza subs.

He'd brought her home only once, when she was visiting the city to interview for a summer internship with UJA (an internship she would indeed be offered, in a letter that arrived one week after the accident). That introduction had gone well, despite the Bernsteins' obvious lack of Our Crowdliness (and despite the fact that Selda Oppenheimer plainly harbored hopes of a Sachs, a Schiff, or even a Warburg for her only son); Mandy was simply that delightful, that charming and powerfully kind, and that in love—pure, clear, and very obvious love—with Salo Oppenheimer. She loved his brain and his manners and his spindly body, tall and frail, devoid of musculature. She loved a goodness she saw in him, which Salo—quite honestly—had never pretended to see in himself. It was not precisely true that she made him wish to be a better man; it was more true that she made him *wish* he wished to be a better man. At the time, that felt like enough.

He hadn't asked her to marry him. They weren't engaged, though later he was deliberately vague on this issue, because he knew it would make a big difference to Mandy's parents; the distance between "She was a wonderful girl, someone any guy would have been lucky to date" and "She was the love of my life, and I was on the point of proposing to her" felt vast, and our father opted (correctly) to let her parents believe whatever might help them bear the pain. That awful winter and spring, and for the next several years, he let the Bernsteins enfold him into their grief as Mandy's intended: future fiancé, husband, and father of the children she would never have. Then he married Johanna Hirsch, their daughter's Lawrence High schoolmate, and all contact abruptly ceased.

Mandy Bernstein had been Johanna's Big Sister, not literally but within the local chapter of the B'nai B'rith Girls. This was a position she had taken seriously, leaving surprise gift baskets (bagels and cream cheese, chocolate-chip cookies) on the doorstep of the Hirsch home when she knew Johanna was studying for a test, and showing up to help out on Johanna's service projects, like the roadside car wash to benefit the Hebrew nursing home recreation fund or the friendship letters to children in Israel. The "Sisters" had all been randomly assigned, but Johanna was ecstatic to find she'd been paired with the popular and pretty Mandy Bernstein. *Mandy Bernstein!* A person she would not have dared solicit for friendship in the halls of their teeming New Jersey high school, where a year's difference in age meant everything, and perceived deficits in looks, wealth, and cool meant everything else.

Johanna was one of dozens of young women at the funeral that day, each and every one of them sincerely, personally in mourning. The identity of the young man with the bandaged wrist had been freely exchanged among them, and it would be fair to say that Salo Oppenheimer was the object of a certain romantic fascination. How must he feel? So young himself, and already responsible for the deaths of two others, just as young? How would he survive the loss of his own beloved Mandy, this glowing, clever (Ivy League!) girl, the jewel of her family, school, and town? Possibly, Johanna was not the only person in the jammed pews of Temple Beth Jacob wondering what kind of person it might ultimately take to draw this devastated Salo Oppenheimer from his eternal vortex of guilt and pain. Possibly she was not the only one imagining the great love and compassion necessary to bring Salo Oppenheimer back to life.

Our mother wasn't remarkable like Mandy Bernstein. She was an ordinary girl from a family so average and undistinguished that she cringed at their inadequacies and then again at her own disloyalty. Her father was an accountant who worked for the famous Lawrenceville boarding school, a job he'd taken so that Johanna's younger brother, our uncle Bobby, might possibly be granted admission (Lawrenceville was still several years away from coeducation, not that our grandfather had ever given a thought to opportunities, educational or otherwise, for his female children). Lawrenceville, and the opportunities it represented, were completely lost on our uncle Bobby, who was a committed anti-intellectual (which you could still be at Lawrenceville in the '70s) and pot dealer (which you could not be, at least not if you were caught, as Bobby certainly was). After a disastrous freshman year he would transfer to Lawrence High where his sisters were already in situ, and there he would add scores of new clients to his thriving business. (In the long run, our uncle's entrepreneurial instincts were by no means disadvantageous. By the early 1990s he was a real estate developer with a McMansion of his own in Point Pleasant. By then, he had retired from acquiring pot for other people, and one day would even—*wonder of wonders!*—send a child of his own to Lawrenceville.) Phil Hirsch, our grandfather, was certainly humiliated by the way things had turned out, but he still remained at the school until his retirement; his way, perhaps, of saving face.

As far as our mother was concerned, her parents had completely missed the true star of the Hirsch family, which was not Bobby and certainly not herself. Our aunt Debbie, the oldest of the three siblings, was very smart and also very ambitious, in the subdued manner of girls coming of age with the Second Wave in the '70s, all too aware of the fact that doors were opening and that she was going to be allowed—if not exactly *encouraged*—to walk through them. Debbie opted for a safe (though quietly roiling) Mount Holyoke for college, and afterward a retail training program at Macy's, chosen for no other reason than the fact that she still got a little trill of excitement from department stores. That trill wouldn't last long, not once she was spending her days unpacking boxes and checking inventory, but things clicked into place as she realized how many ideas she had about adjusting chains of command to streamline operations. Her supervisors, shockingly enough, were not interested in Debbie Hirsch's ideas, so she went to business school and eventually found somebody who was. By the time her younger sister Johanna was settling into married life and embarking on her fateful "fertility journey," Debbie Hirsch Krieger was a full partner in a consulting firm, living in a Classic Six at 1065 Park Avenue with her husband and boys, and summering in Bridgehampton.

Between the unacknowledged star that was Debbie and the perpetual fuckup that was their younger brother Bobby, our mother ducked through adolescence in a furtive attempt not to be noticed. Johanna was an average student, a volleyball team member who mainly sat and watched, and a non-mixer in either of the two cliques that dominated her high school (these were known as the *Beautifuls* and the *Weirdos*). She kept company with a half dozen or so girls from back in elementary school, was generally fearful around boys, and gave her parents not one reason to worry about (or otherwise pay attention to) her. When she was sixteen she joined B'nai B'rith Girls at the suggestion of her sister Debbie, who was about to leave home and who worried Johanna would simply disappear once she'd gone. That was when the wondrous Mandy Bernstein, not only a *Beautiful* but also a *twelfth grader,* had materialized to sprinkle her magic fairy dust over Johanna Hirsch. Months later, Mandy was gone, off to Cornell. A year after that she was gone for good.

"I'm very sorry," said Johanna to Salo Oppenheimer that day after the service had ended. She was one of perhaps forty young women to approach him and extend her hand and say these exact words, and there was no reason for him to remember her, and in fact he did not remember her, though that had less to do with Johanna's ordinariness than with the shrieking voice in our father's head all through the service and burial and reception. Afterward she went in one of the cars to the cemetery and watched Mandy's broken parents and sisters throw red clay on the coffin, and Salo Oppenheimer throw red clay on the coffin, and by the time she reached the open grave there was little left to throw. Afterward, Salo Oppenheimer had been taken away by a dowdy, dignified couple in a Lincoln Town Car, and Johanna would not see him again for several years, until the Rudnitsky wedding in Oak Bluffs.

By then, Johanna was a rising sophomore at Skidmore, not that her heart was in either her nominal major (sociology) or anything else of an educational nature. She also didn't like Saratoga, which was full of dancers and horse people in the summer and brutally cold the rest of the time, and the series of crushes she'd developed on boys at the college always ended in some variation of *It isn't you, it's me,* usually delivered over mugs of terrible beer in one of the town taverns. If you'd asked Johanna Hirsch what, in the whole wide world, she cared about, she'd have been hard-pressed to come up with anything, not even—or perhaps especially not—herself. Basically, she was drifting, as she had always drifted, once in the gully of her family and now in the gully of her college "experience." Until, suddenly, she wasn't.

It was one of those *It isn't you, it's me* young men who invited her to his brother's wedding on Martha's Vineyard. He did not explain that our mother's role would be that of a beard (perhaps he thought he didn't need to), but he did warn her that the likelihood of family meltdown over the course of the wedding weekend was high: his brother was marrying (and this was his parents' word, he insisted, not his) a *schwartze,* and his mother had been on the verge of hysteria all spring. (In other words, no, this would not be an opportune moment to turn up without an unobjectionable female date. In *other* other words, it would also not be the time to make any grand announcement about his own clarifying life choices.) Johanna was game. She had never been to the famous island where, a few years earlier, that ghastly accident had occurred with the young senator and his aide, and she was curious about the family of her nominal date, who would call a Black person a *schwartze,* and the brother who was brave enough (or perhaps antagonistic enough) to marry someone so certain to provoke them. (To be completely fair, she'd taken the opportunity to share the relevant detail with her own mother, who'd reacted pretty much the same way as Joshua Rudnitsky's mother had.)

When they arrived on the afternoon before the wedding, she was fairly swiftly deposited with the bridesmaids: eight women of Spellman plus Wendy Rudnitsky, the only sister of Joshua and Michael, the groom. This was hugely uncomfortable as far as Johanna was concerned, not because she was white (the bride and bridesmaids were gracious and welcoming) but because the women were mostly familiar and affectionate with one another while her own connection to the event was so very tangential. She tried to at least peel off for the rehearsal dinner, but they insisted on bringing her along to the Inn at Lambert's Cove, and that was the place she recognized Salo Oppenheimer, a person she had sometimes thought of in the years since that terrible funeral. After the toasts, as the older family members began to drift off, and only the bride and groom and their friends remained chatting around a long table, she saw him outside, leaning on the porch railing with a glass of Champagne. Our mother went to him and reintroduced herself, extending, for the second time, her hand.

"I'm sorry to have to tell you where we met before," she said.

Our father turned to look at her. "Oh," he said, after a moment. "Daniel or Mandy?"

Daniel must have been the other one, she realized. The friend.

"Mandy. I knew her."

"She was such a good person," said Salo.

"Yes. I'm Johanna. I'm here with Michael's brother. Joshua."

"Oh," Salo said. "I thought Joshua was homosexual."

Incredibly, this was when the meaning of *It isn't you, it's me* finally reached her.

"We're just friends," our mother said, having already expunged whatever notions she'd held (and, let's face it, till that instant maintained) for the brother of the groom. From this moment forward it was all going to be about our father, and the great purpose of her life would be to love him enough to relieve him of his great burden, and to free him from that one, terrible shard of time in which he was so unfairly trapped, and to salve at last that wound of his, that one that wouldn't heal. It didn't occur to her, and wouldn't for years, that she wasn't the one—the only one—who'd ever be capable of doing that.

Chapter Two

The Stendahl Syndrome

In which Salo Oppenheimer tumbles and Johanna Oppenheimer begins to understand what she's dealing with

When our father's Jeep lost contact with the earth, its tether of gravity stretching, stretching, then suddenly, irredeemably gone, I imagine a rasping sound of breath all around him, then a weirdly graceful tumble through the tumbling space inside: four bodies coiling and snapping in a fatal ballet. The feeling would have been bizarrely not-unpleasant if one could manage to excise the actual physical sensations from a broader understanding of what was happening, and it would never leave him. Sometimes, awake or asleep, he might find himself looking into Mandy's surprised eyes, or hearing Daniel Abraham's weirdly pleasant "Hey!" from the back seat, or sensing that fourth person, the invisible girlfriend, somewhere behind him in the confused air: a shadow passing darkly across his right wrist. And all that contributed to his new and very specific and lifelong challenge, which was how to continue drawing breath after having caused the deaths of two people.

He never told us, not one of us, what he'd done. He never gave any of us an opportunity to understand him.

Even before the accident, our father had been a practiced dissembler, routinely allowing significant falsehoods—such as the fact that he was engaged to, or even in love with, Mandy Bernstein—to go unchallenged. Before he killed her the main reason for this was that he did not want to hurt Mandy's feelings; after he'd killed her it was to try not to compound the pain of her family. Also, it was far easier to simply agree when people made certain assumptions, and everybody made the same assumptions, for good reason; Mandy had not only been devoted to him but had been willing (indeed, happy!) to have sex with him in his college dorm room (this was the early '70s, after all, when a lot of nice girls wouldn't do that). And actually, it wasn't at all impossible that the two of them would have stayed together, married, and made a wonderful go of things. *Why not?* You only had to look around to see men who'd settled for far less than Mandy Bernstein! But *in love,* as he himself and at least some of his own children would later experience that—no. The truth was, he had never felt such a thing, and half disbelieved anyone who claimed to have done so.

Anyway, dissembling wasn't the same as *lying,* especially when its purpose was to spare the feelings of the bereaved, of which there were so many, including, as it happened, Johanna Hirsch. Our mother was careful never to ask Salo about Mandy, and she obviously believed that his heart (his *heart!*) could never be entirely hers anyway since it must always belong, in some part, to that poor, lost girl. Also, Salo gradually decided, even a lie wasn't an *egregious* lie when you simply lacked the mechanics for a certain thing (say, doing four-figure sums in your head, or performing a long jump of over ten feet, or feeling a deep connection to another human being). There were many such mechanisms our father lacked, a few of which he regretted far more than an ability to really love the woman he had supposedly intended to marry (or indeed the one he actually did marry). He lacked any musicality, for example; that was a disappointment. He lacked a kind of easy friendliness he could see in other people. Finally, and especially after the accident, he lacked a sense of fully inhabiting his own life, as if he were still, somehow, tumbling through that tumbling air. On it swirled around him as he struggled to right himself, and sometimes fought a powerful urge for it to simply stop. That was the biggest deficit of all. That impacted everything.

Salo's pathetic physical wounds resolved so quickly they were embarrassing. Within weeks he was back in his dormitory, back in his lectures and seminars, though he avoided the people he'd known. He limped through his classes and passed them without much effort (or much distinction), and that summer flew to Europe on his own and meandered. To the strangers he fell in with (as one does, on trains or at museums), he gave only basic information: *New Yorker, Cornellian, future banker,* and did not volunteer the harm that was now at the center of his existence. He wasn't in despair; he was just tumbling, perpetually tumbling, relentlessly at the mercy of that terrible weightlessness and the betrayal of gravity. No one could conceivably understand that, so what could be the point of telling them?

He began his trip in Rome and drifted north through Milan, Geneva, Paris. He didn't mind being alone, though it was clear that the packs of young people, hitching or traveling by the new Student Rail Pass, were a little mystified by him. A tourist their own age and obviously affluent—he slept in hotels, not hostels—traveling alone? But of course he wasn't always alone. He was fine with meeting the people he met. He was content to buy them meals—he could afford it; why not?—or a ticket to some tourist site that could not be missed. And if they were heading somewhere next that sounded no worse than anywhere else, he often went with them, because there was no place in particular he wanted to be, so what did it matter where he was? When the world is tipping beneath you and you are tumbling even when you are sitting, even when you are sleeping (especially when you are sleeping), any place is the same as any other place.

All this, like every other private thing, he would tell only one person, who would one day tell us.

In Bruges he tried cannabis for the first time, even a little bit hopeful that it would help, but it didn't. In Amsterdam he met an art student in a café, and he had dinner with her and even went to bed with her in a flat she shared with a sculptor and a state-registered heroin addict, both amiable guys. Her name was Margot and there was an art exhibition in Krefeld, in Germany, that she wanted to see, so Salo folded his long legs into her brown Peugeot and drove east with her. When he showed his American passport at the border the guard looked sharply at him and held that look, and abruptly the hairs on Salo's arms stood up. It hadn't occurred to him that it wouldn't be innocuous, this trip. This crossing. The car was waved forward, and Margot drove on. It was his first time in Germany.

Krefeld was not so far from the border. Margot was talking about the man whose work she wanted to see, who had once painted soup cans and bananas but was now making movies of people staring or sleeping. She seemed surprised that our father had never heard of the artist, but he told her about the sort of paintings he'd grown up with on the walls of his family's New York apartment, the low-country landscapes and portraits of jolly women and smug, prosperous men. He did not tell her that some of those paintings had been donated to his university the very month he'd applied for admission; possibly he'd understood how crass, how outlandishly American such a gesture would have appeared to her. Instead, he turned to watch the country—this dreaded country—run past, and marveled at how ordinary it seemed: grocery stores, car lots, playing fields with soccer games in progress and parents watching on the sidelines. He thought about these same towns and fields and roads at the time of Joseph Oppenheimer, our mythic ancestor, and at the time of Goebbels's *Jud Süss.* He thought about why anyone would paint a banana, and what you'd have to paint it with to make sure the paint didn't peel off, and he wondered why a film of somebody sleeping was art. He didn't think it was worth asking Margot about either of these things.

The Kunstmuseen Krefeld was actually two side-by-side buildings made of brick, large and flat and blocky, like a middle school in a dreary American suburb. Salo and Margot had been on the road for nearly three hours, and she went to use the bathroom while he bought tickets. When she reappeared she asked the guard where those film pictures were, and then she was off to find what she'd come for. Salo followed. He was there, in Krefeld, Germany, with a girl he was more than ready to part from. He was there, but he was also, as always, in that other place, the tumbling place, the place he was used to now, or if he wasn't used to it he knew he had to figure out how to be, because it was not going to change. He couldn't remember how to walk as if the floor might not at any moment pitch sideways or upside down, but this was simply a skill he would have to master, and also he was getting better at it. He entered the first gallery.

Those paintings our father had grown up with in his parents' Fifth Avenue apartment, rheumy apertures to other continents in other centuries, were as unremarkable to him as the Peter Max posters on the walls of his fraternity house, or the framed Eliot Porter photographs his college friends were beginning to put up on the Sheetrock walls of their New York apartments. Unremarkable, as in: not to be remarked upon, or taken notice of, which was very far from appreciation, let alone admiration, let alone love. And when, two years before the day Salo entered the Kunstmuseen Krefeld, trailing a girl he was fated never to see again, about half of his parents' Old Master paintings departed in a sudden exodus to Cornell University's Herbert F. Johnson Museum of Art, our grandparents never bothered to ask if he wanted to keep one, or a few, or indeed all of them for himself. (Why would they? He'd never asked a single question about a single painting!) He'd simply returned home from his camp counselor job at Androscoggin that summer and noticed the blank wall beside his bedroom door where *Boy with a Spoon* (Bartholomeus van der Heist, 1643) had been hanging ever since he could remember. *Boy with a Spoon* had left the building, along with eleven others, and when it eventually materialized inside I.M. Pei's brand-new concrete building while our father was still an undergraduate, he never even went to see it. That was how untouched he was by even that painting, or any other painting, until what happened next.

With his first step into the gallery, Salo lost his hard-won mastery of remaining upright. The floor playfully darted away, then flipped overhead, and down he went, hitting first with a bony hip and then an elbow and finally a cheek, which landed in near repose along with the rest of his head. Accordingly, he closed his eyes, strangely not unhappy and already marveling at the thing he had seen before he fell, feasting upon it inside his head: imprinted. Then—far too soon—the tug of hands on his own arms. These were guards, tall men in khaki uniforms and hissing walkie-talkies, and they pulled him up like a newborn insulted to be expelled from the womb. One of them set down a folding chair. It was, our father would learn, a special chair, kept precisely for the emergency needs of affected tourists.

"Stendahl syndrome" was the name for this, he would eventually learn. Dizziness, confusion, even fainting, usually by foreign visitors in the act of viewing great art. It was called that because the French writer had given its first and best description: *I was in a sort of ecstasy . . . Absorbed in the contemplation of sublime beauty . . . I reached the point where one encounters celestial sensations . . . Everything spoke so vividly to my soul . . . Life was drained from me . . .*

He thanked them, of course, but mostly he hoped they would go away, so he could look at it in peace, and eventually they did.

The painting was large and square. It had a kind of fawn-colored background nearly obscured by frantic, scribbled loops of orange and red, relentless, swirling in an exhausting scrawl. He could not take his eyes off that orange, that red, those rhythmic loops, their valiant attempt to scribble something away.

He thought: *Is this really art?*

He thought: *Why does it help?*

He thought: *Who gets to look at this?*

Margot came back, escorted by one of the guards. She came to his chair and bent down to look at Salo. "You seem okay," she said. "They told me you fainted."

"Maybe," Salo said.

"Are you sick?" He could tell she didn't want him to be sick. She did not want to drive a sick person three hours back to Amsterdam, and he was pretty sure she didn't want to spend the night with a sick person in Krefeld, either.

"Oh no," he said, trying to sound cheery. The whole time, he never took his eyes off the painting.

"Well, so you like modern art after all," she observed.

"I like that," he confirmed. "I don't know what it is."

She walked up to it and looked at the card. "*Untitled.* That's helpful. He's an American." She tried to sound out his name, but couldn't get closer than "tomb-ley" or "twom-ble." "Oh look, he used house paint and wax crayon. Not quite your Flemish landscapes."

No, our father agreed.

"Do you want to see the rest of the exhibit?"

He didn't, he said, but she should go back. He wanted her to leave him alone with the painting. He wanted the world to leave him alone with the painting.

Basically, he found a way to stay until the Kunstmuseen closed that evening, after which he and Margot (who'd been very disappointed by those movie stills) endured the long drive back to Amsterdam and parted in Dam Square, never to meet again. Our father had recognized that he knew nothing about anything. He had not the first understanding of what he had seen, or where the thing he had seen had come from, or what other paintings by other artists were already in conversation with this one, or what any of this had to teach him. Also, he had no idea when he might live in a place where he might put such an object on his wall and look at it, every morning, every night. Also, he would not, for a few years yet, be in control of the money held in trust for him, and he would not begin drawing a salary from Wurttemberg until after finishing college. But he knew, as he had never known anything before, that he would somehow, at some time, own that painting.

Back at Cornell in the fall, he unenrolled from his fraternity, not because the men were in any way insensitive but because he found that he couldn't stand to enter those rooms and not see Danny Abraham, a person he'd considered almost unbearably kind. Someone told him the girl who'd been Daniel's date that terrible day had left Cornell. Salo could not remember her at all. He could not even picture her face; he was not sure he had even turned his head when the two of them, Daniel and the girl, climbed into the back seat of the Jeep, or if he'd ever been told her name. He didn't ask where she'd gone; he felt only relief that he would not have to meet her in some classroom or cafeteria. For the rest of his time in college he wanted to not make any friends and not make any waves; he wanted only to complete his degree without fucking up another thing. He knew enough not to shift his major from economics to anything else, let alone art. Art was an established tradition within the Oppenheimer family, and that was enough to justify an early-morning survey course, and one on the Modernists, and one on Pollock and his circle. Art was also an acknowledged part of the apparatus of wealth, indeed, a not unuseful vector for *acquiring* wealth. (Selda and our grandfather, Hermann, were not sentimental and they were not stupid: the seventeen Old Master paintings that remained in the Fifth Avenue apartment after *Boy with a Spoon* and the others departed had been earmarked by Sotheby's as having the greatest value and/or potential appreciation.) Salo did not need to have any of this explained to him. If he wanted to own and live in the world of paintings once the business of the workday was done, that was his right, indeed our family tradition! But he would continue to study economics and after graduation he would, without complaint, step into the place prepared for him by his father and the fathers before them—the Broad Street offices of Wurttemberg Holdings—there to serve the business of being an Oppenheimer for the rest of his professional life.

When he turned twenty-one, two months before leaving college, he was given access to his trust, and within days he had enlisted the help of the Marlborough gallery to make the purchase from Galleria Sperone in Turin (for an amount that would forever strike him as absurd). Four months later the crate arrived, and when the movers pried it open and went away, he nearly ran after them, terrified to be left in charge of this object and stunned that they—that anyone—actually trusted him to be its caretaker. Even in such an uninspired setting, it had lost not the tiniest fragment of its power.

The setting in question was the perfectly ordinary apartment Salo had rented, in a white brick building on Third Avenue, just your basic young professional one-bedroom with Sheetrock walls, a Jennifer Convertibles sofa he'd bought right off the floor of the shop, a glass and chrome coffee table, and a couple of chairs from Habitat. Now it was all that plus an iconic artwork by an American master that would one day be worth seventy million dollars. Our father had first attempted to hang the Twombly from a lonely nail he'd inexpertly hammered in (off-center and too low), but the weight of the picture promptly tore the nail and a chunk of Sheetrock out of the wall and the picture fell forward, with Salo barely managing to catch it before it hit the coffee table. (One of us, on learning this detail, would not soon recover from it.) After that, the picture remained on the floor, leaning against the wall and just covering the missing chunk. Salo, quite obviously, had no particular interest in beautiful spaces, let alone furnishings, not even furnishings that might conceivably be more *comfortable* than the ones he had, and he barely used the kitchen. Every corner in his neighborhood had a Korean grocer, and every Korean grocer had a salad bar, so after work he went there and spooned some hot dish into his plastic tray, then he went back to the apartment and sat on his convertible sofa and ate off his lap with a plastic fork, barely taking his eyes off the painting. That's how he spent his first year at Wurttemberg.

The following summer, when our parents met (re-met) at that wedding on the Vineyard, he saw, before anything else, that Johanna Hirsch was a person in Mandy Bernstein's mold. Not quite as attractive, maybe, and not quite as smart, but strangely just as loving toward him, as if he were some great prize to be won. He'd been holding on to the rail as the rehearsal dinner wound down, possibly a little drunk and wondering what it would be like to live here, on the island, when suddenly this person was standing next to him and calling him back to those first appalling days: the somber shaking of hands, the enfolding by strangers who vibrated as they held you, the smells of grief. But she knew what he'd done, and she was here anyway. Something inside him slipped into place: not love, not a sudden recognition of his own terrible loneliness, not even desire. Only he thought, looking at her, noting the obvious nervousness as she spoke and understanding that she wanted, for some unfathomable reason, his good opinion: *Why not?* Here was a pretty, amiable girl who seemed to have decided, apparently on the spot, that the redress of his great personal tragedy—for the record, not his own cosmic view of the matter—ought to be her purpose in life, or at least its priority.

That fall, Johanna returned to Skidmore for her sophomore year and Salo continued to work downtown alongside his father. He didn't dislike what he was doing and he wasn't bad at it. He could sense in the other employees, many of whom had been with Wurttemberg for decades, a collective relief that he appeared to be dutiful in his attitude toward the company, competent as he familiarized himself with a century and a half of holdings, and even creative as he began to put together deals of his own. On the weekends our mother came down on the train and stayed with him, something she was less than forthcoming about with her own parents. Salo hadn't slept with anyone since the Dutch art student he'd been with that day in Germany, when he first saw the Twombly. He'd known it was absurd to be a young man, in the 1970s (when even women were shrugging off old ideas about promiscuity), and living like an ascetic in some religious order, but he'd felt incapable of crossing that abyss. Johanna took charge of the whole thing, somehow, meaning that he was not required to do anything but be accommodating. And once they were having sex (in other words, almost immediately) he was relieved to discover that his body remembered how to do this strange, animal thing, and also how to like it. It comforted him to sleep all night and wake up next to Johanna. He had never actually done that, not even with Mandy Bernstein.

Mainly they kept to themselves, going to museums or movies, sometimes meeting Johanna's older sister Debbie and Debbie's boyfriend (later fiancé, later husband) Bruce Krieger at Maxwell's Plum or P. J. Clarke's. Debbie was a dynamo in shoulder pads who power-walked to work in running shoes, listening to music on a Walkman. She and Bruce had embarked upon big careers and were obviously on their way to being very well-off. (Salo could see that his family's archaic little firm, deliberately shrouded from the public gaze, was somehow suspect to them.) A few times Johanna's brother Bobby came in with whoever thought of herself as his girlfriend that week, and the four of them went out somewhere and struggled to find things to talk about. Bobby was already buying and selling strip malls and commercial spaces, sometimes—through a series of probably illegal holding companies—to himself. He spoke proudly of having been thrown out of boarding school for selling weed to his schoolmates (he had only been caught, he informed them, because he'd cut some preppy's purchase with pencil shavings), but by some suspicious alchemy he already lived in a huge New Jersey house, full of glittery things that attested to his success. Bobby did tend to thump our father on the back whenever they said hello or good-bye, but it was really to his credit that, despite being "in the same racket," he never once asked Salo for anything, or tried to sell him so much as a garden shed.

Gradually, weekend by weekend, little by little, Johanna moved in with Salo, bringing bits and pieces from her dismal little Skidmore room and nothing at all from her childhood home but a wedding photograph of her grandparents, Rose and Lou. Gradually, her weekends on Third Avenue extended on either end—Friday to Sunday, Thursday to Monday—until she was only going back to Saratoga for unmissable classes or exams. (She also ended up switching her major to child psychology, which in time would afford her not the slightest insight into any of her children, at least not when it mattered.) About the painting that dominated her boyfriend's living room she said nothing at first because—incredibly—it didn't make much of an impression on her, but as she watched the way he looked at it and began to understand the real estate it occupied in his head, she did make a sincere effort. Our mother obviously recognized that it wasn't some roughshod picture he'd picked up from one of those street markets in Soho, or a piece of student work he'd bought off an art major at Cornell. A complicated purchase had been involved, and real money spent, and the thing had actually been shipped from Europe. But that only deepened her lack of understanding.

No one had ever taught him how to look at art. Not his parents—if, indeed, they knew themselves—and not the early-morning survey course at Cornell, which in any case ended with *Nude Descending the Stair*. But this—the 1970s—was a time when the wish of an ordinary person to buy a picture matched up easily with the wish of a gallery or auction house to sell a picture, and nobody cared to complicate that transaction. The advent of art advisors was still a decade off (not that that mattered to our father, who would later take special pleasure in sending them packing), and the only collectors attracting much attention were the people buying Pollock and his circle, which meant that Salo could wander into Christie's or Sotheby's, get himself a paddle, and walk out with one of Diebenkorn's Ocean Park paintings, or a slab painting by Hans Hoffman, both things he actually did before the 1970s ended. It was at an absurdly low-key auction that he first encountered Franz Kline and Agnes Martin, and in Andrew Crispo's gallery, while Crispo himself was in the back lavishing attention on a Swiss collector, Salo wrote a check for a large work by Ed Ruscha. He brought the picture home to Third Avenue, tied to the roof rack of an accommodating cab.

"So, what do we know about this artist?" our mother asked him one day as they sat on the couch. The painting was in the place a television would be in anyone else's apartment.

He gave her the basics, and our mother listened, but it was a struggle for her to sustain an interest in someone who scribbled in *crayon* on a background of what was apparently *house paint,* not even proper oil paint. And actually, Salo himself wasn't all that interested in the life or opinions of that painter, just as he would not, in the future, be very interested in the biography of any artist he collected. He knew their stories, in general, and he knew their stated concerns, but he didn't let anything interfere with how a work of art made him feel. Never once, in all the years of his collecting life, did he set out to acquire a work by so-and-so because he felt his collection ought to include a so-and-so, or because someone had told him so-and-so's work would one day be worth a fortune. He wasn't concerned with acquiring a fortune. He already had a fortune.

Usually, no one even spoke to our father when he went to Castelli's or Pace or even Marlborough on Fifty-Seventh (where he'd once sought help acquiring the Twombly), or when he wandered through the showrooms at Sotheby's and Christie's in his weekend wardrobe of chinos and old sweaters, head down, hands stuffed in his pockets. It helped that the artists he found himself drawn to were not well-known, not highly valued, and not considered at all likely to become either of those things. And while he never set out to reject the fashions of the art world or the "guidance" of its critics, he saw no reason to pay attention to them, either.

At first, no individual work provoked in him the magnitude of feeling he had experienced in Krefeld, but he discovered, as he looked, that he was beginning to understand the ideas refracting among these paintings. Then, nearly a year after the Twombly, he found himself returning more than once to look at another square painting, a vertically divided field of gray and different gray, so deceptively simple and endlessly complex, by another painter no one had ever heard of. That became his second purchase, and he put it in the bedroom of the rental, above a brown laminated bureau he had bought on the furniture floor at Bloomingdale's. He could tell that this one didn't just baffle Johanna; this one she actively disliked. But she didn't say a word. His third purchase, when it was delivered, proved too large to get through the door of the apartment, and the super had to be bribed to remove the doorframe. Once inside, only the wall the Twombly was leaning against would be big enough, so the Twombly went to the bedroom. The exposure of that damaged Sheetrock necessitated another bribe for the super, and a delay for the wall to be patched, and—for the first time—a visit from a professional art installer. Not one of the people involved in this process—auction delivery men, superintendent, professional hangers—looked at these three pictures with anything but open disdain.

"What do you think of this one?" he asked our mother.

She was sitting on the Jennifer convertible, looking at the new painting with a certain dismay. It was large, a mustard color with a thin vertical greenish stripe on the left edge and a crosshatch of lines at the top. It clashed horribly with the sofa, which was a light blue flower print, and with the shag rug, which was also blue, but a different blue.

"What is it supposed to be?" she asked.

"His home. He lives in Los Angeles."

"And those are . . . streets?"

So that—the sharing of it, with her, the woman he already assumed he was going to marry—was obviously not going to happen. But then again, our father wasn't sure he wanted to share it. It relieved him not to share it.

One thing Salo really did like about Johanna was the fact that she didn't care much about the acquisition in general. Our mother had never been a shopper and she didn't start then; she wore jeans and Fair Isle sweaters, tall brown Frye boots on her feet, and for dressy occasions there were a couple of wrap dresses that made her already small waist nearly disappear. She had no wish to experience the downtown clubs, CBGB, already legendary for its iconoclastic bands (and filth), or later the game-changing Palladium and Studio 54. She seemed happy at home with a book or watching one of the new cable channels, Cinemax or Home Box Office, or going out with her Skidmore friends who were beginning to drift south to Manhattan. She gamely went along when there was a museum he wanted to visit, but he waited until she was back in Saratoga to do what he had begun to think of as his real investigations. She did not seem to have a comparable interest, let alone passion; or rather, he understood that the chief interest of her life was himself: his comfort, his entertainment, his absolution. Salo had not asked for this, but suddenly he had it, and he could not seem to make himself feel anything about it. Sometimes he wondered who he might have become if his Jeep hadn't hit that rock and sent the four of them tumbling through space, but he could never quite see this theoretical version of himself. That person was as much a stranger to himself as the actual person, the tumbling person, he knew himself to be.

Sometimes, our mother made him think of Mandy Bernstein: her relentless focus on him, the force of her unqualified love. He understood that she thought of him as a good man, a man beaten down by the undeserved tragedy in his personal rearview mirror, but always on the edge of some beautiful redemption. Our father couldn't bring himself to disappoint her, to tell her how wrong she was. He would not destroy another nice young woman who was so ill-advisedly determined to love him, and it was that, more than anything else, more than love for her or optimism about a life with her, that made him propose one night at Maxwell's Plum under one of the ersatz Tiffany lamps, with a ring that had once belonged to his father's mother. It was too big for Johanna—the size, not the stone—but she was happy with it. Wildly happy. She would also have been happy with a small wedding, just their families and the few friends they'd each kept from college, but they ended up with a big ceremony at the Harmonie Club, and plenty of Wurttemberg clients in attendance. His parents paid for everything.

By then, of course, our mother had a firmer grasp of what she was dealing with in regard to the Oppenheimers, their considerable wealth in particular. She had met his parents, the all but silent Hermann and the terrifying Selda (her expression so frozen Johanna truly did not know whether she was being singled out for special disapprobation or was merely a tiny part of a disapproved-of world), but mainly in restaurants, which delayed her complete awareness. Objectively she recognized that the Oppenheimers were people of means, far more so than her own family, but she had grown up in proximity to only one version of American wealth—the one represented by the students of the Lawrenceville school—and Salo's parents were obviously not that. Also, Salo himself was indifferent to any display of wealth, unlike other boys she'd known (and dated) who had far less money but who seemed to require the most expensive version of anything in order to feel good about themselves. Our father, when they met, lived mainly in those elderly chinos and sweaters, sometimes over a T-shirt from his old school, Collegiate. He didn't make any great change in his wardrobe even after he'd begun to work at Wurttemberg, and it was only when his own father spoke to him that he suited up to the appropriate degree. (Johanna helped him pick out a briefcase so he'd stop transporting his papers in a Big Brown Bag from Bloomingdale's.) She was not yet enough of a New Yorker to recognize the significance of some of Salo's touchstones: Collegiate, the weekend house on the shore in Rye, the summer camp long associated with Jewish families of a certain financial stratum, and above all the Oppenheimer apartment on Fifth Avenue, in a 1915 limestone co-op that had once been resolutely off-limits to Jewish people, no matter how much money they had. This mansion in the sky took up fully half (the better half) of a high floor, so its long line of rooms all overlooked the great carpet of trees in the center of Manhattan. There, the sofas were certainly not from Jennifer Convertibles and the chairs were certainly not from Habitat, and the paintings on the beautiful walls, which were certainly not Sheetrock, had little bronze nameplates and discreet lights overhead.

They went there one afternoon when Hermann and Selda were in Rye, to pick up some document from a drawer in Salo's childhood bedroom. As they passed through the living room she happened to look up at the wall above the mantelpiece, and stopped. Then she took a step nearer. The bronze plate said . . . it actually said . . . Édouard Manet.

"Is that . . . ?" She'd been about to say "real," but she already knew it was real. She would never be on intimate terms with her in-laws, but she already knew they weren't the kind of people who'd have the work of a famous painter copied for display in their living room.

"What?"

"No, nothing."

And she followed him down a long corridor, still stunned.

It was just one more thing to fold into the ongoing enigma of her boyfriend's parents. When she went to Salo's office, as she sometimes did, Hermann came to greet her with a smile and a formal handshake. When the four of them met for dinner, always at a restaurant with hushed service and frightening silverware, Selda asked solicitously about her mother and father and brother and sister. But her own boyfriend, then fiancé, then husband, seemed to have nothing at all to say about his childhood, and the details he offered Johanna were mainly to do with the household staff. There had been a housekeeper named Etta who stayed overnight in the apartment, in the small maid's room off the kitchen, making it possible for Salo's parents to travel or go to Rye without him (something they had done a lot). There had been a nanny named Rosa who'd walked him to nursery school, and another named Miss James who took him on the crosstown bus to Collegiate and picked him up, at least until fourth grade. He ate dinner at the kitchen table, sometimes with his mother before she went out, sometimes only with Etta or Miss James, who put a great quantity of salt on everything she was served, which was offensive to Etta, who cooked. His bedroom, far down the corridor from the room where his parents slept, had a green plaid bedspread and curtains and a desk where he was supposed to do his homework and a beanbag chair he used instead. (He hardly needed to describe this to her, since it was all unchanged.) On the wall outside his room there had been a painting of a boy with a spoon which wasn't there any longer. Actually, Salo told her, a lot of the paintings he'd grown up with were no longer there.

But he could barely remember a childhood conversation with his mother and father together, or an outing, let alone a family vacation, only the three of them together. Having produced him they seemed to have retreated to a respectful distance at the edges of his childhood, politely applauding and dutifully accompanying him through those formative years but opting to leave some parts of the business of parenting to people better suited, which in this case meant nobody. He wouldn't fault them, and she was careful not to insist he do so. They had not withheld from him anything he'd actually wanted at the time, or anything he now missed having had. On the contrary, Hermann and Selda had driven to Maine each summer to visit him at Androscoggin, standing with the other parents to watch the canoe skills demonstration and the archery tournament, and they'd stood with him at Temple Emanu-El (another Hermann Oppenheimer, the grandfather of Salo's grandfather, had been a founding member in 1845). And then there was the night those two had swept into Ithaca and packed Salo in ether and taken him away, back to New York, and never once said a thing to him about what he had done. They had even brought him to Lawrenceville for Mandy's funeral and to Newark for Daniel's, waiting in coffee shops while he did what he needed to do, what was the right thing to do, what they themselves would have expected if, God forbid, one of those other young people had been behind the wheel and their own son, their only child, was so suddenly gone.

He never talked about that either, but our mother waited, even so. She perfected the making of safe moments for his profound utterances, should they ever come.

Salo's life at Wurttemberg was precisely what he had expected it to be. The limestone building on a corner near the Stock Exchange had been the shrewd purchase of his father's grandfather at exactly the right moment, that moment being the fall of 1920, shortly after the Stock Exchange bombing. This Oppenheimer forebear declined the opportunity to build upward, insisting that the stubby little limestone corner remain a mushroom among redwoods. Inside, time slowed to a crawl: the quiet dignity of a rigorously private institution with stately reception and meeting rooms on the ground floor and elegant individual offices upstairs (some large, others very large). Floors were swept and woodwork made to glow by invisible nighttime cleaners, and every morning breakfast was arranged in chafing dishes in the dining room for the employees, as if they were all members of some titled family, gathering for kippered eggs and toast before dispersing to their busy days. The firm's culture was somewhat suggestive of certain other institutions which had gone out of their way to make earlier generations of Oppenheimers as unwelcome as possible, and unlike other Jewish firms founded by equally adept and ambitious families Wurttemberg had been steered by a century of like-minded commodores with one eye on family wealth and another on the next generation. Unlike those firms, Wurttemberg resisted every one of the sinkholes that came along to bedevil the industry, among them leveraged buyouts, junk bonds, insider trading, "pumping and dumping," and the occasional Ponzi scheme.

When Salo Oppenheimer assumed possession of one of the third-floor offices, he brought with him only that square gray painting his wife found so distasteful. The painting—its actual name was *Dylan Study II*—went on the wall opposite our father's desk, where its stillness and depth would sustain him for many years. Johanna, making a rare visit at around this time, was relieved to see *Dylan Study II* in its new home, but the office as a whole looked a little dingy. She suggested a coat of paint. Maybe a brighter white? Or at least a pair of lamps from Bloomingdale's? "It's so dim in here."

"I know. It's always been like that, even before all those buildings went up."

"There must be something we can do."

No, he told her. "You concentrate on the house."

The house, their new house, was in Brooklyn, a place where neither of them had ever considered living. Brooklyn in those years seemed much farther away from Manhattan than it later would, and represented a very different city. But at one of her work events Johanna met a magazine editor from *People* who understood the significance of our mother's new last name. She also had a husband who was a young broker at Douglas Elliman, so low on the totem pole that he'd been assigned this Van Diemen's Land of New York City. He called Johanna Oppenheimer the very next day and told her he had something he wanted to show her, in Brooklyn Heights.

Our mother had once watched a scary movie in which a Brooklyn Heights house actually contained the gateway to hell, and she felt a little spooked at the thought of looking out there, even if the Realtor promised it was spectacular, undervalued, and—the key to everything she thought about in those days—big enough for a family. She caught some heat from the driver of the taxi she hailed on Lexington, but an extra twenty persuaded him and he drove her, for the first time in her life, over the Brooklyn Bridge and through the cobbled streets of the Heights. The driver left her a few minutes' walk away on Montague Terrace, unwilling to help her find the right number and so surly it was clear he thought she must be looking for something unlawful. (Drugs? Or a gun?) So our mother gave him his fare and the twenty and climbed out, already worried about how she was going to get home.

The agent was waiting for her down the block, and he came rushing to meet her, perhaps to make sure she didn't flee. His name was Barton Zanes. He was twenty-five, tops, but already completely bald.

She took in the street, which was shabby. Once grand, she could see that, but in 1979 much diminished. "Where does that go?" she asked. There were very dubious people walking on a kind of footpath beside the house Zanes had led her to: a couple with their hands in each other's back pockets, and a tall man with a rottweiler.

"It goes down to the Esplanade. On the waterfront. You know."

Of course she didn't know. She was a girl from suburban New Jersey who'd only just gotten used to the Upper East Side. As far as she was concerned, Brooklyn was where John Travolta went to the disco and Gene Hackman chased drug dealers, and where gangs on the subway roamed at will (not that she ever rode the subway in Manhattan, where gangs also roamed at will). And also, where blind priests guarded the entrance to hell: *Abandon Hope All Ye Who Enter Here.*

"It overlooks all of lower Manhattan. You see?" He was pointing after the rottweiler at a walkway above the open water. She didn't even know what that water was. The Hudson? "Doesn't your husband work in the Financial District? He can walk to work!"

"Walk?" she said, mystified. "How?"

"Over the bridge!" said Barton Zanes. He seemed delighted. "C'mon, let's look. It's completely insane."

And it was, it was. Even she was breathless at the rooms, some of which had broad views of that spectacular water—*New York Harbor!*—and the buildings of Wall Street and the Fulton Fish Market and even the Statue of Liberty. The floors were dingy and scratched, but they were all there, inlay and parquet. The plaster walls were flaking and seemed in places to emit strands of something, waving in the air—horsehair, Zanes said helpfully, as if this were a good thing. (Horsehair? In the walls?) The great carved bannister wobbled. A few windows were cracked or patched with duct tape. Some of the bathroom tiles had crumbled to dust. There was a kitchen somebody had obviously started to renovate, but lost the will to proceed with after the appliances had been extracted. "So you can start over!" said Zanes. "Marble everywhere! A big commercial stove! Gourmet kitchen!"

"I'm not that great a cook," our mother said, as if this had ever stopped anyone from ordering up a gourmet kitchen. "But, you know, I can sort of see a big table here."

She could see more than that. She could *hear* her own children running up and down these staircases, flushing the less than modern toilets and bathing in the oversized claw-foot tubs. She could imagine playrooms and rooms for piling on a couch in front of the television. As she climbed the stairs to the attic rooms and descended to the basement, it seemed that the more rooms there were the more children she might have. She could see a different Salo in this house, as well: a father and husband, a man who felt able to take pleasure in life. That was what she wanted for him, and it might be possible here as it could never be possible in that dingy little apartment on Third. For the first time it struck her that staying in such a featureless and depressing place as their present apartment was somehow preventing her family from coming into being. If we lived here, she thought, our children would be here with us.

Of course, she didn't tell Salo *that*. She told him that the house needed lots of work, but something about it felt right and he should come as quickly as possible to see it. Salo, lifelong New Yorker that he was, did not need to be told what he was looking at when he stood by the west-facing windows, but he was dumbstruck, nonetheless. It happened to be a late afternoon in November, and the sun was disappearing over New Jersey, trailing orange and pink along the water as a ferry headed home to Staten Island. Twenty-five-foot-wide single-family homes with twenty-foot ceilings (on the parlor floor, at least; the rest were a mere fourteen) and four fireplaces had already become both scarce and expensive in Manhattan. And not one of them actually overlooked . . . Manhattan.

He asked again what the price was, and when he heard it his heart leapt. Then he offered 75 percent, cash.

Not surprisingly, his parents were vocally opposed. Where would they shop for groceries in Brooklyn? Some kosher market in Williamsburg or Crown Heights? Where would they find doctors and dentists? What about a gym and a video store and a salon? Salo and Johanna should stay in that nice new building on the Upper East Side, and, when the time came, they could move to Park or Fifth or even the West Side, if they really wanted to go crazy and antiestablishment. There were some parts of the West Side that were just lovely. But Brooklyn? Why not *The Bronx*. Why not *Staten Island*!

"It's absurdly inexpensive," he told them.

"Well, there's a reason for that," his father said.

"It's going to be gorgeous once we've fixed it up."

"I think this idea that you're going to walk across the Brooklyn Bridge to work is very bizarre," said his mother. "Who walks across a bridge?"

"Lots of people."

"If you're in the middle of the bridge and someone tries to rob you, who can help?"

The same no one who'd rush to help you on Park Avenue, Salo thought.

And, our grandmother added, this time to Johanna, and in a studiously offhand way so as not to make a thing of it, if the two of them had children one day, only think how long it would take to cart them into the city every morning to Brearley or Collegiate, and then back to Brooklyn again!

But there was a school nearby, very nearby, in fact, called Walden. And if that school did, oddly, refer to itself as an "educational collective" and was the kind of place where children apparently learned from drum-beating teachers, well, that was all right with her, not that she said this to her mother-in-law. Already—more than once—she had walked dreamily around its periphery, peering through the iron gate at the multicolored playground full of shouting girls and boys. Yes, their children could go to Walden. If, that is, they were ever born.

Chapter Three

Fertility and Its Discontents

In which a rosary is said for the Oppenheimers, with remarkable results

Our mother also had a job, though not, of course, for the money. She worked three days a week as a program director for the American Society of Magazine Editors, a position made available to her through the intervention of Wurttemberg's legal counsel, whose sister was executive assistant to ASME's director. The actual job application and hiring had consisted of a lunch at Smith & Wollensky (at which she'd been so afraid to order anything off that expensive menu that she'd ended up with an onion soup and a waiter who looked at her with open hostility); after that she was basically handed the annual internship program and told that she was in charge. Johanna liked reading the application essays of students from the Midwestern state schools, who seemed starstruck by the prospect of interning at *Progressive Grocer* or *Scientific American*, and the Ivy League girls (women) who she suspected would drop out of the program if they didn't get assigned to *Vogue*, *Mademoiselle*, or *Glamour*. They were only a few years younger than she was, but they were all so focused! In fact, they made her wonder if the rest of her generation wasn't rushing past her into some promised, post-coeducation future she hadn't been told about. In June, when the young people arrived in New York for their orientation, she was the one to greet them in the lobby of their NYU dormitory, offering ASME T-shirts and maps of the city with the restaurant for their welcome dinner circled in red. Waiting for them at her little table, handing them their keys, she watched them approach, already in their Professional-Summer-in-New-York-City clothes, and felt the force of their ambition. The only thing she wanted as much as these college students wanted to work in magazines was to be pregnant.

Then, during her second ASME summer, not one but two young interns (*Seventeen* and *Reader's Digest*) came weeping to her with unexpected and very unwanted pregnancies, and Johanna Oppenheimer walked directly into the office of the sister of Wurttemberg's legal counsel and quit. After that, fertility and its discontents would be her only employment.

How she came to despise the use of the word "journey" to describe this, the grating, grueling, sometimes boring, always excruciating business of trying and failing to become pregnant. It was not supposed to be a thing at all! It was supposed to just happen in the way it had always happened, something along the lines of *open legs, insert penis, bring forth offspring*. That was how it had worked for her sister, and even for the thoroughly unremarkable person Bobby had finally married and impregnated (though not, as it happened, in that order). But not for Johanna and Salo Oppenheimer. For the first year, Salo wasn't even aware of the fact that his wife was actively trying to become pregnant, and she somehow persuaded herself that this made it not count as a year of failure. Then one afternoon she asked him, as if the notion had just occurred to her, whether the two of them were not ready for the next step. And he had said: "Next step to where?"

It wasn't that he was holding back. He wasn't holding back. He wasn't even afraid. It was just that the idea of it, of a pregnancy that might, in due course, turn into a baby and thence into a child, or "person," was so utterly beyond his ken that he could not immediately understand what she was talking about. He was so not there with her in her longing, so not bitterly disappointed each month when it didn't happen. He wasn't a step behind, vaguely believing that it would all work out eventually. It wasn't an acknowledged issue between them, something he'd made his feelings clear about and asked her to concede to. No. It simply wasn't there at all. It was as if the entire notion of procreation would have to be fully reinvented for the sole edification of Salo Oppenheimer.

If she could have moved ahead without his help or even knowledge, she'd have done it in an instant, but the first thing you gave up when you dragged yourself, finally, to the famous infertility doctor you've read about in *New York* magazine was the privilege of keeping a secret from your husband.

"We'll see you and your partner on the eighth, at eleven A.M.," said the receptionist for the famous infertility doctor.

She would have to tell him.

"What do you mean, infertile?" had been Salo's first reaction.

"I don't know. I'm just concerned. I'd just like to get checked out. Both of us to get checked out."

"But we haven't been trying to get pregnant," Salo said. He looked more mystified than anything. This gave her hope.

"I'd like to try. I think we're ready."

He was only twenty-seven. She was only twenty-four.

"I'm not ready," said Salo.

Johanna canceled the appointment and went back to not telling her husband that she wasn't doing a single thing to not get pregnant.

Another two years passed.

She became increasingly, privately, intractably frantic.

"Bobby and Christina are pregnant again," she told him one morning as he was looking through his briefcase for some elusive bit of paper.

"Oh?" said Salo. "There it is. I knew I picked it up off my desk, but I couldn't remember what I did with it."

"Are you still not ready? Because I am ready for you to be ready."

"Ready for what?" he actually said. He was snapping the latches of the briefcase. It was burgundy, made of eel skin, the one she had picked out to replace the Big Brown Bag.

"To have children, Salo. I would like to. I think we would be such wonderful parents."

This was not precisely true. She was full of apprehension when she thought about him as a parent.

"Well, sure. But why is this so important right now?" he said.

Why? Because each individual cell in her body was howling at her, every day, all day, incessantly. Because she walked through their house on the Esplanade imagining children into the empty bedrooms. Because even their dog, a standoffish dachshund named Jürgen, seemed to understand he was only a placeholder for something vastly more significant that might at any moment replace him.

"I'm concerned that something is wrong."

"Nothing is wrong. We're not even trying to get pregnant."

Three years was a long time. She had different priorities now.

"I thought it would take a while, so I went off the pill," she said.

Salo frowned. "And when was that?"

That, said Johanna, doing a rapid calculation in which she omitted the first year of unilaterally not trying to not get pregnant, was two years ago.

After a long moment, he said: "I see."

So this time they made it to the famous infertility doctor, Lorenz Pritchard of Fifth Avenue and Lenox Hill ("and Georgica Pond," Salo would later joke, "courtesy of *me*").

"We'll see you and your partner on the fourteenth, at four P.M.," said the receptionist.

Dr. Pritchard's office was papered with photographs of infants, smiling and drooling infants, infants in color and black-and-white. Johanna shielded her eyes against the glare of these children as she went inside. She took a seat on the leather banquette, eyed the vat of pink ranunculi, and began filling out forms on the clipboard. *Height. Weight. Sexual history. Sexual habits. Drug use.* There was no end to what she was being asked to reveal.

Beside her on the banquette, Salo was frowning over his own form.

"I don't see what my choice of underwear has to do with your not becoming pregnant."

"Really?" Her heart jumped. Underwear? Could this all be solved by . . . underwear?

"Or how many drinks per week."

"I have that one, too," she said.

"Do you have the underwear question?"

Johanna looked. "No. But I have lots of lovely questions about my period and venereal disease."

"Oh, I've got venereal disease here," Salo said. "You know, I'm sure there's nothing wrong. We probably need some hormone shot or something."

The "we" was a nice gesture, and she appreciated it, but she was careful not to look at him. She had been educating herself on these matters for over three years, reading every magazine article and every *New York Times* Science Section update on the new fertility frontiers, and she highly doubted that a simple hormone shot would be the end or even the beginning of things. She had a strong suspicion that they were—or she was—about to commence a long slide down a steep slope of increasingly uncomfortable and frightening interventions, from the aforementioned hormone shots (hers, not his) all the way to the brave new worlds of surrogacy and test tube babies. She had, in her head, a whole list of possible diagnoses, ranked from least to most fearful: a blockage was preferable to a hormonal dysfunction. Hormonal dysfunction was preferable to absent or unviable eggs, which weren't as bad as insufficient sperm, which was better than an incompetent uterus. Of all the things she worried might be wrong, the one Johanna feared the most was "unexplained infertility."

"What if there's nothing wrong?" she asked, whispering.

"There *is* nothing wrong," he answered.

Dr. Lorenz Pritchard was a big guy who seemed to be spilling out everywhere: hair from the sides (but not the top) of his head, flesh at the waist and wrists and neck. He was waiting for them at a long antique desk, covered with files and legal pads and a small plate on which remained the corner of a tuna-fish sandwich on rye and a crumpled napkin.

"Dr. Pritchard," he said, extending a faintly fishy hand. They both shook it.

"I read about you in *New York* magazine," Johanna blurted.

"Okay. Which year? We're so much further along than we were, even a few years ago."

"Well, good," said Johanna, forcing a smile. She knew exactly what he was referencing, of course. The test tube baby, Louise something, was two years old, and that was long enough for an entire genre of TV movies to have been written, produced, aired, and seen by herself. There was a story in *Ladies' Home Journal* about a couple who'd paid a woman to be pregnant with the husband's child, and then the woman had just handed over the baby to the father and his wife after it was born. They all seemed happy about it, but it sounded horrible to Johanna. She wanted to be pregnant with her own baby. And anyway, what if the mother—the other mother—decided she wanted to keep the child after it was born? What then? It wasn't as if you had King Solomon on hand to settle things.

"I'm afraid there's something wrong with me," Johanna said. Then she started to cry.

Dr. Pritchard, to his credit, took this in stride. He'd been a perennial in *New York* magazine's "Best Doctors" issue as long as Johanna had been checking. He had seen crying women before.

"Mrs. Oppenheimer," he said, passing her the Kleenex, "I have treated over five hundred couples, the vast majority of whom are now parents, some several times over. Sometimes nature doesn't go our way, and that will always be true, but I can promise you that everyone in our office is here to support you on your *infertility journey*."

Even in the depths of her embarrassment, our mother found room to despise the term.

Salo reached for another Kleenex and passed it to her.

"So, you got yourselves here, and that's the first step. Also the hardest."

A blatant lie, as Johanna would later be the first to say. A ridiculous lie. Getting herself and Salo into an office where his underwear and her menstrual cycles could be scrutinized had certainly not been fun, but it wasn't by any measure harder than some of what lay ahead. From the hormonal testing to the early-morning sperm analysis to the Clomid prescription she walked out with that very first day (a drug that made her even more weepy, crazy, and scared than before), to the hysterosalpingogram, which Dr. Pritchard's radiologist herself referred to (just seconds before actually performing the procedure) as "having your tubes blown out." It was all terrible, fearful, and degrading.

And useless. Another year of months passed, in rage and depression, so much blood through the cervix, so many filaments of hope gone forever. Her brother Bobby's third child, a boy, was born. Her father had a mild stroke and retired from the Lawrenceville school, shortly after which he and Johanna's mother sold their house and moved out to live nearer their favorite child and his growing brood.

It was with these first (official) steps of her infertility *journey* that Johanna felt the strong embrace of her husband's money for the very first time. In the midst of her great and ambient distress it was at least good to know that they could pay for whatever interventions Dr. Lorenz Pritchard felt like tossing their way, especially since they were both still young, and there were, as he was forever telling them, always new protocols and procedures coming down the pike. "Whatever we need," Salo had told her, before they even got home from that first appointment. "Whatever it takes."

What it ended up taking was the next four years of their lives, beginning with the vindication of Salo's sperm, and moving on to the "blowing out" of Johanna's fallopian tubes not once but three times (she could not be ignorant of the extreme unpleasantness of this procedure after the first time, sadly), and four rounds of doctor-assisted insemination and six of hormone-assisted egg production, extraction, fertilization, implantation, and ultimate disintegration.

It was in Dr. Pritchard's office, during the postmortem on this sixth go-round, that the dreaded S-word was first mentioned.

"I don't want to do that," said Johanna, between sobs.

"It is my recommendation," said Dr. Pritchard. "At least that you explore the possibility. You two are not having a problem producing viable embryos, but they are not surviving the transfer. I've had many patients who have been able to work around this impasse by means of a surrogate. You might have to ask yourself, do I want to be pregnant or do I want my children to be born so that we can be a family?"

Salo, she noticed, was silent. Was he asking himself the question or was he wondering what his wife actually wanted?

"Oh, of course. The latter. I know, but it's hard to give up."

"You've done everything, Johanna." At some point after year two, she had become "Johanna" and Salo "Salo." "Above and beyond, I would say."

"Me, too," said Salo. "I mean . . ."

"One more," Joanna said sharply. "Okay?" She blew her nose and attempted some humor. "One more, for the road. And then yes, I promise. I'll do it."

And so it was back to the injections and the extractions, and four perfect eggs landed in one of Dr. Pritchard's petri dishes, the Cradle of Life, as she had privately taken to thinking of them. Those four perfect eggs, fertilized, began to bubble and brew their way into being, as had fully thirteen of their proto-siblings, and when the time came to transfer these precious final quintessences of Oppenheimers, Dr. Pritchard chose three at random to journey on to the dubious destination of their mother's womb (her much maligned womb) and dispatched the fourth to a freezer in a special facility somewhere in Connecticut, there to wait for the surrogacy they all, even Johanna, expected to ensue.

One more, for the road.

Who knows why it worked, at last and so spectacularly. She'd had the good-news pregnancy test twice before, and once, even, brutally, a stoic little heartbeat, so loudly magnified in Dr. Pritchard's ultrasound room that it hammered like something out of Edgar Allan Poe, but it was still gone only two weeks later (after she had told everyone, including, in floods of tears, her parents). So when she made her way down that long and terrifying corridor in Dr. Pritchard's office at the six-week mark, and wiggled up onto that table of torture with its unforgiving crackle of sanitary paper, and pulled up her shirt for Loretta, the Irish sonographer, to goop her abdomen with gel, she had only the barest hold on her own imminent devastation.

One more, for the road.

Technically, three more. Her three final chances for the only thing she had ever made so bold as to request from the universe. But then Loretta, who had been present at every one of those thirteen embryonic failures, and who, moreover, had seen some of the most powerful citizens of the metropolis wail and weep (sometimes in happiness, sometimes in grief), lowered her magic wand over Johanna's belly and the cacophony of life came thundering through. And not a single thump either, or even a duet, but a crashing, howling trio. Johanna Oppenheimer was, literally, teeming with life.

"Well now," said Loretta, whose Cavan accent had never shifted, despite forty years in New York. She was grinning at the screen. "You folks, everything you've been through. I said a rosary for the Oppenheimers, I don't mind telling you. I don't do that for everyone!"

She heard someone say, "Oh wow," and thought of Andy Warhol, because only a week earlier they'd watched some television program about the artist. He'd stood over a gaggle of assistants as they silk-screened Uncle Sam onto canvas, and said the same thing: *Oh wow, oh wow*. Now, when she turned her head to look at Salo he himself looked silk-screened, and in a shade of green she had never seen before. Or perhaps it was making him actually, physically ill, the news that he was now—and could never for the rest of his life escape being—somebody's father. A whole bunch of somebodies, in fact.

Chapter Four

Triptych

In which Johanna Oppenheimer gestates and Salo Oppenheimer goes further afield

Our mother spent the second half of the pregnancy in bed, allowed up only for careful, increasingly uncomfortable trips to the bathroom and the occasional appointment with the high-risk obstetrician. Hers was an old-fashioned confinement, beginning with heartburn, nausea, and gas, and only getting worse as those babies commenced to mess with her internal organs and the inertia commenced to mess with her head. Downstairs, contractors finished up the house's "gourmet kitchen" and went clomping up to the fourth floor, where they got started on the nurseries: the two boys in the larger front room (with its stunning view of the harbor, a compensation for having to share), the girl in the back, overlooking Montague Terrace. At six months some offset between elation at her long-desired state and profound discomfort tipped, and she began to find that she did not wake in the mornings to contemplate the pure delight of a new day. She did not wake at all, having failed to sleep during the night, as twelve limbs tangled for position inside her and somebody's head pounded her bladder without remorse, and fear—deep fear—coursed through her exhausted body.

The goal was to get to eight months, but eight months undulated before her like a hula dancer in a desert mirage—so far, so unreachably far. Seven and a half months felt just as impossible. Seven months was a daydream, like someday, somehow, loping toward the ribbon at the New York Marathon. She couldn't lie on her left side, where one of the boys sojourned head down, or on her right for fear the girl might be crushed under her brothers. She wasn't allowed to stand except when walking, carefully, to the bathroom. That left sitting up in bed or lying flat on her back, two positions she alternated throughout the day and night.

Our aunt Debbie came once a week or so after work, and our grandmother on Saturdays. One of Johanna's Skidmore friends was a nanny in Park Slope for a couple of novelists; she visited a few times, telling stories about her employers' pretensions, and their dinner parties with other novelists (and their pretensions), but hanging out with an immobile and hugely pregnant woman wasn't a scintillating activity for a nanny's single day off, so Johanna wasn't surprised when those visits petered out. Mainly it was just our mother and Gloria de Angelis, the housekeeper she and our father had hired when the high-risk obstetrician told her to hit the mattress, and the dog, Jürgen (who, being low to the ground, did not enjoy the house's many stairs and preferred to stay on the parlor floor, barking at perceived intruders outside on the Esplanade), and of course Salo, who faithfully came home early and brought dinner upstairs on a tray for both of them: broiled chicken, ravioli, gazpacho, all prepared by Gloria. For nearly four months she stayed where she was, trapped and supine except for those terrifying walks to the bathroom and extremely careful visits to the doctor. Upstairs the workmen clomped and clattered as they readied the two nurseries. She wanted so badly to see the rooms, the curtains and paint color she'd chosen from her bed, the rugs and rocking chairs, the three black-and-white mobiles, which Aunt Debbie insisted had contributed to the genius of her sons, our cousins. But it wasn't worth the risk of climbing the stairs. And the three of them came closer every deeply uncomfortable day.

Facing the bed was a triptych Salo had traveled to London to buy in an auction. The three paintings were of heads, grotesque and distorted on a dark background, each facing in a different direction, each with features swirling into chaos. Johanna, left alone with it (them) day after day, had moved past her initial alarm and even repulsion toward this painting and into an even more problematic way of looking at it. She had begun to think of those three heads as bad fairy counterparts to the three babies kicking her (and one another) throughout each day and night, the warped faces becoming proxies for her fears—fears that plagued her and which must not be permitted to cross the placenta and attach to her actual children. And what, exactly, were the fears of a woman who had waited so long and tried so hard (and yes, suffered so much) to be in precisely the position she now occupied? Simply this: it had occurred to our mother, almost at the moment of those three cacophonous heartbeats in Dr. Lorenz Pritchard's ultrasound room, that for all her yearning and despite the years of pills and shots and blown-out fallopian tubes and egg extractions and waiting and failure . . . she had no idea how to be a parent. None. She knew only, thanks to her own parents, how not to be one. Years of effort, she slowly came to understand, had only pressed her into quicksand, and now here she was, sinking and alone. And what made it worse for her was the fact that our father had found a path of his own—a path he seemed determined to walk without her company and a path she had not recognized soon enough as a path. If only she had, she would have tried harder to understand those squiggles of crayon or the hard blocks of color, or even—though she loathed them—the twisted faces at the foot of her own bed. But it was too late to understand, or even pretend to understand, how these pictures spoke to her husband, and what he heard them say.

By this time our father had acquired fourteen paintings (sixteen, if you counted the triptych as three) and they were everywhere in the house. After work, after the tray and the dinner, after bringing the dishes back downstairs and offering pleasantries to Gloria, Salo's great preoccupation and delight was assigning individual works to the various rooms, and then positioning them within the rooms. This was a ceaseless project, since whatever contentment he felt at the sight of his orange scrawls or gray solid canvases or crosshatch patterns on a neutral wall was always followed, sometimes very quickly, by an absolute conviction that there was a better pairing of room and painting to be found, or a better position within that room, or an idea about something he didn't even own yet which would, on its arrival, topple every domino and set off an epic reshuffling.

Then, one evening as she neared the Holy Grail of her eighth month, Salo set the tray down on the bed beside his mountainous wife and announced that he had purchased a warehouse in some distant wasteland of their adopted borough, and he would be moving every one of his paintings out of the house. A few of them were becoming rather valuable, he told our mother (who was frankly incredulous at hearing this), and he was beginning to get invitations from some of the dealers he'd bought paintings from, a gesture he did not appreciate. Also, a museum in London had actually extracted his name from that Turin gallery and asked to *buy* the Twombly, which felt like a shot across the bow. Our father had found himself worrying about these works, and their safety in the house, with its nonexistent security and fluctuating old-building temperature. Not to mention the combined impact of six toddler hands, flailing, feeling, examining, perhaps adorned with food or grime as they did so. Or three children stumbling into them as they learned to walk. Or, later, the book bags and backpacks, the carelessly handled sporting equipment (they were expecting two boys, after all), or just the number of bodies that were going to share the space with these works of art—passing, crowding, perhaps merely moving the air around them.

"But, if the paintings aren't in the house, you won't be able to see them."

"I'll see them in the warehouse." It was being worked on, he told her then, set up with the proper security, the necessary temperature controls. He could go out there when he wanted to look at them. They both could!

So he had had this in mind for some time, she understood, and the project was well along. She could not say that made her happy, but her job, as ever, was to try to understand, and she did that. The paintings were a joy for him in a way she was quite sure they never would be for her, and in fact there *were* several she would be actively pleased not to have to see every day.

In her seventh month, the art movers arrived and the pictures began to leave: the scribbles and splashes and dark mazes of color. With many apologies and obvious embarrassment, they came into the bedroom and gently removed the triptych and took it, like all the rest, to that other place.

Which brings us, now and inevitably, to our father's warehouse.

The warehouse had previously been part of a portfolio Salo managed, itself descendant through Wurttemberg as part of an estate from his grandfather's time. This had once included several acres of Brooklyn, and even after being forced to sell a portion of its land for the future construction of the Red Hook Houses, it retained a row of structures in Red Hook, on Coffey Street. Red Hook in 1982 was a neighborhood that could not imagine itself becoming anything but what it was: industrial and remote and rudely bisected from the rest of the borough by that massive swath of public housing. Small wonder, then, that it was also a place Salo Oppenheimer, native New Yorker, had never set foot. Until the day he did just that.

The current principals in the estate were a pair of brothers in Fort Lauderdale who had not spoken to each other in a decade and were both childless (or as good as, since the brother who'd actually fathered a single child had gone to extreme legal lengths to disown her). Salo had never met either man in the flesh; he communicated with Abraham Geller of Fort Lauderdale by fax (with a cc to Myron Geller of Fort Lauderdale by standard mail), and with Myron Geller of Fort Lauderdale by standard mail (with a cc to Abraham Geller of Fort Lauderdale by fax), almost always about unremarkable matters. Over time both brothers had expressed their strong desire to "off-load" (in the words of Myron Geller of Fort Lauderdale) Coffey Street, but selling wasn't a straightforward proposition because of one of the trust's more archaic mandates, which was to obtain valuations of every structure in the portfolio every ten years and restrict any initiation of sale to an eighteen-month window following that valuation. Thus, the properties were forced to languish through the '70s as their value declined and the estranged brothers of Fort Lauderdale raised their voices in a crescendo of strangely harmonic (under the circumstances) protest.

In the fall of 1981, as Johanna began her final, magical round of in vitro fertilization, the mandate and its magic outlet rolled around again. Accompanying the appraiser through some of these shabbier Brooklyn locales might have been delegated to a Wurttemberg employee whose last name wasn't Oppenheimer, but our father, now newly resident in this self-same borough, found that he was curious about the addresses he'd known for years. They proved to be old residential buildings abutting a former sugar refinery on a cobblestone street sloping down to the water. The homes were old and basically intact, with rough wooden floors and crumbling walls, and fireplaces that looked far from safe. A couple of them had tenants. The factory building was vacant.

"What do you think of the neighborhood?" our father asked the appraiser.

"This isn't a neighborhood," the appraiser said. "Red Hook? You kidding?"

"It was, once," Salo observed. He had been reading up. Red Hook had originally been a Dutch village, then a busy port, then a warren of tenements full of Norwegian dock workers. That was before the Red Hook Houses, of course.

"Nah. This place'll never come back. If these buildings were in Brooklyn Heights or Park Slope. Even Cobble Hill, maybe, in time. But your clients picked the wrong place to inherit a chunk of the city."

Salo nodded. He didn't disagree. He didn't know enough to disagree, but he was already thinking. And when the valuation for those Coffey Street buildings came in even lower than he'd imagined, he did nothing at first except try to explain to the brothers that neither the firm nor a Brooklyn Realtor he'd consulted at their request felt that any of the properties had a market. But neither Abraham Geller nor Myron Geller, both well into their eighties, saw any reason to wait. Soon, every one of their Red Hook properties was offered for sale to a highly uninterested market.

Salo had no plan, but he found himself thinking about that old factory, and the houses beside it. Sometimes, when he was going out for something for his wife, or heading into Manhattan with the car, he detoured to Red Hook and drove down Coffey Street. The row of run-down houses felt like a memory of another New York, and the adjacent warehouse was spacious. Very, very spacious. And also very, very cheap. And he needed a place to put his paintings, and a place to go and look at them that was, somehow, not the place where he lived with his wife and, soon, the utter strangers they had spent years willing and striving and (for Johanna, at least) suffering to produce. People had begun to open storage facilities designed for just this purpose, Salo knew; one, in fact, had just been built in Long Island City, secure and climate-controlled and expensive and more distant from Brooklyn Heights than Coffey Street. How could this not be a better plan than that? If it was a plan.

"That's an awful idea," said our grandfather, who nonetheless invited Salo to persuade him, and so Salo did. Hermann Oppenheimer was himself spending several thousand a month on storage for only three paintings at a facility in Westchester. "You can't just move a painting into an old building and leave it there," he said, as if his son were an idiot.

"Absolutely not." Salo already had an estimate. Twenty thousand for a climate-control system and the same security the Frick had at its off-site storage in Queens. "And there are four houses adjacent to the warehouse. I'd like to renovate and rent those."

"Who's going to want to rent in Red Hook?" said his father.

Salo shrugged. He still had neither seen nor read a single thing that challenged the appraiser's verdict on the neighborhood, present or future. "It's still New York City," he told his father. What he didn't tell him was what he'd felt as he walked through that empty warehouse, and the small, elderly homes packed with other people's junk and declining fortunes. They were so unlike the gilded and upholstered apartment of his childhood, or the gracious house on the Esplanade a few miles to the north where his wife lay incubating; these humble buildings promised no great comfort or beauty, and yet they called to him. And he was going to continue buying paintings, obviously. If they couldn't be in his home, they had to be somewhere.

Of course the two brothers took the offer. They were mad to sell. They were mad for cash! (One had just been diagnosed with Alzheimer's. The other had a new wife.) It was fast-tracked and over inside a month.

As for our mother, she would spend years of her life perched on the most genteel edge of Brooklyn, but Brooklyn Heights represented the extent of her exoticism. She never troubled herself to learn much about the rest of the borough, and as a result she could never seem to remember the name of the neighborhood where her husband's warehouse was. Coney Island, she called it, in fact, for years—she had heard of Coney Island, and knew it was out there, somewhere, in that general direction—and Lewyn, when he was young, would develop a strange fancy that his father ran some private fun house or waxworks in proximity to Nathan's and the rides, and Sally, who was partial to amusement parks, considered it very unkind of her father to spend so much time in one without her. Harrison never concerned himself one way or another, which was ironic as he was the only one our father ever actually took to the warehouse (once, when he was nine or ten). Johanna herself he took one Sunday morning as soon as the children were on a schedule and secure in the competent arms of two baby nurses, and she had gaped in dismay, predictably, at the neighborhood. Inside the renovated building, she could see that he had already bought more paintings, more pictures of nothing rendered as blocks and scrawls and bright colors hurled against canvas. She took her leave of those, and the familiar ones, more or less without regret and more or less for good. In fact, she would only return to Red Hook once, many years later (a visit with unintended consequences for herself and a number of people she cared about, not to mention a major museum).

That day, in her gestational bed, their bed, with the bad fairy triplets listening in as our father told her about Red Hook, she had asked: "If the paintings all leave the house, though, what will we have on the walls?"

"Whatever you like. I'd say it's your turn to pick."

But there was nothing she would ever want except the faces of her own children. Every year a birthday picture would be taken on the back porch in Chilmark, the three of them holding hands for as long as she could make them, crowded as near to one another as they were willing, briefly, to go. These photographs would climb up the staircase wall, step by step and year by year, three fussy babies, three impatient toddlers, three sullen children, three teenagers who would disperse the instant they heard the shutter click.

Chapter Five

Already Gone

In which the Oppenheimer triplets arrive and immediately commence to grow apart

Lewyn's first memory was of a rocky beach (later to be identified as the one behind our Vineyard cottage), and a long strand of brown seaweed he held up to the sun.

Harrison's first memory was of Jürgen the dog, growling at him.

Sally's first memory was of her brother Harrison grabbing a piece of apple out of her brother Lewyn's grubby hand.

What was the first shared memory? Settling on even that trifling common denominator would have required conversation and the acknowledgment of a shared history, and that was not to be, at least not while they were still children. Harrison, who did most things first, would opt out before the other two, but Sally wasn't far behind. Lewyn, poor Lewyn, held on longer than would be reasonable to anyone else. In fact, he wouldn't give up entirely until his sister dismissed him at the start of their shared freshman year at their mutual alma mater. But without the cooperation of the others, did it ever matter what Lewyn wanted?

Only days before their arrival, the house in Brooklyn Heights had been cavernous and still, classically proportioned rooms full of air, with only an immobile woman upstairs in the bedroom and a lazy dachshund guarding the Esplanade from a couch in the parlor. Now three infants sent forth their existential discontents into the void, and two baby nurses and a housekeeper raced around in an endless cycle of feeding and comforting and changing and bathing as Johanna looked on in pain and disarray. Still, three new souls had entered the world! More than replacing the ones Salo Oppenheimer had taken! Our father might have read in this cosmic redress some whiff of redemption, a tether (three tethers!) to set against his ongoing and incessant ricochet through life, but he could not seem to get there. He stood over them in the NICU, and later in their beautiful wooden cribs at home, sincerely trying to recognize these tiny, wrinkled, angry bundles as being somehow associated with himself, but he failed to do it. He would always fail to do it. Still, our father had been looking at paintings—often quite difficult paintings—for years by then, and because of that he was able to read an essential truth about those three tiny people—that they had arrived as they already were and would ever be: Harrison wild for escape, Sally preemptively sullen, Lewyn full of woe as he reached out for the others. There was no changing them, just as he had no real hope for change, himself.

He made an honest attempt to hold them, to stare into their foreign little faces, but even as he seated himself in the strange gliding rocker and took awkward possession of a baby from one of the nurses, he felt the insurmountability of what he faced. The infant would be at its best, newly bathed and diapered and swaddled, sated from a bottle and drifting toward sleep, but despite such favorable conditions he invariably handed it back and went to find the dog to take him for a walk on the Esplanade. A fair and warm September evening. Across the river, Wurttemberg Holdings was hunched somewhere in the nineteenth-century lowland between the American International Building and the World Trade Center, and everywhere in that dense and frenzied triangle of Manhattan Island young men swarmed the bars, and young women slipped off their office heels and laced on their sneakers to power-walk home. He did not want to be there, particularly. But he did not want to be where he was, either. Johanna, his parents, the fraternity brothers who'd made a point of not shunning him, the colleagues who deferred to him because he was an Oppenheimer, even these three little lives he'd helped to make; he recognized, not for the first time, that he didn't seem to want any of it. But what did he want, instead?

The joint birth announcement was accompanied by the first of the enforced photographs, taken after the last of the babies (Harrison) came home from the NICU: three long infants in matching onesies, one stoic, one sleeping, one in tears. The baby nurses had been standing by when the new family arrived home, all systems at the ready, but Johanna still couldn't settle. She was in a certain amount of *the worst pain she had ever experienced* from her caesarean, but she still had to fight the compulsion to jump up (and wrench open her sutures) whenever one of her children cried, which amounted to a near-constant challenge. The house, indeed, reverberated with infantile unhappiness (largely from Harrison, who gifted them all with his colic) and also stank of all the ordinary baby things. The two nurses didn't get along, and one quickly dispatched the other and replaced her with her own sister-in-law, a silent woman who merely glowered. The dachshund made a point of climbing many stairs, just to soil the carefully chosen carpet in the boys' room. (It was a lot of effort for him to go to, but apparently worth it.) Our mother's maternal anxieties shifted from gestation to lactation, and she spent those first months in an armchair on the parlor floor as one whiny triplet after another was brought to her and taken away. Then, an intervention of nannies, the pediatrician, and her sister Debbie (who certainly had *not* breastfed either of her superior sons) persuaded her that she had done her duty and the children would sleep a lot better if they got a little formula. In a rare show of unity, all three babies instantly declared an allegiance to the bottle, and refused the breast thereafter.

The house on the Esplanade became a twenty-four-hour factory of rocking and feeding and cleaning and airing and rocking again, and feeding again. The various tenders (Johanna, eventually, among them) handed off the various babies to one another when someone needed to sleep (or eat, or pee, but mainly sleep), and the babies did most of what they were supposed to do, in the mainly right order, though Harrison was first at every milestone and either Sally or Lewyn lagged, always. Harrison would only be distracted from his colic when placed in his car seat and set on the dryer. Sally cycled through every conceivable food in search of something she wouldn't projectile-vomit. Lewyn was placid and amiable so long as someone was holding him. Two had eczema. Only one had hair. It was hard to imagine a time beyond this time, with its constant neediness, strong primal odors, and sheer physicality.

Johanna, for once, lacked the wherewithal to think about what Salo wanted, and so her husband fell more and more into the habit of stopping in Red Hook on the way home to sit in the presence of what he had made and was still making: not a thing to be rushed. The first time she paused for breath the children were four and in the pre-K program at Walden.

By then the baby nurses were long gone and also the two nannies who'd replaced them, and she'd downshifted to an afternoon-and-weekend assist from a couple of Hunter College students who came with her to Walden pick-up and helped walk them home or ferry them to activities. All three kids went to a Mommy and Child music class (where they shook little egg maracas and showed a dearth of musical feeling) and attended a Saturday-morning sports program in the little park by Cadman Plaza (where only Harrison agreed to keep running around after the first ten minutes). At home she furnished the basement playroom with every conceivable prop and aid, and waited for the magical creative synergy of her happy children to fill the house on the Esplanade.

And waited.

It meant everything to Johanna that her children be powerfully attached to one another, even *more* attached than some random sequential assemblage of "normal" siblings might have been, but the illusion took every bit of her will and strength to maintain. There was not, for example, one single thing that Harrison, Lewyn, and Sally seemed content to do together—not just at the same time and in the same place but *together*—no matter how she or one of the nannies (later babysitters) might suggest, cajole, bribe, or even admonish them. *Play some game! Cooperate!* Even persuading them to sit on the same couch in the basement and watch the same television show or video seemed to require a Himalaya of effort. The three of them might rise but they simply declined to converge, even if they happened to actually share some interest or preference. Harrison and Sally were both readers, for example, but wouldn't talk to each other about what they were reading, even when they were reading the same thing. Lewyn and Sally had both been affected by the passing of Jürgen, but each came to Johanna, separately, and said they were fine with not having another dog. Harrison and Lewyn both went through a superhero phase—at the same time, no less—but even then had refused to cooperate in play. To call them collectively "quiet" or "self-reliant," for example, was to ignore the fact that Sally isolated herself to feel annoyed, Lewyn to feel wounded, and Harrison to simply escape the other two. So powerful was the mutual aversion, and so ironic, given the triplets had never actually been apart, that you might even have said it was the single thing the triplets actually *did* share.

In the house on the Esplanade, home to three toddlers, then three preschoolers, then three primary-school-aged children, the only time our mother heard the sound of kids at play was when one of her children had a friend over. Otherwise: silence in the basement playroom with its puppet theater and cupboards full of board games and arsenals of foam weapons for active children to hurl at one another, silence in the bedrooms and in the living room, where she not infrequently came across a child with a book or art project or solo game. Her home was quiet—*so quiet*—with not even the shared quiet of a video they all liked down on the basement couch, or the companionable quiet of concurrent reading. When they gathered for a meal conversation might be made, grudgingly, and light chores could be jointly undertaken without too much complaint, but at the first opportunity they parted again, to tend to homework or activities or recreation, and to think separate thoughts about who knew what.

Our mother, who had willed her children into existence (and suffered mightily along the way), would not give up her notion of what they might be. She grew adept at deflecting the "observations" of others—parents on the playground who joked about how the triplets steered clear of one another, or their teachers at Walden, who took some strange delight in describing the children's intra-aversion in parent-teacher meetings. Even her own mother had a way of *tut-tutting* through her rare visits, whenever Sally, Lewyn, and Harrison declined to do something adorable together. So maybe the true, deep bond her children had for one another just wasn't registering in an obvious way, or was something only a mother could possibly intuit. So when Harrison called Lewyn fat and Sally put Harrison's chess medal (which came not from Walden, where everyone got a medal, but from the Brooklyn Chess League, where you actually had to win in order to get a medal) in the garbage, or Lewyn didn't want to share his puzzle with the other two, or Harrison lifted not one finger to help his brother conquer homesickness at summer camp, or Sally refused to agree to any movie or television show that Harrison wanted to watch (even if she also wanted to watch it), simply because *Harrison* wanted to watch it—our mother refused to attach great importance to any of these things, because on some deep, deep level, where it counted, she maintained the fragile notion that all three of her children were devoted to one another. And besides, close intimacy in childhood was no indicator of close intimacy in the fullness of time, which was much more important! (She herself had once been close to her elder sister Debbie, but now Debbie had her own life with Bruce and their boys, and the sisters hardly ever saw each other.)

Into this void Johanna poured routines and rituals—so many routines and so many rituals! Breakfast parfaits and walking to school one way in the morning and home from school another way in the afternoon, stopping at the same bodega for Snapple and OJ, building a family cookbook of recipes they voted on, and taking turns to choose the restaurant on Sunday nights. Disney movies at the Cobble Hill Cinema, stops at Lenny and Joe's on the drive to the Vineyard, the Flying Horses with the brass ring dispenser in Oak Bluffs. She had patchwork quilts made of their baby and kid clothes, so they'd remember. She took Sally for Saturday-morning pedicures and marched Lewyn and Harrison across the Brooklyn Bridge to buy roast-pork buns in Chinatown. On their birthday she took those photographs on the back porch of the Vineyard cottage, and hung them along the staircase wall in Brooklyn so they could see themselves grow up together every time they went upstairs. But if she faltered, even once—one Sunday, one birthday photo, one route home after school—not one of them seemed to notice, let alone care.

When they were six, they departed Walden's nursery school building and entered the Lower School on Joralemon Street, where, for the first time, the three of them were assigned to separate first-grade homerooms and given individual class schedules. The transition would certainly be destabilizing, so our mother set out to prepare her kids, reminding them that the important thing was the comfort and strength of what they shared. She delivered solemn sermons to them over dinner as they approached this traumatic separation, and took them out separately to allay any fears. Harrison she brought to the bookstore on Court Street, treating him to a stack of books; Sally she took to a special lunch at Serendipity. Lewyn got a private walk on the beach, a few days before they left the island that summer. And when the momentous morning arrived, she woke them with excitement and pancakes and asked Salo to go in late to the office so they could walk the kids together, and all the way there she fretted over the approaching moment when two parents would somehow have to divide three children, leaving one or two or all three vulnerable to feelings of abandonment. Harrison was clearly the strongest of the three, so they would all accompany him to his homeroom and leave him, and that would be that. Then she and Salo would split up to take Sally to hers and Lewyn to his, and not leave any of them until each was truly okay. But when they got to the building that morning, the sidewalk and hallways were packed with first-day parents and caregivers and kids, and her boys suddenly announced that they knew where they were supposed to be, and walked off without a backward glance. Only Sally consented to be accompanied to her new classroom, and Johanna couldn't help wondering whether there might be an element of actual pity in the gesture.

When they were nine, all three of them went off to camp in Maine, but only Harrison lasted past the first year. Harrison loved Androscoggin, and would spend many summers there, piling up badges and honors, assembling a pack of admiring buddies, and mastering the arcane skills of the canoe before defecting to CTY at Johns Hopkins, to be with other teenagers who knew what "Supply Side Economics" meant. For Lewyn, though, it was a torment from the moment his parents returned to the car. Oppressed by homesickness, scratching at rashes from plants and insects and sheer anxiety, and only occasionally managing to kick a ball or tie a knot, Lewyn failed to do manly things in the wilderness with the other boys, and begged to spend his summers on the Vineyard with his mother and Sally (who'd also defected, without explanation, after a single Pinecliffe summer).

And then came the September morning when her children, who were no longer children by then, entered the storied stone building that housed Walden's middle and upper schools, and marched off to their separate sixth-grade homerooms for the first time, each having asked Johanna *not* to accompany them. She had stood on the sidewalk, looking after them as they went inside, and then wandered home to her quiet house to spend the day wondering what she was supposed to be doing with herself. Climbing the stairs, she watched the three of them grow up in those magical birthday photographs, just as she had done thousands of times before, but this time she stopped in front of the picture she had hung only days before. Three individuals forcing rictus smiles, waiting for the shutter to click so they could each return to whatever it was they'd been summoned from. Johanna felt herself sit heavily on that top step to the landing, near a spot on the wall that had indeed, as her husband once predicted, borne the brunt of innumerable book bags and backpacks.

Finally, finally, the tiniest pinprick of reality came through the force field of her stubborn delusion, presenting Johanna with the first filament of an idea. That they were two adults plus three children, made concurrently. That they were five humans cohabiting. That they were not, and never had been, a family.

And her husband, what was more, while she hadn't been paying nearly enough attention, had slipped past them all and disappeared—not in terms of his physical self, of course, though his physical self came home later and later each night, after longer and longer visits to his warehouse in Coney Island or Red Bank or wherever it was—but his attentive self, his essential self, which by then lived somewhere else entirely.

Chapter Six

Outsider

In which Salo Oppenheimer remembers some additional injuries, and ceases to tumble

One January afternoon in 1993, Salo Oppenheimer walked into something called the Outsider Art Fair at the Metropolitan Pavilion in Chelsea, and looked around for his wife.

The two of them hadn't visited a gallery together for years, not since before the children were born, in fact, and he had long since moved the slow, deliberate, and frequently joyful perusal of art into the column of things he did away from the rest of them. But this had been Johanna's idea, offered over brunch at their local spot, the previous Sunday.

"Have you been over to see this thing?" She pointed at the Arts Section. All five of them were reading at the table. "Somebody at school was telling me."

"No. I don't know about it."

"She went a few nights ago. This mom. She said the place is jammed full of young people. Lots of energy. It's called Outsider Artists. It's where the art world is going, she said."

"Well, I doubt that." Salo, himself, had just bought another Twombly. Much smaller than his beloved rust-colored scrawl (which, along with its peer-contemporaries, was part of something now being called the "Blackboard Series") and far, far more expensive. Increasingly, it seemed to him, the art world was going where he had already been, for years. That meant there was less to find, and way too many people waving around money.

"So what's an 'Outsider Artist' then?" he asked.

She turned the paper around.

Outsider Artist—the term was so new there was yet to be any strict consensus about its meaning—had something to do with the artist's lack of formal education or training, which didn't make much sense when you thought about it. How many of the artists in his own warehouse had declined or been unable to access formal education and training? Besides, from what this review of the new show described, a truer delineation ought to be based on the artist's sanity, or the lack thereof; they all seemed to be mental patients or street people, laborers building palaces out of toothpicks in their basements at night or self-ordained ministers proclaiming their vision of God. He studied the accompanying photograph: a truly bizarre picture by a Chicago janitor who'd apparently cut pictures of little girls out of magazines and painted them into battle scenes. Some of the little girls even had male genitalia. Sick!

"You should go see it," said our mother. "Actually, let's both go. It sounds bizarre, doesn't it?"

Salo agreed that it did.

"Well," he heard himself say, "that's a nice idea."

Now, at the Metropolitan Pavilion, Johanna was late, five minutes, then ten, then twenty. The entrance area was indeed jammed, with more people pushing past him and into the building. There was no seating, and he was growing irritated past the point of retrieval. Then he heard his name. Over at the registration desk, a harried young person was holding a cordless phone and looking around.

"Yes," he said as he made his way through the crowd, "I'm Salo Oppenheimer."

"Okay," the man said. He looked barely older than his own kids, but was wearing some kind of official badge. "Someone's calling for you. But please don't take long, we need the line."

Salo took the phone. It was Johanna.

"What's wrong?" he said. "What's happened?"

"Oh, I got a call from Aaron's office." She sounded frustrated, not frightened. "They wanted me to come in right away. I went racing over there, thinking something terrible was going on."

"But it wasn't?" He was relieved, and now annoyed. Aaron, who at any other school would be called the "principal" but at Walden was called the "head of school," had always struck him as histrionic and prone to exaggeration.

"No. Well, except that it started with Harrison being unhappy that his class was repeating some material from last year, then suddenly it morphed into serious concern about how the kids aren't speaking to each other at school, and is there something going on in the family that Walden needs to perform some kind of an intervention over."

"You mean an exorcism." This was Walden at its worst, Salo thought. All the drum banging and collective guilt and ethical processing—it was a far cry from his own Collegiate experience, but he had made his peace with that, and besides, he could see that all three of his children, even Lewyn, were reading and writing and doing age-appropriate math. Still, the delight these people seemed to take in breaching family privacy!

"What?"

"What did you tell them?"

He could hear her annoyance, even over the volume of the lobby.

"I said what I always say: Thank you so much for pointing this out, and our whole family will discuss it."

Salo nodded. There had been a similar incident the previous year, with Aaron. That time the instigating concern had been Lewyn's "self-isolation," but this, like the current round, had metastasized into Aaron's all-triplet-all-Oppenheimer expression of Waldenian concern, and the actual suggestion that the family enter counseling.

"So, no list of approved therapists this time?"

"Well, it was offered. But I said I still had the information from last year. I wonder if everybody gets this level of personal attention."

Even such a mild suggestion of fault-finding was noteworthy for Johanna, who having long ago chosen Walden for her children preferred not to question either its principles or its practices.

"Anyway, when I realized I wasn't going to get there at four, I went to the school office and tried to call the show. I ended up talking to some PR office in Soho before they could get me connected to the Pavilion itself. I'm sorry, Salo."

"No, don't worry. I'm sure this isn't our cup of tea, anyway."

The "our" was a gift.

"I'll just take a quick look and come home." Perhaps, he thought, with his now-liberated hours, after a stop in Red Hook.

"Okay," he heard her say. "I'm sorry, though. I was looking forward to it. Let me know if you see the one with the cut-out little girls."

The harried person behind the desk was giving him some very unhappy attention. He was not yet reaching out his hand for the phone, but that had to be imminent.

"See you later."

He expressed his thanks by purchasing a catalog, which indeed featured a cover photograph of a naked little girl shooting a rifle. Then he turned into the shock of another person, standing utterly still before him. Salo was significantly taller than this person, so he looked down.

"I heard your name called," she said, the person. She was looking up at him: a woman, short, slight, African American. She wore the contemporary art uniform of black pants and black shirt, and had a video camera slung over one shoulder. Her other hand held a takeout cup of coffee.

"Yes?" said our father, automatically.

"It's Salo, yes? Oppenheimer?"

"Yes," said Salo, mystified.

"I don't think you remember me," she said.

You don't think? I remember you? He gaped at her. Then it occurred to him: the wedding in Oak Bluffs. Where he had met Johanna. The bride had so many friends. Surely this was one of them.

"Oh, I do," our father said, trying to persuade them both. "Martha's

Vineyard, right? The . . . wedding?" But now he couldn't remember the name of the groom, his fraternity brother, let alone the bride. He'd lost touch with them both. And besides, after that weekend he was with Johanna, and the world had drawn itself around the two of them.

"Martha's . . . ?" said the woman. "No, I don't think so. Not a wedding. I'm Stella. We were . . . I mean, I was. In the car. With you."

It took a moment to land, and then another moment to release him, but by then he was lost to so many things: a clear sense of who he was, and where he was, and what he was supposed to be doing in the world. Because he had missed a signpost, a very, very important signpost, perhaps as far back as that long-ago morning, back past the years of tumbling through space while attempting to pass as a husband and father, back even further to that girl he hadn't looked at, only an extra body in the back seat, only a shadow over his wrist as the Jeep rolled in the air. Here she was, standing in front of him, up to his shoulder, dressed in black and, appallingly, smiling at him. He would never have known her, not on the street or in the lobby of an "Outsider" art fair or anywhere else, but suddenly, now, it all came searing back at him. Her name was Stella.

"Stella," he said.

An impatient man was actually pushing him aside, to get at the registration table.

"Excuse me," this person said, gruffly, after the fact.

That smile. It was small, because her mouth was small, and her teeth were perfectly aligned. Too perfectly, he thought with new horror. Had her teeth been smashed? Were these new teeth, false teeth? He struggled to remember in what specific ways he had damaged her: *arm, foot, concussion, suture.*

"You were in the hospital," our father said, like a fool.

She looked at him. "Well, yes. A long time ago, I was."

Mandy Bernstein, his acknowledged fiancée. Daniel Abraham, his fraternity brother and friend. Their two victim-spirits had been his companions every day since that day, two lost people fastened to him and walking gravely beside him, step by ponderous step, and never once did he imagine they might release him, because he truly did not believe he deserved release.

And not once, not one time in all these years, had he given a single thought to that other person in the back seat, that other body in the tumbling car, because he hadn't killed her and because there was so much else, too much else, in the way: Mandy and Daniel, who were dead. This woman wasn't dead. Had he ever even seen her? Had he turned back, offered a hand or a word of welcome? He had been listening, half listening, to Mandy as she narrated the story of the movie her sorority had screened the night before. He had been wondering if he shouldn't run into the fraternity house to use the bathroom before setting out. He had been questioning whether he'd fastened the canvas roof correctly the last time he'd had the car out and was showing somebody how the convertible top worked, but he was too proud to ask his girlfriend to get the manual out of the glove compartment. He had barely turned his head as the two of them, his passengers, climbed into the back.

Had Danny said: *Morning! This is Stella.*

Had Stella said: *Nice to meet you!*

Had Salo said: *Great to meet you, too.*

But he remembered nothing else, nothing about her at all, not even that she was Black, which was not a non-thing, not in 1972, and then he was turning in the air and they were dead and yoked to him forever, except that here this woman was in the foyer of the Metropolitan Pavilion.

"I'm sorry," he heard his own voice say. "I'm sorry. I'm so sorry."

"Salo," she said quietly, "it wasn't your fault."

And right then, right there, he started to cry, not silently and not with restraint, and this was the first time, the only time, if he was being honest. All those years, not once: never by the roadside, or in the emergency room, or down in the horrible basement morgue with a pathetic Ace bandage on his wrist, or at either funeral. Never, it now occurred to him, with his wife, whose entire purpose, he knew, was to persuade him of the very thing this stranger had just, so matter-of-factly, said. Of course it was his fault. Every moment since that day had been formed around the understanding that it was his fault. He shook with the weeping, he felt its aftereffects on the skin of his cheeks, and chin, and neck. Both of those men, the impatient one who had pushed him aside and the impatient one behind the table, were looking at him now. Salo could see it, from the extreme blurred edge of his vision, but he couldn't get himself to care about it. He might be a grown man in a business suit sobbing in the crowded entryway of the Metropolitan Pavilion, but for the first time in so many years our father was also standing still. Perfectly, beautifully still, and rooted to the ground. The endless tumbling that had been his life since that awful morning: it had all just . . . stopped.

"Do you want to come upstairs with me?" said Stella. "We could talk."

He nodded. He had not one thing to say. The delirium of stasis had silenced him.

He followed her up three flights, barely able to catch his breath as they climbed, his absent wife, his children who did not acknowledge one another at school, the little-girl soldiers somewhere in that building, all now utterly forgotten. Salo kept his eye on her, on her slim legs climbing the steps, on the video camera bouncing against her hip. When they reached the fourth floor she led him through the booths to the back of the building. There were people here, but not as many as he'd expected, not with those crowds in the lobby.

"I thought there'd be more people," he said to the back of her head.

"They're all on the second floor, where the Dargers are. Apparently, no one can resist a female child with a penis and a sword."

Their destination apparently was a square booth in one of the back corners, its walls covered with what looked like large framed blueprints and schematics. There was a glass-topped case in the center of the space, also full of smaller pictures of buildings. Misshapen buildings. The sign above the entrance said SANDRO BARTH, LLC. BERKELEY, CA. A young woman got up from her desk as they approached. "Thanks, hon," said Stella.

"No worries. Hope you found something drinkable."

"Doubt it," Stella said. She turned to Salo. He had stopped crying, which was a great relief to him. "We've invented this thing called coffee out on the West Coast. It's kind of like this," she raised her takeout cup, "in that it's liquid and hot. But it's different because it tastes good. I feel sorry for you guys."

"We're just used to it," the woman said. She left.

"So . . . you live in California," said Salo. He took the seat beside the desk. A group drifted in and over to the glass-topped case.

"I grew up in Oakland. I went back after the accident."

She said this so easily, gliding on without a falter.

"You didn't . . . you mean you didn't graduate from Cornell?"

"Started over at Berkeley." She smiled her beautiful smile. "I love how you East Coast people do that whole Ivy League thing. I get this a lot. *What do you mean, you could have had a diploma from Cornell and you turned it down?* I was thrilled to be accepted there, but I would have gone to Berkeley if my parents hadn't persuaded me. Then, afterward, they were the ones who didn't want me to go back." She paused. "I sometimes think it was all harder on them than on me."

Salo wasn't surprised. The man's daughter had climbed into a ridiculous car with three white students, one of whom had sent the others hurtling into injury and death. And Salo had not even gone to the hospital to see her and the damage he'd caused, whatever it was. It had to have been terrible, but nothing alongside the damage he'd inflicted on the others.

"What," he began. "I mean, what were the . . . your . . . injuries? I can't remember."

She sighed. The topic seemed of little interest to her. "We don't have to talk about this. I want to hear about you! What are you up to? Married, I see! Do you have children?"

Our father looked down at his own left hand. He had come close to denying his children, not duplicitously, but because he'd genuinely forgotten them. "Yes. I have three children."

"Three! How old?"

He explained. It took so little time.

"My gosh, that's a lot to take on."

"I work for my family's company. Financial services."

She nodded. "Do you like it?"

"I . . ." The question didn't immediately compute. "Well, sure. And I started buying paintings, years ago. Nothing like this," he said apologetically. "I mean, they're very nice, but I'm just looking."

Stella burst out laughing. "Please! I'm not here to sell you art. These aren't even paintings, you know. All drawings. I think he's *much* more interesting than Darger, actually."

"He?" Salo asked.

He was a San Francisco draftsman named Achilles Rizzoli. He'd spent his work life in an architectural firm rendering office buildings. By night he'd conjured a fantasy city offering everything from matrimonial matchmaking to reincarnation. The city was weirdly beautiful, but the strangest thing about it was that its individual buildings were real people, transmogrified into architecture.

"Everyone he knew became a building," said Stella. "The thing is, he didn't know that many people. He was odd, very antisocial. And he never showed his work publicly except for one day a year. He put up a sign outside his apartment and charged people ten cents. Then most of those people ended up getting drawn as buildings. A little girl who lived on his street named Shirley became these towers he called *Shirley's Temple.* Another neighbor became a palazzo. And his mother was a cathedral."

"He must have been incredibly lonely," said Salo.

"Oh, he was."

Salo got up. For the next few minutes he walked around the room, looking. The pictures were all identically framed in pale wood, with a broad empty space around each image. The largest ones, the people-buildings, were fascinating; each had a grand title and a few sentences of praise, sometimes conveyed by or interspersed with puns, about the person who'd been remade into stucco or stone. *The Sayanpeau. The Kathredal. The Primal Glimpse at Forty.* There was a definite edge of sexual anxiety over a few of the drawings, too, notably the female ones.

"He was watching his neighbor's daughter playing," said Stella. He turned to find her just behind him. "Her dress went up. She wasn't wearing underwear. This was how he dealt with the shock."

"Schizophrenic?" Salo heard himself ask.

"Interesting you should ask. Never diagnosed, and he held a job throughout his life. But it's not possible to say. I did show the work to a psychiatrist I know in Berkeley. He had a field day, gave me lots of reading on psychosis and manic depression, but declined to give me a diagnosis. Which is only right. There are some very off-kilter letters, and he wrote a massive novel that made no sense, which he couldn't get published. And there are hundreds of the smaller drawings, sketches and schematics for his imaginary city. I'd love to see all of this go to the same place, and stay together, but I don't think that's going to happen."

He nodded. "And you work for the dealer?"

"Oh no!" Stella said. "I'm a documentary filmmaker."

He looked at her. Her eyes were following two women as they moved swiftly past the displays. The women were dressed identically in black, with shaved heads.

The camera registered, then. She had placed it on her desk. It looked very different from the home-use versions Salo had occasionally used over the years, to videotape his children. More like the real thing.

She wanted to make a film about Rizzoli, Stella explained. That was why she'd come. To see people as they encountered the work, to find critics to interview. But the people and the critics were mainly downstairs, gaping at little girls.

"Rizzoli never left California, not once in his life. And of course he died with nothing, no heirs. All of the work was thrown away when his landlord cleaned out his apartment in San Francisco. And somebody, some total stranger, was walking past and saw all of this in a dumpster. And when he looked at it, it just blew his mind, so he took everything home with him and eventually brought it all to a dealer friend of mine in Berkeley. Sandro almost turned him away. He didn't think there was a market for a dead guy whose entire life's work ended up in a dumpster. But then this whole Outsider thing just kind of started to build momentum, so he had everything framed and we drove it all across the country. I filmed some interviews yesterday. The *New Yorker* critic was here, and a few other dealers. But like I said, it's all about Darger at the moment."

Salo nodded. "Your guy should have thrown in a bit of male genitalia." It was remarkable how, without ever having seen a Darger, he felt entitled to an opinion. Well, that was the art world in essence. Outsider *and* Insider.

"Very sad men. Both of them. Very sad and very lonely men."

The collar of her shirt had slipped open, he saw. There was a bright pink scar across her clavicle.

Arm, foot, concussion, suture.

Clavicle. He remembered now. She had broken her clavicle. He had broken her clavicle.

When Sandro Barth returned, the two of them left, first for a bar on Ninth Avenue and then for Red Hook, where he walked her through his collection. She was amazed by it, by what he had done. She marveled at the triptych and recognized the Diebenkorn immediately. ("California artist," she said and shrugged.) She stood before the two Twomblys, hands on hips, silent. When he pointed to the large one and told her it was the first painting he had bought, she nodded. He didn't have to say more than that. They stayed for a couple of hours, then he took her back to her hotel and they had another drink in the lobby bar. The place was dark. They sat apart. She had never married, she said. She had wanted to have children, but she'd spent years filming a single mother in Oakland who was struggling to raise four kids, and she didn't think she could do that, or willfully put a child through it. The documentary, she told him, had won some awards and received some attention.

He went to find a phone booth in the lobby and called home, and our mother was actually pleased to learn that he had run into an old friend from college at the art show. He had lost touch with so many of his Cornell friends, his fraternity brothers. Even the couple, Michael and Dorothy, at whose wedding they'd met. She didn't ask for many details about his evening, but she told him she'd had a long talk with Harrison about his run-in with the head of school. Their son had agreed to stop tormenting Aaron if they'd allow him to go to the Brooklyn Public Library on Remsen Street after school, and come home on his own. Salo nodded. But he wasn't paying attention.

He went back to the table, and Stella, and she told him more about her life and her world, the world of documentary film, which was slow-moving: grants and investment and red tape and eternally ongoing conversations. He nodded. The idea of an ongoing conversation with her was already blooming, uncomfortably, thrillingly. He hoped she couldn't tell, and she couldn't, or so she would say, afterward, and why would she lie to us about something so important?

Just after ten in the evening they shook hands and he leaned down to give her an awkward kiss on the cheek. Then he went home.

His own father, as Salo himself well knew, had for years carried on an arrangement with his executive assistant, a woman precisely as old and objectively as attractive as our grandmother, but single and childless and content to remain so. This person had lived in a tidy apartment on Madison Avenue and Sixty-Sixth, over a gourmet chocolate shop, and whenever Hermann was not at the office, or at home on Fifth Avenue, or at their weekend place in Rye, or somewhere else with his wife . . . well, that was where he was more likely than not to be, for years and years until the lady in question (known to our father as "Miss Martin, from the office") suffered a stroke in her tidy apartment and died alone at Lenox Hill Hospital. It was less an affair than a parallel marriage with different terms, and Salo had no idea what, if anything, his mother knew about it.

This was not that. This was not that, at all.

Our father, for one thing, was not a person given to tracking beautiful women as they walked down the street or gathered in front of the school, and there were many, many beautiful women around Walden, aerobicized in the '80s and increasingly yoga'ed or Pilate'd as the '90s got underway. Some of these women worked, in the parlance of the day, "outside the home"; others took care of their kids and more highly calibrated care of themselves. A few Walden moms were even famous—actresses and media figures—yet they made a good-faith effort to leave their outside lives at the door and be informal and approachable within the school's social enclosure. Salo hardly ever gave any attention to these women. Not even the beautiful ones. Not even the *famously* beautiful ones. "Tell me her name again," he would ask Johanna as they made their way home after the fourth-grade play or all-school fundraising evening. "I know I've met her. She seems so familiar."

"She starred in that movie you liked, about the bank heist," our mother would say. "That's why she seems familiar."

Sometimes he told himself that their marriage worked because each of them ceded the authority of their respective spheres to the other. The fact that they didn't crowd each other or push their way into each other's daily affairs, that was a good thing. Wasn't it? And of course he valued the work our mother did, running the family so smoothly that he could spend his hours in Red Hook or fly to Europe to see a picture or attend an auction, just because he wanted to. From the beginning our father had addressed family life as a party of one, setting a schedule around his personal needs and responsibilities and interests, while she was a many-tentacled creature, staying on top of the vaccinations and tutoring (for Lewyn, who needed help in math) and vet appointments (while the dog was alive) and upkeep on the house (both houses) and oversight of her parents (because her mother was beginning to have some difficulty with language, and her father refused to accept this, and Debbie was so busy and Bobby was incapable of doing a single thing in aid of anyone who wasn't Bobby) and incidentally Salo's parents as well. (Hermann had fallen the previous spring, on the corner of Seventy-Seventh and Park, and the resulting hospital stay had left him with an invasive staph infection leading to endocarditis. He was home now, but much diminished and not all that fun to be around, not that he ever had been. Johanna visited at least once a week.)

So our father certainly understood that he was not what was now being called an "involved" or "attached" father, but naturally he felt responsible for his children, and he approved of them, in general. Sally was fractious but she also had some deep strength the others did not—that boded well for a world in which people were always, essentially, alone. Lewyn was easily wounded, but he had a reserve of human warmth that our father respected.

Harrison he never worried about for one moment. Harrison's dark days were right now, with the constraints of Walden upon him, but once he went out in the world he would proceed directly to wherever his true peers were congregating, and be as content with those people, in those places, as he was capable of being.

The triplets, by this point, had reached the precipice of Walden Upper, home of the legendary Walden creativity and scholarship (and drug experimentation and broadly supported sexual expression); beyond that, the vision of their departure for college began to shimmer in the distance. Neither of our parents was blasé about this symbolic finish line, but beyond that tiny point of agreement they saw things very differently. Even before that day at the Outsider Art Fair, our father had long been aware of a certain excitement in the way he thought about the children's departure, and what the transition might mean for his own future. Sometimes he thought of the houses he himself owned on Coffey Street, a few of them still with tenants, one empty. That appraiser hadn't been wrong about the neighborhood, exactly, but there had been certain intriguing signs in the years since his ill-advised purchase: artists taking over the old buildings, young couples repainting the wood-frame homes. There was a new restaurant on Van Brunt Street that was surprisingly good, not all that different from the expensive places in Brooklyn Heights (or even, for that matter, Manhattan). Sometimes, before he got back into his car at night, he walked down to the empty house at the end, his favorite of the properties. No one had lived in it since his purchase, but Salo had been inside a number of times and he had some recurring thoughts about a renovation: bathrooms, a kitchen, care for the cracked walls. There was income potential there, possibly, especially with the intrepid young people now exploring Brooklyn's nether regions. There was even some vague talk about a regular ferry service to and from Manhattan. But in the end it came to him that no one should live in this house but himself.

Johanna had no such daydreams about houses or apartments. Neither were there excited plans to work again, or go back to school, or even just enjoy herself once the day-to-day concerns of parenting came to an end.

Our mother, on the contrary, contemplated the future with deep and growing dread, and Salo had good reason to worry about how she'd navigate this treacherous passage to whatever came next. Her life recoiled, even as his sped toward an opening.

Stella went back to Oakland, where her life was. Of course she did. Salo, when he thought of her, which was often, had reason to be grateful she lived so far away. But when she came to the city he met her for dinner in some formal restaurant, the kind where people conducted business affairs, not personal ones. And they did have business to discuss, now that the Rizzoli paintings were safe in the collection of a single owner, an owner more than willing to make the works available to her for filming and study. She moved to secure funding from her previous partners: the Arts Council of California, the National Foundation for the Arts. Her project moved at the usual glacial pace, but it did move. Certainly, the film she envisioned was impacted by the public's unyielding interest in Henry Darger, the painter of little girls at war who, to no one's surprise, had become the shining star of the entire genre of Outsider Art, casting all other artists into corresponding shadow. Already there were books about Darger, and films about Darger, and innumerable magazine stories about Darger, and the works themselves were making their way around some of the country's most important art museums. No one seemed interested in a *different* backward, antisocial guy who'd left his life's work in a hopeless pile after his lonely death. It frustrated Salo but not Stella, who reminded him that documentary filmmaking was a long game, and any number of superb, even classic films had taken years of dogged stewardship and suffered many varieties of setbacks on their way to getting made. In the meantime, she had actually managed to find a couple of elderly San Franciscans who'd worked with the reclusive draftsman, and a neighbor who'd once stepped into his apartment on the day of his annual exhibition to the public. (And emerged moments later, mystified.)

Our father lived in torment. We understand this now. We also understand that he tried, for a time, to do what he thought was right—he wasn't Hermann Oppenheimer and Stella wasn't "Miss Martin from the office"—but also that this right thing was untenable. Twice a year, then more often. He always took her to dinner in staid and well-lit places, and he sat as far away from her as he could, because he was afraid of what might happen. This was the person he'd run into at that strange art fair, he reminded our mother when he came home after their dinners. This was the old friend from college, he said, leaving out the detail of what he had done to her all those years ago. It was exhausting to pretend not to feel what he felt every moment they were together and every moment they were not together. He couldn't bear the thought of hurting her any more than he already had. He engaged in diversionary tactics: introductions to potential investors, meetings with curators, notably at the Museum of American Folk Art, who were already planning a major show for Darger (of course). He went back to the Outsider Art Fair with her each year. He even brought our mother out to dinner with Stella one January night when the kids were in eighth grade or ninth—Stella couldn't remember the year and none of us ever asked our mother—the three of them at Aquavit under the waterfall, carefully eating arctic char and talking about this woman's life in California and the movies she'd made and her current documentary subject, a strange and obscure artist from San Francisco who turned people into buildings.

"What a hard way to live," Johanna told Salo in the cab, going home. "Good for her."

It was the last kind thing she would ever say about Stella Western.

Salo, naturally, would have simply handed her the money for her film, but he knew she would never take it, not with their history, which was always between them even if they never spoke of it. The least our father could offer was access to the pictures themselves, to study them, to film them whenever she wanted, a few times to bring in experts to examine them. He had gone back to see Sandro Barth on the last day of that first Outsider Art Fair, intending only to buy one or two of the human buildings, but the Berkeley dealer was anxious to move on, perhaps to other corners of the Outsider market, perhaps to something a little more conventional. By the time their meeting ended later that evening (at one point it moved to the Gotham Bar and Grill), Salo Oppenheimer had purchased the contents of that corner booth two floors above the Henry Darger exhibit, and everything would be delivered a few days later to the warehouse in Red Hook: those strange buildings-as-people and the schematics for Rizzoli's mythic city and the illustrated poems addressed to his dead mother and even the hand-drawn signs the artist had constructed to hang outside his apartment on that one day per year he allowed the public inside. All of it, comprising the entirety of the extant work of the very obscure (and likely to remain so) Achilles Rizzoli, would spend the next decade in an upstairs room of that former sugar refinery on Coffey Street, behind a closed door. And then it disappeared.

Chapter Seven

Warrior Girls

In which Sally Oppenheimer learns something new

Sally was the first of them to find out, and, for a long time, the only one who knew.

She was a newly minted teenager then, and not thinking about our father much, if at all, just as she wasn't thinking about our mother or our parents' marriage, all of which made her a very ordinary thirteen-year-old and, in that respect at least, entirely like her brothers.

Besides, she had other things on her mind.

Fifth grade had been the year of backyard Truth or Dare—a surprising number of Walden kids lived in brownstones, with backyards—and sixth grade had seen the first couples, breaking up and making up in the school corridors, sometimes with the help of intermediaries. By seventh grade there was open speculation about who had gone well beyond kissing, and one particular couple (granted, the boy was a ninth grader) was widely believed to have gone all the way. No boys seemed unduly interested in Sally, which was just as well since Sally was terrified one would be. Three years earlier, she had been so horribly captivated by one of her Pinecliffe counselors, a sweet girl from Shaker Heights who attended Northwestern, that she'd informed her parents she wouldn't be returning to camp. After this, there had been a fallow period during which Sally just about persuaded herself that the counselor was an aberration, but then Lewyn mentioned that a girl from a popular TV show was actually in the Walden class behind them, and this had proved horribly true. It was obvious that Lewyn himself had a pathetic crush on this person, which only made things more stomach churning, and Sally did her best to defang her feelings by loudly and frequently making fun of her brother. It didn't help. The girl was so pretty, with long hair parted along a razor-straight line and falling nearly to her waist, and long legs toned from years of ballet. (According to *Sassy* magazine, she had first been spotted at the School of American Ballet by another girl's mom, who worked in casting.) Now, Sally saw this girl constantly: in every Walden corridor, in the middle school cafeteria, even in combined gym class, which was excruciating. She saw her in the mornings, on the sidewalk in front of Walden, with her mother. She even saw her one Saturday in Bloomingdale's as Johanna force-marched her around the second floor, desperately trying to bond. (The girl, by contrast, was with a couple of friends, carrying armloads of stuff to the dressing rooms.) Of course, Sally never once spoke to her. She didn't *want* to speak to her. But she didn't want Lewyn to speak to her, either.

One afternoon, as she was leaving Walden's signature Ethical Conflict Resolution class, a girl named Willa fell in with Sally and said the strangest thing. It was so strange that Sally actually had to ask her to repeat it, even though she didn't know Willa all that well and didn't much like the parts she did know.

"Sorry, *what?*"

"I *said*. I *saw*. Your *dad*."

Okay, Sally nodded dumbly. She was fighting the urge to roll her eyes. She had as little interest in her father as Willa likely had in her own.

"With his *girlfriend*."

This, undeniably, hit just as intended, and Sally was temporarily robbed of her breath, her speech, and her wits, roughly in that order. More than anything else, the sentence failed to compute, and then, in a great cumulative clanking of pieces sliding into place, it did.

"So?" Sally managed, desperately trying for nonchalance.

"Well, if it was my dad, I'd want to know."

Ah, but it wouldn't be Willa's dad, would it? Willa's dad was a surgeon who was always flying off to war zones to fix the damaged hearts of poor children. He was perfect. He probably had his affairs safely on the other side of the world. (It was remarkable, Sally observed, that she had gone from ignorance to snark so quickly.)

She didn't ask for the rest, but she got it anyway: Willa and her mother and sisters had been coming out of Odeon into a rainstorm, and there were no cabs. Then: there one was, splashing to a stop right in front of the restaurant. Willa's mother waved at the driver and the girls huddled under one umbrella as they waited for the passengers to get out, which was when Willa had recognized him.

Not for one single second did Sally doubt that what her classmate had said was true, or that Willa had correctly interpreted what she'd seen. Willa and Sally (and, of course, Sally's brothers) had been classmates since kindergarten. Hadn't Willa seen Salo Oppenheimer at any number of parents' nights and play performances and holiday parties and Halloween observances? Hadn't Salo Oppenheimer picked her up at Willa's house on Tompkins Place, more than once? There had even, before Sally had decided Willa was a bit of a wuss, been the occasional sleepover at the house on the Esplanade, with her father in the kitchen the following morning. Of course Willa had recognized Sally's father, getting out of a cab and ducking through the rain into Odeon.

Willa had not, however, recognized the woman whose hand Sally's father was apparently holding.

"What makes you think I don't know about it?" she told Willa. Then she went to her last class of the day, fuming.

What really pissed her off, she later decided, was not that Salo had done this—to herself, to "the children," even to our mother—but the notion that he might actually be making an effort with another person, which was something he hadn't ever done with any of the aforementioned people, not in Sally's own opinion. For a technically intact family (and intact families were not the norm at Walden; most people seemed to have steps and halves or a parent who had simply checked out) the Oppenheimers didn't really operate as a unit, and when they did things together they mainly did them for Johanna's sake. Yes, all five of them got dressed up to see *The Nutcracker* every year, because it was a family tradition. Yes, they walked over the bridge to Chinatown on Christmas Day and then went to see a movie, because that was what New York Jews did (if they weren't actually observing the holiday!). Yes, they celebrated the magical anniversary of the (scheduled) birth together on Martha's Vineyard. These were things the five Oppenheimers undertook together, but it didn't mean they had tangible intimacy with one another's lives, or (especially) that they actually liked one another. Sally's family was not given to warm gestures, reassurances, encouragements, deferrals. They were not one another's "biggest fans" or "persons." They didn't have one another's backs. They weren't, you know, *close,* and despite the tragic efforts of our mother, none of them ever tried to pretend they were.

Sally's father had never once, for example, held Sally's mother's hand anywhere, let alone in public. Not that Sally could recall.

That first night she found herself watching him attentively when he came home, which was, as usual, after the three of them and our mother ate dinner. He sat in the living room with Johanna as he usually did, speaking pleasantly to the kids as they passed through, reading his art magazines and looking through his catalogs. How had the eighth-grade social studies teacher liked Harrison's report on John Jay? Had Lewyn made up his mind about Androscoggin this summer? Was that a new shirt Sally was wearing?

Polite enough. Attentive enough. It was basically the way Salo had always behaved toward them, as if the fatherhood protocol had been explained to him by authorities, and he ceded to their expertise. Also, he was a benign sort of person, not at all a mean person. He'd probably never hurt anyone in his whole life.

And at the end of that evening, like any other evening, our mother and father went up the stairs lined by those birthday photographs and closed the door of their bedroom. Sally might hear *David Letterman* as she went up to her own room or down to the kitchen, but she never heard them speaking to each other (or—God forbid—any other kind of interactive activity). They were a quiet couple. We were a quiet family, that was all.

Except, as is now apparent, even to those of us who wouldn't find out for years, that was obviously not all.

She began to pay closer attention. What, if anything, did he say about how he spent his time? And what, in particular, did he do with himself in the evenings?

"How come Dad never eats dinner with us?" she asked Johanna, once she'd worked up her nerve.

"He eats dinner with us," our mother said, which wasn't untrue, but it also wasn't very common. Maybe one night a week.

"Would Dad take me with him sometime to look at the galleries?" she asked.

"Oh Sally, I think he'd love that."

But for something he'd love, he never invited her, or either of the others.

"Dad," she finally said, "are you busy tomorrow night? I thought maybe we could do something. Go to a play or something."

But he had a work thing. He actually seemed genuinely sorry about it, too.

"What kind of work thing?"

"Just a dinner with some clients. They like Delmonico's. Have you ever been to Delmonico's?"

Of course she had never been to Delmonico's.

"Well! We should go," our father said. "It's like visiting the nineteenth century."

Sally, who had no great wish to visit the nineteenth century, just nodded.

One night, as he gathered up his catalogs at the end of the evening, an invitation fell out at her feet. He didn't notice, and she picked it up and looked at it before handing it back. It was for the opening of a show at the American Folk Art Museum, for an artist named Henry Darger. The front of the invitation showed a line of little girls all tied together. Behind them was a row of men on horseback, each holding a flag.

"Who's Henry Darger?" she asked, handing it over.

"An Outsider Artist," her father said. "The most famous Outsider Artist, but not the only one."

Sally had no idea what that meant, but those little girls seemed like more of an issue. "This is kind of sick," she noted.

Salo actually smiled. "You're not wrong."

"They look like something he cut out from a magazine."

"Yes, I think he did that."

"And you're going to buy something from this guy?"

"No," our father said, a little too emphatically.

"But you want to meet this artist?"

Our father shook his head. "No, he won't be there. He's dead."

"Oh." This made even less sense to Sally, because when you went to these art openings, didn't you at least get to meet the artist? "So why would you want to go to this?"

"Well, you know, I'm always trying to learn something new."

That wasn't much of a why, but more to the point, it wasn't an "I'm not going," either. In a little less than three days, this museum was where our father intended to be, perhaps even with the woman Willa had seen getting out of the taxi.

Sally decided that she would be there, too.

The thing with the camp counselor might have been a classic lesbian childhood trope, but Sally was no Harriet the Spy. (She hadn't even liked that book, and following folks around to discover things about them and write it all down in her notebook? It seemed like a lot of trouble to go to, and also a little bit mean.) She viewed her upcoming mission not as a great adventure or some piece of an ongoing fact-finding mission, but as a likely unpleasant task that she just needed to perform, and not for anyone's edification but her own. Pretty much the only pleasurable element of her plan was the fact that she would be withholding information about it from her brothers, and as a result she might conceivably know something they did not know when it was over. For that reason alone, she hoped the woman would be there, and that she'd be able to get a good look at her for subsequent analysis.

On the day in question she called her mother from a pay phone to say that she and a few friends were heading to Manhattan to see *Clueless,* after which one of the dads would be bringing them all home in a cab. Then she went straight to Lincoln Center and lurked, finding the American Folk Art Museum right beside the Latter-Day Saints visitors' center. The museum was closed to set up for that night's big event, so she couldn't go inside to scout out a place not to be seen, but she did go into the gift shop where there were endless postcards of quilts and weathervanes and two apparently new and very expensive coffee table books all about Henry Darger, the "Outsider Artist" of the moment. Sally, seeing more of the man's work, was thoroughly mystified by the weird simplicity of those cut-out girls and cartoony backgrounds, often featured in states of pain or degradation. Just looking at it gave her a funny feeling, and not a pleasant one, but she kept turning the pages: girls being throttled, girls being hung, girls being stabbed. At least the illustration on our father's invitation had merely showed them tied together. She wondered if he knew about the rest of it.

When they closed the gift shop she went to get herself a falafel, and ate it across the street from the New York State Theater, watching the dancers duck-walk to the stage door. Then she went into the Library for the Performing Arts, back behind the opera house, and changed into a simple black dress and a pair of black boots with a bit of a heel. (Even at thirteen, Sally was a New York Woman. She knew how to wear black.) She also put her hair up in a bun, like those dancers going in the stage door. She wasn't in disguise, exactly, but she knew she didn't look like her usual self, the one who attended Walden with her brothers and (official version) hadn't liked summer camp in Maine. The way she looked, it was entirely possible that, even if our father happened to see her, he might very well not recognize her. Not that she intended to be seen.

She'd been worrying about a guard or someone checking tickets, but there was nothing like that, only a woman who wanted to take her coat and a man offering wine and water. Sally darted deep into the galleries, searching for places where she could look at others without being looked at herself, but nobody seemed to be looking at anything but the pictures. They were huge and bright and on all of the walls, but also suspended in the middle of the rooms: long and uncoiled scrolls of paper, some of them painted on both sides; those little girls, naked or with butterfly wings, armed and dangerous against orange or seafoam skies, or spurting blood on the battlefields. She tried to avert her eyes from them as she moved, searching for Salo Oppenheimer's tall and angular shape, but when she looked up it was into the face of an agonized girl being bayonetted by a grim, almost bored-looking man, or some other beautiful outrage. No one had spoken to her, not since the man with the tray of wine and water glasses. No one seemed to regard her with any interest, let alone suspicion. Perhaps the presence of so many tormented children detracted from one not-quite child making a creditable attempt to look even older than she was, or perhaps Sally really had succeeded in camouflaging herself at a New York art event in the year 1995. She nearly felt invisible as she completed her circuit of the rooms.

Just as she returned to the lobby in search of a safe place to watch the door, two things of immense significance happened, almost simultaneously. The first was that Sally found herself immobilized by the exposed back of a woman who happened to be standing a few feet in front of her, near one of the long double-sided panels. This back, narrow but muscled, delineated by a visible spine, warm brown in color, was on display between the slim white straps of a linen dress all the way down to where it curved into hidden places, and its impact on Sally was immediate. She felt this not just in the form of conscious admiration, but in a breathlessness and a bolt of weakness, and, perhaps most distressing of all, in the sharp, hollow feeling between her legs, so powerful and so impossible to dismiss that it mocked every one of her efforts to deny the obvious. Before her eyes, as the woman that back belonged to turned to the person on her right and then to the person on her left, alternately speaking and nodding in agreement, that warm back tensed and relaxed, flexed and straightened. The woman had long dreadlocks, but they had been swept aside and over her left shoulder, obscuring her neck. The white dress was long, but not so long that Sally could not see her calves and lovely ankles. Those ankles confused her. She could not understand why they seemed to matter so much.

Anyway, that was the first thing.

The second thing followed so closely on the first that Sally did not immediately separate them, especially since, in a wave of bonus confusion, there was a certain sensory overlap. That sharp, hollow feeling where her two legs met was moving decisively into a related but distinct sensation, less sharp than dull, less hollow than unarguably . . . moist. Sally had a sudden powerful and unhappy conviction of what it might signify.

She turned and made her way to the bathrooms beside the gift shop, went in and took the farthest stall, and there, with trepidation, she reached under her black dress and pulled down her underpants.

Oh. Naturally.

For fuck's sake.

A year or so earlier, when she'd gotten her period for the first time (at school, between classes, and while wearing very unfortunate white jeans), there had been no rush of delight at having achieved, however misattributed the term, *womanhood.* In fact, Sally had been dreading the great milestone, and was actually enraged at the brown stain on her underpants. That she'd also been completely unprepared, from a practical standpoint, when the great day arrived, was totally her bad, since Walden had been drilling down hard on health and sexuality for years by that point and many of the girls in her class had already jumped from one side of the roster to the other, often broadcasting the fact to their classmates.

Sally had not been one of those eager for public transition. She had not been eager for transition at all. She had no great need to bleed into her underpants every month (a prospect that seemed, at the very least, totally gross) and no desire to be any closer to the awesome prospect of motherhood or, for that matter, sex. (Sex was a thing she'd been trying hard not to think about.) She was generally resentful about the extra burden she would now have to shoulder, and had a particular resentment for the kind of sacred mother-daughter sharing that was a standard scene of Young Adult fiction:

Johanna, who had already burdened her with words about how important this was, and already asked, on more than one occasion, whether there had been any sign of Sally's period. (Sign? What kind of a sign would that be? Surely it had either materialized or it hadn't!) In response to these queries, Sally had issued a silent plea—to whom she didn't know—for more time. More months, another year . . . maybe never? And indeed, at twelve-going-on-thirteen, she'd been one of the last girls in her grade to reach the momentous milestone. So yes, she'd had a decent run, but you couldn't stay lucky forever.

It had come twice since that first time: sporadic, irregular, abbreviated. This was the third time, and once again, of course, she was totally unprepared.

Women were coming into the bathroom now, but there were plenty of stalls. Sally stayed where she was, motionless and silent, trying to play out the various options open to her. The tampon dispenser she'd noted on her way in, beside the door, was useless to her (this being a transition she still hadn't made), but she obviously couldn't do nothing, and another drone of pain was even now surging through her lower abdomen. That pain was a sharp reminder of how deeply unfair this all was. Lewyn and Harrison would never hunch over a toilet seat in the name of procreation, just as they would never be called upon to waddle around with a bloody pad inside their underpants, or shove cotton up their revolting penises. (She assumed they were still revolting. She hadn't actually seen them for years.) All for the privilege of that *greatly multiplied sorrow* in the *bringing forth of children*!

Resigned, she took a fistful of paper from the dispenser, rolled it around her hand and inserted it between her legs, then she pulled up her underpants around it. It felt absurd, like wearing a diaper, but at least her dress was loose. At least it wasn't white, like her jeans that first time, at school. Like the dress that woman had been wearing out there in the lobby.

The memory of that woman's back, its descending spine, momentarily displaced her discomfort and resentment.

She flushed the toilet and opened the door of her stall.

And there, like something preordained, like something totemic, was that very back, contained by those same white linen straps, inclining forward over one of the sinks, only this time the dreadlocks of its wearer were tumbling down to the shoulder blades. Sally stopped where she was, stupidly, in the open door of the stall, just as the woman straightened up with a damp paper towel in her hand and began to wipe the skin under her eyes. She looked up into the mirror and Sally couldn't look away. Apparently, she couldn't keep her mouth shut, either.

"Hi," she heard herself say.

The woman looked into the mirror, into Sally's eyes, and Sally felt again that terrible sensation, less sharp than dull, less hollow than . . .

"Hi yourself," the woman said. Then she stopped dabbing her face and looked again. "You okay, hon?"

Sally, in a perfectly rational response to this question, burst into tears.

"Uh-oh," the woman said. And before Sally could stop her—and she totally, totally would have stopped her—this person had taken three steps in her direction and was giving Sally Oppenheimer possibly the most encompassing and terrifying hug of her entire life.

"You're okay. You're okay," the woman said, as if this were an established fact. Her embrace was horrifying but also horrifyingly not-unpleasant. She stepped back out of the woman's arms, and at that moment the door opened and two other women entered, parting like people in a square dance around Sally and the woman with the beautiful back, and slipping into the stalls on either side.

"C'mere," she said. She meant the little sitting area beyond the sinks: two armchairs and a low table, beneath a framed poster for a show on ship figureheads. Sally sat, uncomfortably crossing her legs over the wedge and trying not to look at the front of that white dress, which, while not nearly as low as the back, was pretty low. The woman had a scar, bright pink, at her collarbone. Sally stared at it.

"Do you want me to get someone for you?"

Sally shook her head, no. Who was there to summon: her father, *his girlfriend*?

"No, that's okay. I came on my own."

"Oh? Just had to see those Dargers?"

"No, no. I mean, well, yeah." Her voice shook. She was horrified by the drivel coming out of her mouth, and also by the tears. She couldn't remember the last time she'd cried. And to cry here? In the women's room at the Museum of American Folk Art? In the midst of her super-brave mission to catch her father in a nefarious act?

"Like moths to a flame," the woman said, ruefully. "Like there's no other Outsider Artist on the planet."

"What?" said Sally, who was remembering that her father had used this exact term.

"I mean, not that he wasn't a genius, of a kind. Of course he was. And he had an awful life. But I mean, those girls . . ."

"Oh, yeah." Sally crossed her legs the other way. The paper in her underpants felt massive, like a rolled-up *New York Times*. "I mean, they're kind of crazy, but they're also kind of beautiful."

"And that's what upset you? The pictures?"

The pictures? The pictures might be both strange and strangely beautiful, but they were just pictures. Whatever weird thing her father had about pictures, she didn't have it. Nothing against a pretty painting or photograph, or even, she supposed, a ship figurehead, but she wasn't ever going to prostrate herself before a work of art.

"I don't even like art," she heard herself say, and rather forcefully. "My father collects paintings. He's always running around after them and fawning over them and spending probably a lot of money to buy them, and then he just hides them away someplace in Brooklyn and goes to look at them on his own. I've never even been there."

It was the most critical thing she had ever said about Salo, at least to another person, and now she was saying it to a total stranger? It made no sense, and of course there was now a barely suppressed look of shock on the woman's face, even if she was trying to cover it up by smiling, as if what Sally had just said were witty or hilarious. Then she said, "My name is Stella. What's your name?"

But Sally didn't want to say her name. She just wanted to keep on doing what she was doing, which was looking into the woman's—Stella's—smile, and at the pink scar at her collarbone, and the long coiling dreadlocks down that lovely back. But she forced her gaze away.

"I'm so sorry," Sally said. "You know, I think you're right about those girls. I guess I didn't realize how upset I was. I'm just going to wash my face." She forced herself to her feet, the wedge shifting uncomfortably in her underpants. She might have missed our father's arrival by now, which meant at the very least that she'd have to repeat her reconnaissance mission around the galleries but which also might mean, if she was particularly unlucky, that Salo was standing near the door to the women's room with his girlfriend, and that there'd be no way to not be seen by him when she tore herself away and went out there.

"Well, okay," the woman said. "If you're all right."

"Of course I'm all right," Sally said. Even to herself she sounded borderline insulted. "I mean, thank you, I appreciate your concern."

Stella nodded, and to Sally's great relief she turned without another word and left the bathroom, and Sally thought what a kindness it would be to never have to see this woman's face (or her back) again for the rest of her life, although she would never forget the humiliation and mystery of this encounter, not ever, even without what happened next.

She went back into a stall and (unnecessarily) switched out the wedge of rolled-up toilet paper, and then, her face still flushed with embarrassment but at least newly washed, she left the bathroom herself. Her father wasn't there, just outside the door, and he wasn't there in the lobby, or in the main gallery, but in the farthest corner of the farthest room from the entrance she encountered, again, the unmistakable contours of that lovely dark back, Stella's back, and the hand on that back—intimate, unhurried, and, even from where she stood, across the room, obviously full of love—was instantly recognizable to Sally, and would have been even without the utterly known body attached to it.

She stood for a long moment watching the two of them, watching the space between their bodies narrow and widen and narrow again as they spoke to each other with unmistakable familiarity and ease, not caring that either or both of them might at any moment turn and notice her. She was as appalled at herself as she was at Salo. She was enraged that his was the hand permitted to touch this woman's back (and, Sally now inferred, every other part of her), which was awful and unfair, and it made her feel sick and it made her feel deeply angry and it made her hate our father, which had never been true before that night but which was going to be true after it, and also she hated the woman, Stella, with her beautiful smile and coiling dreadlocks and kindness. Sally had to fight an urge to rush at them through the crowds and pound them with her newly washed fists, even as she also wanted to run out onto Columbus Avenue and far away from them, and all the others who dressed up to drink wine and look at repellant—but also undeniably beautiful—scenes of tortured children. Either act would have served to bring this ill-judged and horrendously successful expedition—successful because she'd actually done what she'd gone there to do, and learned the thing she'd gone there to learn—to the same pathetic conclusion, but it still took Sally ages to actually turn away from them and go.

Chapter Eight

The Last of the Oppenheimers

In which Johanna Oppenheimer makes a purchase and pays a bill

When the kids began ninth grade, Harrison joined the swim team, mainly because he liked the fact that when he had his head underwater people didn't talk to him. Lewyn retreated to his room, where he indulged in his hopeless crush on the movie star a year behind them at Walden. Sally, who declined to share her secrets with either of her brothers, of course, was the only one with a seminormal social life, and this she weaponized to keep herself out of the house and away from the other Oppenheimers, as much as possible.

What that meant, in practical terms, was away from her mother. Salo had always been thin on the ground when it came to family time, but he had made himself even more scarce, arriving home on a typical weeknight later than ever, and nearly always after the kids had bolted themselves inside their rooms. He could still be seen in the morning, cooking his own eggs, making coffee for his wife and even his children, asking the kind of terribly interested questions all three of them had come to know and deflect. As for the triplets themselves, fourteen years of honest and even benign lack of affinity had naturally solidified into unmistakable avoidance. Truly, all three of them were, in the idiom of the day and of their generation, not just over it but SO over it.

Still, Johanna soldiered on, hopeless forays across the dinner table.

"So, anything interesting happen today?"

Grunts and downcast eyes.

"Anything *not* interesting?"

Silence again, this time with rolling of the eyes.

"You have a lot of homework?"

Nods, at least. But nods unaccompanied by noncompulsory speech.

"I went to see Grandpa Hermann today. He asked if you're going back to camp next summer."

She meant Harrison. Harrison did not bother to answer. His mother knew that he would not be returning to Androscoggin.

"I told him about the program at Hopkins. I don't think he understood why you'd give up Maine for Baltimore."

"Gotta go," said Harrison. "History paper."

That was hard, but ordinary. Harrison had been holding her at bay for years.

"Me, too," said his sister.

That was harder. She could still remember snuggling in bed with Sally on weekend mornings, reading books and watching TV.

"Me, too," said Lewyn.

That was when she knew it was over.

Her family. The salve to her husband's mortal wound and the great work of her own life; the *art* of her life, she might even have said. Those birthday photographs running up the staircase wall: three babies, three toddlers, three children, three young people. Three young people wild to leave.

Johanna spent a lot of energy trying not to think about this. Thinking about this made her take to her bed for long, agonizing days during which she sometimes tried to trick herself into being happy. It was a fine, fine thing that her children were growing up! Children were supposed to grow up, and then they were supposed to go away! It's what you wanted them to do.

Except that her departing children would leave nothing behind.

And she did mean nothing.

She was not, of course, the first woman to forgo the satisfactions of work "outside the home," and she would not be the first mother to feel the sharp emptiness of abandonment, the fog of purposelessness, when her children departed for their own lives. Probably, there were support groups out there, full of people feeling precisely what she was feeling and fording the exact same dangerous waters, but Johanna had never been much of a group person. Actually, now that she was really considering her situation, she hadn't been all that much of a one-on-one person, either.

She was the triplets' mother, which was exactly what she'd sought to be. And lest she forget, it had taken an act of will—many acts of will—to make that happen. Making that happen had been the signature achievement of her existence.

And here it was, nearly at an end, and also—finally, even she was forced to admit—some form of a failure.

Not because the three of them looked incapable of negotiating the world of adulthood, or were not good people. Not because they were hooked on drugs, had criminal records, or ran away from home to spend wanton nights at raves or in Tompkins Square Park. None of the three had so much as lifted a ChapStick from a corner bodega or failed a class, let alone gotten a girl pregnant (or gotten pregnant) or been caught selling a bag of weed (real or faux) like her own brother. Not one of them had even cursed at our parents or failed to present himself or herself for the rare command appearances in the combined Hirsch/Oppenheimer calendar: Hermann and Selda's anniversary, Johanna's mother's birthday dinners (increasingly sad as she retreated into dementia), the Seder hosted by Debbie and Bruce. Harrison, Lewyn, and Sally were normal young people in just about every obvious way, well educated (despite what even she recognized as Walden's worst tendencies), globally aware, and not even particularly acquisitive, despite our astonishing privilege. Individually they were a credit to themselves, if not to her.

But as a family, they were still a failure.

And when they left, which was now on the not-so-distant horizon, they would not come back. They would keep on going.

She remembered something she had once read in the memoir of a famous writer. After he left home for college, he never went back to visit, or even called his mother and father. Why not? *He hadn't known he was supposed to.*

It was her greatest fear, and the anticipation of it her greatest pain. Still, it didn't occur to her that there was anything to be done about it, anything she hadn't already tried, and not even the one thing that would seem so obvious to all of us, in retrospect, and which might have been done at any point while we were growing up, not left to its absurdly latter-day implementation. That, not one of us would understand.

One spring morning in the triplets' eleventh-grade year, our mother went to a parent meeting in the gym on the top floor of the school, where at least a hundred chairs had been set up. This was their introduction to Walden's college counselors: two young people hired from their first admissions jobs at Harvard and Princeton and the department head, a woman named Fran. Fran had been at Walden so long she actually remembered a time before the arrival of the first helicopter parent, a time of "well-rounded" students each submitting five or six handwritten applications (one to a safety school that truly was a safety school). She was a tall and lean woman with a long gray braid, artfully arranged over her shoulder. She stood before the crowd with a beatific smile.

That didn't last long.

The purpose of this meeting, Fran explained, was to make a preemptive plea for calm before the parents hurled themselves, lemming-like, over the cliff of madness.

Maybe it was supposed to get a laugh. It didn't. Even at Walden, that lemming had bolted.

Colleges loved Walden students, said Fran to her palpably tense audience. They always had! Walden students were independent thinkers, intellectually robust and thrillingly creative. Walden students had been admitted to colleges and universities all over the world, some of them with famous names, others less well-known but perfectly suited to that individual applicant. Every Walden student would receive the focused guidance of one of the three college counselors, and individual meetings would commence at precisely the right time, which was now, in the spring of the students' junior year, when a holistic approach to finding the right fit for each young person would be applied. Every Walden student would receive *personal attention* and *custom support*. Every Walden student would be treated as the *unique and capable young adult* he or she was. And when it was all over, every Walden student would be admitted to a college that would eminently fulfill his or her needs. That was a promise she felt very comfortable making!

Any questions?

In a flash, those laid-back parents who had chosen Walden over Brearley, Walden over Dalton, Walden over Riverdale, and Walden over Collegiate transformed into obsessive, ruthless, competitive despots.

Won't it hurt our kids that Walden doesn't grade?

What about class rank? How was an admissions officer supposed to tell if a student was at the top of his or her class or the bottom?

Would transcripts indicate the difference between, say, an advanced seminar and a tie-dye-for-credit course?

Were the college counselors going to persuade certain kids not to apply to certain colleges? And if so, how did they plan to justify that?

"If my wife and I went to Harvard, does our daughter have an advantage there?"

(Just pure nastiness, for its own sake, this particular father being a well-known asshole.)

Fran, of course, had been here before, and "here" was getting worse with every passing year. She reiterated her points, reissued her Zen, and recommended that parents read a recently published book that she herself had been learning a great deal from: *Colleges That Change Lives*. "If you look beyond the name-brand schools there is so much out there! Even I didn't know some of these places! The educational landscape is so *varied and fascinating*! I really look forward to *meeting you*, and *working with your children*!"

Johanna left with the others, spilling out onto Joralemon Street in a scrum of frantic people. Many of these mothers and fathers had been together since their children started pre-K; now, suddenly, they were at the opening bell of a steeplechase, and everyone knew far too much about everyone else. Tommy Belkow was a piano prodigy. Lizzie Wynn had spent the previous summer in China doing a language immersion, and her older sister was at Princeton. Julia Wu was straight-up brilliant, and she had already taken the SAT. Twice. Both of Carla Leavitt's parents—as her father had just reminded over a hundred truly disgusted people—had attended Harvard.

"Poor you," Nancy Farrell said, behind her. "You've got three!"

She said this as if it was news to Johanna.

"Maybe that'll keep me from getting too stressed out about any one of them."

"I'd be out of my mind. I still haven't recovered from Daisy."

Daisy was a sophomore at Brown, where Nancy herself had gone to college.

"I suppose Harrison's going to want to apply to Yale or Harvard."

Johanna had no idea whether Harrison was going to want to apply to Yale or Harvard. Even if he was already thinking about college—and he was the only one of the three who conceivably was—he was hardly confiding in her.

"Wherever he wants to apply is fine."

That felt like a pretty strong statement to Johanna, but obviously not strong enough.

"Where did Salo go? Remind me."

"Cornell."

"Oh! Well, I bet Cornell would take them all."

Johanna looked at her.

"Sammy says he doesn't want to go to Brown but I told him he needs to apply. At least have the option."

"I have to go," Johanna said. She didn't, and she was surprised to hear herself say it.

"Oh. Okay. Where you off to?"

"Bookstore." Another surprise. "I have to get some books."

Nancy laughed. "Well, that would be the place for it. Hey." She leaned close to Johanna's ear. "Carla Leavitt's dad. What a tool."

Johanna nodded.

She took off down Clinton Street, leaving the scrum behind. It was a bright spring day, and she couldn't quite believe that they were really here, all five of them. She'd been grateful for the parents' meeting, the excuse it gave her to walk to school behind the kids this morning, but the day still stretched before her, a long straight line to sleep, itself a preamble to waking again with this same terrible feeling of not one wonderful thing to look forward to in the years ahead. Then, as she turned down Court Street, she found herself circling that thoughtless comment of Nancy's, about all of her children going off to college together, at Cornell. Neither she nor any of the children had actually ever been to Cornell. Salo had never been able to love the place—how could he, after what had happened there?—so there had been no class reunions with the family in tow, no football weekends or visits to show the kids where he had spent four years of his life. Still, as Johanna walked, she found herself consumed by a powerful reverie about the three of them, together at Cornell, and somehow finding one another there, at last sitting together in class, meeting for dinners, even studying in one another's rooms. Could that happen? Had it only, ever, been a question of their leaving home, leaving herself and Salo, to find what had been so *not there* among them all these years? If it were possible, even if it left her out, she would still rejoice at the thought of it: all three of her children, reconciled at last over whatever had driven them so relentlessly apart. Calling home to report that Harrison and Lewyn were joining the same fraternity, or Sally's room was the place they gathered to study, or Lewyn had found a great restaurant in town and they were meeting there for dinner every Sunday night. When she and Salo went up for Parents' Weekends they would find the children waiting, arms around one another and full of love, and at last, at last, the five of them would be that thing she had given herself over to making, and which was *not* a failure.

But then it struck her that Harrison would never, under any circumstances, even apply to a college his brother and sister were applying to. So that fantasy crashed to the pavement.

All New Yorkers walk quickly, even as they daydream, and it took only a few minutes for Johanna to reach BookCourt. Inside, the usual Brooklyn literati, actual and wannabe, davened among the volumes. For a moment she forgot the specific books she had come here to buy; then, as another Walden parent from the eleventh-grade meeting came into the store and made for the SAT prep volumes, she remembered, and followed.

She didn't know this guy, though they nodded to each other. His child—daughter, Johanna thought—had been a ninth-grade arrival at Walden, and by ninth grade even the most socially active among the parents were tired of meeting new moms and dads. He was holding two thick workbooks and seemed to be evaluating them on the basis of weight. She stepped beside him and began to pick her way down the shelf. *The Yale Daily News Guide to the Colleges. Getting In. 100 Winning College Essays.* Then she noticed a small paperback at eye level. *Colleges That Change Lives: 40 Schools You Should Know About Even if You're Not a Straight-A Student.*

"Oh, that's the book she mentioned," said the Walden dad.

Johanna looked up. "Yes, I guess so. Do you want it?"

He smirked. "No. My daughter's Stanford or bust."

Well, I hope for her sake it isn't bust, Johanna nearly said.

She opened the book and read her way down the table of contents. Forty schools, as promised, and, as Fran had mentioned, far from "name brand." In fact, Johanna hadn't heard of any of them: Whitman, Grinnell, Roarke, Reed, Hendrix.

"Happy reading," said her fellow Walden parent. He took his prep books over to the counter. Johanna looked around for a chair.

The college section was adjacent to the children's area, an open space with a bright, multicolored rug and a number of fabric-covered cubes for small people to sit on. There were toys underfoot, and a couple of moms were down there with toddlers on their laps, turning the pages of board books and talking over their children's heads, a maneuver that Johanna remembered as having been all but impossible for her with three kids. These two towheaded children—one with a haircut straight out of *To Kill a Mockingbird* and a pair of Boo Radley overalls to match—were perfect exemplars of the new

Brooklyn, prematurely literate kids with names like Otis and Mabel and parents who made jewelry or kombucha, and still somehow lived in gleaming brownstones on the side streets of Cobble Hill and the Heights. She wondered what it would be like to be starting now, in an obvious renaissance of this sturdy borough, with its new rules and rituals and so much more of everything to fight over. Then a new child walked over to the rug and got down on the floor and began, on his own, to read.

It was Lewyn, though obviously not Lewyn. It was Lewyn as he had been, at two or two and a half: compact, intense, with sharp features and a frown, and curly brown hair cut close to his head, though not as close as this child's. That was a difference. Another difference, obviously, was that this child was African American. (Or perhaps just plain African? There were entire neighborhoods of new immigrants in Brooklyn, though not necessarily *this* particular neighborhood.) But apart from that: Lewyn. Two-year-old Lewyn, reconstituted with taupe-colored skin and reading a book that surely was too advanced for him (and would certainly have been far too advanced for two-year-old Lewyn, the last of her children to read).

Our mother stopped looking for a chair. She stepped closer to the children. One of the moms looked up at her, then went back to her conversation. Johanna was gripping the book, *Colleges That Change Lives,* in her right hand. She felt her left hand want to reach out and she stopped it, of course, but she could not stop her eyes from swallowing him whole. Lewyn. At that moment a half mile away in some discussion group or eleventh-grade language lab, but also here and transmogrified into an alternate version of his earlier self. She understood that it was strange. She could not understand why it bothered her so much.

Then a slender woman stepped between Johanna and the boy, and scooped him up onto her hip, and ran out of the store.

Even in the blur of that instant—red dress, bare brown leg, small head, dreadlocks—our mother understood it all. This child who was not her son Lewyn; his mother, that fleeing woman, was Stella Western, and his father was our father, Salo Oppenheimer.

Johanna stumbled out onto the sidewalk and looked around, still with the paperback book in her hand. She turned first to the right, back in the direction of the Walden School, and saw nothing. She turned to the left and saw Stella Western, far away on the next block and moving fast: a tiny, narrow woman with an obviously protesting small boy jolting along on her hip. The boy was also still holding his book. Johanna felt sick. She watched them go. It would not be possible to catch up with them. Why, for what reason, would she want to catch up? What could there possibly be to say?

She went back inside and numbly paid for her book. *Colleges That Change Lives.*

Then she walked home, down the same streets that had enclosed her life as a mother and as a wife. It was all so ridiculous, the effort she had put into everything, the fiction she had made for herself to live inside. She thought of how hard she must have worked to not know this obvious thing, all the way back to that night Salo had brought her to dinner to meet this old friend from Cornell. The woman had been lively and good-natured. She'd asked Johanna about the children. She'd spoken about the documentary she wanted to make, about some artist who turned people into buildings, and our mother had told herself, afterward, *Well, that was a harmless evening.* Never thought of again, at least not by her. Never mentioned between them again. And yet, Stella Western—her name retained in some overly efficient cerebral locker room inside our mother's head—had slipped from that unremarkable restaurant meal into some netherworld of her husband's life, and implanted herself. All those hours in Coney Island or wherever it was. With the *art.* All of her own compensation, perhaps, for our father's suffering. And now, here was an actual human child with her own child's face and, for all she knew, an equal claim to Salo's time, name, and everything else, which was not fair, not after she had wound her own life around him, like a suture.

This was the flaw in making a bargain with yourself. There is no one else there to agree to the terms.

Her feet were dragging. She fought the urge to stop, to collapse on any one of the famously lovely Brooklyn stoops, where happy families passed warm afternoons together on the weekends, something she and her husband

and her children had never done, not once. And Stella Western, who at the time of their pleasant dinner supposedly lived somewhere in the Bay Area, had looked very much at home on Court Street, rushing past the shops and restaurants that Johanna and her family had been walking past if not patronizing for years. *Their* streets. *Their* shops and restaurants. *Their* neighborhood. *Their* family.

I have given too much, our mother thought. And she had asked far, far too little in return.

Back at the house, and safely alone, she sat down at her desk just off the "gourmet kitchen" and began to cry. This built-in spot was a part of the design their architect had once identified as the "menu planning area," though our mother was no more a planner of menus than she had been a creator of gourmet meals. Over time the location had acquired the less fanciful purpose of appointment arranging and bill paying, and performing all the aspects of family maintenance that she did in fact perform: school trip forms, passport renewals, the pathetic paperwork of being a mother, wife, and person. From this desk and the Power Macintosh that occupied most of its surface, Johanna had overseen the workmen and vendors who made it possible for them to drop in on the Vineyard house and find the pipes running clear and the rooms free of invasive species. She had kept track of everyone's health insurance claims. She had made sure Sally had leotards for gymnastics and Harrison the next size of Suzuki violin, and Lewyn the math tutor he'd needed in middle school. She had scheduled the parent-teacher conferences and squabbled with her brother and sister over the care of their parents in New Jersey. She had managed, in other words, that deflated charade that had been the Oppenheimer family, or at least *her* Oppenheimer family, the one now ticking down to its failed and sad conclusion, after which, she supposed, her husband intended to move on with Stella Western and the boy who looked like Lewyn. All three of her own kids mad to leave, and her husband ready to step directly into his next Oppenheimer family, already in progress, perhaps close by, leaving her alone in this enormous, sad place with its astonishing views of the harbor and lower Manhattan. What more could she have done? What sacrifice had she not made, or effort not spent, in the single-minded pursuit of her husband's remission, the goal she had understood them to share, beyond all others? Something, obviously. But what?

It wasn't fair. It so wasn't fair.

For a miserable half hour more she wept, with no one to see her in that house of five full-time occupants (plus a part-time housekeeper not due till four in the afternoon). For once the emptiness of the rooms felt like a gift.

There was a stack of invoices on the bit of desk not occupied by the computer, things that had come in over the past few days. The caretaker and oil company bills from the Vineyard, the tuition for CTY, for which Harrison would be forsaking Androscoggin this coming summer. And on top, by providence—if you believed in that, which Johanna, long after this day, would claim she did—the annual bill from Horizon Cryobank of Torrington, Connecticut, wherein the last of her embryos resided in liquid nitrogen. Horizon Cryobank had changed names and owners a couple of times, and once, even, its location, since that day in 1981 when the blastocysts that would be Harrison, Sally, and Lewyn had been placed inside a deeply pessimistic (and frankly resigned to failure) Johanna Oppenheimer. That day, indeed, it had been *this* sequestered embryo, and not the ones painfully inserted into her own uterus, on which she had pinned her ultimate hopes; when the transfer failed, as all previous attempts had failed, *this* was the embryo intended for somebody else's *competent* womb, where it would—if she was very, very lucky—turn into a single child around whom she and Salo would make their longed-for family. But then Loretta, the Irish sonographer, had prayed a rosary for them, and lo: the miracle of the triplets had upended everything. And this sequestered child, the one who was supposed to be born, but who had never been born, had become—if not a forgotten thing, then a thing only thought of by one person (herself), and that only once a year, when she paid this very bill. She had never told the children. What would be the point? And for Salo the cloistered embryo had simply ceased to exist once his triplets came thumping into the world through Loretta's magic wand.

But they hadn't been triplets, really, it occurred to her now.

Torrington, Connecticut. Johanna wasn't even sure where that was, nor could she remember the name the storage facility had previously used, before being bought by a company that apparently managed many such facilities across the country. Cryo-Gen? Reproduction Options? Over the years there had been occasional notifications of these changes, all with assurances of the great care being taken and the profound understanding of responsibility, along with the annual rate increases. Johanna was a busy mother, and not sentimental about all of this technology. If anything, she regarded the annual bill as a kind of superstitious rite to be observed, and the embryo itself an inanimate object magically linked to her precious sons and daughter, but it never went further than that. It was a speck in liquid ice in a building somewhere in Connecticut. It was not even a thing in itself, and certainly not a person with any claim on her at all, let alone a claim even remotely comparable to that of her *actual* children.

And yet, the decision to send this one of the four into such an artificial abyss: it had been so . . . random, hadn't it? Because wasn't this one just as entitled to life?

Johanna picked up the invoice. She wasn't crying now.

The goal of Dr. Lorenz Pritchard's interventions had been to circumvent whatever wasn't working, naturally, in her own body. This they had done. The promise of Horizon Cryobank of Torrington, Connecticut, was to circumvent the essential unfairness of human reproduction: that there was, yes, a *horizon* for women, beyond which they simply could not conceive children, but no such horizon for men. Salo, if he wished, could continue to father sons and daughters and to make new families with new women until the day he died in his bed many decades from now, surrounded by progeny.

She, on the other hand, would never be able to have another child.

Unless. Unless.

Here, in her hand: one tiny gesture of redress for all that inequality. If it all worked, of course, as advertised. And if she really wanted it.

She thought of the babies her tall and sullen teenagers had once been: default dependent, wild for her attention. She thought of the years she had been charged with the important work of keeping them alive and safe, years in which no one, herself included, had ever once questioned her purpose or worth. She thought of the wet, toothless smiles, the little arms enfolding her neck and squeezing tight, the reading of bedtime books, the planning of activities, the listening to scales being indifferently practiced on musical instruments, the checking of homework, the discovery of nature, and culture, the making—and remaking—of every choice, past and future, that she had ever made. She thought of how her husband sometimes referred to their family—or at least to himself and the children—as "the last of the Oppenheimers," as if he were solely authorized to make that pronouncement, as if he had been the one longing them into existence and presiding almost entirely over their daily lives and being the parent who was actually there and not communing with modern art in some warehouse in Coney Island or Sheepshead Bay.

As if she had not faithfully paid this very bill, once every year since 1981, for a purpose she had never really understood. Or at least not until now.

Dr. Lorenz Pritchard was still in the same office suite on Fifth Avenue. He welcomed her back, asked for photographs of the kids, and listened to her explain why she had come in. He did her the courtesy of not looking surprised, or ever once asking: *Are you absolutely certain?*

Yes, it was possible, he told her. Very possible, though this time there would have to be a Gestational Carrier; only one outright miracle per family, that was his rule! She'd be okay with a Gestational Carrier, he assumed?

The Johanna Oppenheimer in his consulting room was a far cry from the Johanna Oppenheimer of two decades earlier.

Yes, she was perfectly okay with a Gestational Carrier.

The following morning our mother made the unprecedented request that Salo stay home from work. She told him what she knew, and then she told him what she wanted. She also had forms from the gestational surrogacy agency, ready for his signature, and he signed them. Of course he did. And that was how the person who really *could* be called "the last of the

Oppenheimers," *her hour come round at last,* began slouching toward Brooklyn Heights, to be born.

Johanna and Solomon Oppenheimer
with Harrison, Lewyn, and Sally Oppenheimer
joyfully announce the birth of

PHOEBE ELIZABETH OPPENHEIMER

June 20th, 2000
8 pounds, 2 ounces, 22 inches

Thanks to our wonderful "team" at the office of Dr. Lorenz Pritchard
and of course our fabulous Gestational Carrier, Tammy Sue Blanding

PART TWO

The Triplets

2000–2001

Chapter Nine

Ithaca Is Gorges

In which two of three Oppenheimer triplets leave home, and Sally Oppenheimer delights in the aloneness of it all

Sally and Lewyn both ended up at Cornell, though certainly not out of any shared wish to continue their education, let alone their life journey, in each other's company. Obviously, their father had attended Cornell, though he had never seemed all that gung-ho on the place, certainly not to the point of steering them in the direction of his alma mater. As far as they were aware, the most significant event linking the Oppenheimer family to Cornell University had taken place in the 1970s, when our grandparents had donated a dozen sixteenth- and seventeenth-century European paintings to the just-established Johnson Museum of Art. (This event, by purest coincidence, had narrowly preceded Salo's own application for admission.) They were not aware of the fact that Salo had recently directed another tranche of his late parents' collection—more waterlogged landscapes and red-cheeked burghers—to the selfsame institution. He did this, frankly, in hopes of attaining a similar result for his children. He also did it because he hated those paintings.

As before, it was not a gesture that went unnoticed. Cornell, like other institutions of its ilk and pedigree, was inclined to smile upon the children of its alumni, and if Lewyn's and Sally's test scores were not among the finest of those applying seniors in Walden's class of 2000, then . . . well, test scores weren't everything. Cornell even made an informal inquiry—to Walden's principled team of college counselors—as to the inclinations of the third triplet, Harrison Oppenheimer, which seemed only right, but Harrison Oppenheimer, by then, had his sights set on a place neither of his parents had ever heard of, and where no Oppenheimer, nor anyone known to the Oppenheimers, nor indeed any graduate of the Walden School, had hitherto set foot. Accepted to that very much under-the-radar institution (and, more or less concurrently, to the somewhat less obscure Harvard University, where he would transfer in due course), Harrison had spent the remainder of senior year in his bedroom with the door shut, furiously reading and waiting for the clock on his childhood to run out.

Sally did not fully process the reality of Ithaca's location in central New York State, nor its true distance from New York City, until, in a painfully self-conscious enactment of the parental ritual, Salo and Johanna booked a van and driver to transport the new Cornellians and their boxes of bedding and dorm accoutrements upstate. Both kids were subdued, though Salo did manage a breakthrough of sorts when he attempted, in his tuneless voice, to teach them the school song, first in its parodic version:

High above Cayuga's waters
There's an awful smell
Twenty thousand sons of bitches
Call themselves Cornell . . .

"Ugh," said Lewyn, who had long endured certain concerns about his own personal hygiene.

"Well, it's better than the original," said Salo.

Far above Cayuga's waters,
With its waves of blue,
Stands our noble Alma Mater,
Glorious to view.

"I mean, who talks that way?"

"People in the 1800s?" Sally said with luxuriant sarcasm.

"What's Cayuga again?" said her brother. "A gorge, right?"

"Jesus." Sally rolled her eyes.

They had said good-bye to their brother a few hours earlier, from the doorway of the room the brothers had shared. Harrison, ensconced in the oversized lounge chair he read in, hadn't gotten up. Either he wasn't aware of the significance of the moment or he was declining to acknowledge it, but even Sally felt a brief pang. So this was it. Eighteen years, their entire lives: *done.*

Everyone stopped for the bathrooms at a Cracker Barrel in Binghamton, and Johanna loaded up on Olde Tyme candy for Lewyn's and Sally's future roommates, as if this were a summer camp visit and she wanted to make a good impression on the bunk. No one even attempted to stop her. They reached Ithaca just as a storm swept in off the lake. The freshman registration tent got pounded, and the ground underfoot gave up brown water at each squelching step. The rattle of rain drowned out all but the loudest shouting—*Name? Your name? Can you spell it?*—and Lewyn, in some confusion, put himself on the line for incoming hotel school students, which made for an awful moment when he was found not to exist. There were so many nervous people, students and parents, all wet and all agitated, nobody making eye contact. A friendly pair of girls in Big Red T-shirts handed Sally a packet and Johanna a red umbrella, which the two of them hunched beneath as they dashed to Balch Hall. Inside Sally's packet: a Big Red T-shirt of her own and a folded ITHACA IS GORGES bumper sticker and a Cornell '04 water bottle. She could feel them against her chest, and the dark water entering her sneakers and spattering her legs, and only then did she understand that she had now left Lewyn behind, as well, to find his own way in this strange new place, spinning away from him as she had spun away from Harrison, earlier that day: weightless and free.

The unfortunate reality that Lewyn would also be a Cornell freshman was an inconvenient truth to be carried offstage and stored out of sight, because for all our mother's rhapsodizing about the great adventure she and

Lewyn were about to share—a fantasy that seemed to encompass hot cider at the Dartmouth game or debriefing over weekly (God, perhaps *daily*) sibling dinners—all Sally Oppenheimer wanted from this great adventure of college life was that it be undertaken finally, blessedly, *alone.*

There were so many things she had loathed about being a triplet, but the greatest of these was the way people always gushed about how the three of them would have one another through life and *never be on their own,* as if being forced to share a house and a family and a *womb* were not some contrived human torture on an existential level. True, as "the girl" she had been the most fortunate of the three of them, granted an instantaneous *other* status from her brothers (and not insignificantly, her own room in the house on the Esplanade, and on the Vineyard, while the boys had been forced to share). That was certainly an asset. But the *threeness* of it all, the psychic merge that strangers and classmates and teachers and relations and *even our parents* seemed to assume, had been a source of constant outrage to her. Yes, she had a chip on her shoulder. Two chips, if you wanted to be precise.

How could anyone not born into instantaneous, enforced, and eternal siblinghood, as the three of them had been, understand the joy of turning to one's left, and then to one's right, and seeing *neither of them there?* She had been irritated to discover that Lewyn was applying to Cornell, and enraged to learn that he would be matriculating. Of all the colleges! And it wasn't as if he had some academic or life goal that required this particular institution! (That she, herself, was also basically directionless when it came to her own education, let alone life plans, was not relevant here.) Mainly, Sally was furious at her brother for not just *letting her go.*

She understood, though, why he seemed determined to hold on. She and Lewyn had been cemented in their auxiliary orbit of two since infancy, which was when Harrison had effectively and permanently renounced them, jettisoning his siblings like some no longer necessary engine to his rocket ship, and consigning his sister and brother to the far side of his personal barricade. Harrison being Harrison, it was not enough to merely separate himself; he'd fueled that separation with icy moods and glowering expressions, punctuating it with constant disparagement, loudly or silently doing everything possible to convey to them how eminently superior he was. This intra-triplet excision might have brought the rejected parties closer together, but not even the shared experience of their brother's dismissal had been enough to accomplish that. Sally and Lewyn had learned to vote in tandem on all issues, trivial or profound (travel plans, restaurant choices, kid activities), and it was always gratifying to see the impact of their majority on their brother, but they both understood that they were motivated solely by an aversion to Harrison, rather than any real affinity for each other. In other words, neither their brother's rejection nor their shared loathing of him could make Lewyn and Sally actually like each other.

Now she had gone to this great trouble of leaving home, only to find her brother still beside her, his dormitory literally *next door* to Balch Hall on the handy campus map in her packet. This was intolerable, obviously, but she would tolerate it. And she had already decided how. She would not volunteer, to any of the friends, classmates, dormmates, or study partners she was about to meet, the fact that she had a brother similarly matriculated at the university. Lewyn knew where she was. If he cut off a hand or drank himself into a coma in one of Cornell's fine fraternal organizations, he could come and find her and she would (probably) not turn him away. Short of that, her brother was on his own.

Sally got rid of Johanna as soon as she could by dispatching her to Lewyn's dorm (to have, presumably, a more lachrymose farewell), then she rushed around, trying to get things sorted before her roommate, a Rochelle Steiner of Ellesmere, Long Island, (and possibly additional Steiners) could materialize and potentially express her own opinions about how things in the room should be established. She moved the beds into an L formation, which doubled the usable space of the room, and dragged one of the desks out into the hall and left it there, because (a) it was unbelievably ugly and (b) she wasn't really a desk person. Her sacrifice would be a gift to 213 Balch Hall, she thought. *You're welcome.*

"There's a desk out in the hall," her father said, when he arrived a few moments later, ostensibly to say his own good-bye.

"Yes," Sally agreed.

"Is that your desk? You don't want a desk?"

Obviously, she thought. Her nerves were fraying.

Salo continued to inspect 213 Balch Hall: the Bed Bath & Beyond sheets (denim blue, extra-long), the aqua plastic shower caddy, the brand-new Cornell mug and water bottle.

"I had a girlfriend who lived in this dorm," he said, apropos of nothing.

Sally didn't react. She was, of course, far less concerned with some long-ago Cornell girlfriend than with the girlfriend of right this minute. But clearly this wasn't the time. Not now, with escape so near.

She hugged him. She had to. She also had to confirm, before he would go, that she would check in on her brother that very night, a promise she obviously had no intention of keeping. (Had our father extracted the same promise from Lewyn? Somehow she thought not. It was ever thus, probably because she was *the girl.*) Then, mercifully, he too was gone. She unpacked her clothes and put them away. She broke down the boxes, cleared away the wrappings. She studied the campus map.

Before the hour was out, the Steiners arrived: one slight, intense girl in braids and one fragile and emoting mother, both of them bearing heavy-duty contractor bags, shiny and bulging. Rochelle had a spray of acne across her chin and a cheery voice of Long Island–ese. She hurled her stuff on the unclaimed bed, uttered not a murmur of objection to the desk in the hall or the configuration of the remaining furniture, and reached for Sally's hand. It could have been worse.

"No family pictures?" said Steiner mère, right away.

"Mom," said Rochelle Steiner.

"Not yet!" said Sally, with all the cheer she could muster. "I just got here a little before you."

Her own parents had already left, she informed them, but Mrs. Steiner wasn't quite through with Sally, not yet.

"You're from New York City?" she asked. "Long Island?"

Sally shook her head.

"New Jersey? Westchester?"

"*Mom,*" said Rochelle Steiner again.

"No, no. The city."

Mrs. Steiner gaped, trying to process this apparently incomprehensible information.

"You mean . . . Manhattan?"

"Well, Brooklyn."

What could be more baffling to a Long Island mom than Manhattan? Brooklyn, apparently.

"And you grew up there? And went to school there, and everything? In Brooklyn?"

Yes, she had gone to school there, and everything.

(To be fair to Mrs. Steiner, Sally was about to have essentially this same conversation with many others, equally perplexed and equally aghast. In the world beyond the five boroughs, apparently, "New York" meant Long Island, Westchester, even, counterintuitively, New Jersey. "New York"—as in "the city"—was apparently considered a place one went to work, shop, or possibly see a Broadway show, before "going home," while the notion of actually *inhabiting* the metropolis was both nonsensical and alarming. Also, Brooklyn—which had only just begun its Great Hipster Renaissance—was still an outer-borough equivalent of Siberia.)

"What does your father do?" said Mrs. Steiner.

"Mom!" her daughter said, with finality. "I'm going to walk you out."

And she did just that. And it should be noted that Rochelle Steiner (though under some considerable strain of her own, particularly with regard to her mother) had chosen to act, at this delicate moment, in deference to her own new life, which would bind her so deeply to the fractured heart of the Oppenheimers. In other words, it would all work out far better than Sally had dared to hope, though with far stranger implications than she, on that first day of her long-awaited new life, was capable of imagining.

Chapter Ten

Designated Martyrs and Angelic Forms

In which Lewyn Oppenheimer hears an epic and unsettling story

His sister Sally—fulfilling her promise to herself, if not to our father—had refrained from checking in on Lewyn *that very night* of their arrival, and when Lewyn went to find her in 213 Balch Hall the following day, neither she nor her roommate were there. He felt thoroughly self-conscious standing at their locked door, on a long corridor of identical doors, in a women's dormitory, in all of his own disheveled and possibly malodorous maleness. So he'd used the pen on the string to write a brief message on his sister's whiteboard: *Hi! I stopped by to say hello. L.* She would know who *L.* was, he reasoned. He hoped she would know. But she didn't return the visit or send an email.

They went off on separate freshman trips and after he returned to campus he went to Balch a second time, on the morning of Convocation, ostensibly to ask how Sally's canoe expedition to the Adirondacks had been but really because the Freshman Week activities had left him feeling distinctly alone, which obviously was not their purpose, and this time she was home. The roommate (her bed had a heart-shaped cushion people had scribbled all over, and sheets with butterflies) was fortunately not there that morning, because the ensuing conversation, unpleasant as it was, would have been far worse in front of a stranger. It was nasty, brutish, and short, but even to Lewyn not entirely unexpected. "I just think," his sister said, "that we should act as if we've left home. I mean, we *have* left home. And I'll see you at Thanksgiving, I guess."

So that was how it would be, apparently, and just to show her he was quite capable of getting along without her, Lewyn didn't go to her room again. In the months to come he would only occasionally catch sight of Sally across wide collegiate courtyards, or a dining hall, and once in the first lecture of a massive intro psych course she then apparently dropped. He didn't tell anyone he had a sister at Cornell who was also a freshman and who lived in the dormitory next door, and he only wished he hadn't told his own roommate about Sally, something that happened on their very first night together in 308 Clara Dickson Hall, because what was Jonas (Lewyn's roommate) going to think about the fact that this sister never stopped by once as the weeks and then months passed? Lewyn was prepared to imply that he and Sally met regularly *outside* the room, for walks or meals or parties, even, but in fact Jonas was quickly distracted by a full Cornell life of his own, and never brought it up again.

Jonas was a tall—very tall—and very pale kid from Ogden, Utah, who was studying to be a vet. "Large animal," he clarified, that same first night, which only confused Lewyn. Practically the first thing he had done, on entering 308 Clara Dickson for the first time, was scoop up a small brown object called an "Idaho Spud," part of the candy hoard Johanna had left for them, and actually crow with delight.

"Where the heck did you find this?" he asked. "My brothers said no way on the East Coast."

Lewyn wondered if he should point out that Ithaca was far from any coast, but he didn't want to come off like an ass. "We stopped at Cracker Barrel," he said instead. "My mom went kind of crazy. Too bad it wasn't booze," he said bravely. "Right?"

"Oh, I don't drink," said Jonas. He had already torn open the brown paper and eaten half the spud. "Do you?"

Lewyn frowned. He wasn't sure of the answer. *Yes?* Because there was no reason not to say yes. *No?* Because he didn't, not really. Or he hadn't. But he could, maybe, now, away from home. "Sure," he said finally.

Jonas had traveled light. There was a shiny comforter on his bed, a pillow and sheets in basic white, and on the desk a stack of pristine textbooks: *Color Atlas of Veterinary Anatomy, Diseases of Dairy Cattle, Large Animal Theriogenology.* Taped to the wall above the pile, a single photograph of two parents and six children: all stick-lean, all pale, all yellow-blond and all with bright, bright white and even teeth. He was, it turned out, more than two years older than Lewyn, though this would not emerge until a couple of months into their cohabitation, but he did not seem overly burdened by relative maturity. He had an insatiable appetite for SpongeBob SquarePants, for one thing, and possessed a full DVD library of *Buffy the Vampire Slayer,* which he was stunned to learn Lewyn had never watched. And while he was diligent in his veterinary studies he would also partake, with enthusiasm, of Cornell's robust fraternity culture, dividing his early loyalties between Alpha Gamma Rho and Acacia. He was, by any meaningful standard, a reassuringly normal and inoffensive cohabitant.

Down the hall, by contrast, two roommates were about to begin an appalling fall, with first one and then the other coming out, and first one and then the other falling in love with the other, and then one but not the other falling out of love with the other. By late September they were in a state of constant erotic fervor and not attending classes. By late October they were not speaking. The previous week, one had apparently spent the night with an ice hockey teammate and the other set fire to his roommate's bed, necessitating the 2:00 A.M. evacuation of the dorm into an already frigid Ithaca night. Now, one of them remained in Clara Dickson and the other was at Cayuga Medical Center, bound for a behavioral services facility back home in Illinois.

The two-year hiatus in Jonas's education came to light after a fairly routine conversation about the looming 2000 election, in which Lewyn planned to cast his first presidential vote for Gore and Jonas planned to cast his first presidential vote for Bush. Each had responsibly ordered an absentee ballot, which arrived two weeks before Election Day.

"Well, that's a relief," Jonas said, tossing his onto the bed and cracking a soda from Lewyn's refrigerator. "For the midterms I didn't get it till a month after it was due. Not that it would have made much of a difference in Utah."

Lewyn looked up from his computer. He was clawing his way through the Roman chapters of *Janson's History of Art*. "You voted in the midterms?" It did not occur to him that Jonas could be older. What occurred to him was: *Are the rules different in Utah?*

"Well, I tried. I was in England, on my mission."

My mission. The two words, separately, were innocuous, but together they clack-clack-clacked into something bigger.

Religion, in fact, was another thing that had not come up between them. He and Jonas might be living in close quarters, but they seldom overlapped beyond their room and the occasional trip to the dining hall. Jonas's academic life was entirely confined to the Agricultural Quad, and Lewyn, unsurprisingly, was drifting: a bit of aimless flotsam in a sea of Cornellian drive. When he had nothing to do and nowhere specific to be, he had taken to hiding himself under the dome of Sibley Hall, where the art history library was housed, but only because he was reluctant to go back to the room and be alone there. It probably shouldn't have struck him as strange that the word "mission" hadn't yet passed between them.

"So," Lewyn managed, "where did you go on your . . . mission?"

"Newcastle and Northumberland. The wettest, coldest place you never want to be."

Lewyn nodded, as if this was something he agreed with, or had ever considered.

"What was it like? I mean, what did you have to do?"

Jonas started to grin. "You want the short answer? Or the nonbeliever-is-opening-the-door-so-step-through-it-and-connect answer?"

Shit, Lewyn thought.

"I'm Jewish, you know," he said, instead of answering the question.

Jonas was slitting open the ballot. He did not seem terrifically invested in the conversation. "Yeah, I figured," he said, without taking his eyes off the page.

I figured? Lewyn went a little cold as an alternate narrative began to impose itself on the past weeks: *Church missionary bides his time while planning conversion assault on Jewish roommate.*

"Well. Oppenheimer?"

Well, Lewyn? he wanted to say. Their names had been ridiculously de-Semitized, although each of the triplets had been named, in the Jewish tradition, for a dead relative: Sally for Sarai Braunsberg, Salo's maternal grandmother, Harrison for Salo's paternal grandfather (who, like his father, was named Hermann), and Lewyn himself for Lou, his mother's grandfather.

"Do you know anything about the Oppenheimer family?" he heard himself ask. It landed horribly wrong: on one hand, with undeniable snobbery—*Don't you know who we are?*—on the other, with the appalling prospect of a lecture to come.

"Well, no. Why, should I?"

"Oh, it's just," said Lewyn, trying to remember the script. "Well, my ancestor was this guy in Germany, in the 1730s. What used to be called a 'court Jew,' in a town called Stuttgart. Wurttemberg," he added, though he'd never been entirely sure whether Wurttemberg was like the city and Stuttgart like the state, or vice versa.

Jonas looked up from his ballot. Lewyn wondered if he was considering which way to go with this. There were several he himself could think of. "Okay," Jonas said finally. "So, what's a 'court Jew'?"

"You weren't allowed to borrow or loan money if you were Christian back then. You needed a . . . a Jewish person. To do that for you. So even though most Jewish people were living in ghettoes and weren't allowed to do most kinds of jobs, if you were really good with finance you sometimes got, like, elevated. And my ancestor did. His name was Joseph Süss Oppenheimer, but he was also known as Jud Süss. He was the court Jew for this duke named Karl Alexander, and helped make life better for the Jews in the city, but he also made a lot of money himself. But then the duke died suddenly, and they arrested Oppenheimer and accused him of murder. Also a bunch of other stuff: lying, stealing, sex with Christian women. So they executed him. Actually, they tried to get him to convert to Christianity, but he wouldn't. Goebbels made a film about it."

"Who?" said Jonas.

Lewyn enlightened him.

Joseph Goebbels, in his zeal to imbue the citizens of the Thousand-Year Reich with a moral code, had dug up poor Joseph Oppenheimer *again* in the film version of this story, and murdered him *again,* this time with a few other crimes thrown in, all to remind the *Volk* what happened when they let the *Juden* live among them.

"Yow," said Jonas. He was riveted.

The film, a great success with its 1940 audience, might have retained only a glancing relationship to historical fact, but it packed a lot of oomph. Goebbels's version of Joseph Oppenheimer extorted and thieved just as soon as he'd wormed his way into power, and to make things worse, he persuaded Karl Alexander to open the city gates to a filthy, ailing, and praying horde of his fellow Jews. Those crimes were bad, of course, but not as bad as Oppenheimer's sins against the pure Germans of Stuttgart, who had just been going about their ordinary pure German business, as they had always done, but were now subjected to humiliation, torture, and even rape. (The pretty Rhine maiden Jud Süss assaults will drown herself to spare her family the potential horror of a miscegenated child.) Once the duke dropped dead, the burghers of Stuttgart wasted no time, throwing the malevolent Jew in prison and, ultimately, hoisting his gibbeted corpse aloft. In the film's final scene, the council chairman shoved the Jews back out the city gates, intoning that future generations would be wise to remember what happened in Wurttemberg.

"The point of it was to get people thinking about how great it would be to throw all the Jews out of Germany," Lewyn explained to his roommate. "It was a big hit, all over the Third Reich. Bigger than *Titanic*!"

Jonas nodded. "And that's, like, your . . . what, great-great-whatever-grandfather?"

There was no "whatever" about it. He, like his siblings, knew the precise and documented line from Joseph Süss Oppenheimer in Wurttemberg to the family of Salo Oppenheimer in Brooklyn Heights. The court Jew's immediate family had fled Stuttgart even before his execution seemed certain: wife, sister, and children going first to Heidelberg, where—despite having taken the precaution of changing their name to the ubiquitous Levin—the association was common knowledge. After 1812, when citizenship was conferred on Jews, they moved again, to Prussia, still as Levins, still—even a century later—in fear of discovery. When Hermann Levin, our great-great-great-grandfather, disembarked at Castle Garden in the City of New York, in the year 1838 (a century to the month after the death of Jud Süss, in fact), he had already spent a miserable voyage in contemplation of his new American name. It was a moment fraught with meaning, for the future and for the past. When his turn came, he approached the official, still undecided.

Port of embarkation? *Hamburg.*

Christian name? *Hermann.*

Family name?

Had there finally been enough time, enough distance? Could this immigration official—this Dutchman or Englishman or even fellow German of the New World—possibly know or care what someone so long ago had done, or what had been done to him? For that matter, was this a portal through which he and his descendants might surrender the burden of being Jewish entirely? There were any number of common German names he might take up and not a single person to object. Muller, Schmidt, Hoffmann; in this new world he could be anyone. He could—his family could—begin again.

But that was to deny not only their religion or tribe; it was to deny the crime against that person, a hundred years earlier. Even now, even an ocean's distance away, even at the edge of a continent Joseph Süss Oppenheimer had likely never even heard of.

Family name? *Oppenheimer,* said the first American Oppenheimer.

"It's an important story to my family. And our company, I mean the business we've had since we got to America in like, the 1830s or whatever, is called Wurttemberg. Kind of in Joseph Oppenheimer's honor."

"Well, it's cool to know how far back you go, and all the people in your family tree. Practically LDS, in fact."

When Lewyn said nothing, Jonas looked up.

"I'm assuming you know I'm LDS, right?"

LSD? Lewyn thought, instead. *ADHD?* Was it a syndrome of some kind?

"Uh . . . no. What is that?"

"Really? Latter-Day Saints."

Lewyn frowned, more lost than before. *Seventh-Day Adventist? Jehovah's Witness?* The words swam in biblical gibberish. Wait: Jews for Jesus? Or those Nation of Yahweh people who hung out in Times Square and screamed at everybody? They were *crazy*.

"Or Mormon. I mean, officially The Church of Jesus Christ of Latter-Day Saints. It changed over in 1982, but I don't mind Mormon."

"You're a Mormon?"

He was shocked, himself, by how it emerged: disbelief and . . . was it distaste? He could barely grasp the fact that he'd been sharing space and time with an active proponent of a faith so . . . well, so cultish and strange.

Jonas was laughing. "What? Like, where are my horns?"

"No. I just . . ."

"Never met a Mormon. It's okay. Not so many of your people where I come from, either."

But Cornell was full of Jews. More Jews than any other Ivy, according to Johanna (though a smaller percentage than Yale, when you adjusted for size). This was a colossal development, Lewyn realized: Mormon and Jew, Jew and Mormon. And they were only just getting to it now?

"How come we're just realizing this now?" he asked Jonas.

"Well, like I said, *I* realized. I just figured you'd bring it up if you wanted. And again, not an issue for me."

Okay, Lewyn thought, but "not an issue" as in: *I don't care*? Or as in: *I'm not prejudiced*? And if the latter why should Jonas think it was only his prerogative to be—or not to be—prejudiced? Was Lewyn also entitled to be "not prejudiced"? But even as he conjured this bit of defensiveness he realized that he didn't know anything about Mormons, certainly not enough to conceive of something that might warrant prejudice.

"Well, you're not out to convert me, I hope." He thought he was saying this ironically, but it came out sort of choked, and Lewyn suffered yet another wallop of embarrassment.

"No, man," Jonas said. "Two years on my feet, that's enough. Two years, five converts. It doesn't sound like much, but a lot of people came home with fewer. If Heavenly Father wants more from me, he can let me know, but for now I'm all about fungal diseases of the hoof." He said this with a little flourish of the hand, and with that hand he withdrew one of his spiral-bound Cornell notebooks and flipped it open on the desk. This was to be a caesura in the conversation, apparently. If not an outright severance.

Lewyn was left, as usual, to his own thoughts, and they seemed to be in equal parts apprehensive and self-flagellant. To another person, he now saw, the fact of a very white and very blond young man from Utah, with a large family of similarly white and blond people, might have fairly shrieked MORMON. To himself and his siblings, though, a Saul Steinberg distortion had basically divided the country into New York City, its suburbs, the Vineyard (where the Oppenheimer cottage—not, of course, really a cottage—clung to a fragile dune), and New England, Florida, and California. The rest was, well, *the rest*. Unexplored, but full of people who enjoyed strange pastimes like watching cars drive around a track and shooting things dead. Jonas, it had always been obvious, was some kind of not-Jewish person from *the rest* of the country. But did he truly believe in God? And wait, had he actually just spoken the words "Heavenly Father"?

In fact, Jonas Bingham of Ogden, Utah, did maintain an ongoing (if one-sided) conversation with an entity he referred to, without irony, as "Heavenly Father." It further turned out that virtually everyone Jonas had ever known (and certainly everyone he was related to) likewise held routine conversations with this same "Heavenly Father." It was also true that Jonas, born and reared in Utah, was far less a stranger to upstate New York than

Lewyn himself was, having visited the area no fewer than four times with his large and smiling family. "It's a special place for Mormons, you know."

No, of course Lewyn didn't know. "Really? Ithaca?"

"Not Ithaca. West of Ithaca." Jonas opened a map on his computer and pointed to some random spot, between Rochester and Syracuse. "Where we began," he said simply.

Lewyn frowned. He was thoroughly ignorant, of course, about the vast and foreign territory known as "upstate New York," where people lived without reference to Brooklyn Heights or even Manhattan, otherwise known as the center of the universe. The notion that something had actually happened in this backwoods wilderness which was of critical interest to millions of people around the world would come as something of a shock.

Jonas tipped back in his chair and braced his long legs against Lewyn's bedframe. "You're pretty much in the dark about us, aren't you?" He shook his head, but he was laughing, too. Then he told his roommate a story about a long-ago farm boy and a pillar of light in the woods behind his house, and golden plates dug up out of the ground, which became the Book of Mormon, and which contained everything Jonas Bingham personally believed about the world. Lewyn struggled to control his own face as he listened, and he did listen. The great stories of the Hebrew Bible had never, particularly, stirred him: Abraham and Isaac, Joseph and his troublesome coat, the Exodus and the Red Sea and Moses, hauling the tablets of the law down to the gathered tribe . . . it was interesting, in the way that all history was interesting, as something that had probably happened, in some version, at some time. The Babylonian Exile, which had scattered his ancestors across the globe and sown their centuries of harassment and suffering, had always given him a sad and guilty feeling, since he himself had never been forced from his home. Far worse even than that, of course, had befallen the Jews over the centuries, including the crimes against Joseph Oppenheimer, his own designated family martyr, but even poor Joseph Oppenheimer's story had weirdly not been as compelling as Jonas's unsettling story.

"Is any of this true?" he asked his roommate, an instant before realizing how rude the question must sound. But Jonas only shrugged.

"The thing is, I don't have to answer that. The story comes down to us through our tradition. Not all that different from your family tradition, I guess. And that's enough for some people. But the Book of Mormon actually comes with instructions if we're not ready to believe. It says all we have to do is ask Heavenly Father with a sincere heart if the story is true, and He'll answer us. Which is exactly what I did when I was fourteen. Now I know it's true."

"You mean, you believe in it."

"No. I know it."

Then he got up and asked if Lewyn wanted anything from the common room down the corridor, where the candy machines were, and when he came back he returned to *Large Animal Theriogenology* and ate his Snickers bar. An hour later Jonas closed his ponderous textbook, quietly thanked his Heavenly Father for the day, and turned out the light. Instantly, he was asleep, breathing deeply, his shoulder rising and falling in the light from Lewyn's own reading lamp. But Lewyn couldn't sleep, not even after he'd given up on the Romans and his own ponderous textbook. He lay awake in his bed for hours and thought of angelic forms, hovering in the trees of a sacred grove, only an hour westward.

Chapter Eleven

The Precious Object in the Secret Box

In which Harrison Oppenheimer is enlightened at the Symposium, and gathers with his tribe in a New Hampshire parking lot

Harrison left home four days after his brother and sister, on a bright golden day that seemed to spin the Connecticut River Valley into a lovely autumn haze. At his chosen college there would be no choked-up moms at move-in, no T-shirts and bumper stickers handed out to families under festive tents. There would be no non-matriculants at all beyond the meeting point in Concord, New Hampshire, where the newest Roarke men—all communications, throughout the application process and since, had been addressed to "Roarke men"—were to be deposited for the journey north. Johanna was on edge the whole way, her intensity building as they cut across Connecticut and Massachusetts (states she at least knew and understood) and entered the foreign land of the New Hampshire forests. "If you'd wanted to be in the back of beyond, why not Dartmouth?" she said, trying to make it sound like a joke. It wasn't a joke.

"Don't see Harrison at Dartmouth," said his father.

"No? You see him at this crazy place?"

Harrison, in the back seat, was silent. *One more hour,* he thought. *Then I'm out.*

"If he doesn't like it he can transfer," said Salo.

Harrison smiled. Of course he would transfer. All of the Roarke men would transfer, in fact, because Roarke was a two-year college, after which every one of them would move on to finish at more conventional universities, regardless of whether they'd liked Roarke or not. This piece of the Roarke enigma had been especially baffling to his mother, Harrison knew. If he was resolved to get to Harvard eventually, if, indeed, he already possessed a letter of acceptance and a two-year deferral, guaranteeing his place in the junior class, why this incomprehensible detour? Why were the three of them unpacking the Volvo in a diner parking lot in Concord, New Hampshire, and not an hour south of here in front of some Ye Olde pile in the Yard, with fluttering ivy around the windows? Harrison declined to explain. He could have had that, but he wanted Roarke. He'd wanted Roarke from the moment the school had first been presented to him, like a precious object in a box only special people could open.

Since middle school, Harrison had been begging the two alleged adults in his alleged family to let him leave Walden, where he and his siblings had been ideologically indoctrinated since preschool. Actually, he'd first raised his concerns even earlier, when he discovered that the school's widely stated passion for early language immersion incorporated Mandarin and Spanish but neither of the so-called "dead" languages, Latin and Greek. Harrison went on to rage against the years of repetitive, almost identical instruction about civil rights, women's rights, and LGBTQ rights, while European history was offered only as a senior spring seminar (a class he was preposterously forbidden to take as a freshman, sophomore, or junior) and the fact that he and every other Walden student had to suffer a pointless Ethical Conflict Resolution class each semester. (It might as well have been called "Let's talk about race and gender. Again.") Harrison had pushed back relentlessly against Walden's English classes, in which discussion always turned to the way the assigned poem or novel or story or essay made each person in the classroom *feel.* It drove him insane.

Walden had been founded in the 1920s as a school for the children of laborers, so that the bright offspring of the working classes might have an opportunity to ascend to the better colleges, and beyond, to the professions: business, law, medicine. Walden, always friendly to Jews, would open to nonwhite students decades before it was commonplace, and welcomed girls from the outset, but the school truly came into its own when the culture turned in the 1960s. Suddenly little Walden, that Brooklyn experiment, emerged as a prescient institution, both reassuringly established and utterly au courant in terms of its ideals and methodology. Yes, little girls and little boys could learn together—*should* learn together! Yes, the children of all races, creeds, and colors would find at Walden a common workshop for hungry minds and soaring creative spirits. Yes, making art was central to the life of any developing consciousness, and music must be sampled in forms far more diverse than the narrowly defined tradition of classical European. No, major decisions concerning the institution should not be made without consulting the students themselves, and allowing their voices to be heard.

It. Made. Him. Crazy.

"This? Again?" he'd said for the first time—*but not for the last time!*—in second grade when he realized that Freedom Summer was scheduled to take up *fully a month* of the spring term. "We did this last year," he'd informed the teacher, hoping a simple mistake must have been made. (The teacher was new and possibly didn't know they'd already covered the entire Civil Rights Movement the year before.) A little girl in the back began to cry, and a boy stood up to begin talking about how Harrison's comment made him *feel*. This unburdening would eventually spread to the entire class, after which Harrison himself asked if he could go talk to the head of school, who liked for the students to call him Aaron.

"We did Freedom Summer last year," he'd explained to Aaron.

"You know, Harrison, there are some events in history that are so important they are turning points in our shared humanity. We can't study them too much or too deeply."

Yes we can, Harrison had thought.

"I would like to study something new every year," he tried.

"But we ourselves are new every year. We can see new things in the material."

Harrison wondered briefly whether it might not be a good idea to let Aaron know how he *felt* about that. But in the end he went back to the classroom, and back to the Civil Rights Movement.

He would spend a lot of time in Aaron's office, though never for the typical reasons a restless boy might be compelled to see the principal: cheating, pot brownies, AOL unkindness. Harrison's issues (default obnoxiousness toward everyone at school) mainly derived from his own belief that he was not just smarter than his siblings (a low bar, in his opinion) but smarter than his classmates, his teachers, and the head of school, himself. Tragically, it was far worse than that. He was a superior student trapped in a school without grades (so no one could tell!), a school where no one was ever deemed a "winner" (designed to take the sting out of not being a winner!), a school in which every student marched in lockstep to his or her mandated different drummer. He raged for years, first at his parents (who would not consider letting him go to boarding school, or even to Collegiate, where Salo himself had gone!), and at his teachers (who declined to acknowledge his superiority!), and always at his siblings (because they were there, and so passive, and it was so convenient to do so).

In calmer moments, he attempted to set his own curriculum (one that did not repeat, annually, the same few topics dredged through a muck of human feeling), stringing together classics, history, Latin, philosophy, and religion (religion *was* taught at Walden, but mainly in a spiritual drum-banging way). But it was all so hard without capable guidance and similarly engaged fellow students to push him, and there were moments—not infrequent moments, either—when it seemed to Harrison that he might actually be struggling with the material: concepts that didn't click through the synapses in his head, arguments that fell apart as he attempted to build them, pieces of writing he understood to be eloquent and brilliant but which spun in verbal tapioca as he tried to get through them. For the first time he was forced to wonder if he might actually have been wrong all this time, if—and this was horrible to contemplate—he might not, after all, be that superior specimen of Oppenheimer, only an ordinary teenager, perhaps a little brighter than some but nothing to attract the notice of the world. It was a horrifying concept.

In the end, Harrison managed to get through the eternity of Walden: dressed in a white suit, holding hands with his white-clad classmates in the Community Room on the top floor of Walden's massive stone building as the school song was tearily sung and the students "commenced" down the wide staircase and onto Joralemon Street. And then he was out, with only the summer to get through until he could go off to Roarke, where his people, he hoped, awaited him.

Roarke was the precious object in the secret box, and the secret box had been opened to him by a person named Vernon Loring, BA Harvard, MA Oxon, PhD Princeton, and author of six scholarly works of moral philosophy. Loring, a six-foot-three crane of a man, had turned up at Walden one afternoon the previous fall for what was meant to be an enlightening and civil all-school discussion entitled "How Should We Define and Experience Spirituality?"

First to speak was the school's chaplain, who defined spirituality as the divinity within each and every living creature, no person's (or animal's!) greater than any other person's (or animal's!). "In my yoga class," she said, "my favorite part is always the *namaste,* which comes at the end." And there, she laughed at herself. "As those of us who do yoga know, we love namaste *because* it comes at the end!" (Much nodding and grinned approval in the congregation of affluent Brooklynites.) "But what does namaste actually mean? It means: *I bow to the divine light within you and you bow to the divine light within me.* Now I know yoga is not a religion, though we've all met practitioners we might describe as fanatics. But this little insight contains a great profundity: all of us, bringing our little lights together to form what the apostles of Jesus might have called 'the light of the world.' *This* is the spiritual, and it's within and around us all, at all times. We may find our way to it through a text on a page. We may find it through love or our family and friends or in service to others. We may call this 'God.' It makes absolutely no difference what we call it: it is *our* divinity that makes each one of us deeply special."

Then, after the expected applause, Dr. Vernon Loring walked to the podium, every inch the white cis-gendered male he was, and dressed in a gray tweed three-piece suit and a scowl for the occasion. Before he'd said a word, he was already an object of general disapprobation. Within minutes he'd sent the entire Walden community shuddering into hysteria.

According to Vernon Loring, PhD, the absurd and inadequate interpretation of "spirituality" they had all just been treated to ought to send each and every student home to Papa and Mama to demand they withhold tuition until the school ponied up some capable instructors. The *divine light inside of me* bowing to *the divine light inside of you*? Was he—were any of them—supposed to listen to this garbage with a straight face? Because he had been under the impression that an established school like Walden, with an impressive price tag and a frankly surprising (under the circumstances) 14 percent admit rate, ought to be capable of recognizing the anti-intellectual drivel they had all just been treated to, by a school official—its chaplain, no less!—and banish it to its natural habitat: a student club, for example, alongside the tai chi enthusiasts or the tiddlywinks-curious.

"Fucking hell," someone said, behind Harrison. But he didn't want to turn his head, not even long enough to see who it was. A few rows ahead of Harrison, a woman got to her feet and began moving to the back of the room, her face a rictus of horror.

"The narcissism I will not even engage with," Vernon Loring scolded. "We all are narcissists, myself included, you will doubtless be stunned to learn, but this is an inextricable part of our success as a species. No, what I object to is the fact that you young students are in a position of privilege, with all human knowledge at your fingertips, and yet you are paralyzed by guilt over the moral failings of people who died centuries before you were born." A popular teacher of pottery darted up the center aisle to crouch beside Aaron and whisper furiously into his ear. "Can even one of you explain to me why you are content to wade around in this kind of anti-intellectual muck, apparently without complaint?"

Harrison heard himself make a sound, something primal, deep in his own throat. At the same moment, an entire row of Walden seniors near the front of the community room stood in unison and turned their backs, showing their stricken expressions to the rest of the school. The speaker, blithely ignoring this and every other iteration of audience disapproval, had now begun his prepared remarks by batting aside the very notion of "spirituality" with a rather gleeful reference to Madame Blavatsky (a person Harrison felt certain few of his schoolmates could identify), then compressed into twenty minutes the most cogent yet comprehensive history of Judeo-Christian-Islamic monotheism Harrison had ever encountered, complete with political context and a spattering of references to William James. "Brother of Henry," he informed his audience helpfully.

Harrison observed that this was not, in fact, helpful to his fellow students.

"I will now withstand your criticisms," Dr. Loring announced, with clear delight, when he came to the end of his speech.

Harrison, glancing around the room, could plainly see his sister Sally, seated on one of the oak benches against the wall, looking stunned. Two teachers and a parent, magenta with rage, were surging in Aaron's direction. Harrison himself was thrumming with excitement. For the very first time in Walden's self-described Fulcrum of Enlightenment, he was being enlightened, and by a towering stranger who was also, by his clear reception here, a loathed iconoclast.

Loring stood calmly before the audience for another thirty minutes, parrying the sputtered outrage of adolescents and their "teachers." He was a tree in a maelstrom, bending his strength with the winds, never losing his composure. He calmly suggested books a young man might read to elucidate the notion of individual responsibility, and made philosophical arguments a young lady (young lady!) might turn to for a very clear statement on the subject of personal freedom. Scholarship, books, the record of centuries—millennia!—of human (well, human *male*) thought; before Harrison's eyes, this tall man in his three-piece suit was pulling back a screen to reveal a groaning board of new (old) knowledge. Incredibly, he laughed at his enraged audience. He did not even condescend. In fact, as far as Harrison could tell, he seemed to be looking for something: a capable debater he might set himself against, a young person to whom he might hand over a thing in his possession—a thing of value.

Whatever that thing was, Harrison Oppenheimer wanted it. He was seventeen years old, and he had groped his way alone in the darkness long enough.

Loring wasn't difficult to find. He had an email address on the Columbia University Philosophy Department website, but Harrison opted to contact him in the traditional manner, on paper, explaining that he was a Walden student who'd admired the stand Dr. Loring had taken in his remarks, and would he possibly be willing to meet for coffee and further discussion? The response, also in writing, also mailed, was swift if succinct: Symposium on West 113th, the following Thursday at five. When the much-anticipated day arrived, he lied to his swim coach and headed to Manhattan on the subway, surfacing into a thunderstorm on Morningside Heights.

Symposium was below street level, and Harrison descended in a trill of nerves. Loring, the restaurant's only customer, sat in a green faux-leather booth on the far wall, one of his bony hands wrapped around a china coffee cup, as if for the warmth. The other hand hovered over a short stack of blue exam booklets, the uppermost of which—Harrison saw as he drew near—Loring was liberally annotating with a classic red pen. Somebody was going to be very disappointed with their final, he thought.

"Dr. Loring?"

"Well," said the man himself, giving Harrison a once-over. "I wondered if I'd recognize you when you got here. I don't think I spotted you in that congestion of anti-intellectualism that passes for your high school."

Harrison grinned. He couldn't help it.

"I should have spoken up, but I guess I was too shocked. Please forgive me."

"You're forgiven. Sit down. Coffee?"

"Sure," Harrison said, sliding into the booth. The green Naugahyde was troublingly sticky. "I'm afraid I cut swim practice." He wasn't sure why he'd led with this, and regretted it the minute it was out of his mouth.

"Why afraid? Do you think someone will punish you? Do you think *I'm* going to punish you?"

"No, no," he shook his head. "I just . . . I'm feeling a little guilty."

"Well, that's a waste of your time," Loring said. He was putting the blue books down on the seat beside him. Harrison couldn't help seeing the bright red D on the cover of the booklet on top.

A waiter came with a coffee for him, and refilled Loring's cup. Harrison wanted milk but was too shy to ask for it. Loring, he saw, was drinking his black.

"Tell me about yourself."

"I'm a triplet," Harrison heard himself say. He was surprised he'd said it. He rarely thought it, or at least, he never *tried* to think about it.

"Interesting." Loring nodded.

"In vitro. I mean, not natural."

"More interesting still. And your siblings, do they share your intellectual interests?"

Harrison smiled. "They don't have any intellectual interests."

"Then you are as an only child."

Yes, he wanted to shout. *Yes, yes!* Five minutes in, and this person understood him in a way his own family never had.

"It feels like that, sometimes. I mean, they're not bad people. In a . . . moral sense, I mean."

Loring, for the first time, seemed to smile. At least, it looked more like a smile than not.

"Tell me about the moral sense of your family," he said.

And Harrison did: the sullen sister and doltish brother, the mother who persisted in the notion that the three of them were deeply, intractably bonded, and the father who was seldom present, even when he was.

"You are planning on attending college, I imagine," Loring said.

"Well, yes. I'm working on the applications now. I mean, everyone at my school goes to college. Wesleyan is very popular, and Brown. And Yale."

Loring made a face.

"I was thinking about Harvard, myself."

Harrison was doing more than thinking about Harvard. He was obsessing about Harvard. He had fetishized the school for years, casting it as his personal exit ramp. The notion that Harvard might not lovingly accept him was horrifying, not that he had confessed *that* to anyone. Deep inside him, so deep even he would not have known how to excavate it, was the rank, gangrenous fear that he was not entirely the intellectual being he had long ventriloquized. Obviously, he wasn't stupid. Compared to his siblings he was brilliant, and in relation to his classmates, some of them annoyingly capable, he was clearly running with the pacesetters. But beyond the self-esteem-boosting enclave of the Walden School, where grades did not exist? Beyond the Oppenheimer enclave, in which Johanna showered them all with resolutely equal praise? Beyond a culture that handed out participant trophies, in which making a show of your personal suffering passed for debate? To be honest, he couldn't remember a time when he didn't fear being found out.

The previous spring, he'd walked into the SAT (his first ever standardized test!) under a personal waterfall of terror, and was not at all reassured to come out of it with a perfect score, mainly because certain loudmouths in his own grade were busy boasting of *their* perfect scores. Harvard—and, he supposed, the few other schools he might deign to apply to—would naturally be inundated with kids brandishing the identical credential. Too many people had obviously figured out how to study for the test and perform those simple tricks that defanged it.

"Well," said Loring, "Harvard is still a place where actual ideas can be discussed, I'm happy to say. But I wouldn't advise it for you."

"Oh?" Harrison felt stung. He'd been expecting Loring to encourage him in the direction of his own alma mater, but what was this? Had he fallen short in some way, already? He groped backward in their conversation, weighing, parsing, excoriating himself for every single thing he'd said, wondering where in the wondrous swirl of ideas he had lost track of himself and revealed his deep core of inadequacy.

"And certainly not Columbia. They bring me in every couple of years, because there are fewer and fewer on the permanent faculty who are equipped to teach the core curriculum to freshmen, and I usually say yes. The library is beyond reproach, but the students there get worse each time I return. Still, the fault's not specific to this university. It's a generational failing, I fear."

Harrison nodded, as if he himself were not being indicted. "Oh, I completely agree."

"Apart from a contemporary of yours. A young man from the south, who managed to get himself an education with no help from anyone else. I read his book the other day. It gave me hope. I wonder if you know who I mean? His name is Eli Absalom Stone."

Harrison did know who he meant. He'd known more or less since "contemporary," "the south," the autodidacticism reference and, most of all, *the book*. There was only one person whose story rang all of these bells, and Harrison had been obsessed with him for months.

Eli Absalom Stone was a name you'd be unlikely to forget if you happened to see it, say, in print, which Harrison had first done as the subject of an *Atlantic Monthly* profile, before senior year. A wunderkind writer, Stone hadn't attended school for most of his life. Instead he'd studied at home, and home was a shack on a mountain somewhere in Virginia. (Harrison, who remembered the failure of his own attempts to self-educate, had been especially wowed by the breadth of Stone's autodidacticism.) Before he was even eighteen, this remarkable young person had become the author of a small publishing miracle called *Against Youth*, in which he had called out his own generation (their shared generation) for complacency, anti-intellectualism, and carelessness with the English language. Harrison, naturally—and *not without envy*—had rushed out to purchase this book, which he found to be annoyingly persuasive and unimpeachably well written, and its author the very first of his own contemporaries he might have to muster some actual intellectual regard for, in the unlikely event that they should ever meet. There had been no author photo, Harrison remembered; Stone, whose ethnicity was central to the *Atlantic Monthly* piece, was apparently uninterested in being identified as African American. Apparently, he had the radical belief that his words alone should represent him.

"I read his book," Harrison said now. "It was remarkable."

"A young thinker, untainted by current indoctrinations. Someone who might do some real good in the world."

Harrison didn't disagree, not that he'd ever given much thought to the good Eli Absalom Stone might do in the world. He hadn't even considered the good he himself might do.

"So," he said, reaching back to the last time the conversation had revolved around himself, "you don't think I should go to Harvard?"

"Oh, eventually. You could do worse than end up at Harvard."

Harrison's head was churning now. He felt defeated. If this was another test, he had obviously failed it, too. "I don't understand," he finally admitted. Dr. Loring looked around for the waiter.

"My young triplet friend," he said. He held up his empty cup. "I hope you are not expected home to your unappreciative family just yet."

Harrison frowned. "No, not yet."

"Good. Because I would like to tell you a bit about Roarke."

And this he proceeded to do, right there in that green Naugahyde booth.

Even by American standards, Roarke was not ancient. It had been founded only in the 1970s, as the tsunami of liberalism and enforced diversity began its crest over even the most resistant American universities. One by one they fell to coeducation and quotas, absorbing their sister schools and appending departments that required the word "studies" to have any meaning: women's studies, Afro-Am studies, gender studies, media studies. And what had been shunted aside to accommodate each and every one of these "studies"? All of the subjects that had never required the word "studies" in the first place. Latin. (Latin studies?) History. (History studies?) The much-degraded Western canon that had merely produced two millennia of knowledge, art, and culture!

The school began in a decommissioned Shaker Village in upstate New York, a promising setting with its asceticism and simple beauty, but by the mid-1970s there was pressure from the national historic preservation movement to reclaim the site. Then a Dartmouth alumnus who'd watched the dark incursion of femininity ooze across the Ivy League, and now saw that his own alma mater (the last to fall!) was poised to admit women, offered

Roarke's founder a property just north of the Presidential Mountains and not far from the Maine state line. The first students constructed the buildings themselves; first, in the manner of the earliest American colleges, a single structure in which they lived, ate, and studied, then a barn for the animals, then a library, then a dormitory. Students and professors grew much of their own food and raised their own animals, though not as a faddish or progressive practice. Quite to the contrary! Self-sufficiency and self-governance were traditional principles, reaching back to scholarly monastics, and they were to be essential principles at Roarke, as formative to the very special men the school aimed to produce as intense classwork and deliberate separation from the various distractions of the twentieth century. Thirty years on, with the students' intentional labor more symbolic than strictly necessary, Roarke men were expected to set the annual curriculum, hire the faculty, muck out the cow stalls, and oversee the annual arrival of first-year students in the parking lot of a Concord, New Hampshire, diner.

It was nearly four when the Oppenheimers arrived at the rendezvous in New Hampshire. The parking lot belonged to the Red Arrow Diner, and the bus was an ordinary yellow school bus, not even a Greyhound with video players and a bathroom. The person in charge was apparently a redheaded guy with a clipboard, only he seemed awfully young. Some of the other boys—other *men*—stood around, already chatting or hoisting their boxes and duffels up the steps of the bus and onto its rearmost seats. One had a military haircut and was built like a boulder, another reminded Harrison of his own brother: pudgy and ducking. Looking around the lot, he briefly allowed some misgivings of his own to slip past his considerable defenses. He hadn't been expecting a solemn procession under crossed swords, he told himself. Except that he had, or at least *something* solemn, something ritualistic. Was he heading for camp here? Or the army? Or some backward cult of the Granite State?

But then Harrison thought of Professor Loring, who had once made this same journey, on—quite possibly, from the looks of it—this very same bus. He introduced himself to the person with the clipboard and formed a chain with the others to swiftly load the contents of the Oppenheimer

Volvo onto the bus. He did not like to think of the impression all this stuff was making—he had, in the past weeks, allowed Johanna to assuage her own anxiety by buying him things "for college"—but making a scene with his mother, telling her she'd been wrong to pile on so many purchases, seemed like an unwise use of their final moments together. After this he stoically allowed his parents to hug him and moments later the Volvo did successfully depart without him: south to Brooklyn and their own absurd new lives as parents of a squalling infant.

Alone. At last.

Harrison shook the hands of the others: Paul, Bryce, two Justins, Emmanuel, Gordon. The boulder was named Tony; he was the only one actually from New Hampshire. The one who reminded Harrison of Lewyn (though less and less of Lewyn as he began to speak, since he functioned, quite plainly, far above Lewyn's negative intellectuality) was called Carlos Flores; he had come all the way from Louisiana and seemed excessively interested in everything he saw, even the terribly mundane Red Arrow Diner.

The final student, a slender, fawn-colored young man with a distinct southern accent, introduced himself to Harrison and the others as Eli Absalom Stone. *Holy crap,* Harrison thought, shaking Eli Absalom Stone's cool hand. *It was him! Actually Eli Absalom Stone!* The boy from the shack in the south, the boy who had written a book even Harrison had found remarkable, the boy who had declined an author photo establishing him as anything but a person who'd set down his ideas for the world to take or leave alone. Here: in a parking lot in New Hampshire, boarding the bus with the rest of them, and with the second-year student named John-Peter who wielded the clipboard, and with the actual driver, introduced as Mr. Boudreaux. Shortly after five, they stowed the last of the boxes and duffels and drove north.

John-Peter bounced up and down the aisle, chatting away, delineating his own trajectory (Wisconsin public school, then a year as a congressional page in Washington where a member of his state's delegation took him aside and told him about Roarke). He was planning to transfer to Yale in a year's time and then fast-track to Yale Law, unless he got a Marshall or a Rhodes. Across the aisle, one of the Justins and Emmanuel were discussing

New Wave Cinema as if they were seated at Les Deux Magots, not jolting over New Hampshire roads. Eli Absalom Stone was alone in his double seat a few rows ahead. Harrison watched the darkening forests slip by, and in spite of the landlocked circumstances, the term he kept reaching for, the one that best conveyed—to himself—the terror and thrill of today's events, was *outward-bound.* Outward-bound with these other travelers who, just like him, had opted for actual ideas over the empty rituals of the modern college experience. They might be strangers, but they already had that one very rare thing in common, and it was enough. Or so he hoped it would be.

Chapter Twelve

213 Balch

In which Sally Oppenheimer is once more unsettled

Balch Hall was home to over two hundred freshmen women, most of them clad in Juicy Couture tracksuits and shod in Ugg boots. Their small dormitory rooms were festooned with posters and crowded with text-adorned picture frames (*Sisters Are Best Friends Forever!*), the beds dotted with stuffed animals and jacked up on plastic risers so that extra cases of Diet Snapple could be shoved underneath. That was how at least one half of room 213 began, but barely a week into term Sally began to dispose of many objects supposedly indispensable for dormitory living that she'd allowed her mother to buy. Over the next weeks, mugs, frames, lights, and even items of clothing were carried down the long hallway to the second-floor lounge and left on a table with a handwritten sign: FREE. The women of Balch Hall soon learned to keep their eyes peeled for these expunged items, which began to disperse throughout the building.

"Are you sure?" said one of the girls in the room next door, who stopped at Sally and Rochelle's room with her arms full of Abercrombie sweatshirts and a newish pair of Uggs.

"Completely," Sally confirmed. "I just want to think a little less about what I want to wear."

What she wanted to wear, she'd decided, would come from the minimalist stack of folded blue denim and black long-sleeved shirts on her side of the shared closet. It was, maybe, a little strange, but then again, far more alarming transformations were underway elsewhere in Balch Hall. On their corridor alone a freshman from Texas had inked an arachnid on the back of each hand and taken her septum to some shady place in Collegetown to be pierced. Two fragile girls, unluckily assigned to room together, were already embarked upon competitive cutting. A flautist from Denver had deliberately lost her instrument at a Starbucks in town, after which she had shaved her head for no reason she was able to articulate. All this, and *Sally* still attracted official attention from the RA on her floor? When the senior stopped by she saw that Sally Oppenheimer lacked a standard-issue wooden desk and had not one family photograph or stuffed animal anywhere! On the other hand, Sally herself seemed perfectly healthy and on good terms with her roommate, and there was no telltale herbal residue in the air, nor any alcohol in sight, no new tattoos or fresh scars or radical haircuts or poor hygiene, and both girls talked about their classes with enthusiasm. What should the RA do? Report them for tidiness? She left them to it, and moreover accepted the oversized Cornell '04 mug Sally offered her, because a person could always use another mug.

It encouraged Sally that her roommate seemed to take some cue from the incredible shrinking trousseau on her own side; as the fall progressed Rochelle, too, began to leave some of her more extraneous items in the lounge down the hall or in the trash bins, notably a set of horrible pink-and-butterfly sheets, a souvenir heart-shaped pillow covered in fading Sharpie autographs, and half of the posters she'd initially stuck up with Blu-Tack. She also kept her desk uncluttered and her bed made and her half of the closet—which never emptied out to the extent Sally's did—at least orderly. In fact, Rochelle Steiner had been so generally compliant in domestic matters that it took Sally some time to understand that her roommate was no pushover. What she was, instead:

plainly brilliant (even quite possibly to the elevated standards of Harrison Oppenheimer), tenacious, and powerfully focused on the future—her own future, in particular. Rochelle had a love of discourse for its own sake and took obvious pleasure in arguing one side of an issue and then, equally effectively, the other. In fact, she did this so good-naturedly and so clearly as a kind of cerebral exercise that Sally often had to guess which was her actual opinion, and she was not at all surprised to learn that Rochelle had captained her high school team to victory in the Congressional Debate division of the statewide NSDA tournament, an event that had actually been held right here, on the Cornell campus. ("I took one look and decided to apply. I mean: wow.") Between the two of them, many matters—from the optimal route to Uris Library (distance vs. shelter vs. maintenance of walkways) to George Bush's decision not to appoint an inaugural poet—would come up for this kind of animated but nonpersonal discussion.

Sally had parried her roommate's initial, ordinary, getting-to-know-you questions, evading in general, making no specific statement about her family's sibling configuration, for example. It wasn't something she had strategized in advance about, and this was partly why she'd been surprised to hear herself volunteer the fact of a brother named Harrison, who attended some weirdo college in New Hampshire where the men were men and there were no women at all.

"Dartmouth?" Rochelle had asked, not unreasonably.

"No. It's actually a two-year college."

"Oh. Like a junior college? That's cool. What's he like?"

"Kind of a jerk," Sally said. Then, truthfully enough, she added: "We're not close."

And that ended that, at least on her part, though Rochelle would occasionally insert the elusive brother into a question or a discussion of their prior lives. *What was the brother studying in junior college? Had he gone to the same school as she had, this fascinating source of oddities like the Ethical Conflict Resolution class and the collective open mic rending-of-garment sessions over the school's perceived institutional racism? Had the two of them been bar/bat mitzvahed? Did Harrison share her distaste for pizza?* It wasn't difficult to construct or to maintain this alternate Oppenheimer family, nor to uphold the bigger untruth that a second, unnamed brother lived in the dormitory next door, not after that first week when she had come home to find (and hastily erase) his ridiculous "stopped by" note on their whiteboard. Technology, at least, was on her side; that fall Johanna had acquired an AOL account and quickly developed a fondness for deeply unwelcome in-box fodder: joke lists and medical alerts of dubious origin, chain letters you were supposed to send to ten people you loved, with a gobbet of wisdom or a favorite poem. These were not difficult to parry with a *Thanks!* or *Cute, Mom!* and they served to open enough of an aperture between herself and Lewyn that there was even less of a reason to make real-world contact. Then Johanna figured out how to email photographs to her children at college. She did this a lot.

"Who's that?" Rochelle said one late afternoon in October. She had come back unexpectedly while Sally was in the bathroom and was pointing to a sour infant dressed as a pumpkin for Halloween.

"Who's what?" said Sally, knowing full well. "Oh. Cousin's baby. Chubster." She clicked it away as Rochelle stepped closer.

"All babies are cute, though."

"Are they, though?" She closed her Clamshell iBook. "Are you going for dinner soon?"

"I don't know," said Rochelle, as expected. "Are you?"

Only a handful of times had she even set eyes on Lewyn: once in the first meeting of Cognitive Science 101 (after seeing him she'd dropped the class), and once far across the dining room, where he was seated with a tall, skinny boy. She'd been on her own at the time, and it might have been an acceptable moment to go over and say hello, but she didn't want to, and anyway Lewyn looked okay, perfectly functional. And obviously, he had made at least one friend.

Sally, too, had made a friend. There wasn't anything particularly shocking about that. She'd always had friends, and she'd certainly expected to make new ones at Cornell. What she hadn't expected, though, was that her will to find people to befriend would pretty much terminate at the door of 213 Balch. Given the fact that she'd never shared a bedroom, neutral cohabitation was going to be a pretty big ask, but Rochelle Steiner went beyond what she'd dared to hope for in a randomly assigned roommate. Well beyond. In fact, beyond in a way that, as the term progressed, began ever so slightly to unsettle her.

They were both Arts & Sciences, but Rochelle was going to be a lawyer and Sally, with no professional direction at all, had yet to truly care what her classes were, let alone how well she did in them. As midterms approached, Rochelle—never precisely laid-back—seemed to rev up in intensity, burrowing into some private carrel at Uris in the evenings, which left Sally in the distressing position of having to wait up, or having to decide not to wait up, or ricocheting between these two unpleasant options. That was in addition to Rochelle's impressive array of commitments, each categorized by a different color of pen in her Filofax. Early in the term, she had joined the Center for Jewish Life and then taken on some administrative role, requiring many meetings. Shortly after that she joined a social justice group, and though she ultimately decided against pledging any of the Jewish sororities on campus she still managed to acquire whole groups of new girlfriends in each of them while exploring the possibilities, and these women often came to call, looking at Sally with frank disappointment when they found her home alone. Sally, on the other hand, had yet to discover a campus activity, group, or interest compelling enough to get her out of 213 Balch in the evenings, or even on the weekends, and usually she found herself alone there, doing her class reading and trying not to think too much about when Rochelle was going to get back, or why that seemed to matter so much, or the ways in which her lifelong dream of singularity, now clearly achieved, was turning out to be not nearly as pleasant as she'd imagined.

She and Lewyn both went home for Thanksgiving, then again for the winter break, both times traveling separately by the college's chartered buses but arriving at the house on the Esplanade within hours of each other. Once back in Brooklyn, brother and sister awkwardly (but at least without discussing it, which would have been even more awkward) regressed to high school–era modes of communication, answering Johanna's and Salo's questions about their Cornell lives in a way that definitely implied they were hanging out, at least occasionally. Johanna seemed to radiate anxiety, clasping them both in viselike hugs that went on for far too long. Never a cook, she had ordered in so much food that both of the Sub-Zeros were fully loaded, and her constant fretting about what would be consumed, and when, on which plates, and in which quantities, said everything those painful embraces had not.

The baby seemed distinctly longer than she had the previous summer. Also, thankfully, quieter.

The baby was nothing to her.

Lewyn, confirming the change she had noticed on campus, was definitely thinner, but the transformation of Harrison was truly impressive. Harrison had added a highly unnecessary layer of smugness to his already noxious personality, as if his great superiority had only been confirmed by recent experiences, but he had also become physically hardened from actual bodily labor. This was obvious not only to her but to everyone, and in particular it seemed to fascinate Johanna, who peppered her most highbrow child with endless questions about chickens and cows. To Sally he seemed to have undergone some form of cultish indoctrination, which apparently featured reading by candlelight while watching over baby animals in a barn, or discussing Aristotle while digging up carrots, or some such ridiculousness. He did not have a roommate, as such, since "the men"—*Christ*—all roomed together in what sounded like a bunkhouse. He was maddeningly evasive about his actual classes, except to say that Roarke referred to these as "seminars," not "classes," and that it was a great pleasure to be in a community of fellow intellectuals at last. One of these "Roarke men," for example, had written an actual book: serious scholarship, properly published, widely admired, etc., etc.

"Well, that's impressive," said our mother.

Lewyn, perhaps in response, tried to tell Salo about his art history survey class, which met early in the mornings.

"They always seem to," our father said.

The holidays labored under Johanna's frantic embroidery of family traditions. There was Hanukkah, with the small and bent silver menorah that had—according to family legend, anyway—come over from Germany, and eight days of gifts to be selected, purchased, wrapped, and presented, every one of which Sally was forced to appear delighted about, and lie about needing, and which would then have to be transported all the way back to college before she might deposit them in the lounge down the corridor. There was the defiant New-York-Jews-on-Christmas-Day walk across the Brooklyn Bridge to lunch in Chinatown. There was even, horribly, a performance of *The Nutcracker,* surrounded by hordes of dressed-up children. In the evenings she sometimes ended up in the basement with Lewyn, watching tapes on the still functional VCR from opposite ends of the old couch: Hitchcock, Disney from long ago, Japanese anime that Lewyn liked and Sally couldn't quite follow. Oddly enough these were not unpleasant evenings, though even alone together they never spoke of Cornell, or their classes, or roommates, or anything else related to the shared experience they were supposedly having.

Every morning while she was home, Sally set her alarm for five and went to her bedroom window, which overlooked Montague Terrace and the back gate, and waited there, watching for the lifting latch and the dark shape of her father as he slipped inside. She'd been doing it for years, and not once had he ever looked up to see her, or know that he'd been seen.

Chapter Thirteen

Light Meat vs. Dark

In which Harrison Oppenheimer's taste for chicken is forever compromised

When Harrison got back to New Hampshire after the holiday he learned that three of the cows were down with mastitis. He wasn't sure how he was supposed to feel about this. The cows hadn't been part of his chore rotation yet, so he didn't know much about caring for them, nor had he formed anything resembling a human-bovine connection. He went right out to the barn with the others, though, to get caught up.

Three cows comprised a quarter of the school herd, and the sick ones were being kept apart from the others. The milk itself, in a brown plastic milking bucket, looked weird, with what appeared to be flakes and clots in it.

"What is *that*?" asked Carlos, pointing to the nearest cow's extended udder.

Tony, who'd grown up on a dairy farm in southern New Hampshire, said, in his succinct way: "Pus."

Carlos looked like Harrison felt.

The cow did seem to be very unhappy, but perhaps that was just anthropomorphism. (Harrison had found numerous opportunities to use the word "anthropomorphism" since coming to Roarke.) "Is she in pain?" he asked Tony.

Tony said: "Ayuh."

The milk would have to be dumped until the infection was cleared. The three cows had already begun antibiotics, which Tony and Justin (one of the Justins, the one from Lake Forest) were giving as infusions. Harrison watched Justin maneuver a plastic tube over the first cow's udder and squeeze the fluid up, then remove the tube, pinch off the teat, and palpate the medicine up into the gland.

Not for the first time, he marveled at how he'd managed to get here. Eighteen years of being coddled, overscheduled, and overseen, paid attention to in all of the worst ways (and in none of the ways that mattered), housed and clothed and fed and amused in a manner commensurate with his family's endemic wealth, had somehow brought him to this Spartan community of men: rising early to menial, often arduous, chores, consuming food they'd personally raised or helped to prepare, and entertaining themselves with little more than the combined content of their minds. As far as Harrison was concerned, every single one of his fellow students was of an intellectual caliber that had never once crossed the threshold of the Walden School (either in a student *or* a faculty member).

Given his own buried anxieties, Harrison had not been thrilled, on arrival the previous fall, to be informed of certain perceived *deficits* in his own intellectual preparation, and assigned remedial—*remedial!*—work to address those deficits. Yes, he, Harrison Oppenheimer, *the smart one,* was to be detained for never having studied—wait for it—the King James Bible and the *Confessions of Augustine,* two texts most assuredly not on the syllabus of any class at the Walden School. (He wasn't alone in this disgrace, thankfully; that fall, he met twice weekly with a few of his fellow remedials—Tony, Chaim, and one of the Justins—to discuss these texts in depth with Professor Alcock.) Meanwhile, he studied Euclid's *Elements* and Aristotle's *Nicomachean Ethics* with the others, and his old muddle with philosophy began to dissipate almost immediately. (*This* was what teaching could be, he marveled!) It wasn't even difficult, and there was nothing wrong with his brain. Addressing another Walden-induced deficit, Harrison began to do some Latin and even a little Greek with Mr. Perrulli, a former priest who'd been teaching classics at Roarke since Loring's time, and he read deeply in epistemology with Tony (who despite his dairy-farm upbringing already possessed a profound understanding of the material) and joined a few of the others in the Constitution seminar. Harrison even found himself engaged by Mr. Boudreaux's auto mechanics class, taught as something of a rite of passage at Roarke, and actually learned how to repair an engine.

But when it came to the famous Roarke chores, the physical labor that was as central to the school's mystique as its cerebral prerequisites, Harrison was far less enthusiastic. And who could blame him? No one was especially happy to rise at dawn and greet the day with their toil. (Even Tony, whose life had been spent tending to cows, was known to be short-tempered as he dressed first thing to go out to the herd.) A few of the men had managed to find good fits: Gordon, for example, who came from a restaurant family in Washington State, and who liked to cook, had taken charge of the kitchen soon after their arrival (a great relief to the second-years and the faculty, as the last Roarke student with any culinary aptitude had graduated a year earlier). He had breakfast and coffee ready by the time the others came in from the barns and the fields, and while the food he prepared was an adjustment for Harrison, hunger helped anything go down. Harrison was hungry at Roarke in a way he had never been in Brooklyn. After a while, he was even happy to see certain menu items come up on the rotation—vegetarian chili, baked trout, pasta with autumn vegetables. Anything but chicken, basically. He was pretty sure he would never eat chicken again.

Harrison had not been at Roarke for a month before he was summoned to the coop, cloudy with feathers and slimy with shit, and unceremoniously handed the unsupervised care of the school flocks. The second-year student who did the handing looked utterly delighted.

"But . . . but . . ." Harrison was already sputtering, and not only from the *reek* of his immediate surroundings. Gordon in the kitchen: that made sense. Tony in the cow barn: that also made sense. But a Brooklyn boy—a *Brooklyn Heights* boy—in charge of *this*?

The second-year looked as if he knew precisely what Harrison wanted to say about this situation. Perhaps he had attempted some similar objection a year ago at about this time, and yet these birds had still gotten fed and watered and relieved of their eggs and, yes, butchered and readied for the kitchen, from that day to this. Putting Harrison in charge of these . . . *creatures* . . . was a test, like rebuilding a car engine or achieving some familiarity with the King James Bible or sharing a bunkhouse with twenty-seven other men, or finally, *finally*, gaining liberation from his siblings. If help was needed, he was told, an answer could likely be found on the shelf of animal husbandry books in the library, every one of them older than Roarke itself. Also, would he please bring in eight broilers for dinner?

Yes, killed.

Yes, plucked.

Yes, gutted.

Chickens were beings of little brain. Precious little brain, it turned out, and while this was neither a good thing nor a bad thing when you had to feed them or chase after them or break up their disputes (they could be horrendous bullies, like something out of a John Hughes movie) or insert your hand beneath them to collect their morning eggs, it was an indisputably good thing when you were tasked with terminating their lives. In the end, and after many abortive attempts, Harrison did indeed consult *Modern Poultry Farming* for the best (most efficient? most kind? most likely not to make him barf?) means of shuffling eight unlucky fowl from off this mortal coil. And he managed to get the job done.

Harrison's ability to consume chicken would probably be the greatest casualty of that day: permanent, and certainly inconvenient, given the many rubber chicken dinners in his future. It was not compassion for the bird, or belief in the sanctity of its life; it was the filth and the crap and the flying feathers and the smells and the sounds and the interminable squawking which were to be his lot for the foreseeable future. Or at least until he was allowed to hand off his burden to the next horrified Roarke man.

Sometimes, on those cold mornings, he warmed himself by imagining his siblings at their own pathetically conventional institute of higher education. Fragile Lewyn and caustic Sally, who aspired to nothing and who had produced not one original idea throughout their (enforced) years together; Harrison tried to imagine what they did with themselves all day, in their overheated dorm rooms, alongside their video game–playing, blow-drying, chugging-and-puking classmates. He thought of his siblings in their massive survey courses, doodling their way through PowerPoint lectures, receiving inflated As, learning absolutely nothing. Lewyn and Sally had entered the great education con in which students and their families paid in for four years and were rewarded with a piece of paper, suitable for framing, in return (along with, for those who were not Oppenheimers or of similar alignment, a whole lot of debt). And this appalling proxy for an actual education was what Lewyn and Sally had signed up for while he was here at Roarke! He felt elated when he considered his own fellow students, and the conversations that overran their seminars, trailing them to their chores, their meals, the bunkroom, even the showers. These were men who fell asleep reading then woke up and began reading again. Like him. And he was at home with them, far more than he had ever been with those other two.

A couple of years earlier, tiny Roarke had become more broadly known, courtesy of an influential guidebook called *Colleges That Change Lives,* which appealed to the reader to look beyond brand-name institutions for an exhilarating array of less-well-known colleges and universities. Harrison, who had come home one day during his junior year to find this very book on the dining room table, assumed it had been purchased for Lewyn and Sally, since he himself would obviously be going to one of those selfsame brand-name institutions; still, when he troubled himself to open the guidebook a few months later, he found that Roarke was actually listed among those justly obscure institutions, and praised for its quirky insistence on the canon, its tiny size, and purist intellectualism. The book had led directly to a sharp spike in applications for its fourteen annual places, and while Harrison had no way of knowing exactly how superior he and his classmates had been to the rest of their applicant pool, there was no disputing that they were a bluntly impressive group. Nearly all of them had declined or deferred admission to the most selective universities in the country, for reasons that soon came to light. Carlos (Princeton, Yale) had anchored last year's national champion debate team for his high school in Louisiana. One of the Justins (MIT, Stanford) had made it to the finals of the Siemens Competition the previous year. Bryce (Harvard, West Point) had spent the past couple of years essentially explaining policy papers to the dim-witted congressman from his district in suburban Minneapolis and writing first drafts of much of the congressman's correspondence (not excluding a bill bearing the congressman's name that had recently passed the House). Emmanuel (MIT, Stanford, Caltech) had won the national Math Olympiad, and Gordon (Columbia, Yale, Dartmouth) had coauthored a monograph with his mentor, the chief justice of the Ninth Circuit Court of Appeals. Even Tony (Dartmouth, Princeton), the New Hampshire farm kid Harrison had assumed to be some kind of keeping-the-locals-happy recruit, was deeply immersed in semiotics and intended an academic career.

And then, of course, there was Eli Absalom Stone (Harvard, Yale, Princeton, Dartmouth, Stanford, Columbia).

At no point had Eli been precisely friendly to Harrison, but neither was he notably warm to any of the others. Harrison wondered if his celebrated classmate might show a preference for Roarke's other students of color—a profoundly cerebral second-year from Atlanta named Tyquan, Jonathan Jackson from Nevada, and their classmate Carlos Flores from Louisiana—but he seemed to hold them at the same arm's length as everyone else. Still, Eli was never the least bit snobbish, as—with all of his accomplishments—he might reasonably have been. He stepped up as much as the rest of them when there was some task requiring community effort, and listened respectfully to differences of opinion and even thoughtful criticism, so long as it was properly supported. In the classroom, of course, he was glorious, and watching him eviscerate somebody else's position from the other side of a seminar table—often using only a prodigious memory for printed material, a pincer-like grasp of the relevance of any given passage, and a hypnotically calm voice—was a thing of beauty. The rest of their fellow Roarke men might someday impact scholarship, business, and politics but Eli Absalom Stone, Harrison saw, would require the world to orient itself to *him*.

Harrison had spent the first months of their time at Roarke waiting for the subject of Eli's book, and its critical response, and the *coverage* of its critical response, to arise, and he was more than a little surprised when it didn't. Were none of these brilliant classmates paying attention? Was he the only one whose antennae had picked up this exceptional intellectual, already part of a national dialogue, who was *actually living among them*? Apparently so. He himself had said nothing, except for one November evening when he looked up from his book to discover that he and Eli were alone together, the last two in the lounge after dinner. Before he could actually consider what he was about to do, let alone choose his words, he blurted out that he had read *Against Youth* and had thought it very sound and very well written.

"Thank you," said Eli, barely looking up from his own book.

And then, as if this response had been at all encouraging, which even a dolt could have seen it was not, Harrison heard himself ask about the no-photo-on-the-book-jacket thing, which he totally understood, because the work was the work, and that was what mattered, not some preconceived assumption about ethnicity or a given view of history. But, he stammered, his discomfort obvious, making that choice must have been difficult. Had it been difficult?

"Not at all," Eli Absalom Stone had said, turning a page. This had closed their discussion, and, it seemed, the topic as a whole, and Harrison resolved—*again*—that he was absolutely not going to fawn over Eli Absalom Stone, because Eli Absalom Stone clearly did not wish to be fawned over.

Then one night in January, Carlos—of all people—announced that he'd just found a book in the school library by Eli! Eli Absalom Stone! Like, *their own* Eli Absalom Stone (as if there could be another author by that name), and *Wasn't this so cool?* and *Why didn't you tell us, man?*

Carlos was a person of great enthusiasms, but Harrison had never seen him this excited.

The other students, every one of them, looked mystified.

"Wait, you wrote a book?" Bryce actually said.

Harrison, repelled and embarrassed, focused on his hands.

"What's it about?" said Tony.

Eli looked vague. "Just some preoccupations. Juvenilia, actually. You know," he said. As if they all had collections of essays based on their adolescent musings underway or awaiting imminent publication by major publishers, to be discussed in the pages of the *New Yorker* and the *Nation* and parsed by the likes of Leonard Lopate and Charlie Rose.

"I'm going to start it right away," Carlos assured them all, as if they were anxious about this very thing.

The setting for all this was the regular evening meeting, which took place in the lounge every night after dinner and before they dispersed to final chores, work, occasional leisure, and finally sleep. It was where ordinary concerns were raised, occasionally academic but also related to the practical cogs and mechanisms of the farm and school: library procedures, problems with the milking machine, the hiring of faculty, the reading of application essays by those hundreds of students hoping to attend Roarke the following fall. Sometimes, this time was used to make requests or update projects, like Bryce proposing a trip to see *Angels in America* in Boston or Tony reporting on his experimental fall planting of onions, overwintering in the north pasture. To Harrison these topics were rarely scintillating, and often, by the end of his physically and intellectually challenging days, it was tough to sit still for—let alone care about—things like onions. Sometimes he even found himself nodding off in one of the old armchairs. He wasn't nodding off now.

Carlos did, in fact, start reading *Against Youth* that very evening, and as the weeks passed he took pains to assure the rest of them that *the book was great! really well written!* And say how cool was it that Eli had grown up without television and computers and internet and all that kind of thing, and was still so engaged with everything, their generation and its preoccupations, weaknesses, failings, discarded potential! *I mean, Eli came from, like, a shack. On a mountain. And never went to school!*

Eli's "juvenilia" wasn't particularly long, nor was Carlos a slow reader, but he continued to hold on to the volume, even announcing that he was now rereading certain essays, and he began to say, at some point, that he'd begun organizing his thoughts for what he was calling his "critique." Harrison had a pretty good idea of how little this *critique* was wished for by the author of *Against Youth,* but he himself was so eager to hear Eli talk about his book, and perhaps be forced into the very conversation he had once attempted, and which had been so promptly deflected. Now, if he sat still and didn't disturb the universe, this classmate might just force open that door and haul the recalcitrant Eli Absalom Stone out into the open, and Carlos would ask all of Harrison's own questions, and perhaps even the one about the no-photo-on-the-book-jacket thing, which was obviously related to the race thing. So he kept quiet and waited, but that much anticipated *critique* never did take place, and in fact Harrison would remain unenlightened regarding the full magnitude of Eli Absalom Stone's actual thoughts on *the race thing* for many years to come, by which time it would be far, far too late to unmake certain decisions of his own, and untake certain positions of his own, many of them lamentably public.

One night in early March, as the students and resident faculty gathered again in the backhouse lounge, Eli Absalom Stone accused his classmate, Carlos Flores, of plagiarizing some insights into *Titus Andronicus,* which he himself had composed and left in a notebook on his bed, and which had appeared, without attribution, in an essay Carlos had presented to their Shakespeare seminar.

There was silence. Utter, excruciating silence. Professor Alcock said: "Eli, that's a very serious allegation."

"And I'm making it very seriously," Eli said. "I've struggled with this."

"Wait," Carlos said. He was catching up. "What?"

"Your paper. It was based on my notes."

"It most certainly was not!" Carlos yelled. He was looking around wildly. "Why would you say that?"

"For the only possible reason," Eli said. "Because it's true. And it gives me no pleasure, I promise you. As I said, I've struggled."

Harrison was staring, he realized. Also, his mouth was open—that was easy to fix. Eli himself had not moved. He sat in one of the squishy armchairs down at the end of the lounge, near the kitchen doors, his arms on its shredded armrests. Across the room, somebody emitted a high and nervous laugh.

"I don't know what you're talking about," Carlos said. He happened to be sitting right next to Harrison, but Harrison didn't turn his head. "I never saw any notes. And I'm not in the habit of looking through other people's things."

"I don't know whether it's your habit," Eli said mildly. "I only know that you did it once, because my work was in that paper you submitted. I recognized the material about Roman sources. Seneca's *Thyestes* and Ovid's *Philomela*. My insights. My notes."

Carlos was on his feet. He stepped into the center of the room and began to turn, but he couldn't seem to settle on whom he should be addressing. Eli? Or Professor Alcock, who like everyone else still seemed to be in shock? "I absolutely deny this . . . outrageous . . ."

"May I see the notebook?" Professor Alcock said.

"Wait, is there a protocol for this?" said John-Peter. "Some kind of due process?"

"Due process!" Carlos yelled. "I haven't done anything!"

"Well, that's why there'd be due process," said one of the Justins.

"But if Eli's wrong, shouldn't he be compelled to withdraw the accusation?"

"I'm not wrong," Eli said mildly. "So I won't need to apologize. But obviously I defer to the wishes of the community." This he said with the tonal equivalent of a deep, groveling bow. "Please don't think for a moment that I find any of this easy. I was very troubled when I read Carlos's paper. I took a few days to think it over. I don't feel that I can . . . honorably . . . do anything other than what I've done."

"But it's . . . not . . . true . . ." Carlos's voice was now unmistakably shaking, and Harrison suddenly recalled that this particular classmate had been a national debate champion. "I wouldn't dream of stealing somebody else's work. I never have and I never would. I can't imagine why," he turned toward his accuser, but Eli continued to glare at some spot on the rug, "Eli, why you would say this."

Professor Alcock cleared his throat. "Eli? Can I see the notebook, please?"

With great solemnity, Eli Absalom Stone rose and left the room. They all watched him go, silent as if by agreement. Eli, unlike the rest of them, had acquired no physical traits of the outdoorsman while at Roarke, likely because his nonacademic assignments had pretty much kept him away from animals and out of the fields. Of course, he was no more interested in the workings of the farm than Harrison himself was; he was interested in things like the Roman sources for *Titus Andronicus.* Harrison felt a little chill. He liked Carlos. He liked all of them. Especially Carlos, or was this just occurring to him now, under these rather extreme circumstances? Did he like Eli? It was not the pertinent question. What he really wanted, what he had wanted from the very first moment in that New Hampshire parking lot, what he had likely wanted from the day he sat down with *Against Youth,* eighteen months earlier, was for Eli to like *him.* He had no idea whether Eli liked him.

Eli came back to the lounge carrying a simple marble-cover notebook, and everyone stared at it as if they'd never seen such an object, though this was the type commonly used by Roarke students, not to mention by primary and secondary school students all over the country, and so commonplace that office supply stores and drug stores and even supermarkets stocked them in bulk each August for Back-to-School. Eli himself was likely in charge of ordering a supply of these notebooks for the Roarke community, where students tended to write a lot and no one had a personal computer. Harrison, for example, carried six of these notebooks, one for each of his five seminars and a sixth for egg production records.

Eli handed over the notebook. In Alcock's hands, it fell open easily to a place where pages—possibly many pages—had been roughly ripped out, leaving Eli's distinctive thick and spiky handwriting on either side. "What am I looking at?" he said.

"About ten pages missing," said Eli. "Mainly *Philomela.* But at least a couple of pages on the Seneca sources, too."

"It's absolutely untrue," Carlos said, but his voice was now pleading. "I haven't touched that notebook. I've never even seen it before."

"It was on my bed about six days ago, then I couldn't find it. I just figured I'd misplaced it somewhere. I'd moved on to another paper topic anyway, so I just kind of let it go. When I read Carlos's paper I thought, well, that's a coincidence. But then I found the notebook up in the Stearns Room."

He stopped here. He must have known how this would land. The Stearns Room was one of several study areas around the small campus, outfitted like the rest with tables and chairs and a couple of couches, but it wasn't as popular as the library or the backhouse lounge, both of which had fireplaces. Only a small, regular group opted for the Stearns, leaving their work out on the tables and bringing up mugs of tea from the kitchen directly underneath. This group had always included Carlos.

"Where?" Professor Alcock asked.

"Down the back of the sofa. The pages on Seneca and *Philomela* were missing. Like I said, I just kind of sat with it. I guess I was trying to persuade myself that it wasn't, you know, that."

"I discussed my paper topic with Professor Willem!" Carlos said suddenly. "A week ago!"

Professor Willem was not in the room. He was an adjunct, or what passed as an adjunct at Roarke, which meant that he came in one afternoon a week from Dartmouth to teach the Shakespeare seminar, and a seminar on Milton and Spenser.

"All right." Alcock got to his feet. "I'm going to stop this now. Carlos, Eli, come with me."

"I'm not going anywhere with him," Carlos said.

"This is a community issue," John-Peter said. "We need to process it as a community."

Alcock was nodding. "Without question. But I'm going to talk with these two first. I suggest we end the meeting now."

"Dude," Carlos said, glaring at Eli, "I didn't steal your notes! I didn't take your book! I can't believe you. This is *fucked*."

"Let's calm it down," Professor Alcock said. "We're going to talk about it."

"But it isn't true." Carlos looked very close to tears now. Harrison stole a glance around the room. Heads were down, almost to a man. Gordon alone seemed to be staring at Carlos. "I insist on the right to hold my accuser accountable for this."

"We'll get to that," said Alcock. "For now, though, let's call it a night. Everyone, I appreciate it won't be easy, but I strongly suggest that we leave this until we can convene with more information. Good night, all." And he left, preceded by Eli and followed, a moment later, by an unsteady Carlos. The room was like a tomb. For the first moment, anyway.

"Holy fuck," said somebody.

"Let's not," said John-Peter.

"No way Carlos did that," said Gordon.

John-Peter said: "Gordon. We are not going to discuss this. You heard him."

"He must believe it, though. Eli must. Why else would he say it?"

Harrison looked around. Belatedly, he realized that he was the one who'd spoken. This was how he realized which side he was on. And that there were sides.

"Bullshit, Oppenheimer."

"Guys." John-Peter was losing the battle.

"I'm going out to the barn," said Tony.

A few of the others went with him, and they didn't come back till after Harrison had gone to bed.

Chapter Fourteen

The Gift to Be Simple

In which Sally Oppenheimer experiences rapture by furniture

Sally had hoped her roommate would invite her to Ellesmere while they were both at home for the winter break. Rochelle, however, seemed to parry her many questions about the town, its history and culture, and whether she planned on visiting her old school and meeting up with her friends. Finally, Sally resorted to an outright request. "Hey, you know what would be fun? I could come out to Ellesmere. See where you're from."

"I beg to differ," said Rochelle. "There is nothing remotely fun about Ellesmere."

"Sure, but I'd love to visit you. I've never been to any part of Long Island but the Hamptons."

"Consider yourself lucky," said Rochelle.

Sally didn't feel hurt, exactly, but she recognized an impasse. Besides, she wouldn't have considered allowing Rochelle to enter the Oppenheimer home or experience her own family, with its unacknowledged siblings, including the one who lived in the dormitory next door and the one whose absurdly late appearance screamed family crisis.

Only three weeks after their return to campus, however, Rochelle announced that there was a problem at home, and she had to head back to Long Island for a couple of days.

"What kind of problem?" Sally asked.

"Oh, it's the house. Too boring to go into. Mom just needs me back for a little bit."

"Should I come with you?" Sally said.

Rochelle looked up from her laptop.

"That's kind of you to offer, Sally. But no."

The next morning, a storm over the Finger Lakes dumped a locally modest foot of snow over the Cornell campus. Sally walked Rochelle through that to the bus station and watched her board the eight o'clock to New York. Then, unsure of what to do with herself, she trudged back to Carol's Café for breakfast. The room wasn't crowded. She took the table she and Rochelle often chose, under a poster advertising Cornell's study abroad program in Florence, and bought coffee and a strawberry yogurt. A girl at a nearby table was texting on her flip phone and weeping at the same time. She kept pushing her dark hair back behind her ears, but let the tears fall, undisturbed. Sally didn't know her. She didn't know anyone else in the café, either. Five months into her life as a college student and she felt as if she hadn't met a soul.

The cafeteria overall was emptying, as everyone stomped off to first-period class. Sally had a class of her own—the introductory earth sciences course she was taking for a distribution requirement—but something kept her from getting to her feet and out the door. The next time she looked, the weeping woman had also gone—off, presumably, to text and cry in a less public place—and Sally was the only one left. She continued to sit, looking down at her cold coffee and what was left of her strawberry yogurt, and wondering what it was about this gray Ithaca morning that made it feel so different from any other gray Ithaca morning. But of course this was obvious, even to her. The day was different, and not in a good way, because the diminutive Ms. Rochelle Steiner was on a Peter Pan bus, bound for Port Authority and the mysteries of Ellesmere, Long Island, return unknown.

Gone, in other words. Not here, with her, in other words.

And then, long past time, something began to really break through, something that had been working away at her for months, and Sally Oppenheimer caught an accurate glimpse of her own situation, its dimensions and far-reaching implications. Oh, and her situation was precarious, indeed.

One thing she and her brothers actually *did* have in common was that none of them had ever formed an attachment to another person that might, by any stretch of the imagination, be considered romantic. Lewyn, of course, was a basket case in general when it came to other people, though he *had* moped after that famously beautiful girl a class behind them in high school. Harrison had lost his virginity to a Walden classmate he considered deeply inferior in every way (it had been the girl's idea, he'd made sure to tell them; she had even provided the condom!), but naturally he'd never considered this any form of a *relationship*. Sally herself had felt only twice that hand-in-the-guts disturbance, that sickening catapult into the unknown, first with the counselor during her first and only Pinecliffe summer, and once in that folk art museum where she'd been stalking our father. In both cases the experience had been almost instantly replaced by an equally powerful wave of horror and loathing. So not much baggage, no! And now, in addition to that, there was a brand-new fucking problem, and it was too close for her to ignore, and it was vast, and it consumed worlds.

It went without saying that Sally wasn't going to *do* anything about her predicament. Her goal was to get out from under these very unwelcome feelings, and if that couldn't be accomplished, to learn how to coexist with them, as if they were some form of chronic condition. Management, in other words. Management, through so many of the things she had already taught herself: discipline, order, containment. If anyone could do it, in other words, Sally Oppenheimer could! Anyway, she didn't have a choice.

Sally got up and left the café, heading for Olin Library where she intended to do penance by finding a topic for her women's studies seminar on the Marys, Wollstonecraft and Shelley. She was trudging toward the center of campus, hood up, head down, watching her own feet make their turgid progress through the snow and muck, and there was remarkably little merriment to be overheard among her fellow students, all of them sloshing along through the same wintry mix. As East Avenue curved left past the bridge, a fresh new blast of wind pushed back the edge of her hood, and Sally, squinting into it, found herself with a straight-on view of the Johnson Museum of Art: a right-angled concrete bunker with a Lego-like appendage over the entrance.

She hadn't set foot inside the Johnson since arriving on campus, but she knew about the family paintings that were supposedly there, the ones that had once belonged to her father's parents, Hermann and Selda. They'd been donated to Cornell when Salo was—by purest coincidence, no doubt—a high school senior applying for admission. She had never actually seen those paintings, it occurred to her. Then again, she had never actually cut a class before this morning, so maybe it was just a day for firsts.

Sally turned and walked across the Arts Quad to the museum, unzipping her parka as she entered the sleek stone lobby. Inside, the mess of wind and muddy snow retreated, framed by narrow horizontal windows as something mild and reassuringly traditional: college in winter. She looked around, half expecting to see her own name on a sign or doorway. When she didn't, she went over to the kiosk and took a folding map of the exhibition halls. No Oppenheimer there, either.

"Excuse me," she said, approaching one of the guards. This was a stout woman who couldn't have been much older than herself. "I'm looking for the Oppenheimer paintings?"

"The . . ." The woman frowned, considering. For one awful moment it occurred to Sally that she might have mispronounced her own name. "Oppenheimer is the name of the artist?"

Sally nearly smiled. *As if.* As if anyone in her family could ever produce a work of art on their own.

"The donor was Oppenheimer. The paintings were Old Masters."

"Okay." The woman had taken up a clipboard and was now consulting it. "I don't think we have anything by Old Master. At least not on current display. It could be in storage."

"No . . . I . . ." But words, obviously, had failed her. *That noted artist, Old*

Master? Then suddenly she saw Lewyn, who was calmly emerging from the stairwell at the far end of the lobby, and this took all other thought away with it. She turned her back and hunched her shoulders forward. It was instinctive, involuntary.

"Do you want me to check?" the guard was saying. "We have the Shaker exhibition on now. I know they moved out a lot of stuff, to storage. It wouldn't take more than a couple minutes."

"No, it's okay," Sally said. She had forgotten about the Oppenheimer paintings. Now all she wanted was to get away from her brother. She rushed up the stairs he had just come down, listening to the slap of her wet boots as she climbed, up to the second-floor landing (Art of Korea and Japan, 1800–1910) and then the third (Arts and Crafts Colonies of Upstate New York, 1885–1920), and upward again, as if she still thought they might be up here, the mythic Oppenheimer paintings, that umbilical between herself, her father, her grandparents, and Cornell. Then, finally, she ran out of staircase, and stopped.

THE GIFT TO BE SIMPLE: A SHAKER AESTHETIC read the sign beside the gallery doorway, below a drawing of a spreading tree with large round green and red fruits and a block of text about the exhibition. Not that Sally stopped to read any of that. She was inside the room before she was aware of entering it, and standing, dumbstruck, at the foot of a chair.

A chair, a chair, Sally thought, as if someone were trying to persuade her otherwise.

An ordinary chair. A massively extraordinary ordinary chair, with a seat of rushes woven into a delicate pattern that looked incapable of supporting a fairy. It had . . . finials, she supposed. That shouldn't be much of a talking point. And yet they were so exquisitely perfect, and the slats that made the back of the chair also no bigger than they needed to be, but no smaller, and just plain, beautiful, not at all . . . decorated, was the word that came to her. It was not decorated, not in any way. It needed nothing.

The chair sat (stood?) on a raised white cube, which brought the seat level to her eyes, but there was no glass or plastic around it to protect it from anyone who wanted to . . . what? Touch it? Make off with it? This appalled her, somehow, though she was very far from being able to think why. She only knew that this object, so unadorned and yet so clearly contained by its purpose, its basic and primitive purpose of enabling a human body to relieve itself of its own weight, was a pure expression of beauty. It outshone the sun.

"You an angel?" a voice said. This voice was both low and near to laughing.

Sally looked around. A short woman with unrestrained white hair and a black wool turtleneck, tight across her middle, was looking at her from across the room. The room, she saw only now, was full of other miraculous objects: tables, cupboards, chairs.

"I'm sorry?" Sally managed. She wasn't appreciating the interruption.

"An angel. That chair was made by someone who believed an angel might sit on it. Thomas Merton, don't quote me."

"I'm sorry?" Sally said again.

"Well, don't be sorry. You're the first Cornell student I've seen in here. We get antiques dealers, people up from the city. Shaker has fans, you know. This stuff is like the rock stars of the antiques world." She seemed to consider. "You *are* a Cornell student, right?"

"Oh. Yes." Sally nodded. Now she couldn't take her eyes off the table, just behind the white-haired woman. It was red and very long and might have seated twenty, yet it rested on four of the simplest, most delicate legs, each narrowing lightly as it reached toward the floor. Again, it was elevated. Again, she desperately wanted to touch it.

"You like that?" the woman said.

Sally could only nod. "Like" was a pathetic shade of what she felt about the table, about the chair. And everything else—her eyes swept over it all. The word that sang from the objects was: ravishing.

"I found this, actually," the woman said. To Sally's horror she reached out and touched the tabletop, then tap-tapped it with her short fingers. No alarm sounded. "Down in Homer. In the backhouse of an old place on the village green. It was covered in boxes of eight-track tapes, and I kid you not, it had a dead cat under it. In a suitcase. Not recently dead," she corrected, as if this were an important point.

Sally, mystified, looked again at the table. She couldn't decide which of these degradations was worse: the dead cat or the eight-track tapes.

"What do you mean, you found it?"

"I went in looking for furniture. I'm a picker. You know what a picker is?"

No, Sally did not know. Luckily she didn't have to say so.

"I go to people, ask them if they have any old stuff they want money for. Nine times out of ten they have nothing, it's Ethan Allen or some junk made in China, but it's old to them so they think it's old. And sometimes they have real old, but it's not the right kind of old. Like Victorian, which nobody wants right now. I like Victorian myself, but I'm not the one who counts. And sometimes they have the right kind of old, but they know what it should cost, so that's no good. I have to walk away from that stuff sometimes, and it smarts, I can tell you. But *sometimes* they have it, *and* it's the right kind, *and* they don't know what someone could sell it for. And that's what makes it all worthwhile. Like this."

And again, she touched it. The tabletop. No alarms. No sirens. No one to wrestle her to the ground.

"Do you . . . work here?" Sally asked.

"Volunteer. I'd say it's altruistic but it's business. The people who come to see this, sometimes they turn into my customers. Dealers or collectors. It's just smart."

Sally looked at her. She had a face that seemed at once taut and wrinkled, like someone who had spent a whole lot of time outside, under a weak sun, getting blown around in the cold. Not a speck of makeup. Not a piece of jewelry. She was, in her way, as plain as the furniture.

"You mean, some of this belongs to you?" Sally heard a note of eagerness in her own voice. *I could buy it,* she was thinking. She had been born to wealth, raised in wealth, and yet she had never felt this way about an object. How much could it all cost? A table? A chair?

"Oh no." The woman laughed, this time without restraint. "No, no. I appreciate it, but I'm not stupid. You don't hold on to Shaker just 'cause it's pretty. I sold that"—she pointed at the long table—"to a dealer called Russell, in Westchester. And that"—she gestured across the room, to a rocking chair or a smaller, square table, Sally couldn't tell—"to a lady up in Boston. There's not that many people who specialize in Shaker, and they know all the collectors. Shaker's a very particular commitment. Not something your average Joe would just make up their mind to buy, on the spur of the moment."

"Because it's expensive?" Sally asked, feeling like an idiot.

"You could say!" The woman laughed again. "Not something a college student could afford," she added, almost comfortingly.

This college student could, Sally thought, but she only nodded, and held out her hand.

"My name is Sally," she said.

Chapter Fifteen

Wonder of Wonders

In which Lewyn Oppenheimer introduces a group of muscular Christians to the Seder ritual

Room 308 in Clara Dickson Hall might have lacked a beer can pyramid or a miasma of cannabis, but apart from that it was pretty typical for the temporary living space of two randomly selected college-aged boys. Jonas, for example, had stuck a poster on the wall during move-in and then forgotten about it as it puckered and drooped and folded forward. Lewyn had brought home a plant on a whim, declined to water it, and failed to notice when it died. They both put their stuff down on the floor when they were finished with it—that was what the floor was for—and neither of them saw the overflow of their shared trash bin as a cue to empty it. It was true that Jonas made his bed every morning—that was a mission thing, he'd once explained—but the sheets on both beds were dingy and slippery, and there was a film of grime over every surface. They lived, in other words, inside a tableau of discarded clothing, candy wrappers, and shoes that were often parted from their mates and bearing spring mud. Back in November, Jonas had met a very pretty girl named Lauren, from Arizona, and though he refrained from overnighting at Kappa Delta, Lauren's sorority, he came back later and later at night as the winter term wore on, sometimes slipping into the long bed opposite Lewyn's far nearer to the next day than the day before. When Lewyn woke at his normal time to get himself to art history, Jonas would be there: face to the wall, forearm protruding from the strange long underwear he wore. (For months Lewyn had been under the impression that this sartorial item was an ordinary undershirt, paired with some style of long undershorts favored by people from the rustic lands of the West. The true nature of the thing had been revealed in one of their conversations on Mormonism, ancillary to that first one, in which such topics as evangelism, cosmology, handcarts, and sacred garments had all been touched upon.)

Squalor aside, Lewyn did feel fortunate to be living with Jonas, and on those (increasingly rare) occasions they were both in the room—Jonas cramming for his bovine anatomy midterm, say, and Lewyn drafting an art history paper—they fell easily into their way of being together. After that first magical narrative in the fall it had taken weeks for Lewyn to stop thinking of his roommate as some kind of mystic, an ecstatic possessed of occult knowledge and a personal relationship with angels, but gradually he had managed to draw a kind of curtain around the topic of spirituality in general, and Jonas's religion in particular, and move on into the quotidian business of cohabitation. He and Jonas might represent different political inclinations, different prospects (both career and celestial), and opposite ends of the country, but they were both polite people who spoke kindly to each other as a rule, especially in the morning when they were most often in the same place at the same time. Not infrequently, they even went for breakfast together at North Star, where they were sometimes joined by Jonas's vet school friends and new fraternity brothers.

"Lewyn, my roommate," Jonas always said. He said it the first time he introduced them, and the fourth.

Lewyn wondered if a few of these guys might also be Mormons. He didn't yet possess the expertise he later would, to tell such a thing without asking. He did recognize that they were all some version of Christ-follower, but the distinctions among even the commonplace denominations were a terrible blur. (The Walden School had indoctrinated him with the notion that spirituality was a matter of self-definition, and apart from one wildly out-of-place guest speaker the previous fall, no Walden teacher had ever attempted to impart the actual beliefs of actual Christian people. As a result, Lewyn could barely have distinguished a Baptist from a Catholic. Besides, for all of its vaunted "diversity," Walden students and faculty were overwhelmingly Jewish.) With Jonas's friends he began to observe, if not exactly understand, the commonalities and the distinctions among them. One boy said grace before consuming his breakfast pastry; another did not. One boy was enjoying robust relationships with several willing girls while another had allowed himself only "side hugs" with his longtime girlfriend and presumptive future wife back in Virginia. Several of Jonas's fraternity brothers were heavy drinkers, and one, an ice hockey player from Milwaukee, was so clearly compromised that his fraternity brothers had already (and unsuccessfully) attempted an intervention.

But they were nice enough to Lewyn, and as the weeks passed they began to present an almost uniform interest in him, or at least in one aspect of him. Not one of them, it had become clear, had ever had occasion to talk—that is, *really talk*—with a representative of his *people*.

"So, like," said the Virginian, whose name was Mark, "I can't help but notice that you're eating bacon there, Lewyn. Isn't that, like, against the rules?"

Lewyn explained that his family was not Orthodox, nor even particularly observant. "We're more cultural Jews." What he meant was: dutiful observation of a couple of holidays, correctly sliced Nova from Russ & Daughters, and an extremely broad interpretation of *Tikkun olam*. But what he actually said was: "There are all different kinds of Judaism, you know."

Of course they didn't know, and unfortunately they were all ears. So he had to give them the basics:

Orthodox, Conservative, Reform, Reconstructionist. Also nothing at all, but still Jewish.

And how could you still be Jewish but also nothing at all?

Lewyn, by now mentally exhausted, merely shrugged. *You just could. People just were.* It wasn't like you turned in a card or something. "A lot of the families I grew up with were Jewish but they also had Christmas trees."

This the boys absolutely could not process.

"Are you *serious*? Christmas is Jesus Christ's *birthday*."

Lewyn very much doubted this to be true, or at any rate the whole truth of the matter, but things had been going pretty well so far, and it was nice to be in a group of guys, pounding smoothies and shooting the breeze.

"Okay, but it's also *peace on Earth, goodwill toward men*." (At Walden the lyric had actually been changed to "goodwill toward people.") You didn't have to be a Christian to appreciate that.

"But dude! O Holy Night! Like, you have your own holy night, right? Passover?"

Lewyn shrugged. "Jesus's last supper was a Passover Seder, you know."

From the look of them, they did not know.

"You guys." Jonas was shaking his head. "You should have gone on a mission. What the heck did you learn in Sunday school?"

"Whole lot of Antichrist," said Jim. "And how I was going to hell if I was 'unnatural.' Nothing about Jewish Passover being the Last Supper."

"Hey, can we go with you?" the Virginian said. "It's soon, right?"

Lewyn looked at him. There were so many things wrong with this question. He didn't know where to begin.

Passover, he realized, probably *was* imminent. It had a way of moving around the calendar which Lewyn had never really understood, but it was (duh!) always close to Easter, and Easter was soon—the following Sunday, he was pretty sure. He'd had no intention of attending a Seder at Cornell. As a family they'd always gone to his mother's sister on the Upper East Side for a massive catered do. Still, none of the Oppenheimer triplets, he was quite sure, knew the words to "Dayenu" beyond the word "Dayenu" itself (which, come to think of it, Lewyn could only vaguely define). He hadn't been near any of the Jewish organizations on campus and had never once considered muscling in on one of the Seders that were surely being planned for Cornell's many Jewish students. Was he supposed to invite himself now? And with four or five muscular Christians in tow, to boot?

"I wasn't planning on going," he stalled.

"Why not?" Jonas said. He looked kind of excited. "You should go! It would be so cool. We'd *love* to come."

But I didn't invite you, Lewyn thought.

Obviously they didn't understand that you couldn't just walk into a Seder. There were memberships and wait-lists and fees and probably approvals of some kind. Or wait . . . was that even true? Maybe it was only true of Manhattan, where you had to join a temple, get a ticket for High Holy Days, join a standby list. The Oppenheimers were members of Temple Emanu-El on Fifth Avenue, but they had never, you know, *gone,* apart from that. "I haven't made any arrangements," he shrugged.

"Well, make 'em, dude," said Jim, who was looking a lot better after his smoothie and breakfast sandwich. "My mom is going to have a total fit when I tell her I'm going to a Passover. You should have heard her about all the Jews up here. She wanted me to go to Michigan. I said, *Yo, there's lots of Jews at Michigan, too.* Cornell's the fucking Ivy League!" He laughed. The others, to their credit, looked uncomfortable. A moment later they took their trays and departed, leaving Lewyn in a not entirely unpleasant state of excitement. *I mean: Why not?*

He thought of what Harrison might say. He thought of what Sally might say. But really, where was the harm? Would it be so terrible to actually go out and join a club that he kind of already belonged to? No one back in Brooklyn had called to ask whether he was planning to come home for the Oppenheimer Seder. And anyway, wasn't he here, at college, to partake of that wondrous cross-cultural diversity he'd been raised to revere, *indoctrinated* to revere at Walden Upper (*and* Middle, *and* Lower)? What could be more cross-culturally fecund than bringing a gaggle of Christian frat bros to an ancient ritual delineating the "special relationship" between God and His Chosen? It was almost, when you thought about it, a chance for a bit of *Tikkun olam.* And how hard could it really be to find an adventurous and open-minded congregation on campus with a few Haggadahs to spare?

Not hard at all, it turned out. A belated look through the spiritual (subset: Jewish) offerings on the Cornell website revealed three separate imminent Seders, one each for the Conservative and Orthodox groups (sure to be as alien to Lewyn as to his new pals) and a combined third for the Reconstructionist and Reform groups. When he left an apologetic message for the Center for Jewish Life, a girl named Rochelle called him back on the room phone and said that everyone was welcome the following Wednesday evening at six. All she needed to know was: How many vegetarian and how many gluten-free?

Jonas and his friends dressed for the occasion in sport jackets and khakis and combed back their hair. They looked eager and uncomfortable in equal parts when they appeared in the doorway, and Lewyn figured he should probably upgrade his own clothes. Turning his back to them, he shrugged off his detectably funky T-shirt and put on a button-down and the blue jacket his mother had made him bring to college. Then they set out together.

The combined Reform and Reconstructionist Jews of Cornell were gathered in Anabel Taylor Hall, the mid-century appendage to Myron Taylor Hall, a faux-gothic building of Ithaca stone opposite the Engineering Quadrangle. Lewyn and his goyish party stood for an addled moment in the doorway: five believing Christians and one nonbelieving Jew, taking in the extent of their own overdress.

The students were uniformly clad in some variation of jeans and sweatshirts, about half the robin's egg blue of Cornell Hillel, the rest displaying a broad array of Cornelliana and the Ugg boots that now seemed to cover every female ankle and calf on campus. Institutional tables were set with paper plates, paper cups, and paper towels, and punctuated by bottles of classic Manischewitz.

"Is that wine?" said one of the AGR brothers. His name was Sawyer. He had an Irish last name. O'Something.

"I wouldn't get too excited," Lewyn told them, shouting above the din. "More likely to make you sick than get you drunk." He spoke from painful experience. Once, Harrison had dared him to drink a juice glass full of the stuff, resulting in a blast of syrupy purple vomit all over his aunt's guest bathroom. One of so many warm fraternal memories he cherished. Also: Harrison always found the afikomen.

"Hey, let's sit," O'Something said. "Before we get split up."

It seemed no worse an idea than remaining where they were. The five of them took the nearest end of the nearest table, with Lewyn, to his great embarrassment, at the head. He hoped the position came with no added responsibilities.

"I kind of thought it would be fancier," said Jonas, who had picked up the Haggadah on his paper plate and was thumbing through it.

"What *is* that?" said Mark. He was staring, in some horror, at the Seder plate.

The half-roasted lamb bone did look particularly anatomical, but it was the charoset Mark seemed to be looking at. It emitted a strong, oversweet smell and appeared to have been made far in advance of the occasion, or in considerable bulk, or both. There was an ice-cream scoop of it in a plastic bowl every five feet or so along the table. Lewyn did his best to explain.

"We don't need to eat it, though, do we?"

"Not if you don't want." He didn't really want to, himself. "Maybe pretend to eat a bite. It's part of the ritual."

At the use of this word, Mark looked shocked, as if someone had just drawn a pentacle before him on the paper tablecloth. In blood.

"It's like . . . everything means something," he finally said. "Everything on the table. And then some things mean even more than one thing. Like . . . I guess, Easter. The lamb. And . . . the egg," he managed, hoping he wasn't being offensive. *The lamb? The egg?* "So, the lamb represents the sacrifice to God from back in the days of the Temple. The egg is rebirth. The horseradish is the bitterness of slavery. The parsley is the renewal of spring. This stuff," he pointed to the charoset, "it represents the mortar the slaves had to make in Egypt. Also the sweetness of life."

"What about the orange?" Jonas wanted to know.

Lewyn frowned. Each Chinet Seder plate did indeed have an orange in addition to the usual suspects.

"Haven't the faintest idea," he admitted.

"So this is like a program?" said Jonas. He was turning through the stapled pages.

"Oh, you read it backwards," Lewyn told him.

All five of them turned to him.

"Just . . . how it's done."

And he turned over his own to demonstrate. On the back of the pages, handwritten in black Sharpie, were the words: "Welcome to our Coalition for Mutual Respect Seder!"

Jesus Christ, he thought, before he could stop himself.

To his right, Mark was already laughing.

"Don't," Lewyn heard Jonas hiss at him, but he was laughing, too.

Well, he hadn't promised them a rose garden. What had he promised them?

"Welcome, welcome," said a woman at the far end of the room. She had a cordless microphone, and spoke, initially, in Hebrew, the only words of which Lewyn recognized were *Shalom* and *Pesach.* Then her mic went out and someone brought her a new one. "Such a lovely boy," said the re-amplified rabbi, patting this boy's yarmulke with a tiny hand. "Electrical engineer! Single!" The room laughed.

"Our Chabad friends and our friends over at Koach have their own traditions when they gather for Pesach here on campus, but for those of us who come to Judaism from the Reform movement, or the Reconstructionist traditions, or are just beginning a spiritual journey in Judaism and feel the need for a more open and, dare I say it, personal experience of the Passover celebration and ritual, you have come to the right place! We want to thank Tamar and Rochelle, and David Grodstein—where are you, David? I haven't seen you . . . yes! Shalom, David! Happy Pesach!—all of you, your hard work is so much appreciated by us all. Now, it's a part of the Seder tradition to welcome the stranger to our table, and to link our story to the larger story we all share. When one suffers, everyone suffers. When one of us is still enslaved, no one is really free. That's the big moral of the Seder. Of course, we're Jewish, so we specialize in disagreeing about what things really mean. My mother, for example, used to say, this is what it boils down to: *They hated us. They tried to kill us. We're still here. Now let's eat!*"

Mark, on Lewyn's right, exploded in laughter. Lewyn turned to look at him, a little mystified. It hadn't seemed that funny to him. His own family Seders had been rather joyless, with everyone dressed in uncomfortable "nice" clothes and the table set with special, breakable stuff. There had been long recitations separating the hungry children (he, at least, was always hungry) from the good smells in the kitchen, which would only be served by a uniformed maid once the many speeches and questions and dripping of wine and holding up of green parsley had been completed. His father and his uncle Bruce Krieger, his aunt Debbie's husband, had recited in Hebrew, from memory, while he and Sally and Harrison (and, it was reassuring to note, his Krieger cousins, who actually had been bar mitzvahed) all stumbled along with the phonetic version, printed beneath the Hebrew in their matching booklets. (This reminded Lewyn of the tiny possibility that his sister might actually be here, in this room with so many other Jews of Cornell, and he looked around warily, but there was no Sally to be seen.)

The rabbi, holding her mic delicately between two figures, now said kiddush and things began to move along briskly: the karpas, the middle matzo, the storytelling, the explanation of the Seder plate (that orange, it turned out, had to do with the inclusion of all sexualities and genders, a notion that made one of Lewyn's frat boy guests look vaguely ill), the drip, drip of sickly sweet red wine from their fingertips to their paper plates. Mark nearly gagged when he bit into the maror, and Jonas laughed at him.

The "youngest child" was the rabbi's little boy, who spoke with a lisp that made most of the girls in the room say "Awww" in such unison it might have been rehearsed. The four sons were performed by four students, one on an electric keyboard, as a peppy vaudeville number.

What does the Seder mean?

What does the Seder mean to you?

What is this?

Um . . . what?

(It was supposed to be clever, but it wasn't. Not every musical Jewish boy was Stephen Sondheim.)

Then, finally, it was time to eat. Out from the kitchen they brought trays with bowls of soup, and Lewyn had the indelible experience of watching his guests confront their first matzo balls.

"Oh, I know what this is," said Jonas. "This is that balls thing. But what's it made of?"

Lewyn explained, pointing to the matzo, still on the table.

"Right," said the Virginian. "The crackers."

"The point is that they aren't crackers," Lewyn said.

"These balls are made of crackers?"

"And soda water," said one of the blue-sweatshirted girls. She was leaning forward, between him and Jonas, with a heavy bowl of Israeli salad. "Makes them fluffy."

"So . . . wait, they *are* made of crackers?" said the boy on Mark's other side.

The girl drew back and looked at him, then at their little group, her gaze deliberately rounding the table from one blond head to the next, and finally to Lewyn, on which it lingered.

"First Seder?" She grinned, as if she didn't know the answer.

"I got permission," was all he could think to say.

"And I gave it, if you're who I think you are. Six people, no vegetarian, no gluten-free. Right?"

"I'm gluten-free, actually," said O'Something, and Mark said, "Dude, you should have told Lewyn!" But the girl was already off to the next table with the salad bowl in her other hand. She was short, with wildly curling dark hair. Lewyn stared after her.

The boys fell upon the food: brisket after the soup, and asparagus, and potato kugel. Mark put charoset on his meat. Jonas took a bit of matzo, made a face, and asked if there were any dinner rolls instead.

"No rolls," said Lewyn. "No bread."

"Maybe in the kitchen?" said Mark.

"No, no." Lewyn was shaking his head. "You can't bring bread in here."

"Why not?" said Jonas.

Lewyn's head hurt. It was like having to explain gravity.

Then the rabbi switched on her mic and the lost afikomen was invoked.

For the next ten minutes, the room erupted in childlike glee, as roughly half of its occupants leapt to their feet and tore around the building's ground floor. Lewyn, who seemed incapable of motion, listened to the sounds they made, the yelped encouragement as curtains were pulled aside, books displaced along the bookshelves. Then, a jolt of victorious laughter from the other side of the doorway as a knot of ZBT brothers returned, bearing their prize. This they presented to the rabbi, with a promise that the ransom would be donated to the Jewish Peace Fellowship, so she should feel free to double it. The negotiation continued for a few good-natured minutes, with a circle of cheerleading onlookers.

"I don't get this," said Mark.

"Wait," said Sawyer. "Are they doing a deal or something?"

"Technically it's a ransom."

The girl in the blue sweatshirt was back. Lewyn looked up into her face. She was laughing through her disapproval.

"Didn't you prep these guys?" She stood between Jonas and Mark. She was so little, she barely rose above their very blond heads. "Never mind, we're all strangers in a strange land. All away from home, so we try to make it fun. Witness the stampede of regressed adults crawling under the tables. You didn't want to try?"

"I didn't realize," said the Virginian, with what looked like real regret. "But you know, I'd have felt bad if I'd been the one who found it."

The girl raised an eyebrow. "Non-Jewish guilt," she said. "How refreshing."

"Is it over now?" Mark asked, and the girl shook her little head.

"No. There's a bit more. You should stay if you can."

"Of course we're staying!" he assured her. "I wouldn't miss a minute. It's a privilege. So grateful to all of you. And Lewyn, of course."

All of them looked at Lewyn, then. All of them. He felt himself get hot, as if someone had turned a knob at his ankle and the flame climbed upward: knee, hip, breastbone, temple. He stared helplessly at his plate, with its unlovely smear of brisket and carrot, feeling faint and ill and thinking, as had always been his curse, of how much better his brother and sister would be parrying this absurd combination of circumstances. As for the boys—his friends, he supposed—they looked on in bland affability. Jonas even clapped him on the back. And she slipped away again.

At last, the door was opened and shut for Elijah and for Miriam, whose his-and-hers cups were held aloft at each table. The tiny rabbi reminded them that the Seder was an opportunity to recognize and express solidarity with the victims of modern-day oppression and injustice, "just as we once were slaves in the land of Egypt. For while our story looks back to ancient scourges like cattle disease, locusts, and frogs, we also recognize contemporary scourges like racism, sexism, homophobia, and the war on women's right to choose."

Lewyn felt—or was it his imagination?—the slightest of chills at his end of the table. There wasn't a man among these "friends" who recognized, let alone defended, a woman's right to choose. But it was nearly over, and nothing awful had happened. Surely they were home free.

"Every Passover should call us to social justice," the rabbi's reedy voice concluded. "The Seder reminds us that the political is personal, so take it personally and do something about it."

This, with its ring of finality, was met with good-natured cheering, and Lewyn, relieved that escape was nigh, chanced a quick look around him at the boys, like a camp counselor making sure he hadn't lost any of his charges on a wilderness hike. But none of them met his eye. They were all looking at Jim, the hockey-playing subject of that failed intervention, who was now, unaccountably, on his feet with one hand in the air, as if about to swear himself in. But to what end?

"Excuse me," Jim said in a shockingly calm and very steady voice. "Excuse me, everyone. May I say something?"

No one immediately responded. And then the rabbi herself came over, smiling, extending the microphone. It took her a while, on her little legs. "Of course," she told them all. Lewyn, paralyzed anew, merely gaped upward.

Yo, there's a lot of Jews at Michigan, too! Lewyn suddenly recalled. Jim had said that, to his mother. His heart was thudding.

"Thank you so much . . . ah . . . Rabbi," said Jim. He was so tall and so lean and so very, very blond.

"I only wanted to say, on behalf of myself and my friends here," he gestured at their little group, as if anyone looking might have doubted he meant the overdressed specimens at their end of the table, "how very much we appreciate being welcomed like this, even though we are strangers here. Like it says in Matthew twenty-five: *I was hungry and you gave me food. I was thirsty and you gave me drink.*"

A palpable ripple of unease ran through the room. Lewyn felt it. His face began to burn.

"If it's all right, I would like to offer a prayer from my own tradition, and from my own heart."

The eyes of the room, hundreds of needles, pricking every inch of his slouching body. And hers. Jesus fucking Christ.

"Well . . . certainly," said the rabbi, sounding unnaturally chipper. "You are most welcome."

Then the others rose, so smoothly it might all have been planned out beforehand, but somehow Lewyn doubted it was. They were supporting him, that was all. It was Jim's show. They took his hands. They bowed their heads. They closed their eyes.

"Heavenly Father," Jim said into the mic, "we thank you for the fellowship we've been shown this day, and the good food that has been prepared for us. We thank you for the welcome and the generosity, and for the lessons we've learned here. We thank you for allowing us to celebrate the fact that we are all your children. We thank our friend Lewyn, who made it possible for us to experience this Passover Seder." Lewyn looked up to meet the stricken gaze of the rabbi, her rictus grin. Yes, it was clear, he was none other than the "friend Lewyn" who had made this moment possible, and which of the four sons would that make him?

The wicked one, obviously. Jews-for-Jesus wicked.

"Father, we know that it was part of your heavenly plan to bring us here today, and we humbly wait to understand that plan. We cherish this opportunity to spend time in the circle of your chosen people, the children of

Abraham and Sarah, Jacob and Joseph, Moses and Joshua and the great King David, and we praise the special bond you share with the Jewish people. We who have accepted your son Jesus Christ as our personal savior live in the certainty of your eternal kingdom, and know that our purpose is to serve you and your son, Jesus, who suffered on the cross to wash away our sins. In His name we thank you. *Amen.*"

Amen, said the others at Lewyn's end of the table.

Amen! said the rabbi. Brightly. Too brightly.

Amen, said Lewyn, but only to himself.

Chapter Sixteen

78 East Seneca

In which Sally Oppenheimer discovers the meaning of the term "brown furniture"

Her name was Harriet Greene. She was the last of five generations of Ithacans named Greene, the family having been right here in central New York since disembarking at Montreal in the 1840s. Harriet's forebear—four or five or who knew how many greats back—had had something of a foundational role with the Ithaca Paper Company Mill, which enriched the family until the business ran out of road in the mid-'50s. Their family home was in a part of town Sally hadn't yet set foot in, between downtown and College Town. A few weeks later, on a bitter March afternoon, she walked through the campus and out the other side, to get there.

Sally, of course, had grown up in a house just as large as the one she found at 78 East Seneca Street, more or less as old (mid-nineteenth century), and precisely this style (resolutely Federal, resolutely grand), but Harriet Greene's house was dilapidated. She could see that it had most recently been yellow, but also that that wasn't very recent at all. The shutters were black, about half of them still intact, the other half partly detached or with missing slats. A lot of the windows appeared to be blocked. She stepped up onto the porch, and the floorboards dipped beneath her. One of the porch posts did not seem to be fully in contact with its roof.

Harriet had the door open before she rang the bell. "Oh, it doesn't work," she grinned. "I was keeping an eye out."

There was a large front parlor to the left of the central hall, classically symmetrical and jammed with furniture: tables, bureaus, wing chairs, and cupboards, mostly wrapped in plastic. Canvases, some framed, many unframed, leaned against the walls, but there wasn't a single piece of art actually on the walls (to the extent Sally could see the walls). In the center of the parlor, a patch of floor about the size of an area rug remained uncovered: room to stand and turn around, assuming you could get there.

"It's a bit crowded," said Harriet, stating the obvious and moving down the hall.

The kitchen, too, was jammed, not with furniture but with large Rubbermaid tubs, stacked and labeled, reaching up to the plaster ceiling. Sally read her way upward as Harriet rummaged in a cupboard for two elderly mugs: *Linens (Table), Linens (Table), Linens (Bedding), Linens (Rickrack), Linens (Barkcloth).* She was on the point of asking what rickrack and barkcloth were, when Harriet asked her what she had come to Cornell to study. Not an outlandish question, but it still kind of knocked her back.

"I don't really know," she answered. "Most people do. I don't."

"Most people?" Harriet had extracted an open box of Entenmann's orange donuts from the fridge and put it on the table between them. She started eating one right away.

"Oh, well, your basic Cornell student has everything planned out to retirement. My roommate's going to be a lawyer. I have a brother who's plotting world domination, God help us."

Harriet laughed, showing gray teeth. "Older brother?"

"I wish. He'd have been out of my life sooner. No, he's my . . ." Annoyingly, there was no simple word for this. You couldn't say twin; it wasn't that simple. "Actually, we're triplets. Came out of a test tube."

"Test tube!" Harriet looked mildly scandalized. "I've heard about that. I never thought I'd meet one . . ." She trailed off. "Sorry. My mother used to tell me I was so rude, I'd offend Jesus."

"It's okay," said Sally, trying to excavate a teaspoonful of sugar. It was rocklike in its bowl. Evidently Harriet Greene didn't take sugar in her own tea, or have frequent guests who did. "Actually, it's not all that uncommon where I come from. The sidewalks are crowded with double strollers. Of course my parents had to go even further and have three of us."

Harriet pursed her lips, though whether in disapproval or to simply blow over her tea, Sally wasn't sure. The wrinkles along her cheeks deepened into ridges.

"Well, that couldn't have been cheap. Sorry. There I go again."

Of course it hadn't been cheap. "I imagine," was all she said.

"So," Harriet added half-and-half to her tea, "you and the world domination one. What about the third?"

"He's a little . . . off. I mean, not crazy or anything. Just weird. Doesn't play well with others." She gave up on the ossified sugar and took a bite of a donut. Maybe the excessive sweetness of that would magically merge with the tea. "What did you . . ." She was going to ask what Harriet had studied in college, but it occurred to her that the question might be offensive. Had women her age gone to college? Could she have gone to Cornell, in fact? There'd been women there since the 1870s, after all.

"What did I what?" Harriet said. The table was a far cry from the glorious Shaker she had plucked from something called a "backhouse" in someplace called "Homer," but it was lovely in its own way: dark, with legs of twisted wood and a surface that was honestly marked by age.

"Um . . . I was going to ask what you studied in college? Did you study furniture?"

"God no!" Harriet yelped, finding this, apparently, hilarious. "Nursing at the University of Rochester. I was a nurse for nearly forty years. I stayed up near Rochester for a lot of that time, but I started picking around on the weekends. Didn't do a course or anything, just learned as I went. I'd plan my shifts so I could take off for three or four days at a time, all the way out to Buffalo and up to the Canadian border, knocking on doors. I just loved everything about it. The driving and the little towns and the people you met. How strange people are. Always so mystified when they figured out you're offering actual cash for old stuff they consider junk."

"Did they just say come on in, help yourself to whatever?"

"Almost never," Harriet said. She was on her second orange donut. Sally broke her own into smaller and smaller sections on her plate. "Best-case scenario, they get the basic idea you're there to offer money for something they might have, and they're willing to let you inside. Worst-case, they got an arsenal and they think you're from the government or a holy roller or something. Got chased away from people's houses, more than a few times. Once, this old guy on a farm up near Geneseo nearly shot at me when I drove up his driveway. Didn't believe I wasn't a missionary from Palmyra! Just kept yelling he was going to shoot me if I took another step. Less than a month later they wheeled him into my cardiac intensive care unit. I had to take care of that old man for seven weeks, but he finally apologized to me. Actually, he ended up having a nice Sheraton table and a very early piece of mourning silk work. He sold them to me for so little even he must've known he was getting the short end. I guess he was embarrassed about the shotgun."

"Wow," Sally said. Everything about this story was fascinating to her.

"Did you find this in a house somewhere?" she asked, tapping the table.

"No. Family piece. From my father's side. I'm not sentimental. I'd sell it if there was anyone to buy it, but nobody wants this stuff now. Victorian, Empire. All pretty worthless. They call it 'brown furniture.' When this was my grandparents' house the table was in the dining room. We had Christmas dinner here."

"Wow," Sally said again. She was starting to feel ridiculous. To be so moved? By a table? Or was it imagining the Christmas dinner in the once-formal dining room next door, now crammed with draped furniture? Covered in an embroidered linen tablecloth, set with china, silver, glass. To sit at a table one's ancestors had sat at; it was an insane notion, and it thrilled her. This humble example of "brown furniture" was singing to her just as sweetly as the Shaker table had, albeit a subtler tune.

Harriet was extracting another orange donut from the box. She was a solid woman, thick in the middle, with her white hair (loose that day in the museum) now in a single braid pinned to her head in a coil. She looked intrinsically out of place in the year 2001, as if she knew she would not tread too far into the new century and wasn't overly interested in acclimatizing herself. She must be . . . Sally wasn't good at guessing people's ages past twenty or so. Then again, few women in her hometown went naturally into the good night of aging. The moms of Walden wouldn't have dreamed of greeting the day without a slather of sunblock, preferably at blackout SPF, and if they ate Entenmann's orange donuts they did it in secret. She wanted to know how old Harriet was, and she opened her mouth to ask this very thing, but what actually came out was something else entirely.

"Say what?" Harriet turned her head. Evidently, one ear was sharper than the other.

"I said: Next time you go out picking, can I come with you?"

Chapter Seventeen

Messy Things

In which Harrison Oppenheimer briefly considers escape, and a surprising invitation materializes from an equally surprising source

In the wake of Eli's accusation and Carlos's denial, everything began to unravel.

There was debate, then argument, then outright fighting, with roughly one half of the students arrayed in vigorous defense of the accused plagiarist, roughly the other half crouched in an outraged scrum around the alleged victim, and a few leftover guys with their fingers in their ears, trying vainly to tend their gardens and get in some quality time with the Stoics until this messy thing resolved itself.

But here was the sad truth about messy things: they did not resolve *themselves*. They got resolved, if they got resolved at all, by grunt and confrontation and maybe a little screaming, followed by (gruesome as this was to contemplate) deliberate and redemptive *hugging*. Mostly, though, as history effortlessly demonstrated, messy things just jolted on until they shuddered to a halt in exhaustion. And so, when it became clear that debate and argument were just so much treading of mud, the students of Roarke commenced not speaking across the lines in their little community, and whatever bonds they'd forged in Plato and animal muck throughout the fall and early winter began to degrade in earnest.

By the end of March the damage felt irreversible. Carlos and a few of the others were no longer sitting down for meals; instead, they loaded their plates in the kitchen and went off to eat in one of the seminar rooms, while the rest conversed in a state of general suppression around the dinner table, sticking to the universal and the strictly academic and absolutely avoiding the topic on everyone's mind. In the classrooms a fragile pact held longer but it waned soon enough, discussion splintering into first veiled then open hostility and disagreements beginning to feel, for the first time, *personal.* The center, in other words, was not holding, and as the student body fractured, the systems themselves began to break down, little fissures opening everywhere. Class meetings started after their appointed times or stopped abruptly before they finished, and there was a strange epidemic of oversleeping, which distressed the animals. Some nights, the school even ran out of food due to imprecise planning and indifferent safeguards, and more than once they drifted dangerously low on things the animals needed, like straw and even feed.

At the center of it all, Eli Absalom Stone—prime mover of the crisis, or its victim, depending on your affiliation—remained a still point. Eli had not deviated from his own routines and responsibilities, which now included oversight for the current applicant pool and an active search for a new faculty member to teach the history of science. He still rose at his customary time, took his shower, visited the kitchen for black coffee and a single piece of fruit, then went to one of the classrooms or to the cubicle in the administrative area and began his day's work. Occasionally he could be seen walking with Emmanuel, or one of the Justins, out along the road up toward Jackson, and he could often be found in his preferred armchair in the meeting room, the one with the shredded arms, powering through a book at his normal, accelerated pace. By evening he'd be at the dinner table, passing the salt, genially complimenting the cook (Gordon, who would now only glare at him), and resolutely not acknowledging the tension. He declined, outside the meetings dedicated to the subject, to mention Carlos or his alleged crime. He declined to give the slightest indication that he held any responsibility for the mire in which they all found themselves. He declined to show his hand, and he never, ever broke. But the damage crept steadily outward, ensnaring them all.

For Harrison, it was the breakdown of camaraderie that hit him hardest. For the very first time in his life he'd found himself actually enjoying the company of male humans his own age, and this was after thirteen years of school, eight years of camp, and the incessant presence of a brother. At Roarke the clarifying notion that these men had first self-selected to apply to the school, then been selected *by* the school, and finally opted *for* the school (despite, in every case, such attractive alternatives) had gone a long way toward binding them together, and he had happily been a part of this group of twenty-four, eating with them and reading with them, treating cows for mastitis with them and discussing semiotics with them. For all the years he'd spent in the enforced comradeship of the Walden School, it was Roarke that had finally filled him with a sense of virtuous fellowship. Now all that was gone, or at least going fast.

It was just at this delicate moment that Harrison received a letter from the Harvard Admissions Office, asking whether he would like to matriculate that fall or whether he intended to extend his deferral, as originally indicated, and transfer the following year. He found himself giving this serious consideration, revisiting his earlier decision for the first time since he'd sat opposite Dr. Vernon Loring in that Naugahyde booth at Symposium. While he'd been chasing chickens and rolling hay, hadn't his contemporaries at Harvard been forming lifelong bonds and getting a pretty good education of their own? Harrison was missing all that. If he transferred as planned the following year he'd be as legitimately enrolled as any other undergraduate, but the reality promised an experience that was decidedly off-brand. Harvard would probably slot him into a random suite with an opening, assigning him the room of some loser on academic warning or in a psych ward, and his new roommates would be guys who'd actually wanted to room with that selfsame loser! And also, what if the university wanted to burden him with all the prerequisites he'd have missed, meaning entry-level classes, probably with teaching assistants leading the seminar discussions.

How annoying would that be, after a year of the education he'd been receiving here?

So it was tempting to just go now. This year at Roarke might still be recast as something quirky and transitional, a Gap Year Experience in which he learned about poultry production and agrarian self-rule and linguistics, deep in the New Hampshire forest. He could go off to Harvard only a few months from now as a sophomore or even a freshman with a few extra credits, a do-over his parents—certainly—would celebrate. He could, annoying as it might be, even to himself, *change his mind.*

But then, and suddenly, into this moment of uncharacteristic vacillation and self-questioning, there stepped a new, thrilling, and thoroughly unanticipated factor.

One morning, as Harrison was stamping his way out to the henhouse with his definitely emasculating egg basket, he was stunned to see the author of *Against Youth* giving every appearance of a person who was waiting for another person, and there was no person other than Harrison himself who might conceivably turn up at that place and time. He was just working this out when Eli Absalom Stone raised an arm in greeting.

"Harrison," he said.

For some reason, Harrison's idea of a proper response to this was to put his basket down on the chicken shit–stained ice.

"Oh, hi," he said, just to ram that point home.

"I apologize for the intrusion," said Eli. "I should have found a way to bring this up in a more pleasant setting."

"More pleasant . . . than this?" Harrison said.

"It does have a certain bucolic charm." Eli did not exactly smile as he said this, though there was a gesture toward the *idea* of a smile.

They were both breathing steam. Harrison, illogically, felt himself on the verge of offering some excuse. For the hens? Or the general state of tension?

"I feel as if I should have given you some warning before I brought my concerns about Carlos to the attention of the community," Eli said.

"Oh?"

He'd had generally amiable feelings toward Carlos, he supposed. But nothing special. The only one who'd truly stood out to him was the one currently standing in front of him.

"You're a kindhearted person," Eli observed, and Harrison nearly erupted in laughter. He was thinking of his brother Lewyn, and his sister Sally—how they would have writhed and scoffed at such a notion. Kindhearted! As if the two of them controlled exclusive access to kindness! Sally had written her college application essay on the wildlife sanctuary that just happened to border our Martha's Vineyard property, effortlessly adding eighty pristine acres to coastal view. Lewyn had been unable to come up with a community service project (a graduation requirement at Walden) so our mother had phoned up a woman her sister Debbie knew on the board of Dress for Success. He'd spent his required hours in the shoe closet, doing his homework. And he, Harrison, was supposedly the uncharitable, self-serving one? He was as "kindhearted" as they were, even if that was, basically, not so much.

"S'nice of you to say," is what he actually said. Where was his wit? He felt pathetically tongue-tied, as if a pretty girl had just declared an unexpected romantic interest in him. He looked down to find his silly basket on the hard ground, one edge unmistakably smeared in brand-new chicken shit.

"I'm impressed by how you've handled this. Your friendship with Carlos. I'm sure it hasn't been easy for you."

"Oh, we're not friends, really," Harrison heard himself say. And lo: he and Carlos were defined as not-friends, if indeed they ever had been friends.

"I know it's challenging," said Eli Absalom Stone. "In a community like this. If only the principles weren't paramount, but they are. They always are."

"Yes," agreed Harrison.

"I've been asked to a conference this summer, in Virginia. Sort of a think tank some people I know are involved in. It's in July, near Monticello." Harrison's thoughts were racing, both to keep up and to interpret—*conference, Virginia, Monticello?*—and Eli was still talking. "They're kind of intentionally under the radar. But really wonderful people. So supportive of my education, and what I want to do."

Then Harrison was confused. Eli's education—famously—had been self-administered in a shack on a mountain in West Virginia. Then he realized what Eli must mean.

"Is that how you heard about Roarke?"

Eli nodded.

"Anyway, I thought you might like to come along. I expect you'll want to be with your family over the summer, but . . ."

Be with? His family? He nearly shuddered. But then he was already shuddering in the cold, on the iced-over ground. "No," Harrison managed. "Not at all."

"I'll be giving a talk," Eli said. "You could give one of your own, if that interested you. It's not a formal thing. Everyone who attends can speak on any topic they like. I've generally talked about education, my experience as a self-schooled student. Perhaps you'd like to talk about your exposure to progressive education, and what that was like as a young conservative intellectual. I think this group would find your account fascinating."

But Harrison was still a sentence behind. Not just on "intellectual" (the word he had long embraced within himself, though it had never once been used aloud, in his presence, to describe him) but on "conservative," which had not yet entered his lexicon of self-determination. It fell, at first, like a spatter of acid, and he recoiled from it, but that—he realized right away—was Walden, not him. Walden, where the very notion of conservatism (and intellectualism!) was poisonous, initiating a knee-jerk repulsion devoid of engagement. Though not him. Never him! Never, from the moment he'd begun to think critically, independently, and as a sentient being accountable to himself, not some inherited or institutionalized notion of *worth*. It was an almost comically head-smacking moment, the moment Harrison Oppenheimer understood that he himself was a young conservative intellectual. Naturally Eli Absalom Stone had seen that first. It was final proof, if proof were somehow necessary, that Eli was smarter.

"That'd be okay," said Harrison. He wondered if they were supposed to shake hands or something, or if he needed to show his gratitude—his wild, deep gratitude—in some even more expressive way, like jumping up and down or throwing his arms around Eli's slender brown neck. But while he was resisting this impulse they both were interrupted by a shout from the main lodge, where breakfast was not underway and no coffee awaited them or anyone else, because Gordon and Tony and Carlos himself had all, apparently, departed Roarke in the night, leaving a single letter of principled withdrawal for their former classmates and faculty, and never to return.

Chapter Eighteen

Anyone Else

In which Lewyn considers the grave responsibilities of guardianship, and the seat beside the toilet turns out to be the best one on the bus

Lewyn was the only one of them who went home for spring break. Harrison had skipped the vacation (perhaps his weirdo school didn't believe in vacations?) and Sally, he learned on his arrival, had apparently opted to stay at Cornell over the break to do some kind of internship with a local antiques dealer. This left Lewyn in a situation of exquisite discomfort, with our mother and the small person (though less small, even he could see, since the winter break) relentlessly present, and our father home even less than usual.

Johanna was in an especially bad way; this much was plain, even to him. The baby's needs fell squarely on her, except for the four hours each afternoon when a woman named Marta arrived to perambulate it to sleep on the Esplanade and then do laundry in the basement. These were the hours our mother might appear in his room, asking about school and his new friends, or even his old friends, or—worst of all—Sally, who'd apparently been even more withholding from Johanna than he'd been, himself. Who were Sally's friends? Our mother wanted to know. Was Sally dating any boys? And what did he know about this antiques person his sister had taken up with, who was some kind of a townie and not connected to the college at all? (Leave it to Sally, Lewyn thought, to find a non-Cornell person in a town jammed with students, faculty, and staff.) To these and many other queries Lewyn could provide no satisfying response, nor could he offer the slightest insight into his brother's activities in New Hampshire, since the only information he possessed came from Johanna herself:

Harrison now knew all there was to know about chickens!

Harrison could drive a truck—a stick shift, no less!

Harrison would be spending part of the summer at some institute in Virginia, where he was giving a speech!

Lewyn had not one thing to say in response to any of these things.

"If you're free on Thursday," our mother said, "I'd like you to come with me on an errand. I could use your help."

"Can't Marta?" he asked. It was instinctive. He didn't mean to be oppositional, and it wasn't as if he had something else to do.

"No, she's visiting her brother in the Bronx. Won't take too long."

So he agreed.

On Thursday, Johanna made him hold the infant while she and the car service driver adjusted a baffling number of straps and buckles to fasten the car seat to the middle of the back seat. There wasn't adequate room for all three of them back there, which meant that he had to sit up front in the same seat that had recently hosted the driver's breakfast, and the man made little effort to suppress his annoyance at having to clear away the detritus. A Hindi radio station was turned down low, and the baby objected loudly when her toy fell to the floor and Johanna wasn't able to reach it. When they set off across the Brooklyn Bridge it began to rain heavily.

He realized, when they came to a stop on Park Avenue, just north of the Pan Am Building, that he'd never asked where they were going or indeed why they were going there, but it seemed clear from the neighborhood that Johanna's errand was going to be either financial or legal in nature. Now, with the driver and his mother reversing their efforts on the car seat, seemed not a great moment to ask, so Lewyn stood on the sidewalk, awkwardly holding an umbrella over the stroller, waiting for the infant's cradle to be snapped in.

Then, still wielding the umbrella over the two of them, he walked behind his mother into the building.

When they reached the waiting area for Burke Goldman Finn & Emerson, Johanna stunned Lewyn by putting him in charge of the now dozing child.

"What?" he said, with great alarm. "But what if she wakes up?"

"You'll figure it out," said Johanna, not looking back as she followed a young man down a corridor.

Wait, he called after her, though perhaps not aloud. His heart was thudding. Before him, clammy, slumped in her plastic cradle, the nine-month-old person, shiny in the face with something unspeakable emerging from a single nostril, made him want to gag.

"Ooh! Can I peek?" The receptionist had stepped out from behind her desk. She leaned forward from the waist, her back remarkably straight, as if she'd spent hours in a yoga practice preparing for just this maneuver. "What a sweetie!" she whispered. "What's her name?"

"Uh, Phoebe," said Lewyn.

"Pretty! What does it mean?"

He looked at her. What did it mean? Who asked a question like that of a stranger? He'd been told that the *P* of the baby's name was for our grandfather Philip Hirsch, Johanna's father, who'd collapsed the previous winter at our cousin's wrestling match in New Jersey and never regained consciousness, but Lewyn hadn't known what it meant then, and he didn't know what it meant now.

"No clue," he said.

The woman stared at him. After a moment she said, "Well, she's certainly cute."

She returned to her desk and her computer.

"Ba," said Phoebe, his sister, from the plastic chair, but she hadn't woken herself up, not quite. His sister's fat lips and little chin were working against an imaginary bottle. "Nipple," the word came to him, bringing with it another involuntary wave of nausea. She was still zipped into her padded down garment, the hood over most of her face, her fists only half protruding from the once-white cuffs of its sleeves. He wondered for the first time whether our mother was breastfeeding this baby, then he realized she couldn't be. Had she breastfed him and his siblings, though? He'd never thought about that before, and he wished he weren't thinking about it now, since the idea of it, of them, *sharing* her, maybe *simultaneously* two at a time, posed a violent threat to what remained of his composure. What if it woke up and wanted food? What if it wanted to look at him, and he was forced to look back?

"Mr. Oppenheimer?"

The receptionist was holding the mouthpiece of her headset away from her very red mouth.

"Would you go into the conference room, please? It's the fourth door on the left. Mr. Goldman will meet you there."

Lewyn gaped at her. "I . . . well . . ." he managed. She only smiled, rictus red.

"Please, they're waiting for you."

"But, what about her?"

The receptionist eyed him. "I'm afraid I can't watch her here."

The infant chose this moment to wake. She took a look around the unfamiliar room, and then at her barely less familiar brother, and prepared to wail.

"Fine," he said, grabbing the handle grip. The baby arched up to get a better look at him. If they truly wished for a screaming infant in the "conference room," then that was what they'd get. Ahead of them, down the carpeted corridor, a man with closely cropped red hair stood in the hallway.

"Good," he said simply. "Thanks for waiting."

Lewyn pushed the stroller into the conference room.

"Oh," Johanna said immediately. "She needs a change, doesn't she?"

Did she? Lewyn thought. The other person in the room, a bald man, or nearly bald but for a semicircle of white at ear level, looked unmistakably horrified. He was seated on the other side of the conference table and hadn't gotten up.

"I didn't realize," Lewyn heard himself say.

"If guys had a sense of smell they wouldn't be able to stand their own company," said the redhead. He was closer to Lewyn's age.

"I'll go change her," said his mother, taking the stroller as Lewyn stepped instinctively away from it. "Lewyn, this is Mr. Goldman." She meant the nearly bald man. "And, I'm sorry, please tell me your name again," she said to the one who'd waited in the hall.

"Evan Rosen," he said, extending his hand. Lewyn shook it.

"Can I get you anything?" Evan Rosen said.

It took Lewyn a second to understand that this question was directed to him.

"Oh, no. Thanks." He took the chair his mother had vacated. There were some pages from a white legal pad, covered with her familiar cursive. He saw the name of a company or, he supposed, a person named S. S. Western. Before he could see more, Mr. Goldman had cleared the pages away.

"Understand you're on your spring break," he said as he did. "No South Padre Island for you?"

"Oh. No. Not my scene."

"I think Evan here made his way down to Florida on a couple of occasions."

"Cabo," said Evan Rosen, with a nostalgic smile. "Better class of individual."

"You're at Cornell, I think? Or are you the other one?"

Lewyn briefly considered claiming to be the "other one." But his mother would be back soon.

"Cornell, yes."

"You like it? I went to Dartmouth." This was Rosen, and something of a non sequitur.

"Yeah, sure. Cold winters."

"Not as cold as Hanover!" He said this as if there was a serious competition underway. "And you're studying?"

Yes, of course, he nearly said. Why, because everyone, even these two who knew him not at all, believed that only *the other one* had any aptitude at all. Then he realized.

"Oh. I don't know yet. Maybe art history."

"Art history!" said Evan Rosen. "Now that's unusual."

Lewyn could hear the stroller squeak-wobbling toward them along the hall. Maybe they could leave now.

"No, it's a good idea," said Mr. Goldman. "In this family, to have someone who knows about art."

Johanna was maneuvering the stroller into the room. The baby now had her juice cup, and all seemed temporarily well in her world.

"Right," said Mr. Goldman. "Lewyn, there are a few things that need your signature."

"Ba," said the infant. She had grown tired of her juice cup and let it drop to the floor. Then, abruptly, she was outraged by this turn of events.

Goldman stood to take some papers from the tall man who'd just entered the conference room, then set them down in front of Lewyn. There were Post-its every couple of pages, feathering the right edge. "Sign here," he told Lewyn. "Wherever there's a Post-it, it's either a signature or your initials. Here's a pen," he said, handing Lewyn his own. He kept the cap, as if he didn't trust Lewyn to return it when he was done.

"What am I signing?" he whispered to Johanna.

"Guardianship," she said. "It's not why I came in, but Mr. Goldman reminded me we need to do it. With you here in the office he didn't want to miss the chance. He had the paralegal work on it while we were doing the other thing."

He stared at her, but she wasn't even looking at him. She was reaching down beneath his chair for the plastic cup, which she returned to the baby with a maternal cluck.

"Guardianship," he finally managed.

"Yes?" said Evan Rosen, the Spring Breaker with the 4.0.

"Well . . . of what?"

Mr. Goldman let out a single choke of laughter. "Of your sister," he said deliberately, as if Lewyn were stupid, which, in this particular instance, wasn't far off. At the word "sister," he had thought, of course, of Sally. And if Sally was somehow in need of his guardianship, was Johanna also asking her, or—even worse—*Harrison* to sign guardianship papers for Lewyn himself? Was this more of our mother's eternally enforced togetherness, absurdly reaching into some future past even her own demise?

Then the baby tossed her cup onto the parquet floor again, and they all looked at her, and Lewyn understood. "Wait, for *her*?"

"Don't worry," our mother said, as if they were discussing where to order takeout. "Just a way of making our wishes known."

"And this is your wish?" he asked her with true disbelief. "Me? That I'm her guardian?"

"Well, not *just* you," our mother said, sounding the slightest bit impatient. "All three of you. The three of you should be responsible for your sister. I mean, who else?"

Anyone else, Lewyn thought. He had a horrible image of himself, Harrison, and Sally sitting at the family dining table as the baby masticated its dinner. Which of the three of them could conceivably care for this? Which of the three of them would want to? It seemed incredible that Johanna didn't recognize the state of her own family, which was that he and Sally and Harrison couldn't get far enough away—first and foremost from one another, but equally from our parents, and *it should go without saying* from this unasked-for and utterly ill-advised extraneous Oppenheimer. Not one of the triplets was coming home again, not in any sustained way. Was she out of her mind?

But he signed. Of course he signed. What was he supposed to do in front of these very competent and professional people?

Four days later he repacked his bag and took a cab to the Cornell Club to pick up the chartered bus back to campus. It was brutally early on a morning that promised very little for the day ahead, and he shoved his suitcase into the hold and went up into the bus to find a seat. Even on this less-than-social occasion Lewyn couldn't escape the sense that everyone else in the group seemed to know one another and be on friendly terms. Chatter hummed down the length of the aisle as he passed, moving closer to the back and the remaining empty seats. People looked up, decided he was not worth smiling at, and went back to their conversations.

He took a seat at the very back, just beside the toilet; a deliberate move, meant to discourage company, but as the seats continued to fill, his gamble looked less and less promising. He kept his head down, reading then rereading the same page of his book on Mary Cassatt for his art history seminar, willing himself not to look up as first one, then another, then another shadow preceded a new arrival down the aisle, until finally one stopped, indisputably beside him, and a little voice said, "Well, hello."

Lewyn, reacting in his every nerve ending, looked up—but barely up—into the glowing face of the girl from Jewish Life. In the supernova of that moment, he could not remember her name, a fact made even more appalling because, incredibly, she remembered his.

"It's Lewyn, right?" she said merrily, wedging her backpack under the seat beside him.

Lewyn nodded, stricken and mute.

"Who brought the Jesus freaks to our Seder."

"I'm sorry," he said. It was all he could think of, and it was amazing he was able to say anything at all.

"Oh, it's all right. We thought it was hilarious. Well, the rabbi was a bit freaked, but she's kind of uptight. You don't mind if I sit here?"

Of course, he nodded. "I mean, of course not. Is it full?"

"Is that the only reason I'd want to sit with you?"

He stared at her. Her pointed chin, those thick braids, the dark eyes a mite too close together for perfect symmetry. She was beautiful. Heart-stoppingly beautiful. Already Lewyn was terrified of what might happen if he stopped looking at her.

"Please, sit." He had no idea how he was even making words.

She folded her short legs into the seat, kicking the backpack forward under the seat in front, then sighed. "I love the smell of industrial-strength bathroom air freshener in the morning."

"Sorry," he said, as if he had entrapped her in this awful position.

"Remind me how your name is spelled? I remember writing it down when you called CJL about your friends. Something unusual."

He spelled it out for her. Never had his name seemed so ridiculous. "After a relative named 'Lou.'"

"Naturally," she said with extravagant sarcasm. "So many Aidans named after Avrahams, and Tiffanys named after Tzipporahs. I'm sorry."

For his name? Lewyn wondered. Or for teasing him? Was she teasing him?

"No, it's okay. We don't choose our names, after all."

"Very true," she said. "I certainly would not have chosen Rochelle."

Rochelle. *Rochelle, Rochelle,* he thought, ramming it into his brain.

"It's a nice name," he said at last, because it was. Whatever her name turned out to be would be a nice name.

"Sure, for 1925. So. Lewyn what?"

"What?"

"Your last name. Lewyn what?"

"Oh," he said. "It's Oppenheimer."

The girl—Rochelle—turned to him. "You're kidding! That's my roommate's name! That's crazy!"

Into the awful void of this moment a number of insights came rushing, each dragging behind it a careening wave of numbness and horror. *Not possible.* But clearly possible. *Not likely*. But somehow the case. And *horrible, horrible, horrible,* Lewyn's thoughts were screaming, but on the other hand how could it be that this girl was his sister's roommate, that she had slept as close to Sally as Jonas slept to him, and still had not just offered him the slightest recognition: "That must make you the mystery brother!" or "I've heard a lot about you!" Or something, *something* that implied she already knew her roommate had a brother—also named Oppenheimer, if not, in fact, Lewyn!—who lived a stone's throw away in the dormitory next door. He had long understood that Sally had written him out of the life she wanted to live at Cornell—Lewyn wasn't even hurt by that anymore—but now he saw that she had written him out of her life in its entirety, because it was clear as day that Sally had lied to this marvelous person from the very beginning. *She must hate me,* he suddenly thought, and then he realized that he barely cared, because he didn't care about his sister. Not now. Maybe not ever, after this.

It was all too shocking to get his head around. It was cruelly dealt. It was a disaster.

And yet, he also felt a dizzying jolt of freedom, because what this also meant was that Rochelle, this lovely, small person looking across at him with a kind of open, amused, but thoroughly genuine *interest,* didn't know who he was. And *that* meant that Lewyn was allowed to be somebody else, and not whatever pre-set character Sally might have conjured for him and viciously communicated to her. (He could well imagine the deficiencies of *that* character.) It was an astonishing opportunity, and he would be a fool not to take it. And he wasn't a fool, despite what his sister thought, and his brother.

"Not crazy," Lewyn said, lying to her for the very first time. "Oppenheimer is kind of a common name."

Chapter Nineteen

Thresholds

In which Sally Oppenheimer is not invited inside

The visit Sally Oppenheimer made to Ellesmere, New York, over spring break was not communicated in advance to Rochelle (something Sally had decided would "ruin the surprise"), and not well thought out in general, but in her own defense, Sally was aware of no specific reason Rochelle wouldn't welcome a visit. Yes, there had been that time back in the fall when her roommate had gone home due to a "family problem," and Sally's offer to go along (to support or assist with whatever it was) had been declined. And that other time Sally had asked to visit over Christmas? Also declined. But she had put these prior events out of her mind, and besides, why shouldn't Sally see where her roommate and closest Cornell friend had grown up? And meet Rochelle's friends and get to know her mom and maybe even treat her to a few frolicsome adventures in the city, the kind any Long Island girl must secretly long for?

Rochelle had left early in the week, directly after her econ midterm, but Sally had a term paper due for her Writing and Sexual Politics class. When she finished it a couple of days later, she walked it over to the office of her women's studies professor, dropped it through the slot in the door, and went directly to the student center to pick up the next New York–bound bus. Five hours later, still full of fire and intention, she boarded the LIRR at Penn. Destination: Ellesmere.

Sally might have been a lifelong New Yorker, but Long Island remained a land of mystery. She knew F. Scott Fitzgerald characters lived at one end and Oliver Stone characters at the other, but in between the two was truly a foreign country, and as far as Ellesmere itself was concerned, Rochelle had told her very little: a few choice anecdotes about her big public high school (the degenerate football team routinely harassing the girls from the Catholic school across town, and a single college counselor for the entire grade!). The Ellesmere skating rink and bowling alley had been mentioned, and Sally had heard about the basements of certain friends, where herbals were smoked (though not by Rochelle), and the Saturday-night pack gatherings at the almighty Ellesmere Marketfair Mall, to which the girls wore Ralph Lauren polo shirts and Mudd jeans and the boys dressed like Kurt Cobain. It was this exotic Shangri-la of Rochelle's past that Sally found herself summoning as the train wound eastward, a pastiche of teen movies and magazine stories about bad behavior in the suburbs. But the skies were gray and the afternoon already well underway, and she felt the first stirrings of apprehension, because Rochelle did not have any idea she was coming, and no one would be waiting for her at the Ellesmere station.

There were a few SUVs in the parking lot when the train pulled in, but they picked up their passengers and moved off quickly, leaving a disassociated woman in a trench coat, walking up and down the aisle of cars in a stiff, internally regimented gait. There was a single taxi, which Sally approached.

"Do you know where this is?" she asked the driver, showing him the piece of paper on which she'd written Rochelle's home address hours earlier in their dorm room.

"Yeah," said the man, who might have hailed from Long Island central casting: intentional mullet, chains of gold nestled comfortably in abundant chest hair. "Five bucks. Hop in."

Five bucks sounded pretty good. At home, five bucks wouldn't have gotten her to the Brooklyn Bridge.

They set off, away from the miniscule downtown and along streets of small houses. Eventually the road began to coil through woodland, passing gated communities with names from an Anglophilic epic: Hunter's Chase, Squire Estates. Some of the houses glimpsed past the guard booths were huge. Some had gates of their own. Then, on the right, a football field with a billboard of an Indian brandishing a tomahawk and the legend: *Redskins on the Warpath!* (At Walden this would have instigated a school-wide crisis. Then again, Walden didn't have a football team.)

"And here we are," the driver announced, turning into a cul-de-sac called Lorelei Circle. He came to a stop in front of the farthest house.

"Thanks," Sally said, paying him. She pulled her bag from the trunk and got out.

Five houses facing one another: white, white, white, light blue, and white, all split-levels, all with black shutters. Rochelle's house had a miniscule front porch and, though it was too early for flowers, tidy beds where flowers had once, obviously, grown. No one seemed to be home anywhere, but inside one of the other houses a dog was yapping. Sally looked around, then back, and in that single, small moment of distraction she understood what was different. In the other houses, windows showed glimpses of rooms: a living room, an entryway, a lit kitchen. At Rochelle's house, every curtain was drawn.

She knocked gently, and after a very long while heard sounds from inside.

"Yes?" Rochelle's mother's upper half emerged from the crack of the open front door. "What is it?"

"Mrs. Steiner?"

Sally saw relief on the woman's face. Though it didn't last.

"Mrs. Steiner? I'm Sally. Rochelle's roommate."

"Sally!" She stepped out all the way, onto the doorstep: a slender woman in khaki pants and a Fair Isle sweater. And slippers. "Of course! Sally! But Rochelle didn't tell me."

She took Sally in her open arms and squeezed, and there was the briefest emanation of something sour and sharp. "I thought of surprising her," Sally said.

Rochelle's mother stiffened. "Then she doesn't know you're here?"

"I . . . well, no. Surprise! I mean, I thought, I'd love to see my roommate's hometown . . ."

And I knew she'd say no if I suggested it, Sally thought, or rather, she admitted to herself for the first time. Because this had been a mistake, she already understood. A bad one. Rochelle would *not* be happily surprised to have her turn up unannounced this way, with a bag on wheels and a full ten days of uncommitted time until they both had to be back in Ithaca. All at once, she wanted to get away from this oddly *different* house before Rochelle emerged.

"She's gone into town," Rochelle's mother said. "But she won't be long. Would you like to wait for her on the porch?"

Sally frowned. It wasn't precisely cold outside, but it wasn't porch weather, either. And it was now undeniably getting on toward evening. "Uh . . . okay," she managed. She took the handle of her bag and walked behind Mrs. Steiner to the little porch. There were two plastic chairs there, behind the railing, with a small wooden table between them.

"I'll bring you out some tea!" said Mrs. Steiner, as if this hospitable gesture offset the strangeness of not being invited . . . actually . . . *inside.*

Sally sat, the old plastic giving, slightly, beneath her. She drew her wool cardigan around her shoulders, pretending she was comfortable—which, as the sun's warmth continued to drain, became increasingly challenging. After a few moments, Mrs. Steiner emerged with a green ceramic mug full of tea, or more accurately, water with a tea bag trailing from it. The water was barely hot.

"Now, you come from the city, I remember."

"Oh. Yes," Sally said. She wondered if she should take a sip to be polite.

"I met you, the day you girls moved in?"

She seemed to be reminding Sally, or herself. "Yes."

Mrs. Steiner nodded. Sally wasn't sure what she was agreeing with, exactly.

"It makes a difference, seeing the sort of person your child will be living with. You'll see one day, when you take your daughter to college."

Sally made herself nod. In the dark obscurity of her own future, this was one scenario she felt certain would never occur.

"I'm sure that's true," she said instead. "You know, Mrs. Steiner, this was kind of a last-minute idea, this visit, and I'm thinking I'd better be getting on home. I didn't have a very good grasp of how far out of the city Ellesmere was, so I miscalculated how long it would take to get back. If you could tell Rochelle I just stopped to say hi, that would be great . . ."

"Oh no! Don't go," said Rochelle's mother. "That's her now, I think. That's our car."

And there was indeed a car, a once-white station wagon, turning slowly into the cul-de-sac and drawing nearer, and then pulling into the driveway. On the front seat, an indelible view of Rochelle, staring at them both, but especially her, in utter bafflement and dismay. Sally felt ill. She thought and for the first time ever truly understood the words: *I wish I could disappear.* But some other force took hold of her right hand, the one not clutching the mug of tepid tea, and waved it in the air. "Surprise!" she heard herself call, like an idiot.

Rochelle got out of the car. She had her customary red nylon backpack slung over her shoulder, and reached back into the passenger seat for a plastic shopping bag: ShopRite.

"Okay. I'm surprised," she said.

"Your roommate came all the way from the city!" Rochelle's mother said. Her nervousness, always discernible, had slipped some bond. It was fear, obvious fear.

"Um . . . from Ithaca, actually," Sally interjected. "I mean, I was on my way home, and just, suddenly at Penn, I saw a sign for the Babylon Line and it was so poetic!"

"The poetic Babylon Line," Rochelle sighed. She had walked over to the porch. As she approached, her mother stood to free up the seat, and reached for the grocery bag.

"I'll take these inside!" she said brightly. "You sit with your friend."

Sally watched her snatch the bag away and move swiftly to the front door, which she opened, a bit, and ducked around. It closed behind her. The oddness of it all came over her in a wave. Beside her, Rochelle took the vacated plastic seat. "I gotta be honest," she said wearily. "I wish you'd asked."

"I wish I'd asked, too," Sally said, honestly enough. "It was very spur of the moment, at Penn. I just . . . I saw the Long Island Railroad, and all the names of the towns. And I saw Ellesmere and I just, I thought . . ." (Here she ran out of steam, because she had run out of honesty.)

"I'm not even mad," Rochelle said, and even to Sally, who was now horrendously mad at herself, she seemed not precisely mad. Though there was something else. Definitely something else.

And she remembered then, from when her roommate had gone home suddenly, earlier that winter: *Oh, it's the house. Too boring to go into.*

Without thinking, she turned and looked at it, and it looked almost completely normal, not so unlike the other houses in the cul-de-sac, at least apart from those drawn curtains. White-painted vinyl siding. Black shutters made of something that wasn't wood. The porch had been swept—in fact, there was the broom, leaning against the little porch railing. There was a garage door, but it was closed.

"You said you needed to help out your mom, a couple of months ago. Is she all right?"

Rochelle sighed. "By any reasonable standard, no. But it's how she's lived for the past ten years, at least. After my parents divorced, and then my dad died, she just lost control of this one thing. It's very difficult for her. Wait," she said, eyeing Sally, "you've seen inside?"

"Inside? No. We were . . . she brought me some tea outside."

Rochelle frowned. "Oh. Well, she's ashamed, you know. You need to try to think of it as an illness. It took me years to do that, but I do, now. I had a good therapist. And I still see someone at school, of course."

Of course? Rochelle had never mentioned a therapist, at Cornell or anywhere else.

"Oh, that's good," she told Rochelle. "But, what about the house?"

Rochelle sat in her own plastic armchair, hands oddly open in her lap.

Across the cul-de-sac, a woman emerged from another white-and-black house with a little boy, his legs zipped into woolly boots, unzipped parka flapping over a martial arts uniform.

"Hi, Mrs. Hennessey," said Rochelle. "Hi, Barry."

Barry, about eight or nine, ducked his head. Mrs. Hennessey emitted a faint smile. The two climbed into their car.

"Drinks," said Rochelle. Then she pointed her way around the cul-de-sac: "Smokes pot every single day. Batshit crazy. Husband tried to grope me after I babysat for his daughter a couple years ago. Kid hospitalized for depression. I'd be tempted to call it just this cul-de-sac but it's everywhere. My mom started bringing things home when my dad left, and she couldn't let anything go, I mean ever. So, room by room, it just filled up with junk. It's so sad, and nobody hates it more than she does. Well, I do, I guess. But whatever I tried backfired horribly. Like, once I tried to take out a bag of trash, and she went out in the middle of the night and brought it back inside and put it under her bed."

"Trash?" Sally said. She was having trouble getting her head around this.

"Yeah. And then once I just told her I'm doing this, I'm clearing it out, and I spent a weekend not listening to her even though she was crying and yelling at me, and I hauled stuff to the dump so she couldn't bring it back, but she got so horribly depressed after I did it. I was afraid to leave her alone. I mean, I didn't go to school for almost two weeks. And I ended up apologizing to her and telling her I'd never do it again, never even sneak anything out of the house without her permission, which of course she'll never give. At least not without therapy and medication, which she'll never consent to."

"But . . . what does she do when she's finished with something? Like, I don't know . . . a candy bar wrapper. Or a bottle of conditioner?"

"She's never finished," Rochelle said shortly. "She's never prepared to be abandoned by a candy wrapper or an empty bottle. It's too hard for her. My leaving the house is unbearable. I'm actually really proud of her that she's been able to let me go, and so far away. Weirdly, I think of her as brave." She looked out past the pot house, the groping father house, to the road beyond.

"But I can't let anyone in. I'd say I wish I could, but I don't wish it, and you wouldn't either, if you could see it. Or smell it."

Sally recoiled. She couldn't help herself.

"You mean, it's dirty?"

Rochelle gave her a queer look. Then, with real compassion, she said: "Yes, Sally. Very dirty. Very smelly. Very uncomfortable for you, trust me. I would never have brought you here voluntarily, for your own sake. On the other hand, I'm not going to be embarrassed. Like I said, it's an illness. People get ill, and sometimes they're lucky and recover. But sometimes not. This is a not-recovery situation."

"But . . . do you understand it? I mean, in therapy, did you figure out why?"

Rochelle crossed her arms. She was cold, too, Sally saw. She was still focused on the road beyond, the darkening sky over the trees. How late was it now?

"I thought I had, at various times. At one point I convinced myself it had to do with environmentalism—you know, keeping things out of landfills, or the ocean. Then I thought: it's art. She's making some kind of art. She's expressing something she's never been able to express. I tried very hard to make the world fit what she was doing, so I could make it acceptable, if maybe not exactly normal. I just thought: okay, my mom is unique. She isn't the typical Ellesmere hausfrau, keeping up with the Joneses. She didn't care about the Joneses, she cared about saving the wishbone from the chicken in a special wishbone jar. That was quirky. But then also the rest of the chicken in another jar. And then our neighbor's chicken in another jar. Anyway, I gave up. Or no, I didn't give up, exactly, I just downshifted to maintenance. Psychic maintenance."

"Hers?" said Sally, crossing her legs.

"No. Mine. Hers is out of my control. Or so my therapist—my multiple therapists—tell me." She sighed. "Sally, I wish you'd called. I wish I could invite you in. I wish you could stay overnight and we could sit on the couch and watch *Letterman* and eat popcorn, but none of that is possible. All I can do is drive you to the train station and wait for the next train with you, and see you back at school in a couple weeks. If you'll just hang on a minute, I need to pee," said Rochelle, who got up, opened the door, and disappeared inside, leaving Sally more uncomfortable than before. It was nearly dark, the leafy dark of the suburbs, with the flickering lights of the cul-de-sac televisions. She felt levitational with loneliness, and so terribly sad. And desperately, she too needed to pee.

Back at the train station, she persuaded Rochelle to go home: *no harm, no foul, no worries!* She would head on into the city and her own house, with her parents, and maybe even the weirdo brother from the two-year college in New Hampshire would be home for spring break, and it was fine, it was all fine. She gave her roommate an awkward hug and again insisted she not wait, though the next train was at 8:10, nearly forty-five minutes away. The station was locked and the coffee place opposite was closed. Sally sat on a bench, by the track, thinking and thinking. She wondered what mystical objects were behind the door Rochelle and her mother had slipped around, scattered over the floor or rising up to the ceiling. Jars of wishbones and old chicken carcasses and every single thing she herself might have thrown away. She imagined going inside, extracting an object and carrying it out, liberating a tiny space within. Then she thought of Harriet Greene's house, its rooms jammed with furniture and the plastic bins stacked high in the kitchen, objects also liberated from crammed and filthy houses, but only to be hidden away again.

She hadn't actually told Johanna she'd be coming home for the break. She'd thought vaguely she might turn up after her visit to Rochelle in Ellesmere, perhaps with Rochelle herself in tow (though the chance Lewyn would also be there cast a definite pall on that scenario), but now the idea of returning to Brooklyn Heights made her almost physically sick. And so, as she sat on the dark and quiet platform, she took out her phone and composed a long text to our mother about an exciting opportunity to intern with a local antiques dealer, which was maybe the right thing for her to be doing at this peculiar moment, anyway, not that she'd ever once raised it with Harriet Greene. But in fact people did stay on campus during the breaks—not everyone disappeared to be waited on at their parents' houses or to party on the beaches of Florida! They remained behind to work, to decompress, and some, she supposed, because they had projects to undertake and viable things to explore, as she had apparently begun to explore her own viable thing, her project: that little glimpse of a way to be alive in the world that actually made sense to her.

And when the train arrived, she followed her own breadcrumbs all the way back: to Penn Station and Port Authority and the wait for the bus to Buffalo, which stopped in Ithaca at 3:37 the following morning. A long night's journey into day.

Chapter Twenty

Revel and Dread

In which Lewyn Oppenheimer enters the netherworld of "in love," and learns something important about his sister

By the time the chartered bus had departed the island of Manhattan, he was cataclysmically in love. It wasn't merely that he had never experienced "in love" before; the truth was that he'd never quite believed the state not to be mythical, something solely evoked on a Grecian urn or a Hallmark card, or rapturously on a stage or a screen. But when *in love* happened to him, Lewyn recognized it at once for precisely what it was. Lewyn Oppenheimer, an ordinary guy with an apparently common last name (God!) and a whole lot of things he suddenly, desperately wished not to reveal, was in love with Rochelle Steiner—so wondrously sharp, and funny, so outgoing and energetic, so full of plans and intentions! Not, perhaps, conventionally "beautiful" or "pretty" but a dynamo of adorability, magnetism, and attractiveness (at least in the sense that she attracted people to her) whereas he had always understood himself to be . . . whatever the opposite of that was.

For the first time in Lewyn's life, his physical body was utterly alive, its myriad parts wondrously interconnected, and he walked and climbed steps and lay down at night to rest with a feeling of deep health and a hum of energy he had never before experienced. His brain, also, was alive, not only to Rochelle (though she was ever at the forefront of his thoughts) but in class and even now in the populated human world of the university beyond his fetid little room in Clara Dickson Hall. When he walked the walkways, fed himself with an art book open in front of him (or Rochelle Steiner across from him!), stopped to greet acquaintances (hers, nearly always, but sometimes, as the spring term wound on, also his own), he felt alive, energetic, engaged, and free from care. He might still lack the laser focus of his Cornell contemporaries—already thinking ahead to their shiny professional lives—but he was no longer without purpose. His purpose was Rochelle Steiner, and to be happy with her, always.

Of course, she had wanted to know things. Of course, there had had to be some evasions. Before their first bus ride had ended Rochelle asked him more questions than he'd been cumulatively asked in years. Where did he come from? Who were his people? What were his plans and who were his friends, apart from that strange group he'd brought to the Seder? (*Not his friends!* he'd insisted. His roommate's friends, though nice guys. *Not his friends!*) And while Lewyn did take refuge in some circumventions, he only lied about one thing outright: when Rochelle asked if he had any siblings he said, ferociously and without hesitation, no.

Obviously, there was plenty to worry about. In fact, Lewyn would spend the following months in a near-constant state of worry. What if she asked him to pick her up at her room? What if she pressed him about his parents? Or even asked to meet them? Should he compound his earlier evasions with new and even more labyrinthine evasions? What if he forgot his prior statements and contradicted them—Rochelle was exactly the kind of person who would remember and investigate. Or the most terrible scenario of all, and the one that tormented him: What if he and Rochelle actually ran into Sally on campus, or Sally and Rochelle actually ran into him? The fact that neither of these things had happened already, not once since the previous September, gave him absolutely no comfort, and he lived with a thrum of terror at all times. He knew his luck could not possibly hold forever, and he understood that he truly would have to do something, say something, to head it off or at least mitigate it. More than once he even attempted to compose a letter to her on his computer, explaining that he had made an awful mistake in not telling her, that he'd been afraid of what she might think of him, or of Sally, or of their sibling bond (or lack thereof), which was so normal to the two of them that it seemed benign, but to the rest of the world he imagined must appear anything but. These letters did not progress past their torturous first paragraphs, and were all abandoned, but he continued to compose them in his head. They were a dark cloud, perpetually overshadowing his happiness. And the weeks passed, and he got deeper in, and then too deep to ever fully apologize or explain.

Rochelle, in contrast to all this self-inflicted torment, seemed to take real joy in telling him things. Her father was dead, but not until years after leaving her and her mother in that town he'd never heard of before meeting her. She had no siblings, but had run in a pack of girls, all scattered now at colleges around the country (except for one, who was apparently nearly six feet tall and a fashion model in Tokyo). She had deliberately chosen not to replicate that dynamic in college, declining no fewer than three invitations to join the Jewish sororities and addressing herself to individual connections she made in the course of her life at Cornell: in class, at meetings for Tzedek (the Jewish social justice group), or in the dormitory. Her only hesitation seemed to surround the topic of her mother, with whom she was obviously deeply connected, and he had the sense that she was in some form her mother's supporter, possibly even caregiver, necessitating long and intense phone calls, often several times a day. When they came through on Rochelle's flip phone, she moved automatically away from Lewyn to speak, hunched over, whispering. The calls left her uncharacteristically dull, and sometimes plainly sad. He didn't ask her about them. He was pretty sure she didn't want him to.

He also didn't ask about her dorm room, or the person she shared it with, so afraid to find out anything that would render his psychic affliction even more acute. Once, on the walkway between their dormitories, when she said she needed to run back upstairs for a book, he invented some forgotten thing in his own room so as not to accompany her. Thus far, Rochelle had only come to his own room once, and in anticipation of this occasion he cleaned (or "cleaned") to the best of his abilities. There was nothing personal on display, and most of her attention, in any case, had been directed at Jonas, who happened to be home, studying for an infectious disease midterm.

Always, he reveled in her. Rochelle Steiner! Who could not cross any bridge, quad, or street on or near the Cornell campus without running into someone who was happy to see her, and who might have a question about the exam for the Bill of Rights class or the individual presentations for the postwar international relations seminar. Lewyn, a half step behind, would watch her reach back into her ponderous red backpack and retrieve her much-inscribed Filofax to insert or scratch away some upcoming item in the appropriate color: red for academic, blue for extracurricular, yellow for gym appointments (and other leisure and social pursuits), and black for notes to herself. He, who did not possess an agenda, paper or otherwise, who was still carrying around the official sheet of his class times and locations he'd received at the beginning of the term, and who had yet to visit the Cornell gym or join a club or arrange to meet friends for dinner on campus or in town, could only marvel at the expansive brain in Rochelle Steiner's small head, and that it had somehow selected for companionship his own far less impressive brain in its own much larger head.

And yet: this proved and was continuing to prove to be precisely the case.

In the mornings they ate breakfast in Willard Straight Hall, in Central Campus, drinking coffee and eating fruit salad and sharing the *New York Times* before parting (with a hug!) on East Avenue for their classes (the eternal art history survey for him, the Bill of Rights seminar for her). In the evenings she came to meet him at the Green Dragon after her meetings (she had so many meetings), and they finished the night with more coffee and more talk, unless her mother called. The first time she took his hand was on the bridge one night in May, as the wind blew through the gorge, and this was thrilling, not least because it felt so natural and so innocent. Spring had taken forever to warm up, and people were walking around as if there was still snow on the ground, in parkas and layers of sweatshirts and those ubiquitous Uggs.

Lewyn himself had not much altered his wardrobe of T-shirts and sweat-shirts, but one morning after the weather finally started to change, he was shrugging on the same Big Red shirt he'd been handed six months earlier at registration and found that it was large, in fact huge on his frame. With an almost clinical curiosity, he gathered and lifted the length of it and looked into the mirror mounted to his closet door.

Ribs. And below them, nothing, by which he understood that the padding of fat—not rolls of fat but padding of fat—was no longer there. The shirt was so far gone that it had lost a good portion of its lettering, and the hem was shredded. He threw it away. After his morning class, he went to the Cornell store and bought four more shirts, all of which hung in proximity to the actual new dimensions of his actual new body. It was neither good nor bad, and he attached no sense of accomplishment to it, mainly because he hadn't been attempting to accomplish anything at all and hadn't even been aware that it was being accomplished. This was just how things were, because of her.

That first time, on the bridge, when she took his hand, Lewyn was assailed by the strangest memory of being forced to hold hands with his sister and brother while posing for the obligatory birthday photograph on the back porch in Chilmark, and what followed this memory was an unmistakable wave of unease. He held tight to resist that, and then it passed and he breathed deeply and was calm again. He was more than calm. He squeezed the hand of Rochelle Steiner in his own hand, even as she called hello to someone walking across in the other direction and waved with her other hand.

One day, a little before the end of term, she asked him what he was planning for the summer, because she herself was intending to take a job resident-advising the high school students who came to Cornell for the experience of "college" life (and something to write about on their own applications for admission). It was decent money, and wouldn't it be nice, after exams, to relax on the campus and take a bit of a break? The spring had cheated them out of that brief (but legendary!) time in Ithaca when winter could barely be remembered, and people took to the quads and the gorges and showed their sun-starved bodies to the sun. Perhaps, if Lewyn wasn't rushing off to some job in the city or a holiday with his parents, he might like to take a summer class or get a local job and stay on with her. And Lewyn, who of course had no summer plans at all, who could barely think past the next time he would see Rochelle Steiner, eagerly agreed.

I'm going to stay in Ithaca this summer, he emailed his mother.

"I'm going to stay in Ithaca this summer," he told Jonas, who surprised him by saying that he would also be remaining in upstate New York after the semester ended.

"Really?" said Lewyn. "In Ithaca?"

"No, I'm going to Palmyra, for the pageant."

Lewyn had a brief and hilarious vision of Jonas Bingham walking across a stage in a bathing suit and high heels, a sash inscribed *Miss Ogden, Utah* knotted at his hip.

"I'm sorry," he said, "but what?"

"It's an LDS thing. At the Hill Cumorah. You know, where Joseph Smith found the golden plates?"

Lewyn nodded. Now, the vision was of Jonas Bingham, in his bathing suit and heels, walking across the summit of a hill. "But what kind of pageant?"

"Oh, like . . . kind of like a Christmas pageant, you know? Acting out the Christmas story, except it's the Book of Mormon, and hundreds of people are in it. I saw it when I was a kid, with my family. I always wanted to be in it, so I applied and I'm going. You should come out and see it. Bring that girlfriend."

Jonas had known about Rochelle even before her visit to their room. He had known since Lewyn returned from spring break so radically altered not even a normally myopic male college student could fail to notice something major had taken place. Moreover, Jonas had declared himself not very surprised that the object of his roommate's affection was Rochelle Steiner, the tiny girl from the Passover Seder.

Don't be stupid. You couldn't take your eyes off her. She's just so cute!

"Oh, well . . ." Lewyn said now. "I don't know."

"I bet she'd find it interesting."

Lewyn doubted this very much, but he didn't say so. It was morning, and Jonas was loading his textbooks into his backpack.

"Okay. Maybe."

Jonas turned. He had also changed over the long months at college. He had come in clipped and neat, but now sported a few leisurely patches of beard and his blond hair drifted south of his chin. Lauren apparently approved of this length. Lauren was their spectral third roommate; consistently invoked, if seldom present in the flesh.

"Maybe what?" he said.

"Maybe we'll come see you. In the pageant."

"Oh. Cool," said Jonas.

They had been good roommates, in the end. They had not fought or held resentments toward each other, and they had tolerated each other's less than optimal personal habits with equanimity (or, viewed slightly differently, with a mutual lack of consciousness). Still, they were not moving on together. Jonas had a room picked out on the third floor of AGR for the following year. Lewyn, with a good housing lottery number, had selected a single in 112 Edgmoor Lane, a small dorm in an old house near Collegetown. He had compelling reasons to want a single now.

After the exams were done and the final papers turned in, after Jonas had stored his boxes at the fraternity house and left town, and—crucially—after Rochelle reported that her roommate had already moved out—Lewyn accepted Rochelle's invitation to come see the room where she and his sister had lived since the previous September. For the first time since Freshman Week, he opened the door to Balch Hall and stepped onto its black-and-white-tiled lobby. He climbed the gray speckled stairs up to the second floor and turned right past a paneled living room with a baronial (if clearly non-working) fireplace, and into a carpeted corridor, where the door to Sally's home away from home stood open.

Inside, Rochelle was seated cross-legged on a twin bed, her flip phone to her ear. She was nodding rapidly, and didn't immediately look up, but

Lewyn knew this posture and this tone; she was talking with her mother, or more accurately, listening to her mother talk. He took in the room: dingy walls and grimy floor and the same institutional off-white roller shade. The view was of a far-off corner of his own dormitory, though not the corner he'd actually lived in.

"Hi!" Rochelle said, snapping shut her phone. She got up, stepped to the doorway, and embraced him. He closed his eyes. His chin rested on the top of her head.

"So this is where you've been living," he said.

"With my roommate, Sally. Also named Oppenheimer," she agreed.

He cringed at the strangeness: his sister's name in Rochelle's voice.

"So. Do you want to go get dinner?" He glanced at the door. It occurred to him that they could close that door and stay inside. When had they ever been this alone together?

"Okay. If you're hungry," she said.

"Oh, I'm not," he told her. So they didn't go out after all. And very late that night, still mainly clothed but sprawled across the now pushed-together beds, with her head on her pillow and his head on—incredibly—the left-behind pillow of his sister Sally, Rochelle said something that seemed unattached to anything that had happened in the previous hours, or been said in the previous hours, which had themselves been crowded with a wild array of incredible things and profound sensations. She said:

"I've thought this for a while, actually, but mainly since March, because something happened in March, and I didn't say anything to you, because I felt, I wanted to separate this, I mean you, from that. She never actually put it into words or made any declaration or anything like that. But I know."

"What?" Lewyn asked. He was suddenly so sleepy, and the idea of falling asleep with her, in a bed (two beds) with her, pulled so strongly at him that he had to make himself listen, which is how he knew he was absolutely hearing her.

"Oh. That she's . . . I mean, I wish I knew another way to say this or something else to call it. But: in love with me. She was. I mean, she is. And I feel really terrible for her, because I could see how unhappy it made her, but I never knew what to do about it. It's kind of why I never wanted you to meet her, or come to the room, if I'm being honest. You must have wondered about it. Didn't you wonder?"

No, he thought. "Yes," he said. "But now I understand."

Chapter Twenty-One

Go Down, Moses

In which Harrison Oppenheimer ventures below the Mason-Dixon Line for the first time, and is compelled to relate "The Watermelon Affair" to his new friends there

Roarke didn't have anything so banal as a summer vacation, but students were given leave as needed in June and July, subject to their responsibilities on the farm and pending written application. Harrison and Eli submitted their requests together, with a joint letter of invitation from the Hayek Institute.

The invitation encompassed not only travel, lodging, food, and inclusion in what Eli promised would be an enlightening intellectual conclave, but also, as he had implied, a presentation of Harrison's own, on any topic that might contribute some insights into his generation. Harrison spent many evenings in the Stearns Room in May and June, trying to settle on a subject, and finally, in the absence of any better idea, he decided to write about the political journey of American Jews from the early nineteenth century to the present. Harrison didn't ask Eli's opinion about his topic. He was afraid to be told it was too general, too well-trodden, or, worst of all, too obvious for a young conservative intellectual who happened to be Jewish, and besides, both of them were already inundated with academic and administrative work: end-of-term projects in history and philosophy, not to speak of his final generation of chickens (soon, blessedly, to be handed off to an incoming first-year), and Eli was preoccupied with the search for a history of science faculty member, and the winnowing of fifty-three finalist applicants for the next Roarke class down to fourteen brilliant young men from eight states, England, Canada, Italy, and Iceland. The farm, meanwhile, turned a corner to summer, and as it did, the last foul remnants of the plagiarism charge, and the taint of their departed classmates, Carlos, Tony, and Gordon, seemed finally to dissipate.

In the middle of July, Eli and Harrison flew to Charlottesville. Harrison had long been taught that the south was a foreign country, and one to be vilified. (How many units on slavery? How many spirituals solemnly sung by the children of wealth?)

"First time below the Mason-Dixon Line," he told Eli as they descended. Then, reflexively, he apologized.

"What for?" said Eli.

"Well, I don't mean to be . . . insensitive." He halfheartedly tried to make it a joke, but there was too much Walden in him, after all. "Actually, my forebears weren't exactly first-class citizens here, either."

Eli looked at Harrison. "You're referring to postwar carpetbaggers?"

"I was thinking Leo Frank, actually."

"You know, it's interesting," said Eli. "I think this is the first time you've self-identified as Jewish."

It was an observation, not an insult, but Harrison cringed, nonetheless.

"I don't 'identify.' It's more of a genetic factor. Like being Aboriginal, or a Pict. You don't go around feeling good about it or bad about it. It just is."

"But still," said Eli, though he was smiling, "the sacred brotherhood of the Negro and the Jew. *Go down, Moses.* Two peoples bonded in suffering. Do you think that explains our friendship?"

It was the reference to "friendship" that landed first. It distracted Harrison for a joyful moment, but then he had to address the question.

"I wouldn't think so. Besides, my family's had a pretty sweet couple of centuries. I did have this ancestor, though . . ." he heard himself say.

The landing gear was down. Below them, the legendary soil of the Commonwealth rose to meet them.

"What's that?" said Eli. He was handing his plastic cup back to the flight attendant.

"My ancestor. Joseph Oppenheimer. Court Jew to a nobleman in Stuttgart in the 1730s. Arrested and executed for almost certainly nonexistent crimes."

Beside him, his friend was frowning at some spot on the airplane floor. Harrison recognized this expression; it meant that Eli was searching his own cerebral accordion file. "You don't mean Jud Süss," he suddenly said. "Goebbel's punching bag?"

"The very same," said Harrison.

"You never said."

"Why would I? There's no sense in churning over these old events, however horrible. Despicable things have happened to lots of people, ever since human beings figured out how to harm one another. We're alive now. Until someone invents a time machine, that should be the focus. Or do you disagree?"

"I don't disagree. I'm just surprised. It would be like . . . well, myself descending from Nat Turner."

The plane dropped onto the runway, bounced, and dropped again.

"Both targeted for what they were trying to do, to help their own people."

Harrison shrugged. "Well, how much more fortunate are we, to be living today?"

After a moment Eli said: "Indeed."

The plane shuddered to a stop at their gate.

"Will we get to see Charlottesville itself?" he asked Eli. "And Monticello?"

"You will. A couple of Monticello board members are involved with Hayek. Some are on the faculty at the university."

Harrison turned to look at him. Unlike the other passengers, who were furiously unpacking the overhead bins, he remained in his seat with his eyes closed, and the light through the window lent his skin a distinct note of rose. He had gone for a haircut in town a couple of days earlier, and now it was very short, almost buzz-cut. "How did you meet these guys, again?" asked Harrison.

"Dr. Gregories and I corresponded when I was just starting to think about my book. He teaches at UVA, so I came down to Charlottesville to meet him, and a couple of the others. He suggested I defer Harvard and apply to Roarke. I'd never heard of Roarke. Then again, where I grew up, no one had heard of Harvard." He smiled, but still didn't open his eyes. "I was here last summer. These are people with a sincere interest in ideas. Especially ideas we don't see often enough in the mainstream."

From the airport they were driven south through farmland and past manor houses, some old, some built to look as if they were, but given away by their overblown dimensions and attached garages. A sign informed Harrison that they were on the Thomas Jefferson Parkway, and he turned to look up the drive toward Monticello. Just before Simeon they pulled off onto a gated property. The massive building came into view as they drove a slow, rising curve: a great estate unfolding along the base of a wooded hillside. At its heart was a white frame plantation house with porches on all three of its floors; on either side, modern extensions.

"I hope you won't object to a few creature comforts," Eli said. "I could use a break from Roarke privations."

It seemed an odd thing for someone who'd grown up in a shack to say, Harrison thought. He himself, emphatically not raised in a shack, was absolutely open to such luxuries as a bath, a soft bed, and an opportunity not to feed chickens twice a day.

They were welcomed by two men not much older than themselves, who took their bags upstairs. Harrison watched them ascend and, at the landing, turn in separate directions, settling one of his lesser questions about whether they'd be sharing a room. A moment later, the kind and supportive Dr. Gregories himself materialized and shook Eli's hand.

"Young man," he said to Harrison, when they were introduced.

"Hello," said Harrison. Then, to his own great surprise, he added: "Sir."

"Please. Call me Oren. Hello, my friend," he said to Eli. The two shook hands almost gently, with a kind of mutual contemplation. Professor Gregories was lanky, tall, and clubbable. He had ash-colored hair in retreat, whisper thin across the pate, scalp glimmering between the remaining strands. He wore immaculate khakis, a dark green belt, and a shirt so blindingly white it might never before have been exposed to air. A broad gold watch emerged as those two hands rose and fell. "How goes the new book?"

Eli had not mentioned that he was writing a "new book."

"Slowly, but I'm encouraged. I am looking forward to making some progress these next few weeks."

"Good. I hope you'll stay as long as you like. You as well, Mr. . . . Oppenheimer."

Yes, without doubt, the tiniest of pauses before his surname, which meant . . . what? Quite probably nothing, and yet, here they were: a young Black man and a young Jew at the hearth of obvious traditional entitlement, on what was quite possibly a once-plantation, snug in this most presidential terroir of American soil. Somehow they had slipped back into the source of it all.

Harrison's bed was four-posted with a piece of linsey-woolsey stretched across the top. An adjacent study housed a six-foot-long desk in front of a window that overlooked woodland. He went to take a bath, his first since going home to Brooklyn at Christmas break, and there, embraced by the heat and the steam and the lavender smell of the soap, he drifted off for a few minutes or possibly longer. When he woke, it was time to go downstairs.

Later, he would think of that first evening as an irremediable transit from one state of being to another, so momentous and so permanent, not because he couldn't go back but because he could not, for many years, imagine a reason to do so. The men he would meet that night—and that first night they were indeed all men—were powerfully intellectual, powerfully focused on impact, and just plain powerful, and as he was introduced to them and spoke with them, he began to read his own promise in their reflected interest.

The rest of them arrived over the following days. Two were senators from Midwestern states. One was a governor, another a pundit who wrote historical fiction, just for fun. Harrison met a recently retired member of the Harvard economics department and a rail-thin man with an accent he recognized from his Vineyard summers—moneyed New England, redolent of sailing and boarding schools—who declined to say more than that he worked in Washington. Eli introduced him to a squat man whose very round head segued directly into broad shoulders. This was Roger Fount, the chairman of Hayek.

Harrison spent the next days working on the meandering political journey of American Jews, exploring Charlottesville and Jefferson's magnificent UVA campus, and visiting Monticello for a tour and a rose garden reception. After the seminars began, he attended every one, elated to find himself in room after room of robust thinkers and incisive questioners. It became commonplace, if never for one moment dull, to meet the authors of books he'd read, who might materialize in the bus seat beside him as they drove to a nearby winery for an outdoor dinner, or ahead of him in the buffet line at breakfast. A certain Princeton historian (for whose sake Harrison had once considered applying to Princeton) had the bedroom next to his and could be heard snoring through the wall. On his other side: a former ambassador to China.

A few days later, Vernon Loring turned up.

Harrison had not seen Loring since their meeting at Symposium, when he'd shared the good news of his Roarke acceptance. If he was surprised by their reunion here in Virginia, Loring himself did not seem to be.

"My young triplet friend," he said mildly, in greeting.

They shook hands, and Loring held on to Harrison's for a moment too long, actually holding it up for closer examination. "I am looking for evidence of physical labor," he said.

"Oh, well, I'm in charge of the chickens, if that's what you mean."

"And does that suit you?"

"Frankly, not at all. But everything else about Roarke does. I'm so grateful to you."

"Not at all. By now, I'm sure you understand the importance of steering the right people toward the college. You'll do the same, I would hope."

Harrison nodded. But it would be rare indeed to stumble across a young person with a mind like Eli's, or—he supposed—his own, who'd be willing to be diverted from a Yale or a Stanford.

"Forgive me, but I had no idea you'd be here," he said.

Loring smiled. "Still asking for forgiveness? We have a ways to go, I see. I understand you've made a friend of that brilliant young man we talked about. I wonder, would you introduce me?"

Harrison did, and the two of them began an animated conversation that gradually relocated to one of the library's dark corners. By the time Harrison rejoined them, hours later, they were discussing St. Augustine.

"That's an interesting guy," Eli said the next morning when they sat down together for breakfast. "He found you, I take it?"

"Found me?"

"Well, yes. Not everyone at Roarke, but some of us. Sought out. Pointed in the right direction. It's a tradition, I understand."

Harrison refrained from noting that he had been the one doing the seeking, but he confirmed the part about the pointing. "I'd never heard of Roarke until Professor Loring," he admitted.

"He and Gregories were at Princeton together. Before that, he was at Oxford with Roger Fount. I enjoyed talking with him."

"Well," said Harrison, "he's a fan. Your fan. The first time I met him we discussed you. You were the only one of our generation he had any time for."

"Oh. Well," Eli said with his usual vague amusement, "that's gratifying."

"Did he check out your hands?" asked Harrison.

Eli's fork, laden with the end of a sausage link, paused in midair. "What?"

"Oh . . . it's just, he wanted to look at my hands last night. Something about evidence of physical labor. In the Roarkian tradition."

Eli continued to look at him, and as he did, Harrison felt his own face begin to tighten, and the absolute conviction that he had offended Eli started to pulse through him, horribly. But after a moment his friend shook his head in an affable way. "No, he did not. We're not all meant for the fields, I suppose."

Harrison flinched. Then, in relief, he managed to smile back.

Most of the sixty or so men (and handful of women) who ultimately converged at Hayek were older than Eli and himself by two decades at least, and Harrison got used to being introduced as "our delegate from the land of youth" or "young Mr. Stone's classmate at Roarke." He was asked constantly about his origins, his forebears, his experiences, and how they had brought him to Roarke, and where they might lead him next. "I've deferred at Harvard," he said, over and over, to general approval. (Though the Yalies and Princetonians seemed, amusingly, to still nurse old rivalries. "Lord, make me a Harvard man. But not yet!" said one.)

"After that, I think," said Roger Fount one evening, "you ought to go to Oxford. I've said the same to Eli. You appear far too impressed by that," he told Harrison, looking amused. "There were very few of us, actual intellectuals among the so-called 'Scholar Athletes.' You'd be amazed, some of the idiots they took. Squash players who could read. Rowers who could count. At Oxford you should do PPE. And we can help you land in one of the better colleges."

PPE? Harrison had asked.

Politics, philosophy, and economics. The only course worth studying while on a Rhodes.

He wanted to ask why Fount thought he could actually plan for a Rhodes Scholarship, but he didn't. Uncharacteristically, he didn't want to know.

By the second week, in the gloaming of a rich and fragrant evening among the Monticello fruit trees, he found himself ruminating on the notion of family, and how smoothly the word had begun to slide over these new relationships with these amiable and fascinating people, and how fractured and abrasive that same word had always seemed in connection with his actual relations: mother, father, sister, brother. (He did not, at that point, include his more recently acquired sister.) When he considered how the three of them had been made (something he certainly did not make a habit of doing!) he thought of nameless lab workers, gloved in latex and leering over their innocent cellular divisions through a microscope. It was . . . well, it was many things. But what it wasn't? *Familiar.* Maybe the reason he had never felt anything real for any of those people in his nominal *family* was that he had not actually *chosen* them. And why, by the same token, should they love him? *Did* they love him? He had been every bit as forced upon them as they on him, and at the end of the day, none of it meant anything.

This, on the other hand, meant something.

These remarkable people! They wore their brilliance so lightly and were so passionate in their contemplation of America: the ongoing experiment, their country. He inclined toward them, not only intellectually but, he realized, actually physically, and not only from an affinity of mind but through a surge of natural affection that felt revelatory. The relief from pretense, it was so freeing that he floated along with it, released at last after all the long years. He loved everything about this place, and what was happening to him here.

The two of them, himself and Eli, were to speak on the same evening. Following dinner, the group took their seats in the library, some balancing decaf in gold-rimmed cups and saucers on their laps, others holding heavy crystal glasses of whiskey. Harrison knew nothing at all about what Eli had prepared, and was not the only member of the audience to react visibly when his friend announced that the theme of his talk was a reconsideration of Booker T. Washington, nearly a century after his death.

"Oh! *Ha ha,*" said someone behind Harrison.

Harrison didn't turn around.

Eli began with Washington's 1895 "Atlanta Compromise," in which he'd urged Black Americans to delay direct engagement with the white establishment (aka "the establishment"), both in general and on the issue of civil rights in particular, and focus instead on their own education and financial security, in order to become such hardworking, wealth-accumulating model citizens that even the most recalcitrant racists in even the most Confederate states would see no reason not to share the harvest of American liberties with them. Eclipsed in due course by W. E. B. Du Bois's more aggressively oppositional outlook, Washington had fallen, over time, into a historical trench of Uncle Toms, to the point that he and his Tuskegee Institute stood for nothing so much as a notion of self-negation. The Walden School had entirely written Booker T. Washington out of the shining story of the Civil Rights Movement, suggesting that the rise of Black Americans jumped directly from Sojourner Truth to Frederick Douglass and Harriet Tubman to Martin Luther King.

Booker T. Washington's long game, Eli argued, had been perfectly calibrated. In 1895, American Negroes (as Washington identified this group, and self-identified) were not in a position to oppose, let alone impact, white America; indeed, that would remain the case for decades to come. The notion of using those intervening years to build power and self-reliance within their own community was sound strategy, not capitulation. And, said Eli, looking out at his audience, Black Americans' abandonment of this strategy in favor of Du Bois's alternate path had only demonstrated this to be so.

"It's perhaps an American trait," said Eli, in conclusion, "that when we want something, we want it now. Separation from England? Dump the tea in the harbor. Somebody turns up a nugget of gold in California? Everybody head west. It's understandable that freed slaves should want the whole menu of rights and opportunities before the ink on the Emancipation Proclamation was dry. But Booker T. Washington played what we might call today a multilevel game of chess, always aware that he had opponents on all sides of the board, including the one that was nominally his own. Now, could his vision for Black progress have held? If those generations had risen through education to the professions, and then to politics and wealth and influence, would American society at the rim of the twenty-first century truly be equal, colorblind, and meritocratic? How can we know, because we went another way. So we shouldn't be surprised that the goal is further away now, in 2001, than it was in 1895.

"But still!" Eli said, gathering his pages. "We beat on, don't we? Because we believe in the green light, this American utopia where we're judged by the content of our character and our work ethic and our God-given abilities.

You know, I'm frequently asked if I'm trying to be some kind of example to 'my people.' This is a serious question, so I want to be very precise when I answer. I ask them: *Do you mean the people of western Virginia?*"

The two men behind Harrison chuckled.

"Do you mean people born under my astrological sign, Aquarius?"

Applause and laughter. Harrison sat up in his chair. His neighbor, none other than the lauded Princeton historian, was thumping his hand down on Harrison's forearm, unable to contain his own mirth.

"Or perhaps you mean my people, the left-handed. *A sinistra*? Or we of the tribe who delude ourselves into thinking the Orioles will one day win the World Series! Or those of us born in 1982, the Chinese Year of the Dog. So I'm confused. Because all I want is what Booker T. Washington wanted. I want an America in which it wouldn't occur to anyone to suggest that my accomplishments are anything but fully my own. No lower standard. No . . . affirmative action. You want to know who my people are? People who work hard, and innovate, and take pride in their accomplishments, *those are my people.*"

"Yes!" someone to Harrison's left shouted. The Princeton professor had removed his thumping hand from Harrison's forearm. He was standing, clapping loudly.

"Told you," said a voice, somewhere on his other side.

"Fuck, yes," someone else responded. Harrison turned to see who'd spoken, but they were all on their feet, banging their hands together, and no one seemed to be talking.

They broke for more drinks, more coffee, the audience drifting away to the bar. Harrison stayed in his chair. He told them that he wanted to go over his talk one more time, but in fact he couldn't even bear to look at what he'd written about American Jews and their political shape-shifting. It wasn't that he took no pride in what he'd pulled together, just that now he couldn't remember why he'd settled on this topic. There was a reason he was here, and surely it wasn't to explain how socialism was relinquishing its grip on American Jews. They probably knew that already, and if they didn't there were any number of scholars, far better credentialed than himself, to tell them. No. He wanted to tell them something he was better equipped to tell than anyone else in the room.

He left his pages behind in his chair when he went to the podium, and over the clinking of new ice cubes in replenished drinks, he explained that he wanted to tell them a story about watermelon. "Not just because it's a ridiculous story, and you're going to be entertained, but because it demonstrates so much about what's wrong with the education I had, until a year ago."

The Walden School, he told them, had been his alma mater all the way back to kindergarten, and represented, in his hometown of New York City, the bright shining lie of progressive education. At Walden, they'd been taught about the European genocide against Native Americans, about the enslavement of Africans, about eugenics and lynch mobs and the unmitigated evil of the Republican Party, all while fanning the flame of their own goodness. They'd been taught to genuflect before the notion of free speech while shunning anyone who didn't agree with them. They'd been encouraged to trample traditional values, denigrate the Western Canon, and generally amplify the non-white and non-male and non-heterosexual and non-traditionally gendered, informing those of European descent and Caucasian ethnicity and normative sexuality that their opinions were not required.

In the audience, many of them nodded as he spoke.

"My friend Eli wrote, in his wonderful book, that autodidacticism is a gift, from ourselves, to ourselves, but also a response to the vacuum where an institutional education is supposed to be. In his case, there was no institutional education. In mine, a completely inadequate one, because there was such a powerful orthodoxy at work in my school." Unlike Eli, he told them, he'd had an upbringing of privilege, with a front-loaded expectation that he'd graduate from high school, attend college, and likely earn a graduate degree. Yet even in his premier institution, with its low admission rate and absurd tuition, with its credentialed teachers and penchant for the seminar table and "politically alert" student body, he'd still reached the hard conclusion that he'd have to educate himself. And because, at Walden, there had been no celebration of disagreement, educating himself had meant learning both sides of every argument. That, it turned out, had been a very useful thing.

The watermelon story had begun as a senior prank, a few days before his own graduation. Senior prank was a Walden tradition, in which graduating students would arrive early to string toilet paper through the trees on either side of the school's front door, or paint the elegant iron bars pink with poster paint. One year a pet ferret had been loosed in the Commons, and Harrison remembered a vat of viscous red slime strategically hidden inside the faculty lounge. The plan, when his own class was about to graduate, was for each senior to bring in a watermelon, delivering the fruit to a hallway outside the art room where the rinds would be coated with oil. From there the watermelons would be distributed around the campus and left to be discovered (and hopefully lifted!) by persons unknown, leaving cracked-open explosions of red flesh and seeds everywhere in an obvious expression of senior pride!

What could go wrong?

Teenagers, tearing toward the end of school, have a lot on their minds, which possibly explained the fact that only four seniors remembered their watermelons. (Another possible reason, which Harrison did not add, was that they had already received their college acceptances, and were stoned out of their wits.) When the pair of students in charge saw how few watermelons they had to work with, they made an executive decision to consolidate them, placing all four in the office of their class dean.

Who happened, Harrison informed the members of the Hayek Institute, to be Black.

Crisis and horror. Devastation and dismay. Before an hour had passed, Walden's principal had emailed the community, canceled classes, and set out the microphones for a public (and attendance *mandatory!*) all-school rending of garments. That Walden students, so relentlessly schooled in the narratives of oppression, had committed an act of such thoughtless, callous denigration! How was it possible? What could it mean? All of that consciousness-raising, all of that decency, and yes, all of that tuition, and they had still ended up wielding a particularly vicious racist trope to make fun at a Black teacher's expense. Was there not one Walden senior well enough informed to have intervened and prevented this?

In fact, there was one Walden senior. A *single* Walden senior. Harrison explained to the members of the Hayek Institute that having effectively wrested his own intellectual life from the exclusive dominion of the Walden School, and having read widely from an index of forbidden texts, and having thought deeply outside the bubble of sanctioned ideologies, he himself was fully cognizant of the powerful symbol that was . . . the watermelon, and would have been more than capable of communicating what a bad, bad idea this was to that pair of pranksters, if they had happened to ask him. Harrison had read Goldwater's *The Conscience of a Conservative* and Buckley's *God and Man at Yale*. He'd read Thomas Carlyle's 1849 "Occasional Discourse on the Negro Question" and John Stuart Mill's thunderous reply, "The Negro Question." He had even read *The Turner Diaries* after the Oklahoma City bombing, just to discover what puerile fantasy had addled the brain of that moron, Timothy McVeigh, and he had found it absurd, laughably manipulative and, incidentally, appallingly written, but also, in its way, illuminating. (None of these books, of course, had been in the collection of the Walden library—which, by way of contrast, had no fewer than three copies of *Heather Has Two Mommies* in the K-5 section. He'd had to purchase them, in the case of the Goldwater and the Buckley. For *The Turner Diaries*, he'd had to fill out an interlibrary loan request at the Brooklyn Public Library, under the baleful and plainly suspicious eye of a librarian.)

It was in the notorious Carlyle essay, also a work that could never have been assigned in a Walden class, that Harrison first encountered the stereotype of the lazy, shirking, watermelon-sated "Black persons," whose liberation or continued enslavement was—at the time of its writing—under debate in the parliaments and parlors of the United Kingdom. Talk about offensive!

> *Sitting yonder, with their beautiful muzzles up to the ears in pumpkins, imbibing sweet pulps and juices; the grinder and incisor teeth ready for every new work, and the pumpkins cheap as grass in those rich climates; while the sugar crops rot round them . . .*

After this noxious debut, the "pumpkin"—sometimes "punkin," and ultimately recast as *Citrullus lanatus,* or common watermelon—would spend the ensuing century and a half infiltrating folklore, art, story, song, film, and, notably, advertising as a food powerfully suggestive of uncleanness, laziness, and ignorance. Harrison was no expert, of course, but this was kind of a *duh* when it came to your nastier breed of symbolism, something on the order of painting your white face black or using a certain word that began with *N. No,* he might have told his former classmates, *it was not very smart, and would also not be at all funny, to leave greased watermelons in the office of their Black class dean, a humorless man at the best of times.*

How profoundly had you failed your students when institutional myopia prevented them from learning things that might actually *support* their already indoctrinated opinions?

Profoundly.

And that was just not all right with him. He had too much to learn to waste time coloring inside the lines, and he fully believed that—demented losers like McVeigh aside—people with different ideas from one's own were not the enemy; they were simply people with different ideas. Hearing them out carried, he supposed, some small potential for having one's mind changed, but it was far more likely to strengthen the opinion you already had, so why all the fear? The point, he informed his Hayek audience, was and had always been to *learn,* and then to form an *opinion,* which should not have been considered so very radical, and should not have required such personal tenacity on his own part, but it was and it did, and it had been worth it, because learning things was the whole point of being alive.

He himself had not—full disclosure!—"forgotten" to bring in his fruit that morning. He had made a very conscious decision to ignore the instruction, and to remain at home to prepare for an oral exam in his French class (pointless in itself, as Walden would give him the identical "Pass" grade whether his work was just good enough or outright spectacular). By the time he'd arrived at school later that morning the test, along with every other Walden activity, academic and nonacademic, had been suspended for the all-school gathering, and there Walden was decried from every corner as irreparably racist, sexist, and homophobic. One by one, students rose and approached the microphone with fresh new stories of cultural insensitivity that they themselves had suffered. A Black sophomore, six feet tall, had been invited to try out for the basketball team: she'd been stereotyped! A Korean American boy was always sought out to help other students with calculus: he'd also been stereotyped! A girl with very large breasts had to put up with the staring of classmates, male and female, whenever she chose not to wear a bra: that was triggering! A certain teacher continued to use the phrase "ladies and gentlemen" in her classroom, and for one young person who said they weren't either, this environment was so hostile, and caused so much distress! Was this a class at the supposedly most progressive school in the city or a seminar at Liberty University, taught by Jerry Falwell himself?

Naturally, lunch was canceled that day, and as the afternoon wore on, Harrison had begun to eye those watermelons (which had been carried—carefully!—into the Commons to serve as a backdrop for all this guilty prostration) with sincere hunger. He had always liked watermelon. He still liked watermelon.

Of course the shameful tale would spread, and not just through the Walden community but out into the broader circles of private-school New York, including some highly critical media accounts ("Walden School Roiled by Racist Student Attack"; "42K Tuition School's Toxic Atmosphere for Black Students and Faculty"). But there was one piece of information that never, somehow, emerged.

That pair of students, the ones who'd decided to bring the watermelons to their class dean's office, for maximum impact? Were also Black. One was Harvard-bound, intending to study neurobiology. The other was a powerful young woman heading to Spellman, who'd chaired the school's Black Student Caucus for the past two years and had landed an internship with Eleanor Holmes Norton that summer. She was also the daughter of a prominent Black novelist who'd won the Pulitzer Prize.

Clueless. Both of them.

"What I couldn't get over," Harrison told his audience in summation, "was the failure of it all. On one hand, we'd spent years not really learning because our school couldn't risk exposing us to anything but the prescribed material. Like, it used to be if you were studying the Holocaust you'd get assigned *Mein Kampf* to read—I mean, primary source! But if a teacher at my school tried to include that in the curriculum he'd be tarred and feathered. So what we end up with is exhaustive detail about terrible things that happened to the victims, but no idea of *why* any of it happened, because you wouldn't want to expose a sensitive, empathic young person to the unfiltered ideas of a person who actually *is* racist, sexist, or homophobic. Because apparently we just can't trust a reasonable teenager to be appalled by . . . I mean, we're talking about *Adolf Hitler* here! And not only that, but we have to be these wounded birds, too. *I'm offended! I'm insulted! I'm triggered!* Because what we learn about the world is that it's racist and anti-Semitic and anti-gay and culturally insensitive, but all we can seem to do about it is go into a fetal position. How are we supposed to get up on our feet and actually accomplish anything? It's absurd!"

Harrison paused. He had become aware of the fact that he was losing, ever so slightly, his own thread. The shake in his voice, he didn't like that, either.

"Well," he steadied himself. At some point in the story, he had taken hold of the podium and was gripping it so tightly his fingers actually hurt. "Well. That's what I wanted to say. I'm not claiming racism and all the other isms haven't always been a part of life, just that I don't feel I need to apologize for something that was done in the past, by somebody else. I didn't slaughter any Native Americans. I'm not burning any witches or lynching somebody because I don't like the way they looked at my wife. I honestly don't care if you're a lady or a gentleman or a Vulcan or a Hobbit, and to be completely honest, I also don't care what bathroom you use. I just kind of wish you'd shut up about it."

From the front row, Roger Fount was barely suppressing his laughter. A few others were laughing as well, Harrison saw.

"I'm sorry," he said. "I guess . . . I guess I should stop."

Fount rose to his feet and stepped forward.

The others were clapping, all of them, Harrison realized. He felt very warm, and kind of high. Somebody brought him a drink. Somebody's arm landed across his shoulder.

"That school of yours," said Vernon Loring, who was suddenly beside him and shaking his head. "It's a bit of a miracle you made it out."

"But he did," Roger Fount laughed, taking Harrison's hand in his own doughy hand. "And here he is. Which is all that matters."

Chapter Twenty-Two

Deus ex Machina

In which Lewyn Oppenheimer gets lost in the Sacred Grove, and acquires a new secret

Lewyn had an array of fine reasons for remaining in Ithaca that summer, but the greatest of these was the room at the end of a corridor in Jameson Hall where Rochelle had moved, shortly before the summer program teenagers arrived. Reluctance to see his family, of course, ran a very close second. Sometime that spring, Johanna had mentioned that Harrison was going to be in Virginia for part of the summer, and Lewyn had no idea what Sally's plans might be, but he certainly hoped they involved her leaving town. Neither of his parents had been especially vocal about having him home over the summer, either in Brooklyn or on the Vineyard, but his presence at the cottage, for the ritual observance of the birthday in early September, was nonnegotiable: the Oppenheimer triplets would gather and they would observe and they would, in all probability, be photographed together, and there was no possible way out of any of that.

Except for one year, when there'd been a hurricane and the planes wouldn't fly, this great event had taken place at our Martha's Vineyard home, with some kind of a catered meal on the beach and a big cake, and at some point of the day or evening our mother would provide a ritual, teary retelling of the whole epic, arduous progeny-making ordeal. So when Lewyn called home in early June to say he'd be staying in Ithaca for the summer, his mother went directly and predictably to the matter of the birthday, and once he'd assured her, she seemed incurious about the rest. He had been ready with a description of the important summer class he'd registered for in his now-likely art history major, but she didn't ask. Also she didn't ask where he'd be living, which really would have necessitated a lie or at least an evasion. He noticed these things. He was not especially sensitive when it came to members of his immediate family, and what they might be going through in their own lives, but even Lewyn was forced to note the current in his mother's voice, so dissonant and so discomforting and so unpleasant to hear that he instinctively closed his mind to it and what it might mean.

Really, the only thing of any importance he was "doing" that summer was being with Rochelle Steiner, because the world had divided into a small circle of time and space within which the two of them abided, outside of which was, simply, everyone and everything else. He did not care about people who were not Rochelle Steiner, and he resented the notion that he should try. Why should he try? For the first time in his entire life he was truly *with* another person, and this was so cataclysmic, so all-encompassing, that the least the outer world could do was stop reminding him it was there.

All Lewyn wanted was to be with Rochelle, to curl his length around her small body in the single beds they had pushed together at the end of that corridor in Jameson Hall, and learn the topography of her skin, and read silently with her, and bring her her favored chai lattes each morning and afternoon, and generally express his love for her in any and every way she would permit. It was Rochelle who let him know that her roommate was also in Ithaca for the summer; she had run into Sally at the Hot Truck one night in early June when Lewyn was mercifully elsewhere, and the two of them chatted as they waited for their pizza subs, or at least "chatted" was the word Rochelle had used. Sally was apparently living off campus, in some house with—Rochelle wasn't sure she'd understood this correctly—a woman who bought and sold furniture. Lewyn listened, concentrating on his own expression, and wondering if his thudding heart was audible to anyone but himself. It was certainly a disappointment that his sister was still in Ithaca, but at least she was no longer right next door, and also the Cornell campus was vast, and the town around it also vast and sort of amoebic in shape, coiling around its baffling congregation of rivers and gorges, which was a gift to people hoping to avoid certain other people. (He'd been here nearly a year already, and half the time he'd had no idea where he was in relation to anywhere else, or in which direction he was walking. The other half he did have some idea, but was often wrong.) And also—ever since Rochelle had told him that thing she had told him, he had taken a measure of weird comfort in the fact that she, too, had been working to keep Sally and Lewyn Oppenheimer apart. Theirs was a mutual project, in other words, undertaken separately, in mutual ignorance, and for very different reasons, but still it comforted him. Somehow, they had been in it together, and perhaps their combined will had averted the crossing of paths they both, apparently, dreaded.

Even so, Lewyn couldn't help feeling a certain unease about Sally, herself: aimless in Ithaca, done with the dorms, living with a woman who bought and sold furniture? What did this mean for the remainder of Sally's Cornell career, let alone for the life his sister would live after college? It had never been difficult to imagine Harrison in the world. Harrison would find some corral of smarmy, clever types, in international finance or business consulting, where he and they could convene to be superior to everyone else, but Sally . . . Sally he could not imagine with select comrades. Let alone a partner. What Rochelle had said, a few weeks earlier, in the room she and his sister had shared . . . well, to be honest it had shocked him, but afterward he'd begun to wonder if this might not explain certain other things about his sister: her secrecy, her compulsion to withdraw. And also he could not fault Sally for falling in love with Rochelle. He, obviously, had fallen in love with Rochelle. It seemed to him that any sane person would.

Those summer weeks were as near to bliss as any he had ever spent. Rochelle had somewhere procured an old Handybreeze electric fan for the room in Jameson Hall, ponderous to lift but, once switched on, deliciously effective. (The dorms were not air-conditioned, something she was at pains to explain, again and again, to the mystified youngsters in the pre-college program, most of them from families of means, away from home for the first time, and unable to comprehend why the temperature in their rooms should not be magically comfortable.) The two of them lay on their pushed-together beds with the windows open and the shrill air pulsating above them, and the din the fan made effectively obscured their own noises from the ears of others.

He'd enrolled in an art history course when the summer term began. It was on Flemish painting, and those gray, flat lowland skies and pasty, pock-marked faces made a kind of invigorating inversion of his own happiness. He loved them for that, but then again, he loved everything then; there was simply no bringing him down, not on days he woke to the peculiar position of Rochelle in sleep (hands palm to palm and wedged between her bent knees) and spent the rest of the hours parting from and reuniting with her around classes, study, mentoring (hers), and his own hours in the art history collection, only to end with those hands, once again palm to palm, once again between her angular knees, as she curled away from him and the fan blew over their warm bodies, drowning out the rest of the world. It took Lewyn no time at all to persuade himself that this could be his life in perpetuity, a nonterminating and thoroughly normal existence for the two of them, as if "normal" might feature the conveniences and ease of a college campus in summer, with low-stakes classes in a subject he now felt a genuine interest in and this wondrous girl who, miraculously, inexplicably, returned not only his affection but his desire. He was fine and he was normal and he was in love with Rochelle Steiner.

One night, the two of them came out of Moosewood (feeling virtuous but also still hungry) to find Jonas and Mark in one of the outdoor cafés on Cayuga. They had half-eaten hamburgers on their plates. Lewyn fought a powerful urge to grab one and stuff it in his own mouth.

"Thought you were gone," he said to his now-former roommate. "Doing that pageant."

Rochelle's laugh sounded slightly like a bark. "What does that mean?"

"I am," said Jonas. "We had a night off rehearsal. Decided to drive back for a real meal. There's not much in Palmyra."

"Not a beauty pageant," said Lewyn. He and Rochelle were holding hands.

"Still planning on coming?" said Jonas. "Mark's driving up next weekend."

"We haven't discussed it yet," he said to Rochelle, echoing a phrase he'd heard one of his parents say to the other too many times to count. It made him feel strong and partnered, saying it.

"Discussed *what*?" Rochelle said, with a definite edge to her voice.

"Uh-oh," said Mark, with obvious delight.

"I get to play a Lamanite, which is a lot more fun than playing a Nephite, though my mom wasn't happy. She was holding out hope I'd get cast as Nephi or Joseph Smith himself. I'm like, Mom, I get that you think I'm the greatest thing since sliced bread and I love you for it, but I'm having a blast. We do these warlike grimaces and gestures, because we're actually so far from where the audience is sitting that everything has to be kind of exaggerated. But the best part is we're doing it on the actual hill where Joseph Smith found the golden plates. The ultimate site-specific."

Rochelle was looking up at Lewyn. Her eyes said paragraphs.

"C'mon, Rochelle. You're a student of religion. You'll get a kick out of it."

"I'm not a student of religion," she said. "I'm going to be a lawyer."

"I mean, you respect the traditions. We're the fastest-growing religion in the world, did you know that? Plus, we're super fun," he grinned. "Plus, we crashed your party. You should crash ours."

"You were invited," Rochelle said. "And we were glad to have you."

"And *you* are invited," said Jonas heartily. "And we'll be glad to have *you*. We're even glad to have the hecklers."

"What hecklers?" Mark said.

"Oh, they yell about how we're apostates and we're not Christians and blah blah. We get it. Oppression is nothing new for members of our church, you know. We've had it constantly, literally since the church was founded."

Rochelle, again, gave Lewyn a look of the most exquisite disgust. She might not know this particular history of religious persecution, but she knew how to compare an elephant to a gnat. "I see," she said. "Yes, nearly two centuries of oppression."

"Take a chance, Rochelle!" said Jonas. "Give it a try. Besides, Lewyn wants to come."

She turned her sharp little face up to him.

"And Mark can drive you out with him. Right, Mark?"

"Happy to," said Mark. "Happy for the company."

Lewyn could imagine how much less compelling Mark's company would render the prospect for Rochelle, but Jonas was right: he sort of did want to go. He wanted to see Palmyra, and the hill where Joseph Smith dug up the golden plates, and maybe that Sacred Grove where angels had supposedly appeared. It would be up to him to persuade Rochelle, and he didn't want to go to a religious pageant without her. He didn't want to go anywhere without her.

It wasn't straightforward at all. Back in their room that night, Rochelle subjected him to a vigorous interrogation.

Why did he want to go? Golden plates? Talking angels? Jesus astral-visiting America for three days while his physical body lay in an Israeli tomb? And the politics of these people! What about that?

They were interrupted then by a sad girl from Lake Forest whose roommate was apparently spreading malicious untruths about her all up and down the corridor. *And she had never been anything but nice!* Also, the roommate was too lazy to go to the bathroom and insisted on putting her used maxi pads in the wastebasket! And was there no empty room on this massive campus where she could spend the remaining five and a half weeks away from this evil and repulsive person, whom she furthermore suspected of stealing her pink Reeboks?

When Rochelle returned, he took the opportunity to observe that pink Reeboks should be stolen as a matter of principle, but she was not in the mood. On the other hand, she was too depleted to continue arguing against their trip.

They left four days later in Mark's Toyota, driving north along Cayuga's western edge and then west on the Thruway.

"Remind me why we're going this early?" said Rochelle. "I thought it doesn't start till the sun goes down."

"Well, there's a Sacred Grove somewhere," said Lewyn.

"A what?" Rochelle turned in the front seat to look back at him.

"Where Joseph Smith saw God and Jesus."

"Well, look at you," said Rochelle, not kindly.

The little road to the Smith Farm was crowded with SUVs and RVs, most of them bearing license plates from points far west. Not surprisingly, when they reached it, the parking lot was jammed. Inside the visitor center, the three of them were ushered into a room where a sturdy missionary with an Australian accent related the story that was likely already known to everyone in the room: the Smith family had come to Palmyra after earlier struggles in Vermont, and when young Joseph prayed about which church congregation was truest to God's word, an angel led him from his bedroom to the woods, and there God himself, and Jesus, had delivered the answer—none of them.

"And so, before you exit to the farm, and before you enter the Sacred Grove, I want to testify that like Joseph I once struggled to understand what God wanted from me, and so I did pray with an open heart and real intent, and my Heavenly Father spoke to me, just as I was promised. I know that the Gospel is true and I am loved by my Heavenly Father. I welcome you all to this glorious and holy place. Now, does anyone with a mobility issue need the golf cart?"

Lewyn got up. Outside, the light had become something mottled and a bit strange, as if rain clouds were gathering and dispersing at the same time. "Are you coming?" he asked Mark and Rochelle, who had remained seated.

"To be honest," said Mark, "I'm thinking not. I'm not feeling good about this. I can't really explain it. I mean, not in a way you'd understand."

Lewyn frowned. "Rochelle?"

She shook her head.

"Okay," Lewyn said. "I mean, I would like to see that Sacred Grove. Since we're here."

So Lewyn left them together, an odd couple united by their very different aversions, and he walked with the other pilgrims down past the Smith family's home, and into the woods. He felt the first drop of rain and turned up his face to an unaccountably glowing sky. It was not unpleasant, though the family in front of him instantly produced umbrellas. Everyone, apart from himself, was in a group or holding hands with somebody else. It was deep green, and it all got quiet once they entered the trees.

In the woods, to his confusion, he saw no signs or guideposts pointing the way. People dispersed along a web of paths, as if they knew where to go, which frustrated Lewyn more and more with each turn he took. Surely these faithful had some piece of information not available to him, and all were congregating at the Sacred Grove, the corner of this forest where their mystery had taken place, while he himself meandered. He walked for a good while, occasionally passing others, sometimes hearing the sounds of people on other pathways through the woods, as the rain gently came and then halted. He wasn't warm and he wasn't cold. The ground underfoot was soft. He could have gone on forever if not for the awful feeling that he was still in the wrong place, and everyone else had already arrived, experienced the magical thing, and then departed, and also that Rochelle was waiting for him and growing more disgusted with every passing moment. Finally, he found that he had come around to the lane again, and he could see the farm buildings beyond. A wave of deep disappointment went through him.

On the path not far ahead was an elderly couple, the man drawing a windbreaker hood tighter around his face, the woman waiting under her plastic umbrella. He didn't realize he was going to speak to them until he heard his own voice, embarrassingly reedy.

"Excuse me, I'm trying to find the Sacred Grove."

The woman turned to him. She had thin hair, crossing the border from blond to gray. The man frowned.

"I'm sorry?"

"The Sacred Grove. I've been walking around but I can't find it."

"But," said the man, "you're in it. This is the Sacred Grove."

Lewyn looked around himself. Something about not seeing the forest for the trees occurred to him, but that wasn't quite right. "Isn't . . . I mean, I thought it was a place in the forest. Like, a particular place."

"Well, there is a particular place," said the man with admirable restraint. "Not many people know the exact location. President Hinckley does, of course, but the church believes that everyone should have a personal experience of the Grove."

"So . . . I can't find it?" Lewyn asked.

"Well, you can't find it if you don't know you're in it," the man said, not unkindly. "Are you a member of our church?" he asked.

"Uh, no. No." It was the first time anyone had actually asked him that, he realized.

Outside the visitor center he found Mark on a bench beside the parking lot looking deeply unhappy. Rochelle was in the car, making use of the air-conditioning.

"I'm sorry I took so long," he said as they walked across the lot. "I kind of got lost."

"I think all these people are lost," said Mark.

At six they drove to the outdoor stage, a massive structure that bore no resemblance to the proscenium stage Lewyn had been imagining. Built into the hill itself, it looked more than anything like a massive gray hamster habitat, with too many levels and surfaces to easily count. Lewyn wondered how they were going to get through the evening, the three of them, when it was clear that he was the only one of them who even wanted to be here. But he did want that, even if he had no idea why, or what was the tug that had been working at him all day, pulling him along like the strongest undertow off Chilmark. Rochelle and Mark, with nothing in common but their profound unhappiness about the afternoon they'd spent together and the evening ahead, would each have leapt wordlessly into Mark's car and gunned the engine for Ithaca and their utterly different lives there, if only it weren't for himself and his unfathomable wish to go further in. It was something he would still be thinking about, years later. It was something he would uncoil his path back to, always stopping short of understanding.

They had to walk past a corral of protesters shouting that Joseph Smith was an apostate and Mormons weren't Christians. "Shame on you for attending this unholy event," said a woman to Rochelle, who grabbed Lewyn's hand. "You're going to burn in hell, you know."

"Oh I know," Rochelle said tersely. "But not for this."

"Freedom of speech at its finest," said Lewyn, trying for lightheartedness.

"WhatMormonsDontTell.com," Rochelle read from the group's signs. "What don't Mormons tell? Something to do with history or science?"

"Something to do with Satan," said Mark.

The field was teeming with people dressed as if they'd walked straight out of a swords-and-sandals epic but without having shed their American health, corporeal padding, and straight white teeth. Everywhere Lewyn looked he saw blond and blue-eyed shepherds, double-chinned warriors with leather-like breastplates and what looked like cut-up rugs on their shoulders, giddy kids straight from the mall or the soccer field, dressed as child soldiers and desert maidens. There was a tall man in a vaguely Aztec getup featuring a green dotted skirt with a fringe of beads, a fake black beard, and a towering headdress that might have looked over-the-top on Carmen Miranda. He held the hand of a small child in a dust-colored shift and a green headband, absently sucking on a juice box, and chatted with a guy around Lewyn's own age who was obviously meant to be Joseph Smith. People kept coming up to "Joseph Smith" and posing with him for pictures.

"I see him," said Mark. "Over there, in front of the stage."

Jonas was with a large group of goatherds or nomads, some with oversized faux beards, most with scarves wrapped around their waists and heads and heavy beaded necklaces, as if the whole group had been routed through a Moroccan bazaar and not allowed out until they had piled on the inventory.

"This is my cast team," Jonas explained, when they reached him. "We're all in the Prophet Lehi story and later the Prophet Abinadi."

Rochelle, Lewyn could see, was struggling to process this information.

"It's quite a production," she said, truthfully enough.

"It is! It is! Hey Susie!" he called out to an extremely pretty girl who was walking past with a partner, each of them holding a Book of Mormon and a handful of cards and pens. "It's my friends from school I said were coming."

Susie and her friend stopped and turned. They were both so tall, Rochelle had to peer sharply upward.

"Hi," said Susie. "This is Eliza, my friend from home."

"Where's home?" asked Rochelle.

"Provo, but I'm at BYU. We both are. You go to Cornell with Jonas?"

Rochelle had likely never before thought of herself as someone who "went to Cornell with Jonas," but she nodded.

"Are you studying to be a vet, too?" said Eliza, the friend. She had light-brown freckles all over her nose and cheeks. Her blond hair was woven with beads, now glinting in the light from the retreating sun.

"Uh, no. Lawyer. What about you?"

"Oh, marketing, I think," said Susie. "Are you a member of the church?"

Rochelle shook her head. "I am not. Full-blooded Jewish atheist here."

Eliza's eyes widened. Which was it, Lewyn wondered: the atheist or the Jew?

"Cool," said Susie. She looked as if she were trying very hard. He felt a pang of sympathy for her.

"Maybe, if you have questions after the pageant, we can talk about them."

Rochelle looked briefly at Jonas. She was wondering, Lewyn knew, how she had come to merit this special honor.

"That's kind," she said, after a moment. "I must say, everybody's so colorful. What are you supposed to be?"

"We're all Lamanites," said Jonas. He leaned forward and said, conspiratorially: "We're the bad guys."

"Well, sometimes the Nephites went wrong, too," Susie said, very seriously. "I mean, everyone wanders from the righteous, I think that's the point. What are you two studying?" she asked Lewyn and Mark.

Mark, it turned out, was going into finance. It had never come up in conversation. Lewyn said he was thinking about majoring in art, which sounded downright strange when said aloud.

"Like, painting?"

"Uh, no. I don't paint. Other people's paintings."

"Did you see the painting of Moroni in the Welcome Center?" Susie asked. "It makes you feel, like, the pain and the loneliness of being the last one of his whole line, and the faith that one day Heavenly Father would bring the right person to dig the plates up. Right there," she said, turning to the great gray stage behind her.

Lewyn didn't know what to say, though he was already sure he knew the painting she meant. He had seen it at the Smith farm.

"I love that one," Eliza said. "And the one of the angel next to Joseph Smith's bed, and the one of Joseph in the Sacred Grove. They were in all the books, and the sacrament meeting presentations. It's a beautiful thing that Heavenly Father uses his gift of art to sustain our faith."

Lewyn was about to say that this wasn't the purpose of art, but the exact truth of that notion had just then struck him for the very first time: For centuries, for millennia, hadn't this been precisely the "purpose" of art? "I must go back and have a look at those pictures," he heard himself say.

The three of them found seats far back on the right. Again and again, cast members and missionaries approached, always with the same general script—*Where you folks from? Is it your first time here?*—till Rochelle started heading them off at the first intake of breath: *Ithaca. Our first time, yes. Yes, we are looking forward to it. Nice to meet you.* Did they have any questions? Would they like to fill out a card because missionaries could come visit them at home to talk about some of the messages in the pageant. Rochelle declined for all three of them, as Mark remained brutally silent. They seemed to have found an unspoken mutuality, and a determination to keep these eager, insanely dressed people moving on to the next mark in the next seat. When it was finally dark, a tall missionary with a buzz cut led an invocation—Mark, on Lewyn's left, bowed his head and Rochelle, on his right, did not—and then swarms of actors raced for the stage, coiling up hidden stairs or ramps onto the many levels, filling the hillside with hundreds of now tiny bodies, a vast needlepoint of color.

The people on the stage were so far away from even the nearest audience members that they could not possibly "act" as Lewyn had always understood "acting"; instead, they gestured in great, exaggerated movements as the recorded dialogue, music, and narration washed over the field from massive overhead speakers. He tried to follow what was happening, but it kept jumping around from ancient Jerusalem long before Christ to someone's vision of a future crucifixion. A ship was assembled onstage to take a righteous prophet and his sons to a new world, but once the first protagonists disappeared there were new characters with unfamiliar names, and generations of Lamanites (who were mainly bad) continued to fight generations of Nephites (who were mainly but not always good). Volcanos exploded and violent storms sprayed water all over the stage, and each new prophet called for the wayward to repent and remember the promise of Christ.

Then, suddenly, there he was: the savior himself! He was dangling from a slender cable high above the enormous stage, lit in brightest light with only a bit of the moon, dull behind clouds, in competition for the eye, and the rest of the world of the play and the rest of the real world suddenly still.

Christ stayed with the Nephites (or Lamanites, Lewyn wasn't sure) for three days, then left to return to the story he already knew: the tomb in Jerusalem with its stone rolled aside. Then, the end of the pageant became a metanarrative about the golden plates: containing this very story, buried right here on the crest of the Hill Cumorah. The music soared and the voices of the Mormon Tabernacle Choir rolled over the audience as that same Joseph Smith Lewyn had seen hours earlier, talking to a pretty girl in a BYU Rugby shirt, became a tiny action figure up there on the stage. Behind him, the first faithful took their places, radiant with belief.

Rochelle, on his right, was rolling and unrolling her program between her hands. Mark's eyes were shut in furious prayer. Then Lewyn looked past them down the long row of people: all glowing, many in tears, reaching for one another. Everywhere around him families embraced, scrums of bodies pressed together in celebration, and he was mystified. When, in our own family, had we ever held one another this way? When had any one of us, apart from our mother, reached out with love, and when had any of the rest of us not pulled back? The faintest hint of affection, the palest expression of warmth, was enough to make each Oppenheimer triplet recoil; this

Lewyn understood, with deep sadness, for the very first time in his life, as the waves of applause and the shining faces and the powerful evidence of roiling human love surged all around him. Was it God, after all? Not one of his own relatives believed that the God of Abraham and Sarah and Moses knew them personally or took any special interest in their welfare, or imagined they would someday enter a Jewish paradise and embrace as a family, for all eternity. *Embrace? As a family? For all eternity?* How had we been made so differently from these people? Lewyn wondered, with dismay. Were we even capable of feeling what they felt? These thousands, weeping and cheering and swaying in their unfathomable ecstasy, had crossed some great divide from the place he was and had always been to some other place where people were at peace with one another and themselves, and at that moment, and for many years to come, he would have done nearly anything to be there with them.

Chapter Twenty-Three

Summer Lovers

In which Sally Oppenheimer discovers her brother's snakeliness, and contemplates the entire baffling mosh pit of adult life

Sally was at the kitchen table on East Seneca with half a glass of lemonade in front of her and our mother on the phone. The house, empty on a late Friday afternoon in July because Harriet had gone up to Rochester to see a friend, was very still, though overhead a desultory fan circled, moving the warm air around. She was drumming her fingers on the tabletop, the now-worthless "brown furniture" table once given pride of place in the Greene dining room. It had recently been treated with some homemade wood paste of Harriet's, and was glowing. Over the past couple of months, Sally had acquainted herself with every piece of furniture in the house (covered *and* uncovered) by means of this special concoction. It wasn't about banishing dirt, either; it was about resurrection.

"I told you I had an internship," Sally said when Johanna stopped talking. Our mother was on an island off the coast of Massachusetts, and she wanted to know why Sally wasn't there, too.

"That was months ago. If you're that interested in antiques, I'm sure we could have found you something in Edgartown. Are you?"

"What?" Sally asked. She wasn't *not* listening. But she wasn't completely listening, either.

"Interested in antiques."

"My tastes are developing," Sally said. "I mean, I'm being educated. It's what happens here in college."

"You're studying . . . furniture?"

"No, of course not. I'm just interested. I still haven't decided on a major. Has Lewyn?" she asked, hoping to change the subject.

"Oh, Lewyn. He said something about art back in the spring."

"Art? Like, painting?"

"No, art history. You know, Daddy and I have never pushed you to pick something practical. We want you to follow what gives you joy."

Sally rolled her eyes. Joy had been one of our mother's great themes. So very ironic, given Johanna's noted dearth of it.

"Well, I'm sure the boys appreciate that just as much as I do," she said.

"Have you talked to them?"

Sally rolled her eyes. She hoped Lewyn was getting this same question from our mother, at least. Or did the responsibility attach only to her, possibly because she was *the girl*?

"I don't want to speak for the boys, but maybe we're, all three of us, kind of feeling out the being apart from one another. You know?"

"No, I do not know. We've always been a very close family."

On what planet? Sally nearly said, but she stopped herself. They had all failed Johanna, all three of them.

"But it's something we're each going to have to do, don't you think? Find our own way? I'm not surprised if the boys aren't talking much, or that neither of them is keeping in close touch with me."

From far down the line, she caught the faintest gasp, then another.

"Mom?"

"I took Phoebe on the carousel in Oak Bluffs," Johanna said. "She was absolutely entranced by her horse. But she never even looked up! You were like that, too, remember? Your brothers were throwing themselves at those stupid rings."

"Lewyn actually fell off his horse once," Sally said, relieved.

"We'll all go back when you get here."

Sally closed her eyes. She could not get out of going to the Vineyard, but she wanted to spend as little time there as possible. Arriving on the birthday itself was too obvious, and certainly too cruel. She would have to get there a day before, if not a couple of days. At least, with more than month to go, she still had time to . . . what? Prepare herself? Figure out the answers to our parents' inevitable interrogations? She couldn't even answer the questions *about* the questions. Harrison, Johanna had told her, was in Virginia, or West Virginia, on some kind of retreat for rich assholes: a perfectly on-brand summer activity. Even Lewyn, with an actual intended major, sounded marginally less directionless than before. All Sally herself seemed to want to do right now was think about furniture. The actual birthday, that year, fell on a Monday, which wasn't ideal but at least it came before the beginning of classes. She told Johanna it was a pity she could not stay longer, but it was all she could spare from her busy, busy new life.

Then she said good-bye and went back to her room on the third floor.

The invitation to move into the East Seneca house had surprised her, though it was also clear to Sally that her new friend required basic help at home. Back in the spring, Harriet had asked Sally to take a look through the bedrooms on the third floor because she was certain there was a corner cupboard up there that a dealer she knew in Deposit had once sold her. Now, apparently, he wanted to buy it back for a New York client in search of that very size, shape, and untouched blue surface. The third-floor staircase was far too steep for Harriet to easily climb, so Sally ascended alone to find four rooms of generous size, each one jammed with heart-stopping objects. Wooden trunks were stacked to the sloping ceilings, and beds on their sides had been slotted under and over other beds. In the dust-filled light she caught the edges of wood everywhere: dark wood, painted wood, stenciled wood. Against the walls, gilt frames leaned against other gilt frames, some empty, some occupied by cracked and dirty canvases.

"D'you see it?" Harriet shouted from the second-floor landing.

"I see a lot of things," Sally called back truthfully. Then she had to say it again, even louder.

"Big tall piece, maybe eight feet!"

It wasn't in the first room, or the second (which was weirdly occupied by a line of back-to-back cupboards), or the third (piles of hooked rugs and old blue coverlets), but it was impossible to miss in the fourth. Stately in the corner between the room's two windows, it had been given an actual cleared space in which to reside. It was a lovely object, tall and triangular with a steel-blue surface and a hand-carved knob. She couldn't imagine how Harriet had gotten this up here to begin with. Or how they would begin to get it down.

"Those are nice rooms up there," Harriet had said when she descended a few minutes later. "There's a bathroom, too."

"I saw," said Sally.

"If you wanted to make some space you could move into one. Nicer than that dorm, probably."

Sally thought of Rochelle Steiner, her randomly assigned roommate. Months before, the two of them had spoken about rooming together again, perhaps in one of the Collegetown dormitories for upperclassmen, but then had come Sally's aborted visit to Ellesmere over the spring break and somehow an unacknowledged cloud had begun to obscure their time together. Rochelle, while never anything but cheerful and solicitous, was in the room less and less, and had less and less to say, let alone inquire about, on evenings she was present. When asked about her state of mind (and Sally *had* asked, though not without trepidation), Rochelle had only said that she was worried about her Bill of Rights seminar grade, and how it could impact her choice of upper-level classes for sophomore year. The class was demanding, and she had to study with a few of her classmates on an almost nightly basis if she was going to get an A, which she needed to get into the Functions and Limits of Law seminar next fall, which was completely necessary because that professor would be overseeing selection for the junior year program at the London School of Economics. Rochelle had her heart set on the LSE program. She had never been out of the United States.

Sometimes, when Rochelle went to bed before her, Sally had watched her roommate sleep. She had a peculiar position she always found her way to, no matter what position she started in: hands together and wedged between her knees, as if she needed to fold and lock herself in place to stay asleep until morning. There she breathed, her eyes jittering beneath their lids as Sally looked and thought.

Then it was over. Rochelle announced that she'd be mentoring or advising or something during the summer high school program, and when the subject of continuing as roommates was raised (by Sally, obviously), Rochelle had asked her advice about going to a single in one of the Collegetown dorms or maybe in one of the cooperative houses, where a woman she knew from Hillel apparently lived. "I don't know," she'd said to Sally, who was struggling to keep control over her face. "I don't know if I'm the 'cooperative' type. I'm not that great at reaching consensus, I don't think."

"You and I reached consensus," said Sally feebly.

"Well, that wasn't hard. It was a pleasure living with you, Sally."

That—the finality of that—had been a very terrible blow.

"What have you decided?" Rochelle asked then.

Sally, of course, had not decided anything. Sally had thought the two of them would be continuing their quiet tunnel through the university. Now, not having taken the precaution of making any other friends, she was suddenly alone and without prospects.

By then, Sally had been going to visit Harriet Greene for months, working her way through the furniture, piece by piece. There was so much of everything that Sally couldn't help beginning to understand what was indifferent, good, and better than good, which wasn't always a matter of value, though value was important to Harriet. To extract a fine object from a barn full of rusting cars or a basement of criminal dampness was to do good in the world. Harriet believed that. Sally came to believe it, too.

"Can I come with you?" she'd asked that very first day over the orange donuts, and she asked it every time Harriet disappeared to Elmira or Watertown on a picking trip. Somebody just north of Albany wanted her to look at a table he said was Shaker. (*Yeah right,* Harriet told Sally, but you had to go, for the slightest chance of something Shaker.) The brother-in-law of a woman she'd bought a cupboard from back in '92 had a set of chairs he thought might be old, though two (he admitted) were in pieces. She wanted to go back to a farm near Alfred where an old man had once turned her away, threatening to call the cops on her for trespassing, but not before she'd managed to spot a tantalizing green paint surface in the parlor behind him. Maybe the guy was dead by now, or incapacitated. Maybe he'd be more open to the notion of trading an unadmired sideboard for cash, or maybe he'd have a kid or a caregiver who would. Maybe a lot of things. But Harriet had a large and silent employee named Drew who drove for her and did the loading, and there wasn't really room in the front of the pickup. And besides, "You got your schoolwork," Harriet said, always with obvious mirth, still so entertained that a college girl, a city girl, would want to spend her days hauling all over the state's various backs of beyond, just for a few old boards of furniture.

So she had stayed in class and done her work and continued to visit 78 East Seneca. She told Rochelle that she'd met an older woman who was a bit of a shut-in and who appreciated the company, and Rochelle said something about how it was a mitzvah and an act of *Tikkun olam* and that was the only time either of them mentioned it.

Those are nice rooms up there, Harriet said.

What have you decided? Rochelle said.

Then, as if to close the circle, she was finally allowed to drive Harriet's car to a place called Horseheads, near Elmira, where a job that was apparently meant to last a few hours now looked likely to stretch to another day. Drew could stay over but Harriet wanted to come home, so Sally was asked if she would take the key to the old Ford from its dedicated nail in the garage and drive down and bring her back, which was not quite the same as being invited to come along on a picking jaunt, but it wasn't being told to stay behind, either. Sally spent a good long while letting the engine wake up and going over all of the knobs and switches. Like her brothers, she had learned to drive in her parents' Volvo on the sandy summer roads of the Vineyard, and she was the proud owner of a barely used Massachusetts driver's license. This machine, at least, didn't have a manual transmission, but it felt primitive. At last she pulled out of the drive and set off along Route 34 with the windows down, self-consciously aware of the privilege this represented, and hoping she wouldn't do anything to screw it up.

She found Drew's silver pickup in front of a barn that listed gently, and the massive Federal farmhouse behind it looked as if it might cave in at the next puff of wind. Beside these, however, a clean and bright-blue mobile home sat sparkling in the afternoon sun, a folksy WELCOME FRIENDS! sign on its front door and a couple of garden art cows faux-grazing in the yard.

"Good," Harriet said simply when she reached the car. Sally was still taking it in.

"There's furniture in the barn?" she asked.

"And the farmhouse, though I'm not real happy about going in there. Feels like it's only the junk holding it up."

"What junk?" said Sally.

"Come see," Harriet said. "And don't breathe."

The front of the house had once been meant to invoke the classical. Now its Grecian columns were cracked and even shattered in spots, and the fanlight window was entirely without its glass. The old door was open, but its swing had been impeded by some object or objects unseen, inside. And a thick carpet, or what looked like a carpet, on the floor.

She stepped cautiously inside. She didn't get far.

The thick carpet was not a carpet at all but an impacted layer of something she couldn't immediately make sense of. It was deep, pliable, and soft, but it contained multitudes of harder objects, some with sharp edges, and individually dense items that looked ominously moist, as well as papers, cans (opened, their lids pried up), cloth, more papers, and scatterings of unopened mailers and boxes that looked weirdly recent.

Also, the smell. It had passed beyond the outright foul to something darkly rich and loamy, but also horrible.

"Like I said," said Harriet, at her elbow, "don't breathe."

"There's an alternative?" said Sally. "What *is* that?"

"That is at least two generations of people losing their way in the world," said Harriet, and Sally, even amid the sensory assault she was undergoing on multiple fronts, had to pause to admire the metaphor. "I stopped by her granddaughter's place in the village this morning. She said, if I wanted to come out here to her grandmother's home it'd be a blessing. House was full. Barn was full. These people don't want to be paid, they just want all this erased."

"But you can't clean it up," said Sally, dumbstruck. Harriet could not be trusted to clean her own house, which compared to this poor specimen was a minimalist and antiseptic dwelling.

"No, but I can help get things sorted out with the county. These structures need to be formally condemned before they can get taken down. It's what these folks want, and they don't have wherewithal to do it themselves. They just want to live in that new house out there, with everything new."

Sally looked over at the shiny mobile home. "You've been inside?" she asked.

"In and out, most of the afternoon. Everything is spic and span in there. This mess is something they don't want to even think about."

Sally shook her head. "So, you're going to be like their social worker?"

"If I have to be," Harriet grinned. "I got an old highboy in the barn that's one of the best I've ever seen. I got three tables at least that my friend in Deposit will want for his shop, and I'm only halfway in. They have no idea what's in there because they don't care about any of it. If I told them something they've got might be worth a fortune, I don't think they'd believe me."

Sally was having trouble breathing. There seemed to be a path of sorts, further into the hallway, but it ended at a staircase that tipped upward and disappeared. She wanted to go there, but she wasn't at all sure she could get there. Another moment and she had to reach for the doorframe to steady herself. "Can you . . ." Sally felt backward. Harriet took her by the wrist and pulled her back out onto the doorstep.

"Uh-oh," she heard Harriet say. "I shouldn't have let you stay in there. We'll need boots and masks when we come back."

Sally was breathing deeply, hands on her knees, concentrating on getting the air in. "Back?" she managed, finally.

"It's a three-day job, minimum. Drew'll keep working as long as there's light, and he'll stay over at the Quality Inn in Horseheads, but this is enough for me. I can come back tomorrow. You can, too, if you like."

Tomorrow was Sunday. Of course she wanted to come back. With boots, this time, and rubber gloves. And her hair in braids, under a bandana.

In the end, she spent nearly a week on the site, missing two meetings of her Writing and Sexual Politics seminar and a precept for her English lit survey, and helping to excavate a veritable catalog of eighteenth- and nineteenth-century American furniture, much of it (not surprisingly) in pieces and all of it in need of TLC in one form or another. But even Sally, by now, could see the many forms of value contained in these things. Bringing a seven-foot-long harvest table into the light, taking a rag to its surface, and showing its pale limbs to the sun for the first time in many decades—that felt like a form of spiritual midwifery. There was an early wing chair some animal (or generations of animals) had nested in, but when Drew cut away the fabric and webbing the skeleton of it was beautiful. Inside a high chest so dark it wasn't immediately clear its surface had been japanned, Harriet showed her the ghost of a signature (Eliphalet Chapin) and a date, 1787.

The woman in the mobile home was named Mary Willit, but she asked them to call her Merry because everyone did. She came out every couple of hours with mugs of coffee, sweetened with some pumpkin-flavored concoction Sally found vile, and something newly baked on a tray, which she left on the hood of the car. At first, Sally had wanted to cover up whatever treasure had just emerged from the barn, worried that the glory and the value must be obvious to anyone, in or out of the profession. Certainly the Chapin chest or the harvest table would give anyone pause, no matter how anxious they were to get the buildings cleared out and possibly even demolished. But no: to Mary/Merry Willit, every single object not already transferred to her sparkling mobile home was ancient junk, and Sally, Drew, and Harriet were angels from the planet Ithaca, come to remove a hundred shades of eyesore from her property—all for free. One day, when asked how she'd managed to unpack her massive barn and clear out her foul-smelling old house, she would offer up the name and number of Harriet Greene, that pleasant and hardworking lady who hadn't charged her a cent. And so it would continue, farm to homestead to crumbling manor house, all through the valleys and canal towns and farmlands of the Empire State.

Except that Sally already knew "one day" wouldn't reach all that far into the future. Harriet, not the type to indulge discomfort (Sally had seen her bang her thumb with a hammer and respond with a "Crap" and a rinse of her bleeding nailbed under the tap), was not a healthy woman. She took, with her morning orange juice, a fistful of mysterious medications, and at the end of a list of numbers taped by the kitchen's wall phone (the friend in Rochester, a cousin in Plattsburgh, Drew, and half a dozen dealers and restorers) was the ominously scribbled entry: Upstate Cancer Care. And she was losing weight. The dense round person Sally had met over a Shaker chair at the Johnson Museum of Art was slowly diminishing, as if someone had punched a tiny hole in her foot and let the life force begin to drain. She did not seem to be in pain, or even in distress, but that didn't stop Sally from wondering whether Harriet might need some help.

Those are nice rooms up there, she'd said.

What have you decided? said Rochelle.

She'd found, all that spring, that she was back in 213 Balch earlier and earlier at night, sometimes even in the afternoon with no plans to go out again. Whole evenings in the small room with the window cracked open, sitting cross-legged on her bed with her homework at the ready, waiting for the doorknob to turn and Rochelle to enter. Which, she now understood, was happening later and later, sometimes very late indeed. Sally began to understand that this was not simply a case of general attrition, a peeling away of their friendship in a sad but noneventful way. No. Something had happened, something she'd missed, something of significance. Because she had been distracted by her excursions to East Seneca? Because she was selfish and myopic and hadn't been paying attention? No. Because it was being deliberately hidden from her.

But why hide? They were friends, weren't they? And until that bad mistake she'd made, foisting herself on Rochelle at her mysterious and sad home, they had been the kind of roommates who might say, for example, *I met somebody* or *I might be in love,* for surely that was the something, the deliberately hidden something, that was happening in Rochelle's life, Night after night, with the relentless party room down the corridor in perpetual jamboree and the stubborn stink of bulimia nervosa (multiple cases) in the shared bathroom across the hall, Sally studied for her English lit final and drafted her passionless women's studies term paper and tried not to think about the thing that was happening in Rochelle's life, and why that mattered to her so much.

What have you decided?

She had decided nothing. This had been decided for her.

She began to move well before the end of the term, clearing out the largest of Harriet's third-floor rooms to leave for herself only an epic four-poster, a highboy, and a Victorian marble-topped table by the bed, and scrubbing the bathroom back to its porcelain basins and tile. (The shower ran brown water for nearly an hour at first but righted itself in time.) Each day, she walked an item or two—a few books or a change of clothing—across the campus from Balch Hall and up the hill to East Seneca, and it was so gradual that even with what little remained in the room after the common room purges and giveaways, Rochelle didn't seem to notice any transition was underway. Finally, a week before finals ended, she packed up her sheets and her computer and left for good.

What's up? Rochelle wrote in an email late that night. She must have only just arrived back at the room. *Are you ok?*

Got a place off campus, Sally wrote back. *Lease started on the first so I thought, might as well go now.*

I would have helped you move!

Sally was ensconced in her new four-poster. It was massive with a dark carved headboard and twisted pillars, and she felt tiny in the middle of it with her laptop open.

That's ok. You've been busy.

Studying for finals, Rochelle wrote. She wrote it quickly. Too quickly. *So worried about my law seminar. I'm sorry, Sally. Can we meet up for coffee?*

Sure. Just say when.

When I come up for air, wrote Rochelle, backtracking immediately.

She must not have come up for air at all, judging by the fact that they never did manage to meet up, for coffee or anything else, or at least not the way Rochelle might have intended. Sally would finish her academic work in that bed on the third floor and spend the days and summer weeks that followed with Harriet on East Seneca Street and on the back roads of New York State, being drawn deeper and deeper into the world of old houses and the mainly old people who lived in them. Houses stuffed with sadness: filled up room by room with sadness, each enclosure silenced in sadness behind a closed door until the house itself was jammed and filthy. Some of the houses smelled terrible. Some had owners who barely opened the door, or spoke through a crack, or slipped out and closed the door behind them like Rochelle's mother had done, reeking of shame and fear. Sally wanted to push them out of the way and charge in with bins and tape and rubber gloves and ammonia, but she held herself back. She was there to learn.

They knocked on doors and brightly introduced themselves to suspicious veterans and addled retirees. They weren't always let inside, but if they were, Harriet seemed capable of spinning a connection out of the air, talking crops with the farmers and nursing with the infirm. She could claim kin with anyone, Sally thought, watching her talk and talk with the sullen and the shy, filling up the silences with chatter. Loathing of the Democrats in Albany was a common and unifying theme, and the tyranny of downstate New Yorkers also popular. House after house Harriet filled with warm conversation as Sally, doing her best not to mess things up, smiled and nodded and tried not to give herself (and her New York City–ness, and her Democrat-ness, and very often her Jewishness) away. She followed Harriet into stifling kitchens to make what seemed like hours of insubstantial small talk, all for permission to see Aunt Lee's old family painting that supposedly came over from England long ago, or a late husband's desk he'd sworn was worth a fortune.

More often than not, they came away with nothing, or with a face-saving purchase of some valueless Eastlake armchair or Victorian coatrack. Sometimes, though, the very kitchen table beneath their coffee cups would depart with them, or a miraculously intact hooked rug depicting George Washington and his cherry tree would be taken from the floor and gingerly rolled up. A cracked bucket that held matches or knitting needles would turn out to have the words "Ancient Fire Society" painted over a building in flames, and the knitter would be stunned that Harriet wanted to give her fifty dollars for it. Once, they'd had to spend a good hour listening to a couple enumerate the many items another picker had hauled away, only a few months earlier. Once, they'd been subjected to a terrible story about the addict son who'd stolen every single thing of value from his parents (except, it turned out, the 1850 first edition of *The Scarlet Letter* Harriet found in the drawer of a reproduction vanity, which she'd only opened to be polite).

"But is it fair to them?" Sally asked more than once, as they drove away with some such spurned treasure in the back of the car, wrapped in a towel.

"It wouldn't be, if I lied," said Harriet. "If I said, 'Oh, that's a worthless thing.' Or 'Don't bother showing that to a book dealer or looking it up on the computer.' A book in the back of a drawer is a book in the back of the drawer until somebody wants to buy it. I'm not stopping anyone from doing anything with their property, you know."

"I know," said Sally. "So if after all that, she'd said, 'You know, I think I'll drive down to New York and show this chair to Sotheby's. I mean, if you want it maybe they will, too?'"

"Then I say, *Go with God!*" Harriet sighed. "That's the way the cookie crumbles. At least I got to see the inside of the house and I won't have to come back."

They were out west near Chautauqua on graduation weekend, and when Sally returned to Ithaca the summer-session students were moving into the dorms and roaming in packs. They looked shockingly young to Sally, who felt so displaced by them that she made a conscious decision to avoid the campus. The only time she went back was to meet with her women's studies professor. Sally had done well in all of her courses, but her work on the Marys had earned her not only an A but a mug of horrible herb tea in an office in Goldwin Smith Hall and a probing conversation with MJ Loftig (interpreter of Virginia Woolf) about whether she intended to continue in the program. Sally had no answer to this. Of late, she'd been making every effort to merely open the course catalog for 2001–2002 and actually look at the classes, but the many many words describing the many many courses swam before her eyes, and none of it spoke to her. Not one of the majors or concentrations or disciplines or career paths or study-abroad opportunities spoke to her. Cornell itself was not speaking to her, obviously; the thought of a lecture hall or a seminar room seemed to imbue her with a coiling cloud of alarm. *I just don't know,* she told MJ Loftig, thanking her for the terrible tea. *I just don't know.*

Then, as she made her way back to East Seneca, she looked through the window of the Starbucks on College Avenue and saw something that upended her afternoon and changed the direction of her life.

Well now, thought Sally.

Her stomach felt as if it were falling to the pavement. She didn't stop. She never even broke her stride, but her brain began to pound out each step as she walked on. *Oh,* with each expelled breath. *Oh,* with each slap of foot on cement. The street tilted up the hill. She hadn't seen this coming. Not this. Not *this.* It defied all logic and all fairness, and by the time she got home—to her new home—she felt terminally lost.

Flat on her back on the four-poster, looking up through where the canopy had once been but wasn't anymore, she tried to make sense of the sight of Rochelle, her roommate, her friend, hunched over a textbook with a fat highlighting pen in her left hand and the hand of Lewyn Oppenheimer in her right. That hand, which Sally had been made to hold so often, instantly recognizable, even had it not been attached to the oddly altered body of her brother. A leaner body, longer limbed, longer haired, somehow more at ease with itself than Sally had ever known it to be, but still . . . Lewyn.

Could they just be friends, acquaintances from somewhere, studying conveniently together, holding companionable hands at Starbucks? No they could not. Because Rochelle had kept it a secret. Because Lewyn hadn't given her the courtesy of a heads-up, which even he must have understood was bedrock decency befitting a stranger, let alone a sister.

She passed a terrible night and then another, then she got out of bed and drove Harriet's car to Watertown, following Drew's shiny truck through Adirondack forests, and back through Pulaski, Oswego, and Syracuse (where they relieved a thrift store of a three-piece painted cottage bedroom set), and the following morning she decided she didn't know enough to be as angry as she was or as sad as she feared she was becoming. She walked across Ithaca, across the campus, across the Thurston Avenue Bridge, and past the scene of her own crime, Balch Hall, to Jameson, where she knew Rochelle was resident advising for the high school students in the summer session, and found a discreet seat on a bench with a good view of the entrance.

At half past eight they emerged together, each wearing a sweater against the morning chill, her brother's arm distressingly across Rochelle's shoulders. (She came up only to his shoulder, which made this a logical posture, but still.) They headed into town and Sally, after a moment, followed, trailing them to Café Jennie where she was forced to watch her brother bring two smoothies and a copy of the *Times* to their table, dividing the paper between them like any couple at ease on a leisurely morning. After this, they parted for separate classes and reconvened, again at Café Jennie, this time for sandwiches and coffees. The afternoon they spent at adjacent tables in the law library: Rochelle engrossed in her work, Lewyn restless, checking on her frequently, always with some accompanying touch. Then they ate dinner and returned to Jameson—in for the night. Together.

Sally walked back to East Seneca through the campus and town. Even after this, and the easy intimacy she'd seen between them all day, she still could not fully process the transformation of these two singular persons into coupledom. She kept running an imagined conversation through her head, over and over, as she ascended the hill to East Seneca, churning her humiliation and anger into a froth and then changing something and doing it again, making it worse.

Oppenheimer! That's my roommate's name.

Well then, you must be my sister's roommate. Sally Oppenheimer?

What do you mean, your sister?

My sister. Sally Oppenheimer.

Wait, are you the twin brother? You go to some . . . college somewhere. In New Hampshire? (Rochelle would be too polite to say "junior college." She was a far nicer person than Sally herself.)

Not a twin. A triplet. She never told you she had a brother at Cornell? I've been just across the courtyard since the day we moved in.

She never told me. She never told me.

And then, of course, quite naturally, Rochelle had decided to make this hidden brother her boyfriend—her . . . *God! Lover!*—because what could be more transgressive, more thrilling, than taking somebody else's secret and making it your own secret? She'd never suspected how angry Rochelle must have been, for months now, and must still be, or how thoroughly her own subterfuge had obviously festered, ruining everything: their friendship, their continued journey as roommates, Sally's entire capacity to navigate the university, perhaps to navigate the entire baffling mosh pit of adult life.

Why had she even done it, back at the beginning? What would have been the harm in owning her millstone brother, maybe even inviting him over to the room for a desultory chat and an awkward introduction, allowing him to make his own unimpressive impression on Rochelle? Lewyn, left to his own devices, would certainly have done that, and Sally wouldn't have spent the better part of a year hoping her roommate wouldn't find out. She had done this to herself, in other words. There were layers and layers of closeness she had denied herself—herself and Rochelle—all stemming from this original decision. And yet, it wasn't hard at all to remember why she'd made it: the desperation to be away from her brother, from both her brothers. To be, just, finally, *left alone.*

Well, she was alone now, in an admittedly stately room in an old Ithaca house with an elderly and ailing woman downstairs, unregistered for the fall semester, untethered by other friends, cast off from the only fellow student she'd even tried to know in college. She spent the better part of a month stewing in her own regret and sharpening her resentment at everyone else.

Then, one morning in the middle of August, she woke up in a magnanimous mood and thought she might be capable of some form of apology, or perhaps of giving Rochelle a chance to make an apology of her own. She wisely chose not to sit with this epiphany but sent her former roommate an email before she could dissuade herself, asking Rochelle if she wanted to meet up for coffee (not at the contaminated Starbucks but at Café DeWitt off Buffalo Street). Rochelle emailed her back right away and arrived just as promptly (and alone) at three, joining her at her table. Sally (who was nervous) was on her third cappuccino. "Hey," Rochelle said simply, sliding into the chair opposite. She looked tan and rested. She looked . . . unpleasant as this was to contemplate . . . *loved.* "I'm so glad you emailed," she said without further preamble. "I've been thinking about you."

"You have?" Sally asked with what she hoped was benevolent indifference.

"Well, I was so crazed, running around at the end of spring term, and then you were gone."

Sally let this linger for a moment, not because she didn't have a response but because she was not above pressing this apparent bruise.

"Yes, it's too bad," she said finally. "You want something to drink?"

"No, I'm good," said Rochelle, who had likely just walked over from Starbucks. Starbucks was the common setting for Rochelle's and Lewyn's afternoons, as Sally now knew. "So, you're settled? In your . . . off-campus apartment?"

"Yes, complete with four-poster bed and an immense claw-foot bathtub."

"Well, that sounds swank."

"Yes and no," said Sally. She had a sort of summer internship, she explained, helping a local antiques dealer. This was the dealer's own house, and full of inventory. "So it's kind of a full immersion. Like if you were living in the law library," she noted.

"Sometimes I think I am," said Rochelle.

"You said you were doing that advising thing this summer?"

"Yeah. I'm living with the youngsters over in Jameson. How can I possibly be only a couple of years older than these idiots? They need to be scheduled and entertained at all times. I mean, Christ, read a book! Have a conversation! We have board games in the common room, even. But they knock on my door constantly: *Susie told Alice I like Peter but I don't like Peter, and even if I do like Peter I never said I like Peter and now Alice told Peter I like him and they're all laughing at me and I want you to call my mom and tell her she has to come get me and then you need to call up my instructors and tell them I need a medical excuse for my midsession test on the French Revolution . . ."*

"Yow," said Sally, momentarily distracted from her own drama. She missed talking like this. She had loved talking like this. When would she ever talk like this again, if not with Rochelle Steiner?

"Oh," said Rochelle, "and I kind of have a boyfriend."

Sally, punctured, said nothing. She tried to prepare herself for the next thing.

"I know. Hilarious, right? I mean, who has time? But it sort of just happened. I should have mentioned it back in the spring, but . . . you know, I wasn't sure where it was going, and I just . . . I guess I didn't want to share my inevitable humiliation. But now I'm sorry I didn't. I'd have liked you to meet him. I mean, of course you can still meet him anytime!"

Sally stared. *She could still? Meet him?*

"He's a bit shy. To be honest, he hasn't made a ton of friends here, but that's okay. He kind of hung out with his roommate, and his roommate's friends. They're all, like, born-again Christians. Well, the roommate's a Mormon."

Sally didn't trust herself to speak. Luckily, she didn't have to.

"Oh my God," Rochelle said, "a couple of weeks ago we went to see his roommate in this Mormon thing, this religious pageant thing, way out in the middle of nowhere."

"Palmyra?" said Sally.

She and Harriet had passed Palmyra on the way back from the Chautauqua trip. *Where the Mormons came from,* Harriet had said as they drove by.

Rochelle looked at her in surprise. "Yes. The most bizarre thing I've ever seen in my life. Hundreds of corn-fed Americans in a field, dressed up like extras in *Ben-Hur,* reenacting the Book of Mormon. I mean, I understand why we went. For his roommate. And you need to be respectful. But it was so bizarre. Oh!" she said, "this is the weirdest thing, but he has the same last name as you. My boyfriend, not the Mormon roommate. I had no idea it's such a common name. That's what he said, when I told him about you."

When I told him about you.

Sally, working her way through this, said nothing.

"And what about you? Are you seeing..." Rochelle seemed to falter. "Anyone?"

Nine months on the other side of their little room, and it was the first time this question had been asked. It was so banal, so pedestrian. Sally wanted to hurl it back.

"What do you mean, 'seeing'?" she said unkindly.

"Oh, you know."

A long and uncomfortable moment passed.

"Sally," said Rochelle, "I'm so happy we were roommates. I felt really lucky. And sometimes I thought, how would I have ever met Sally if I hadn't been matched up with her by some computer or something?"

"But you didn't want to keep rooming together," she said. She was a little surprised to hear herself say it out loud.

Rochelle looked around uncomfortably. "I didn't handle that very well. I think I just wanted some privacy..."

"For the boyfriend."

"Well, yes. Partly. And I wondered if... if we were becoming too dependent on each other."

If I was becoming too dependent on you, Sally thought. *That's what you mean.*

"We could have talked about it," she said.

"Yes. We should have. I take responsibility for that. But it's why I was so glad you got in touch with me. Because I'd be incredibly sad if I thought we weren't going to be friends anymore."

She felt something inside herself soften, but even as it did the volume of her outrage was rising. Rochelle had been victimized no less than herself. More than herself! And by Lewyn, that snake, more snakely still by virtue of the fact that his snakeliness had lain dormant all these years. Cruelty from Harrison: that was a given, a no-brainer. Harrison could smell weakness in his siblings, track it to its source, then lay the perfect trap to reap the most exquisite harvest of sibling distress, all without dropping an Oxford comma. But Lewyn? Lewyn, indolent in his loser role, his weirdo role, too passive to even contemplate a vicious act against anyone, let alone the triplet who was not the triplet who'd been such an asshole to him since birth—who would have guessed what depths of vicious calculation he'd harbored, all these years!

"What's his family like?" she asked, more to cut Rochelle off than anything else, but also because she wondered how Lewyn had managed to handle that one.

"I haven't met them yet," Rochelle admitted. "Well, he hasn't met my mom, either. I think you understand the freak-out potential there," she sighed. "I thought I might get invited home with him at the beginning of September, but he has to go on some family retreat or something, and it doesn't sound like the kind of thing where you invite a friend."

Sally frowned. *A family retreat.* That was one way to describe the mandatory observance of the birthday at the Martha's Vineyard house. Harrison would be coming from New Hampshire, she supposed. Lewyn, obviously, from Ithaca.

And then it came to her, that rare, perfect synthesis of calculation and raw emotion: the loss of her friend (because no matter what happened now, her friend was lost to her) and the repudiation of her brother, and the bleakness of what she saw when she looked into those packed and filthy houses, and the dying woman who lived downstairs, and the father back in Brooklyn she could not bear the sight of, and the mother, playing out her long-debunked theory of what our family was supposed to be.

"You know," Sally said, curling her damp hand around her cappuccino cup, "why don't you come out to Martha's Vineyard with me? My mom and dad would love to meet you, and we can go to the beach and relax for a few days before we need to get back here for fall term. I mean, if the dates line up with your boyfriend's family retreat, that is."

Interestingly enough, they did.

Chapter Twenty-Four

An Inescapable Assembly of Oppenheimers

In which Sally, Lewyn, and Harrison Oppenheimer converge on the eve of disaster, for an evening of disaster

Early in September, all three Oppenheimer triplets turned toward Chilmark for the ritual observance of their birth. Harrison, only recently returned to Roarke from Charlottesville, had stopped long enough to interview candidates for a faculty position in philosophy (and a good thing, too, because several of them were idiots) before taking a bus from Concord to the New Bedford ferry. Sally drove Harriet Greene's car straight to Woods Hole and onto the boat. And Lewyn paid an Ithaca taxi driver to take him to the Albany airport, where he got a flight to the island. Not one of them even considered coordinating with the other two, not even Sally, who had a car at her disposal, a long ride ahead of her, and a sibling starting from and going to the exact same places. Especially not Sally.

Johanna and the baby had been on the island most of the summer. She'd tried enrolling them in the very same Parent and Child Musical Jamboree! program in Edgartown to which she'd once hauled the triplets, but now her fellow moms (only moms, despite that supposedly post-patriarchal "Parent and Child") were thirty-year-old attorneys and entrepreneurs, still maintaining their Dartmouth crew or Swarthmore squash bodies, and they all seemed to know one another. They were pleasant, of course, and cooed at the baby, but there was none of the laughing and talking and commiseration Johanna remembered from years before, or maybe there was, but it was happening somewhere she wasn't. Besides, a lot of them didn't actually stay for the class, opting to hand off their babies to an au pair or a mother's helper so they could get in a Pilates session before the weekend guests arrived, or taking their laptops to one of the cafés in town. Johanna had no one to hand her baby off to (Marta had wisely declined the invitation to accompany them for the summer), and the weeks on the island, accordingly, had been exhausting. It was the first time Johanna's true situation, the actual impact of her decision, had fully come home to her: she was a forty-eight-year-old woman with an infant to raise, and all the money in the world could not adjust the very long horizon before her, nor the lonely road she would need to walk in order to reach it. That road, as it turned out, would be even lonelier than she had reason to fear.

The three of them—Harrison, Lewyn, and Sally—arrived within a day of one another to find our mother frantic, our father sequestered behind the closed door of the upstairs room he used as an office, and an unsteadily toddling toddler who wept at the sight of them. They gave one another perfunctory nods where possible, and perfunctory hugs where required, and they patted the infant (no longer, obviously, an infant) on whatever part of its body seemed least repellant. Sally's bedroom overlooked the eroding sands of Long Point Beach. Harrison and Lewyn's bedroom was under the house's eaves, looking east. The infant was in a small room across the hall from the boys and next to the bathroom the three of them shared, which was far too close if it was doing anything besides sleeping.

On the night of the birthday itself, Johanna told them, Lobster Tales would be coming to make a clambake on the beach.

Harrison immediately claimed some crucial work project and retreated to his and Lewyn's room. He might possibly have been hoping that someone, perhaps Salo (whom he still had some interest in impressing), would ask him more—or indeed anything—about where he had been all summer, and what he had done there, but Lewyn was the only one who seemed at all curious about his time in Virginia. Lewyn (naturally) had never heard of Friedrich Hayek, but he did seem capable of lucid questions. What was the retreat and who went there? What kind of activities went on and who paid for it all? (Harrison did not answer this last. He wasn't entirely sure of the answer, and besides, it wasn't any of Lewyn's business.) He said more than he'd expected to say about Eli, managing to convey that Eli was (a) their own age and yet (b) supremely accomplished and (c) fated for great achievements and positions of deep influence and, most surprising of all, (d) someone Harrison actually admired.

"Where's he from?" said Lewyn.

"Virginia. Well, West Virginia. I mean, western Virginia. Right on the border, actually."

He said this as if his brother cared about the specifics.

"Okay," said Lewyn.

"I mean, down there, the state and county lines are much less important than the geography. People identify by the valleys and ridges. They've been populated since the eighteenth century."

"By whites," said Lewyn.

"What?"

"Populated by whites since the eighteenth century. I imagine they were populated long before the eighteenth century, by people who were not white."

This was a very Walden thing to say.

"Well, of course. Also by Blacks, if it comes to that. Eli thinks his family migrated from Georgia. Before the Emancipation Proclamation there were Black families hiding in Appalachia. People left them alone."

Lewyn frowned. He had never heard of escaped slaves being "left alone" anywhere in the Antebellum South, but for merely the thousandth time in his life, he decided Harrison must know better.

"So Eli is Black?"

"I can't believe you even asked that," said Harrison unkindly. "Race is irrelevant." He picked up his book and pretended to read it, but Lewyn could tell that he was too irritated to actually read.

"Well," Lewyn said, "I couldn't care less if your friend is Black or white or green, but it's relevant to *him*, surely. A Black person growing up in Virginia or West Virginia has de facto had his life impacted by hundreds of years of endemic racism."

"Oh?" Harrison sneered. "So basically, whatever Eli has accomplished, and everything he's going to accomplish, is irrelevant in the face of his eternal victim status. *My ancestor was enslaved! My ancestor was killed in a pogrom!* So what? At some point, we get to stop holding a grudge, Lewyn."

A grudge? Lewyn thought.

"Well, our ancestor *was* killed in a pogrom, as a matter of fact," he said. "A pogrom for one. I mean, throttled, gibbeted, corpse displayed for six years. That's pretty bad, I think even you can agree. Hard not to hold a grudge, if you ask me."

"Throttled! Gibbeted!" Harrison grinned. "Big words, Lewyn!"

Lewyn, annoyingly, only shrugged. "I mean, you have to feel for the guy. I feel for the guy. If Joseph Oppenheimer had agreed to convert to Christianity he'd have been home by dinnertime."

"I doubt that. Our great-great-whatever was done for the minute his boss dropped dead. In any case, as usual, you fail to see the bigger picture. Yes, this very unfortunate thing happened to our ancestor, but as a direct result of this same unfortunate thing, his descendants left Germany and ended up in America. So, good for us! If he hadn't been killed, he'd probably have stayed right where he was, and also his kids, and their kids, and on down the line till Dad's father ended up guess where in 1939? And you and I wouldn't be sitting in this nice house on Martha's Vineyard having this conversation."

Lewyn stewed. As usual his brother was persuasive, but only because he himself had somehow agreed to stand still as Harrison ran around him. On this particular subject, he had only one argument, and it bent toward the emotional.

"Don't you feel sorry for him, though? Don't you feel we owe those people something? The ancestors who suffered so you could . . . I don't know, have a nice house on Martha's Vineyard? It's like . . . it's a responsibility."

"Don't be pathetic, Lewyn," his brother snapped. "We're responsible for fulfilling our own potential, and that's it. If Eli had sat around thinking about how his forebears were slaves, I doubt he'd have had the wherewithal to do what he's done."

"Well, it's great what he's done," Lewyn said carefully. "I mean, writing a book before you're even out of high school, and getting it published . . ."

"He didn't go to *high school*." Harrison said "high school" as if he meant *reformatory for the incorrigible and pathetic*. "He educated himself better than any high school could have educated him. And he didn't just get his book published. Some of the most important innovators we have in this country consider his work critical to the intellectual conversation we're having. Or should be having," he added. But Harrison was already unsure about the conversation the two of them were actually having, let alone the one they—or . . . somebody else?—*should* be having.

"I'm glad you've made such a good new friend," was all Lewyn could think of to say, though this, predictably enough, only made his brother turn from him in evident disgust. There would not, of course, be a reciprocal query from the other child's bed under the peaked ceiling. No *How was your freshman year?* or *What are you going to major in?* let alone *Have you happened to fall in love with a person who may just possibly be as clever as I am, and much, much nicer to boot?* Lewyn, the aimless and pudgy brother who'd taken his leave one year earlier, bound for a college of least resistance and without a single affinity or interest, let alone a vision for his future? Lewyn, who'd never kissed a girl let alone had sex with one (whether or not she provided the condom)? That Lewyn was not the Lewyn who had reappeared, and there was much about him of potential interest to Harrison (even if that interest were of the teasing and disbelief variety), but Harrison never asked him a question and Lewyn, who had some pride now in addition to his other new attributes, declined to make an unforced offering.

"Must be nice for you and Sally," Harrison said pointedly on the morning of the birthday. "Having each other so close by. *To lean on*," he finished with a kind of flourish.

"Yes!" said Johanna. They were all—except for Salo—in the kitchen, drinking coffee. The baby was in her highchair, and Johanna was feeding it something vile and brown. "I'm happy thinking of the two of you, meeting up to study or have coffee. Even just running into each other by accident."

"Weirdly," Lewyn said, "it never happens."

"Big campus," Sally said, blowing into her mug. "Anyway, we were both doing our own thing. Busy. You know."

"Busy doing what, exactly?" Harrison said. "I'm curious. What's a *real college* like? What do people *do* there?"

Then he grinned, in case either of them might have thought he was sincere.

"Well, it's like this," Sally said. "People spend years keeping their heads down, working really hard so they can get into an Ivy League school, doing sports and music and community service and getting straight As. It's been the only thing for so long, and then they get in, and now here they are together in the same place, all these high-achieving good boys and good girls who've delayed adolescence, and they're like, *Now what am I supposed to be trying to accomplish?* And they kind of realize they're on their own—no more parents or coaches or advisors keeping them on the straight and narrow, and suddenly it's *Billy has a keg in his room.*

"Well, not your room," Sally said. "'Cause you had a Mormon roommate."

Her brother nodded. Then he frowned. Had he told his sister that his roommate was Mormon? He tried to remember, but there was nothing there.

"Wait," said Harrison, "you had a Mormon roommate?"

Beside him, Sally let out a breath. It was only ten in the morning with the rest of the day to get through, somehow, without showing her hand. Or exploding from sheer stress.

"Yes. Very nice guy. We got along great." Even to himself, he sounded defensive.

"Great with a Mormon," said Harrison. "That makes sense."

"What do you mean?" Johanna asked him. "You think your brother's like a Mormon?"

"No!" Lewyn said, perhaps too quickly.

"Are you?" said Harrison.

"No!" he said again. "But there's nothing wrong with being a Mormon. It's no stranger than what we believe."

"I believe nothing," said Harrison. "I believe people are idiots with a pathetic need to feel special. Apart from that . . ."

"Well, that's not nothing," Sally observed.

"You know what I mean."

"Do you not have a pathetic need to feel special, Harrison?"

"Sally," said her mother.

"I'm going for a walk," said Sally, and she left the kitchen and went down the old log steps to the beach and began to plow furiously west, grinding her bare feet into the sand. There was a knot of people at Gilbert's Cove but apart from that she was alone, her thoughts churning. For the first time since waking up that morning, she thought about the fact that she was now nineteen, perilously close to an age without a "teen" at the end of it, and what would that be like? Incontestably an adult, no mitigation of youth available (or tolerated), no excuse for the kind of unmistakably bad act she was about to commit against her brother, who—she hardly needed to remind herself—totally deserved it. She moved even faster, losing her breath to the wind, putting more and more distance between herself and them. One final year of "teen" and then beyond to the open country of adulthood, where she would be, at last and forever, without the brothers she loathed and that baby she had not enough feeling for even to pity, without deceitful Salo or countdown-to-hysteria Johanna—our parents in their pointless facsimile of family life. Liberated at last. She was terrified.

Johanna shushed her when she made it home; the baby, apparently, was asleep. Our father was still in his little office upstairs, and the boys (she was nonchalantly informed, as if it weren't a colossal deal) had borrowed her car to go to the Katama General Store in Edgartown.

"I'm sorry, *what?*" Sally howled.

"Quiet!" her mother said. "I told you, she's sleeping!"

She's sleeping. Dad's in his office. Harrison and Lewyn took my car.

"You let them take my car? I told you, it's my employer's, not mine, and I gave her my word no one else would drive it."

This was not true, but it might have been true!

"They won't be long," said our mother, as if this were the relevant point. "I thought I might need the Volvo."

"Mom!"

She imagined the elderly Ford blowing a tire on a stone in the road, or just giving up the ghost at some random traffic light in Edgartown: a line of Mercedes going wild on their horns, a Vineyard cop requesting the registration and some irate hedge funder calling up Harriet in Ithaca to berate her, all of which was bad enough.

Rochelle's ferry was due in ninety minutes.

"Relax," said Johanna. "They know how to drive."

"Perfect," Sally said, with extravagant sarcasm.

"Could you come out and talk with me for a bit?"

Johanna meant the full-court press: more coffee on the back porch, in Adirondack chairs painted gray to match the ubiquitous gray of Vineyard shingles and relentlessly uncomfortable to sit on. The porch overlooked the beach she had just steamed up and back, trying—and failing—to exhaust her nerves.

"What is it?" she asked. She had sixty minutes to reclaim her car and pick up her roommate before Armageddon. "I had some things I wanted to do later. I mean, if I get my car back."

"I thought you and I might take Phoebe over to the carousel," said our mother. "We talked about that, didn't we? On the phone?"

"Sure," Sally nodded. "But not today."

"Why not? I can come with you on your errands. Give us a bit of girl time. Do you need anything for school? There are a couple of new shops in Edgartown."

Sally winced. It had been a full year since the last time Johanna had tried to take her shopping. "Mom, no."

"Well, there are some antique stores. I'd be glad to buy you something nice for your room. I love that you're getting interested in beautiful things."

"That's okay. The place I'm living in is furnished." (Like Historic Deerfield, she nearly added.) "But maybe tomorrow?"

By tomorrow, who knew whether anyone in her family would still be speaking to her. The thought of it filled her with a kind of horrified giddiness.

"Maybe. Also, I need you to come and sign some papers. There's an attorney in Edgartown who works with our firm in the city. I just need for you to sign them while you're on the island. Lewyn took care of this back in the spring."

Sally looked at Johanna. "What kind of papers?"

"Well, guardianship for your sister, in case anything happens, God forbid."

She felt, suddenly, very cold. "That's what you want? Me?"

Johanna nodded, but she seemed reluctant to look Sally in the eye. "Yes, of course. Who else?"

"Well, you might have asked. I mean, I wouldn't choose me to take care of anyone."

"This is not anyone. This is your sister."

She could be anyone, Sally thought. "What about Uncle Bruce and Aunt Debbie?"

"What about them? They barely know her. They even asked me not to bring her to Passover last spring. They said they weren't set up for a baby. You're her sister. Harrison and Lewyn are her brothers."

"And you want all three of us to take care of her? That's insane, Mom."

"Well, it's not desirable," our mother said tersely, "but these aren't things you leave to chance. You can't do that with a baby. You have to dot the *i*'s and cross the *t*'s. I don't know why I'm always the only one thinking ahead. The rest of you just waltz along without ever once considering our family. Just sign the fucking papers, Sally. For me."

Sally looked at her. This Johanna was not the same Johanna she had left behind, only a year before.

"Mom? Are you okay?"

"Don't be ridiculous," said our mother.

"Just tell me, why the urgency to do this now? You aren't planning to hand over our sister and disappear, are you?"

The "our sister" was a gift to Johanna.

"Wouldn't you take care of her?" our mother said.

I'm in college, was all Sally could think to say in response, but her heart was beating so fast, she could barely follow her own thoughts:

Is this my responsibility?

Is this mainly my responsibility, because I'm the girl?

Are you making Harrison promise, too?

Where was our father in all this?

But she knew exactly where he was. He was somewhere else, with someone else: a beautiful woman with a lovely back who had once—it was unbearable to remember—overwhelmed her with kindness in a museum bathroom. For years she had carried the burden of our father's secret. She might have shared it with her brothers at any point, she might have wielded it against both parents as a powerful weapon, but she never had. Perhaps the satisfaction of not telling had been one tiny bit greater than the satisfaction of telling. The thought of it now, though, nearly made her explode.

"And what about Dad? I mean, if something should happen to you, shouldn't he be the one to raise his own daughter? I mean, you have a child together!"

"We have four children together."

"You don't have to stay," she told Johanna, and it was only when she heard it out loud that she thought she might finally understand what this conversation was about.

"I know that," Johanna said, confirming it.

"Mom."

"We have the Lobster Tales people coming over around four. We should be here for that, they might need help carrying stuff down to the beach. Will that give you time for your errands?"

Sally looked at her watch. Rochelle's ferry would dock in forty-five minutes. And the boys, where the fuck were they with her car? With Harriet's car.

"Can I borrow the Volvo?" she asked.

She would pass Harrison and Lewyn on the Edgartown Road, but her head was so full she didn't notice, and the boys, in Harriet Greene's old

Ford, didn't notice her, either. They were on their way back from Katama with two bottles of Champagne for that night's "celebration" of their birth. The Champagne was Veuve Clicquot. Harrison had developed a preference for Veuve Clicquot in Virginia, he informed his brother as he handed over Johanna's credit card.

"So that's what you did down there?" asked Lewyn when they returned to the car. "Guzzle Champagne and toast the little people?"

"I don't know that I'd waste good Champagne on the 'little people.' I think sharing ideas with thinkers who are focused on improving our country is pretty much all I've been wanting to do since they let me wash off the finger paints in elementary school. Not that there's anything wrong with art."

Lewyn eyed his brother, who was driving. Harrison's hands were not, he noted, in the sanctioned ten-and-two position.

"Well, I'm glad to see that college has broadened your worldview."

"College has *extended* my worldview. College has *deepened* my worldview. I think that's how it's supposed to work. Is that how it's working for you?"

Lewyn smiled. "I'd say so. I've made some interesting friends. I've found something I care about, intellectually."

Harrison snorted.

"And I have a girlfriend."

His brother flinched. Yes, there was pleasure, deep pleasure, in the moment. Lewyn saw Harrison struggle not to turn his head.

"Really."

"Really. Thanks for your good wishes."

"No, I'm just . . . well, little Lewyn. I can't say I'm not a mite surprised."

"You don't need to say it. Because who could possibly be interested in me, am I right?"

Harrison smiled. They were passing the airport. A private plane was gliding in to land.

"Is that how you feel about yourself?"

Lewyn set his jaw. He could catch Harrison off guard, for some fleeting advantage, but he could never outmaneuver his brother. Not in the long game.

"You're such a charmer, Harrison."

"Thank you."

"I mean, who else could say something like 'a mite surprised'?"

"Who else indeed," Harrison agreed, grinning at the road ahead.

"And your own love life, if I might inquire?"

"Well, I had some *very* pleasant evenings with one of the young ladies at the center in Virginia."

(This was a considerable exaggeration. Harrison had indeed flirted with a cute Sweet Briar junior named Maddie, an intern in the director's office. He had even considered asking her out on a date, but there wasn't a single evening of presentations or even unscheduled conversation—*especially* unscheduled conversation—that he had been willing to miss. So he'd let it go.)

"Well, that sounds . . . *a mite pleasant* indeed."

"Yes. But no. This is not so much on my radar right now. I'm more concerned with the cerebral. And as you're well aware, I got an earlier start on this type of thing."

The light changed. They turned toward home.

"I believe it has been mentioned," said Lewyn. "What was it, sixth grade?"

"Don't be absurd."

"And she provided the condom."

"That is hardly the salient fact," said Harrison, taking obvious pleasure in not denying this. "Please don't think I'm unhappy that you've caught up a bit. I'm relieved, actually."

"Well," Lewyn shook his head, "I'm sorry to have worried you."

(It was here that our parents' Volvo sped past them in the other direction.)

"Not *worried*," Harrison said. "But of course I was ever so slightly concerned about you both. You ripped your heart out over that airhead actress at Walden. What was her name?"

Of course Harrison knew her name. The girl, by then, had starred in two independent films and been on the cover of *New York* magazine. Not even Harrison could miss that. Besides, she hadn't been an airhead, more's the pity.

"And Sally of course. I worry about Sally. She's never even had a boy ask her out."

Lewyn's antennae rose. It was right there. Right there. And he was helpless against it. And the words hammered away inside him, howling for release—*say it, say it.* It wasn't a question of whether it was right. He knew it wasn't right. But he was operating on a far more primitive level. *Say it, say it, say it.* So he did. What else was he capable of doing, really?

"I wouldn't read much into that, Harrison. Sally's a lesbian."

Silence. More explosive than anything even Harrison could have thought up to say, and Lewyn listened to that, feeling the pleasure *rush, rush,* all through his body. Speechless, both of them. Lewyn sensed the tightness in his cheeks and knew he was smiling. No, grinning. Madly.

"How do you know that?" said his brother through clenched teeth.

"My girlfriend told me." This was a grace note, a twist of the dagger, with a flourish!

Harrison was looking over at him. This was unsafe driving.

"Yo, watch the road," said Lewyn.

"And how does your *girlfriend* know?"

He sounded skeptical, but of which element—the revelation about Sally or the fact of Lewyn's girlfriend—it was hard to say.

"That, I decline to answer," said Lewyn, settling into this wholly unfamiliar perch: the upper hand.

"Well, how do you know it's true, then, *Lewyn*?" said Harrison. He seemed to be reaching for his customary smugness, but he couldn't quite get there.

"We both know it's true, *Harrison*," he said.

He loved this. He was admiring the words even as he said them. Then he started admiring the words he didn't say: *You mean you never figured that out? And you, The Smart One? Maybe not quite as smart as you think you are . . .*

"I can't say I've given Sally's sexuality much thought, to be honest."

"Clearly."

They turned off the road onto the long, shared driveway, passing the Alberts', the McConaughys', the Lowells', and the Abernathys'. The Abernathys were long gone, but none of them had ever laid eyes on the new owners, Houstonians who had vastly overpaid for their overblown "cottage" but were never there.

"Not that it matters," Harrison tried one last time before the final turn to the house.

"Obviously," Lewyn parried. "Except, you know, to our sister."

And maybe, it occurred to him, to our parents. He wondered if Johanna and Salo knew about Sally. True, they hadn't had the advantage of intimacy with their daughter's roommate or known the strange and wondrous pleasure of Rochelle Steiner's sweet head close by on a shared pillow, slipping into sleep but still speaking, confiding, connecting. But perhaps they'd noticed something Lewyn and his brother had been too obtuse or uninterested to see. Salo, so fixated on his solo navigation through life, and Johanna, frantically absorbed in her Potemkin family—they were probably as clueless on the matter of Sally's inner life as her brothers had been, though it did seem to Lewyn that they must *care* more about Sally and her prospects for happiness than he and Harrison did, and perhaps be paying closer attention. *A mite* closer attention.

All summer he'd been dreading the enforced fiction of these days in early September, as much as he dreaded the inescapable assembly of the Oppenheimers itself. He would gladly have skipped the observance of his own nineteenth birthday, and he knew Harrison resented having to leave that all-male bastion in the forest he went to. Sally might be marginally more sentimental about their milestone, but then again she'd apparently passed up an entire Vineyard summer to stay in Ithaca and do whatever weird thing she was doing with the owner of this elderly automobile. He'd struggled with how to explain his impending absence to Rochelle, considering and rejecting a sick relative (too much concerned interest) or a reunion of high school friends. (What friends? He'd never mentioned anyone in particular.) He despised having to lie to her, which was another way of saying he despised having already lied to her, and having continued to lie to her every single moment of every day, as they rose together and ate together and walked together and studied together and ate together again and, finally, lay down beside each other in their pushed-together beds, with Rochelle's stalwart fan blowing over their pale bodies. *Liar, liar,* the whir sometimes seemed to coo, after she had fallen asleep in her distinctive position, hands together in prayer and trapped between her knees. *Liar, liar, liar.*

At last, he had hewed as close to the truth as he dared and told her that his family went on a retreat at this time of year, and it was something he couldn't get out of or bring a guest to. He wasn't sure what was being planned, only that he would have to leave Ithaca for a few days, and he couldn't wait to get it over with and come back. He hoped she wasn't upset with him for going away.

She said she wasn't, and she didn't seem to be. In fact, the mildness of Rochelle's response made Lewyn worry more than he had at any time since that strained trip to Palmyra earlier in the summer. Rochelle had plenty to take care of on campus, like packing up her summer room and getting early access to Triphammer, the cooperative house she'd finally decided on for sophomore year. Where was the family retreat to be? she wanted to know, and Lewyn, caught off guard, and thinking, perhaps, of Harrison, said something about New Hampshire. The White Mountains. (Or were they the Green Mountains?)

"Oh, that sounds nice," she'd said. Then she went back to her book.

When they were together again he was going to tell her. He was. Because he had to and also because it was the right thing, and because he had suffered under the lie every single day since that early morning in the back of the bus. And then he would apologize. A lot. And he'd tell her he wished he'd made a better choice, back when he'd had the chance. And sure, he'd try to shift the blame, or some of it, to Sally, who had denied him long before he'd denied her back. That Sally had chosen not to tell her roommate he existed was painful, of course, but it was no excuse for his own lack of disclosure. Now, he wanted to go forward with transparency, if Rochelle would absolve him and allow it. Honesty, complete honesty, from this point forward.

He and Harrison carried the Champagne inside and promptly separated, Harrison to their room upstairs and Lewyn to the back porch, where Johanna had the baby on her lap.

"Oh good," said our mother. "I wasn't sure that car could make it all the way to Edgartown and back."

"No, it was fine," he said. "A truly vintage driving experience."

When the people from Lobster Tales pulled into the driveway a few minutes later, Lewyn was conscripted to haul coolers, bins, and the big rectangular firebox down to the beach. He alone, it appeared: Harrison declined to emerge from the bedroom (though he could hardly have missed the big truck in the driveway beneath their window) and Sally had apparently gone off somewhere in the Volvo. Our mother, after greeting the caterers, had retreated. He didn't know where Salo was.

When they got the cast aluminum pan settled on the sand, Lewyn stood back to watch them work. They lit the wood fire and started to layer in the corn, clams, mussels, lobsters, and seaweed. It was far too much food for the five of them, and he wondered again how Johanna had decided on this particular form of festivity, but he could only imagine they must once, in the misty past, have appeared to enjoy some similar event. Johanna was a collector of moments like that, Lewyn knew. Sally favored a certain green T-shirt: she must have an Emerald City–themed party! Harrison went through a pretentious bow tie phase: off he went with Salo on a father-son trip to Savile Row, to have matching three-piece suits made! (Where was an eight-year-old supposed to wear a three-piece suit? Plus, he outgrew it in a matter of months.) Our mother, as long as Lewyn could remember, had hoarded and imbued with great significance such tiny moments, all while seeing so little of who the three of them actually were, and even less as they'd each learned to deflect her oversight. Johanna had been happiest when they were small, he thought, all three dependent on her and competing for her attention. He wondered if the baby had made her happy again, but he suspected not. He suspected our mother was slipping down a long and rough decline, grabbing as she went and very possibly calling for help. And all of them—

himself, his brother and sister and father, and even the impervious toddler, herself—were watching Johanna slide away and doing not a thing to stop it.

These were Lewyn's thoughts as the last of the summer sun departed and, upstairs in their bedroom, Harrison typed away at an email to Eli Absalom Stone, detailing the recent revelation that his sister was apparently gay and his brother, Lewyn, the chubby one (chubby no longer, in fact, though Harrison left this out), was claiming to have found himself a girlfriend in college, and it was a sad, sad day when one had to confront the notion that one's family were wholly uninterested in the dire impact of a generation of liberalism on a once robust notion of American integrity and so forth, and he could not wait to get back to Roarke and impart some of his ideas for the project he and Eli had (eagerly) agreed to take on for the Hayek Institute, a coauthored collection of essays in which two young conservatives addressed the deficiencies of liberal American academia. Johanna was also upstairs, rigid on her back in bed with her arm slung across her eyes, grasping at sleep as she listened to the baby. The baby was banging away on a toy xylophone across the hall, the single Oppenheimer whose state of being approached anything remotely like contentment.

But she was fourteen months old and would have no memory of this day, or the next, no matter how significant they would appear in hindsight.

Salo, in the little upstairs room that everyone called his office, was on the phone. He had been on that phone for most of the day.

Across the island in Vineyard Haven, Sally watched Rochelle Steiner walk off the ferry, a small person further dwarfed by the overstuffed red LeSportsac duffel slung over her shoulder. Sally's resolve, which might on another day have evaporated at the sight of her friend and roommate, did not even falter. All afternoon she'd been stewing at the bickering of her brothers, Johanna and her cataclysmic neediness, and Salo so maddeningly absent. The whole house was humming, not with reunion or connection or, God forbid, family love, but with intractable individual agendas. Well, she had one, too, and if it hadn't been subjected to a high degree of internal examination, and if it hadn't risen to the level of any real self-awareness, well that was just too bad. She had a quiver full of Fuck You's and enough spleen to send each and every one of them on its merry way.

The ferry hadn't been crowded. It was a Monday in early September and the great island exodus had been underway for about a week, with scores of families departing for home and their Vineyard houses closed for the season. Sally had spotted Rochelle right away, walking briskly behind a pair of teenaged boys she vaguely recognized from Cronig's, and waved when Rochelle spotted her. Then she went forward to greet her guest and ask the usual questions—*Was the journey hard? Was Rochelle tired?* She barely listened to the answers. Now that the thing was actually in motion, now that Rochelle Steiner of Ellesmere and Balch Hall was actually here, walking beside her up Beach Street toward the Oppenheimer Volvo, it was as if some injunction had been lifted and the rest of the prospect suddenly illuminated. How firmly should Sally try to steer what happened now? And what, exactly, was she aiming for? Sally couldn't decide whether it would be better for Rochelle to encounter Lewyn alone or with the rest of them. She couldn't decide whether to unleash the full force of her own intentionality, her planning, her *design*, or maintain a very plausible deniability. *How was she supposed to know that Rochelle's boyfriend and her own enforced lifelong companion, Lewyn Oppenheimer, were one and the same? You'd think one or the other of them might have provided her with that detail! But wait—hadn't her brother, who actually was in possession of all the relevant information, failed to disclose it to his own sister and actually lied outright to poor Rochelle Steiner?* If anyone was responsible for tonight's inevitable unpleasantness, it was Lewyn! If anyone was culpable for the unfortunate collateral damage to Rochelle herself, it was also Lewyn!

I didn't realize Oppenheimer was such a common name!

News flash: it wasn't.

For such a smart person, Rochelle ought to have been smarter, Sally thought unkindly. She did not expect their friendship to survive the evening, which was certainly a shame. But she had signed up for that.

Wait . . . you mean . . . this is your boyfriend? But this is my brother Lewyn!

Rochelle would look at Lewyn and possibly even cry.

Lewyn would definitely cry.

Her thoughts ran through scenario after scenario. She saw herself watching mildly, letting the two of them figure it out, or not, and the farther she traveled down the rabbit hole the less she cared which of them would be more wounded or incensed than the other. She could turn her back right now and walk away from them both.

Rochelle, at any rate, was not in a rush to get going. She wanted to buy a T-shirt at The Black Dog. She wanted to pick up a house gift of some kind for Sally's parents. A candle? A book? Sally patiently walked her up and down Main, as the harbor behind them turned orange in the sun's last light. She helped her friend select a bottle of wine with a pretty label.

"Can we drive past that carousel?" asked Rochelle as they climbed into the car. She had read about the carousel somewhere. Sally experienced the briefest wave of remorse, but it passed.

"Of course," she said. The Flying Horses was still running, if sparsely occupied with children and toddlers and their parents, the scene unaltered from the younger Oppenheimers' own years of rides. She saw her personal long-ago favorite mount, painted the same palomino shade as the others yet distinguishable to her by the slightly deeper red of its saddle. She'd always insisted on waiting for that one, stubbornly sitting out a turn if some other child had already claimed it, even as the boys competed to get mounted first, even if her pickiness meant everyone would have to wait for her. She didn't care about the brass rings, extending in their dispenser from the wall, just out of reach. Harrison always managed to grab one more than Lewyn, probably by placing himself strategically as the ride began, and Lewyn always suffered, pathetically wounded at having been beaten, again, every time. They were ridiculously competitive when they were small, before Lewyn had simply conceded inferiority in all things: intellectual, physical, interpersonal.

This was when it occurred to her that Lewyn might well have told Harrison he had a girlfriend. He would not have let *that* opportunity pass.

Good, she thought.

"Let's go," said Sally.

"Okay. Maybe we can come back tomorrow and ride it."

"Sure," said Sally, but even knowing nothing else, she knew that wouldn't happen.

Chapter Twenty-Five

Illumination Night

In which plans are made for an earlier departure, and either a farce or a revenge tragedy reaches its inevitable conclusion

Our father, who had finally decided that morning to leave his marriage, spent much of his afternoon on hold with American Airlines. From the window of the upstairs room they all referred to as his office, he had watched the movements of his family: his daughter leaving for the beach and returning, his sons taking off in that risible car Sally had arrived in, the appearance of the truck from Lobster Tales, the catering company. He'd heard, but hadn't seen, his wife and the baby as they squawked through the rooms. Nobody bothered him. It was almost as if they understood the metamorphosis taking place behind this door.

Wednesday had been the day they were all supposedly departing—Harrison back to New Hampshire, Lewyn and Sally back to Ithaca, and Salo himself, with Johanna and the baby, home to Brooklyn, but that morning Stella had called him from the beach in Santa Monica and held up her mobile phone to the sound of the boy's laughter, and something inside him just broke open. And he understood: it was past time, and it would never get easier than today—or, to be more precise, tomorrow.

This was what he wanted, but he wasn't gleeful about it. He had appropriate sadness, appropriate regret, and even appropriate guilt. Johanna, he absolutely understood, had devoted her life to him and to their children. She had been loyal, even single-minded, in her devotion, and he had no wish to devalue her years of kindness and comfort, though they had brought him no nearer to forgiveness than he'd been on the day they met, at the funeral of that girl our father had killed. She had done everything within her power to salve his wounds, but there had only ever been one person capable of forgiving Salo Oppenheimer, and it wasn't his wife. *Poor Johanna,* he thought now. It was the great flaw in her life that she had met him afterward, when everything was set in stone, and while it was also true that she had forced a late child into the world and their lives, he could see that the baby was good: full of life and sharp as a tack, and Johanna would have the purpose of raising her, and that was also good. Of course it was sad that Phoebe wouldn't grow up with married parents in a so-called intact family, but she would have the boy, who wasn't much older than she was. This, Salo would absolutely require. After the dust cleared, all of his children were going to know one another. After this, he would never again partition his life, not under any circumstances.

It was obvious to our father that none of his older children were in an especially good place. Harrison had already declared his intention to leave as soon as he was—his word—allowed. Sally could barely look at Lewyn. And Lewyn, the most agreeable of his kids, seemed deeply on edge. He did not know why they were this way any more than he'd ever known. Hostilities might be at a peak, but they weren't new; from the very start his children had turned away from one another. Maybe now, at least, they would come together in support of Johanna and the baby, even at the cost of his own good relationships with them. Not that he had good relationships with them, but perhaps that, too, could change. He had not been a good husband for the same reason he had not been a good father: because he had not known how to love another person. But he was learning now.

American Airlines, in its wisdom, had selected "In the Hall of the Mountain King" as its hold music. Maybe it was their way of punishing people who bought their tickets at the last minute, but all he wanted was to give them his money and he already knew the Boston flight he wanted, the first he could get to after the first flight from the Vineyard. Even so, it had already taken ninety minutes to speak with not one, not two, but three American Airlines employees, two of whom would ask for and be read, slowly and deliberately, his American Express card number. By the time they were finally through with him, the afternoon was nearly gone.

Tonight, after the festivities, he would tell them all what he was about to do. He would answer their questions. He would explain who Stella was, and what had happened between them so many years ago when he was the age they were now. He would tell them how sorry he was, because he truly was sorry. He would tell Johanna that he loved and respected her, and that he would continue to be Phoebe's father, just as he would continue to be the father of the triplets, though he could see that they were launched on their own mysterious lives. He wanted very much to set a tone of kindness and respect that he hoped would continue through the years of co-parenting that still awaited them. He wanted her to know that she had done nothing wrong, but also that he would not accept the role of destroyer, certainly not of willful destroyer, of their family. The harm he'd caused in his life, he had never *not* acknowledged it, but surely that was enough for one lifetime, and even a person who had killed two people was entitled to happiness if fate went to the effort of dropping happiness into his path.

The past years in particular had been difficult, and not just logistically. His youngest son and his younger daughter were growing up only a few miles apart, but even after the triplets left home Salo never once attempted to bring his two lives together. He went to Red Hook after work as he had done for years, and then he went home to the house on the Esplanade. He shook a rattle in Brooklyn Heights. In Red Hook, he played pirates and lions. He made love to Stella and went out for dinner with Johanna and the same three or four couples they had always gone out to dinner with. Occasionally, once the triplets were gone, he spent the night with Stella, but even then he returned early in the morning. It had all been managed far longer than he'd thought possible.

Maybe what Johanna needed more than anything else was the psychic slap of an ending. Maybe the Vineyard was actually the best of all possible places for her to absorb the impact she needed to absorb, for her own well-being. Perhaps she would opt to stay here with Phoebe for a few days or a month, or even for the mythic overwinter the islanders liked to go on about. After all, it wasn't necessary for her to be in Brooklyn. The triplets were up and out and the baby could be a baby anywhere. Off-season on the Vineyard, with scores of folks who were very hirable to take the edge off the childcare and give Johanna time to herself . . . well, she'd come around to it. Or else she wouldn't. And if she never did, if she was determined to be unhappy, then what did it matter where she was?

Our father was still at his office window when Sally arrived home with an extra person in the car, a small person who exited the Volvo from the passenger door, pulling a large red bag behind her. This fact did not overly engage him. The small person, clearly female, clearly young, might have been an additional employee from the catering staff whom Sally had fetched from Edgartown, or perhaps a local teen his wife had hired to watch Phoebe, and since these were not matters that preyed overly on his thoughts on an ordinary day, let alone on a day of such consequence, he turned away from the window and resumed his other task. This was the letter he was drafting to one of the estate specialists at Wurttemberg about the Rizzoli drawings in the warehouse which he wanted to gift to Stella in some formal way, separating them from the other art. The Rizzolis had no great value, not like some of the paintings which were now—even to him—astonishingly valuable; in fact, they hadn't appreciated at all since that first Outsider Art Fair. But he wanted them to belong to Stella, who was in LA meeting with someone at LACMA about funding for her documentary. And while he doubted things with Johanna would deteriorate to the point that she made some claim on the pictures, he still wanted to take them out of the equation.

But it was getting dark, and he could already smell the fire down on the beach, and the distinctive suck and slap of the fridge downstairs being opened and closed. There were feet on the stairs beside his office. There were voices down in the kitchen. And the stress of the day, and the worry about later tonight, and *absolutely* "The Hall of the Mountain King"—all of it had worn him out. He shut the laptop down and put it into his travel bag. He would look at the letter again as soon as tonight was behind him, maybe even during the long flight tomorrow. But now he thought he had better go down and celebrate the nineteenth birthday of his oldest children, and be with them for what would likely be the final night in the life of our family, or at least this current iteration of our family. He supposed that we would all come through it, one way or another, sooner or later, though not without harm. No one ever got through without harm, and no one knew that better than himself.

• • •

Outside, from the driveway, Sally looked up to see our father turn away from the window.

"You called it a cottage." Rochelle was gaping up at the house, hands on her narrow hips, and shaking her head.

"Everyone calls their house a cottage on the Vineyard. It's like reverse snobbery. There's plenty bigger than this. And this one's older than most. I think it was built in the thirties. That's like the stone age here."

"It's so pretty. I love this color gray."

"They're all like that. Seriously, it's an ordinance or something. You have to ask permission if you want your house another color."

She could smell the good smells of the lobster bake, coming up from the beach. Rochelle was looking over at the path down between the dunes. "What is that?"

"Oh. We're having a family clambake tonight."

"That sounds so fun! It was so nice of your parents to let me come. And I can't wait to meet your brother."

"My brothers," Sally said automatically. Then, realizing what she'd done, she said: "My brother's around here somewhere. I don't know. Let's go inside."

Inside, she watched her friend take in the main room with its shiny wooden floors, and the built-in corner cupboard which held an older and bulky television no one ever watched and a stack of crumbling board games no one ever played, and the glorious spectacle of the ocean, visible through the living room windows. She noted, through Rochelle's eyes, the basket of baby toys at the bottom of the stairs, and wondered what she should say about them, but the question didn't come, and they went upstairs. Somewhere, a sink was running, and the door to the master bedroom at the end of the hall was closed. Our father's office door was also closed.

"We're in here," she said.

Rochelle put her red bag on the twin bed Sally obviously wasn't sleeping in, and went into the bathroom.

I'm doing this wrong, Sally thought, watching the door close behind her. Though it was probably nearer the truth that there wasn't a right way to do what she was doing, or had already done.

From out in the corridor she heard our parents' door open, and the descending clomp of an unhappy woman carrying a child. "Salo, are you coming downstairs?" Johanna called up from the bottom of the stairs.

"When I'm off the phone," she heard our father say.

He had been on the phone when Sally returned from her walk on the beach. He had been on the phone when she left for Vineyard Haven. Apparently, he was still on the phone. Whom was he talking to?

She had a pretty good idea whom he was talking to.

In the bathroom, the toilet flushed, and with that utterly pedestrian sound something inside her clarified. The house, and all the people in it, known and unknown, known *but* unknown; hers was not the only story underway, she understood. *I need to go talk to Lewyn,* Sally thought. *Like, right now.*

"Listen," she said when Rochelle came out, "I'll be right back. I want to go ask my mom something."

"Should I come?" said Rochelle.

"No, no, I'll be right back. Make yourself at home." And Sally left her there, rooting around in her shiny red bag for a sweater.

She went downstairs to the kitchen, where she found Johanna pulling Champagne out of the fridge: two bottles that hadn't been there this morning.

"Have you spoken to Dad?" our mother said.

"No," Sally said. "Not since this morning."

"I'm very irritated."

Yes, that was plain. She was jerking wineglasses off the shelves and slapping them down on the countertop, which was marble and probably not a good surface to slap things made of glass down onto.

"Mom, listen, I should have mentioned this, but I have a friend I just picked up at the ferry. She's upstairs. I wasn't sure she'd come. I mean, I invited her, she didn't just turn up, but I wasn't certain she'd actually get here."

Johanna turned to her. "You invited her for your birthday? Who is she?"

"She's my roommate. Rochelle. I don't think you ever met her, but we're friends."

That only sounded additionally aggressive. *You, my own mother, never met her and yet we still managed to become friends?*

Johanna nodded. "Okay. But why didn't you tell me she might be coming? Those sheets on the other bed in your room, I have no idea when they were last changed."

"Don't worry about that," said Sally. She thought, inevitably, of Rochelle's own Ellesmere home, so unclean that Sally hadn't even been allowed inside. "The bed's probably fine, and if it isn't we'll change the sheets. And I'm sure there's plenty of food."

"I'm sure there is," said Johanna, sounding a little sad. "I might have forgotten how much it takes to feed us when we're all together. When were we last all together?"

Sally considered. The conversation had taken an unexpectedly morose turn, but at least Johanna didn't seem angry at her.

"And I might have said we were six people, when I talked to the caterers. I always think: I have four children, as if Phoebe could put away a lobster and a couple of ears of corn." She paused to smile, more to herself. "So yes. We have enough."

"Okay," said Sally.

They both heard a door open upstairs, and the slap, slap of shoes heading along the corridor. Too heavy to be Rochelle, Sally thought. She braced herself for her father, but it was only Harrison, pulling on the bright red sweater with the Anglophilic crest he'd brought back from Virginia. He'd worn it constantly since he arrived.

"Oh," Harrison said to Sally when he entered the kitchen, "I thought you were in your room. I just heard you upstairs."

"I have a friend visiting."

"A *friend*," said her brother with a distinctly lascivious edge.

"Yes. I do have them, you know."

"Do I know that?" Harrison considered.

"Harrison," our mother said, "do you think wineglasses are okay? We only have four Champagne flutes, and we're six adults. I don't think it matters."

Harrison grinned. "You're right. It doesn't matter. Except, there is a right way to drink Champagne, and it isn't in a wineglass. If it had been, the flute wouldn't have been designed to enhance carbonation by reducing the surface area for it to escape."

There was no limit to what her brother Harrison could convert to pure assholery, Sally thought.

"You're right," our mother said sadly. "I'll take down the four flutes and two wines. Daddy and I will take the wineglasses. You three, and your guest, should be able to toast your birthday properly, even if we won't all match."

"It's too bad. Appearances are so important at a clambake, too," Harrison observed, arguing against himself for the pure pleasure of it.

Johanna picked up the baby and zipped her into her woolly cardigan. "Try to get your father out of that room," she told them. "And Lewyn."

"Lewyn's down there already," Harrison said. "He's not upstairs, anyway."

"Oh no?" said Johanna. "Okay, I'm going now." And she left with the baby on her hip and four Champagne flutes wedged upside down between the fingers of her other hand, probably not the wisest way to travel over slippery sand, but neither Sally nor Harrison made any effort to stop her.

"So. Tell me about your *friend*," said Harrison when she'd gone. This time his tone was deliberately flat and decidedly unprovocative.

"Her name's Rochelle," said Sally. "She was my freshman-year roommate. You might actually like her, Harrison."

"Oh?" He opened up the refrigerator door and looked balefully inside.

Then, as if he were settling for something far beneath his intentions, he pulled out a carton of Newman's Own lemonade and drank from the spout.

"I mean, she's very smart."

"Smart? Or educated?"

"I don't even know what that means," said Sally.

"I know you don't," said Harrison, sounding triumphant. He raked back a forelock of his thick brown hair. This had been a habitual gesture, almost a tic, since middle school, but it looked sillier than ever just now, and the hair fell back over his eyes almost immediately. But maybe that was the point.

It did smell good out there, a mix of shellfish and roasting corn coming up through the dunes and in through the kitchen window. She hadn't eaten since that morning.

"Did Mom say anything to you about papers?" Sally asked.

"What kind of papers?"

Newspapers, dummy. Academic papers.

"Legal stuff. Guardianship for the baby."

He stared at her.

"I'm not going to be a guardian for that baby."

"By which you mean our sister, Phoebe."

"I'm not going to be a guardian for any baby. *Including* that baby."

"Okay," Sally said. "Glad that's clear. I'm actually more concerned about what it means for Mom, her wanting us to sign something. She doesn't seem okay to me."

Harrison shrugged. "What's wrong with her?"

Sally shook her head. "I don't know. But I'm concerned."

He faced her and crossed his arms. "She shouldn't be dumping this kind of stuff on us, now. She should have worried about it before she did such an asinine thing. Nobody told her to do it. Nobody said, 'Hey Mom! Why don't you defrost that kid you left behind eighteen years ago and hire some lady in a trailer park to give birth to it?'"

Spoken with his trademark Harrisonian compassion and empathy, thought Sally. And it hadn't been a trailer park. Though how she knew that she wasn't sure.

"I'm just saying, I'm worried about her."

"And I'm saying: *Don't be.* The whole point of growing up is to put away childish things. If she can't do that, the best her children can do is model responsibility."

"Really? That's the best her children can do?" Sally shook her head. "The parent-kid handbook doesn't say anything about caring for your aged mom and dad if they're sick or incapacitated?"

He hauled open the Sub-Zero, which made its usual sucking sound, and shoved the lemonade carton back inside.

"Mine doesn't. Not that that's what we're talking about. We're talking about rewarding her for a selfish and insane and utterly immature decision by reassuring her she can abdicate her responsibilities anytime she wants."

But that wasn't it at all, thought Sally. Or not entirely. Our mother had so loved being a mother, the Maypole around which her little ones danced, perpetually competing for her attention. Who wouldn't feel alive and necessary under those circumstances? The basic responsibilities for food and shelter and safety, the encouragements and rituals, the special time with each of them. And what came after that? Only the frantic appeasement of her meandering partner, the children peeling off to begin their separate widening gyres, and then their outright, heartbreaking departures. When Sally thought of it, she wanted to cry, despite the fact she herself had howled to get away. She was still howling. She was howling right now.

"Hello."

Rochelle was there, shockingly, in the kitchen doorway, one hand on the doorframe, the other holding that bottle of wine they'd bought in Vineyard Haven. Sally was dumbstruck to see her. For a blessed moment, in exercising her generous loathing for Harrison, she'd forgotten all about Rochelle.

"Hello," Sally heard Harrison say. "And you would be the roommate."

"And you would be . . . I'm guessing here . . . the brother?"

"I am that," Harrison said. "Most assuredly."

"Then I, most assuredly, am the roommate. Rochelle Steiner."

Harrison took a step toward her. He had always been the taller of the boys, by a significant margin, but now, with Rochelle as the yardstick, Sally suddenly realized that Lewyn had surpassed him. Harrison wouldn't like that. "A pleasure," said Harrison, extending his hand.

She watched the two of them shake hands. It was surreal, but not, she supposed, as surreal as it might be about to get.

"I guess you're ready for this," said Rochelle, holding up her bottle and nodding at the pair of wineglasses Johanna had left on the countertop.

"I'm always ready for good wine," said Harrison, sounding like a complete git.

"Actually, there's Champagne," said Sally. "We just didn't have enough flutes, apparently. Would you like something now?"

Rochelle shook her head. "I'm so happy to meet you," she told Harrison. "I can't say I've heard too much about you. I just know the basics. You go to college in New Hampshire, right? I don't know the name of it."

"It's called Roarke. For another year, yes," said Harrison. "Then I transfer to Harvard."

Rochelle's eyes widened. She herself, Sally knew, had applied to and been rejected by Harvard. But who hadn't?

Harrison hadn't. And leave it to him to insist on saying so.

"That's very exciting. You know that already?"

"Most of us know where we're going after Roarke. A couple of the others are also heading to Harvard."

Sally watched her as she attempted to process this: a two-year college sending multiple graduates to Harvard? It did not compute, obviously.

"A few to Yale and Stanford. And," Harrison smiled, with deeply disingenuous rapport, "other Ivy League schools. A couple."

"That's quite the student body," Rochelle said. "What do you study there, nuclear physics and advanced game theory?"

He shrugged. "Well, you can study whatever you want. I'm doing a fairly strong core curriculum, but I'm mainly interested in economic and political philosophy. Also, I'm in charge of the chickens, so I've learned a good deal about poultry in general."

Rochelle looked at Sally. It was hard to tell whether she was angry or merely mystified.

"Roarke? That's the name of your school?"

"Yes. I'm not surprised you don't know it. It's all male, and somewhat off the radar."

She nodded. "I see."

And now you know why I never talked about him, Sally nearly said. But that hadn't been why she'd never talked about him.

"Our mom's gone down to the cookout," she told Rochelle. "We could go, too, if you're ready."

"Don't forget Dad," her brother said.

"Oh. Dad." She weighed her options. She didn't really want to leave these two alone in the kitchen, not even for as long as it took to go upstairs. "Would you do it?"

He paused. She saw him entertain, then reject, some caustic word or rebuff. It struck her with some horror that he was actually attempting to be less awful than he naturally was. Because of Rochelle? Because—and this was nearly incomprehensible—he had some wish to appear to his best advantage, for her? Rochelle? That Rochelle Steiner could seem to have such a power over not one but two of them (not two but all three of them, if she was truly, for once, being honest with herself) was a notion in utter conflict with anything rational. But what did it matter, the effort to be rational? It wasn't rational to have told her roommate she had one brother, not two, or that one of those two might have been living in the next dorm over, all through the past year. It wasn't rational to have lured Rochelle here for some ill-thought-out act of aggression, against whom she still wasn't sure. Also, it wasn't exactly rational to be dropping out of college in spite of the fact that your grades were fine and you weren't even leaving the town where your college was located. (And this—it now, somewhat belatedly, occurred to her—was precisely what she was about to do. Or had she already done it? And without any clear idea why.)

Harrison went upstairs. Sally reached for Rochelle's wine, took a corkscrew from the drawer, and opened it. She poured two generous glasses.

"Technically that was for your parents," Rochelle reminded her.

"I'll make sure you get the credit." Sally took a gulp. It seemed to taste very good. For a bottle they'd chosen for its label, that was lucky. "Come on," she said. "No telling how long those two will take."

They stepped outside. The night was windy and more fragrant than before, and the ocean made its ambient *whoosh, whoosh,* the soundtrack of her childhood summers. She felt for the familiar log steps and heard, from below, the laughter of strangers: the caterers, probably, happy in their work. She was grateful for the dark.

"Oops," said Rochelle behind her.

"You okay?"

"I spilled some wine in the sand. I forgot what it's like to walk on sand."

Her mother and the baby were together on an unfamiliar blanket near the long aluminum pan, which was heaped with ears of corn and foil-wrapped bags of mussels and clams, on top of which were the lobsters and mounds of seaweed. She made herself not look around for Lewyn, but went straight to Johanna and said, "Mom, this is my friend, Rochelle. She brought you a bottle of wine."

Rochelle stared at Phoebe. She was trying, Sally knew, to place her. "Mrs. Oppenheimer, so nice to meet you. And who is this?"

The baby was fussing a bit. She had a fistful of our mother's shoulder-length hair in one hand, and a partial ear of corn in the other. Her cheeks were covered in butter.

"This is Phoebe," said Johanna. "Sally's sister, of course."

Oddly, Rochelle nodded, as if the "of course" settled everything.

"It's so kind of you to let me come," said Rochelle. "I'm sorry we're only meeting now."

"I am, too!" said our mother, with an eagerness that stung. "I wish we'd been able to come up and visit, but . . ."

"There's not much to do in Ithaca," Sally pointed out. She was, only now, looking around for Lewyn. And there he was on the other side of the firepit, his back turned, talking to two of the cooks. The waves were louder here. He hadn't heard them. He didn't know yet.

"Well, I don't care about that. I care about seeing my children."

"And how old is Phoebe?" Rochelle asked brightly.

"Fourteen months. Walking up a storm." The baby was set down in the sand, whereupon she released both hair and corn and made for the fire. "No you don't," said Johanna, going after her.

Rochelle turned back to Sally. "I didn't know you had a sister."

Sally shrugged. She had momentarily run out of words. She was waiting for Lewyn, now.

"She's adorable."

Whoosh, whoosh.

"I know! I love all my children, obviously, but from the minute this girl arrived, she was: *Now the party can get started!* It's so interesting how they come out, isn't it? Sally liked to be still. She didn't like anything fussy or anything touching her. Her brother was so cuddly, we called him the baby-barnacle."

To Sally's surprise, Rochelle laughed. "I just met Harrison," she explained.

"Mom?" said Sally. But she had nothing to say after that, so she went silent again.

"Oh, Harrison. He learned to read at two. It was ridiculous. I'd take him to the bookstore on Court Street and get him a whole stack of books, thinking, this will keep him busy. The next day he'd come in and say he was done and needed more. He read like my father used to smoke, just end to end. He still does, probably. Harrison, not my father."

Johanna was standing over the baby, holding her by the arms, and Phoebe was babbling, swinging, leaning toward the packed aluminum tray. "Let's get you another corn, cookie," said Johanna. "No, I meant Lewyn. Lewyn was the baby-barnacle. I miss that."

"Mom," Sally said. "You should try some of Rochelle's wine."

"No, I've got Champagne somewhere. We opened one of the bottles. It's over on that table. Do you want any?" Then, without waiting for an answer, she called out, "Lewyn! Come meet Sally's friend."

And then they stood—Sally, Rochelle, Johanna—the three of them in a row, stock-still between the fire and the churning sea, as Lewyn turned and turned to stone. He gaped at them, his mother and his sister and Rochelle, trying to make pitiful sense of how they could possibly all be in the same place, all at the same time, all here, all now. Sally nearly felt sorry for him. She nearly felt devastated for him.

"I don't understand," Rochelle finally said.

"I'm sorry," said Lewyn, going right to the quick of things. He was still far away, but they all heard it.

"You know each other?" Johanna said brightly. "Oh, well, Cornell. Of course."

Rochelle said nothing. There seemed to be an entire interchange underway between her and Lewyn, and Sally, watching it, felt herself become not more regretful but more inflamed. This was connection, and it was obvious: the two of them, staring at each other as if everyone else—our mother, the baby sister, herself, the caterers, for God's sake!—were somewhere else. That the two of them should have gotten so far, buoyed by Lewyn's great lie, was appalling. Yes, Sally thought, he deserved this moment. He deserved every single awful thing he was obviously feeling, and she had nothing to regret.

"Well, Lewyn," Rochelle said at last. "And I guess this is the family retreat you mentioned."

"I'm sorry," he said again. Maybe it was all he was capable of.

"And Sally is your sister. It's ridiculous, actually."

It was many things, but not, Sally thought, ridiculous. The wine she'd gulped, and the wind, and the smell of the food. She felt as if she might be sick.

"What is?" said Johanna. "Do you know each other from a class?"

"From the bus," Rochelle said, recalling her manners. "We met on the bus back to Cornell, back in the spring. He told me—" She broke off, shook her head at her own stupid credulity. "He told me Oppenheimer was a common name. But why, Lewyn? I mean, what was the point?"

"I wouldn't mind knowing that, myself," said Sally. "I mean, thanks a lot. Am I such an embarrassment you couldn't admit we were related?"

Rochelle turned to Sally, and she was full of ice. "Oh no. You don't get to be the victim, Sally. This may be a surprise to him, but it isn't to you. So who's ashamed of whom? And why would you tell me your brother went to a junior college in New Hampshire?"

"She said that?"

Unnoted, Harrison and Salo had arrived.

"A *junior* college? *Really?*"

"I told you a two-year college," Sally said lamely. "Which it is. You just inferred it was a junior college. Which it actually also is, kind of."

"It absolutely is not!" Harrison scoffed.

"If you don't mind, Harrison," said his brother, "this really has nothing to do with you."

"What does it have to do with?" our father asked. He'd accepted a flute of Champagne from one of the waiters. The waiters, Sally saw, had all gone quiet now. "I know I came late, but could somebody catch me up?"

"Well, I might have a few of the details wrong," said Harrison, now with his own Champagne flute to hand and a definite note of merriment in his voice. "But unless I'm mistaken, and I don't think I am, that young lady is your son Lewyn's girlfriend, and also your daughter Sally's roommate, and neither of them saw fit to tell her they were related or even knew each other. Which means that this is either a farce or a revenge tragedy. But if I were her I would be extremely pissed."

"I am extremely pissed," Rochelle confirmed, nodding. "But I'm mainly sad. I'm sad that neither of them could share something so . . . well, *basic* with me. I mean, why?"

Lewyn shook his head. He had come closer, step by step through the sand. He was nearly on Rochelle's side of the aluminum tray now. All that food. He couldn't imagine who'd eat it now.

"You're not a triplet," Sally heard herself say. "Maybe you'd understand."

"What's that supposed to mean?" said Johanna. "You have no idea how lucky you've been to have one another. Some children grow up without anyone to lean on. They have to take care of their parents alone, and deal with horrible situations alone. And you've always been so close!"

All three triplets turned to look at our mother. All three looked away. In this, at least, they were in accord.

"Wait," said Harrison. And there was something in the sound of it that made Sally grow cold. "Wait a minute. Lewyn, didn't you say your girlfriend was the one who told you Sally was a lesbian? That's what you said!"

Whoosh, whoosh. Sally had to lean over. A moment later she was spitting up red wine onto the sand. Well, this is punishment indeed, she thought. The wine and spit sank into the sand. Had Rochelle really said that word? About her? And to Lewyn, whom she would never, ever look in the eye for the rest of her life? Or Harrison, for that matter. Never, never, never.

"Don't be absurd," Johanna said, but she sounded horribly uncertain.

"Lewyn," Rochelle said. Then she slapped his hand away. Somehow he had gotten close enough for that.

"Well, it makes sense," said Harrison. "I mean, you live with a person for a year, there are things you know."

"Jesus, Harrison, shut up." It was Lewyn. He was weeping.

"That's not true," our mother was saying to no one in particular. The caterers had backed so far away they were out of the ring of firelight. "I mean, she had a boyfriend in high school, didn't she?"

In point of fact, she had not had a boyfriend in high school. She'd had a friend who was a boy who liked other boys, and who was as deep in denial as Sally had been until about sixty seconds before right now. Her life as a lesbian ought to have begun years earlier, but it hadn't. It was beginning now, and in full familial glare, and with this terrible feeling of longing upon her like a net. *I wish,* she thought, but she couldn't wish. It all got drowned in the sound of the waves and the terrible drone screaming in her head.

"Is this true, Sally?" our father said. "It's fine, of course, but is it true?"

She couldn't move her head. She managed only to raise her hand.

"I'm not staying," Rochelle announced. "I mean, just to get that out of the way. Thanks for inviting me. If you did invite me." She directed this to no one in particular. "But I'm going to leave now."

"Don't do that," said Lewyn. "We can talk."

"We can't talk. We're not going to talk. Jesus Christ, Lewyn, what is there to talk about? You have a lot of shit to work out, obviously. And it's not that I don't sympathize, because I do. I think you're a sweet, wonderful person, but there's a seriously big hole in you, and if you don't figure out what that is you're just going to start stuffing it with, I don't know, a crazy religion or some other bullshit."

"That's not true," he said. Though he suspected it was.

"What crazy religion?" Harrison said with what sounded like actual interest.

None of your fucking business, Lewyn thought.

"I'm not discussing this with you," he said. "I need to talk to Rochelle."

"No. No." She actually held up her hand. Then she walked over to Johanna and said, with bizarre politeness, "It was nice meeting you, albeit briefly. You have very interesting children."

Harrison, on the far side of the feast, guffawed.

"And you, Mr. Oppenheimer," said Rochelle, picking her way over the sand to him. "I'm sorry we didn't get a chance to talk. Or, actually, meet."

"Me, too," said Salo. He took her hand and shook it. "Who are you, exactly?"

Rochelle, unaccountably, laughed. "I'm the complete idiot who's been living with your daughter and in a relationship with your son."

Sally wouldn't look at her. Sally had, at some point, gone down on her knees in the sand and was holding her own arms so tightly that her wrists ached. She was still in the terrible loop of what Rochelle had said to Lewyn, and Lewyn to Harrison, and Harrison to every person here, from our mother and father to the four members of the Lobster Tales catering crew. Now each of them knew something about her that no one else had known, until a moment ago.

Never, never, never.

Whoosh.

"Good-bye, Sally," said Rochelle Steiner, and she plowed on past, her short legs nobly struggling through the deep sand.

"Wait!" Lewyn rushed after her. "I need to . . ."

Rochelle didn't even turn. Away she went up the log steps to the house, with Lewyn flailing behind her.

"Most entertaining!" Harrison said brightly, after a moment.

"You are such an asshole!" Sally exploded.

"Sally," our mother said pointlessly.

"How could you say that!" she howled.

"Say what? You don't have to be ashamed, Sally. It's 2001! Nobody cares."

I care, she wanted to say.

I wasn't ready, she wanted to say.

I didn't know, was what she really wanted to say, but not to him. That would only make it worse.

"It's none of your fucking business. Anyway, never mind. I'm leaving in the morning, and I hope you have a lovely life. Go play with the white supremacists in Virginia. But stay away from me."

"You don't know the first thing about what I'm doing," Harrison said. "You have no concept of what's going on in this country."

"Very likely," Sally said. "But I have a super clear concept of what's happening right here. I never want to see you again."

"Oh, Sally," Johanna said. She was crying. Phoebe, in her arms, was also crying, but likely not for the same reason. "Please don't say that. He's your brother."

"He came out of a petri dish!" she howled. "So did I. So did *that.*" She flung out her hand toward Phoebe, propelling a handful of sand that fortunately did not reach either parent or child. "I don't think that constitutes a bond. I never did!"

"Don't talk to your mother like that," said Salo, who had stepped closer to Johanna.

"Oh for Christ's sake," said Sally. "As if you have any authority here."

"I beg your pardon," our father said, more angry than she had ever seen him.

Sally hauled herself up, dripping sand, then she stepped close to him and said, very quietly: "Please tell me you don't think I'm that stupid. You are a terrible father. And I've known for years."

"What did you say?" Johanna said.

"What did she say?" Harrison said.

Salo, the only one who knew what she'd said, said nothing.

And for a long, excruciating moment no one moved or spoke again.

"Right," said Sally at last. "I think that's everything. I'm out."

"Sally, don't leave!" our mother cried.

"Been nice knowing you," said Harrison, with glee, and Sally wanted to tell him what an appalling person he was, too, but someone had blocked her exit, and he did it first.

"Harrison," said Lewyn, from the bottom of the log steps. He looked terrible, deflated, obviously devastated, but somehow not yet through with either of them. "That was a horrible thing to do."

"Oh, please. You don't need any help from me, fucking your life up. Either of you."

"I meant about Sally. Why did you have to tell everyone that?"

"Why did you have to tell *me* that, Lewyn?" Harrison said cruelly.

"I shouldn't have," he said.

"No, you shouldn't have," said Sally. "In case you want to put this all on him. He's a cruel bastard and always has been, but I might have expected more from you. Or is this radical truth some part of your religious conversion?"

Lewyn turned to her.

"Because you're not the only one Rochelle confided in, you know. I mean, could you not have picked a less asinine thing to want to be than a Mormon?"

"Yow!" said Harrison. "That shit actually rubbed off on you? From the roommate?"

"What are you saying?" It was Salo. He hadn't moved or said a word since Sally had leaned close to him and spoken. "What does he mean, you want to be a Mormon?" And when his son said nothing, he looked at them all, one by one by one: the weeping wife and toddler, the trio of flailing young adults. Not one of them would ever know what he was thinking, though much time would be spent, and considerable pain derived, from wondering.

They went back inside, the triplets into their bedrooms, where they commenced not speaking to one another, and it was nearly silent on the upstairs floor of the cottage apart from a whimpering Phoebe Oppenheimer, who was nobody's immediate priority, and the hushed scene unfolding in Salo Oppenheimer's office as a marriage of twenty-five years jolted to its end.

For the record, he did apologize. He said that our mother had not deserved this. He said that she would have whatever she needed, for the rest of her life, and the kids, too, of course. It wasn't like that. In fact, he honored her and every one of her choices. Every one. But he had an early flight: 6:20 from the Vineyard to Boston, 7:45 from Boston to LAX.

Outside on the beach, the caterers waited for nearly an hour after the last Oppenheimer had departed and failed to return. Then they began packing all that food into plastic tubs. Johanna, who would remain for hours in Salo's office, long after her husband had gone to bed, could hear them downstairs in the kitchen, and for years she would associate those sounds—the suck of the Sub-Zero door being dragged open, the smack of it closing—with the worst night of her life, itself a mere prologue to the worst day.

A cab picked him up early, and the only person he might possibly have said good-bye to was the only one who was awake. I've always been an early riser, and I have believed in that, in the thought of him in my doorway, holding his bag and looking down at me with love, for my entire life, but the truth is that I can't rake up a single shard of real memory, not of him and not of what happened after. In the morning, all three of my siblings would also try to leave, but only Sally was out early enough to make it off the island. She caught the last ferry before they shut it down, and disembarked at Woods Hole into a new world, by which time our father was dust over lower Manhattan.

PART THREE

The Latecomer

2017

Chapter Twenty-Six

We Might as Well

In which Phoebe Oppenheimer makes an unsettling discovery

For most people, a Primal Scene happens when they open the bedroom door and Mom and Dad are making weird noises in their bed. Not me. I don't remember my father, of course, and my mother has been a nun since the morning of September 11, 2001, though not because I ever asked her to be. Also, for reasons far beyond my control, my so-called Primal Scene would call for certain high-tech adaptations and a level of personal maturity I wouldn't attain till my teens. If, that is, you can ever really be ready for the version I got.

I was seventeen and a Walden School senior when I found out—ready or not!—on a late afternoon in October, post–school day, post–track practice, post–walk home, and post–collection of the family mail, which was not my job, strictly speaking, but which had become my habit. Of course, by 2017 there was less and less mail being sent in the old way, but this being my twelfth-grade year (and having, if I may humbly note, scored not too badly on the previous fall's PSAT) the haul from the mailbox was nearly all for me that fall. Mainly it consisted of glossy college brochures, many from places I'd never heard of, sometimes with baffling attributes: *Christ-Centered Performing*

Arts! Computer Sciences Aligned with a Progressive Outlook! I wasn't sure how they found me, these places. I certainly wasn't asking to be found.

In fact, I might have been the only one in my grade who hadn't gone over the cliff with this admissions thing. Most of my classmates had been vibrating with anxiety for years, one hundred–plus teenagers triggered by the words "application," "deadline," "essay," and even, impractically, "college," driven to herd panic by their panicky parents (who naturally, this being Walden, all insisted they were completely chill about the whole thing). For some reason it just hadn't hit me yet. When I thought about where I would be in a year's time, I thought of one thing only, and it wasn't a destination. It was simply: *not here.* That was terrifying enough.

Here's the embarrassing truth: I wasn't at all sure I was ready to leave home, in spite of the fact that home wasn't such a party at the moment. (Or, indeed, had ever been.) So while I might be circling the drain of my time at Walden, and time with my classmates, many of whom I loved, I had zero idea what I was doing, collegewise, and less than zero about the exciting and fulfilling life I was supposed to live after that.

Our house was on the Esplanade overlooking New York Harbor and, on clear days, New Jersey. It was old and beautiful but way too big for Mom and myself, though I had been expanding my range of possession for years. The room I slept in was the one my sister Sally once occupied, but I'd converted the room across the hall, which had belonged to my two older brothers, into a lounge and study space. I also had solo access to the mother my three older siblings had theoretically been forced to share, which meant that I was privileged, but zero access to the father the three of them had known, because he had died on the country's bloodiest day since Antietam, which meant that I was also tragic.

Privilege and tragedy. A perfect storm for any adolescent.

I was carrying my backpack, and it was even heavier than usual. One of the straps slipped as I reached into the mailbox, and somehow it trapped a bit of my hair. I kept crooking my neck so it wouldn't pull, and trying to keep the catalogs and magazines and windowed envelopes and brochures from slipping to the ground as I also looked for my key, but a few of them fell anyway, and when I bent to pick those up off the back steps, everything else fell, too: *New York* magazine, ConEd, the College Board. After I unlocked the door, I had to gather it all up again.

"Phoebe?" I could hear my mother croak. She'd had a root canal earlier in the week and was perhaps making a bit too much of her discomfort, but it was impossible to know.

"Yeah." The brochure on the top of my pile was from Webster College: iconic New England clapboard, statue of stern founder rendered verdigris by time.

"Aunt Debbie's visiting," said my mother, from the living room. I went in to them. Aunt Debbie didn't get up.

"Hi." I put the mail on the coffee table and gave my aunt a squeeze around the shoulders. Aunt Debbie wore an awful floral perfume, and way too much of it. She always had.

"Hi, doll," Debbie said. "Your mom's a trouper."

"Mm-hm."

Mom, I noticed, was holding a bag of frozen peas against her jaw.

"Is it bad?" I asked her.

"How was your day?" she said, instead of answering.

"Bio quiz. We did sprints in track."

"The only one of my kids who runs intentionally," Johanna said, slurring a little.

"I like to run."

I did. I ran at school, because it made more sense to me than any other sport I'd attempted. I ran in the summers, on the beach at the Vineyard. I ran on the weekends, across the bridge and over to the West Side Highway, and then back. I'd always found, when I ran, that my thoughts got really still, which is a highly desirable state for me, and which desisted the moment I stopped running. Unfortunately, I wasn't especially fast, and there seemed to be nothing my coach could demand or suggest that made me any faster. It was telling, for example, that neither he nor my college counselor, Shura, had suggested I write to track coaches at any of the colleges I was supposedly already at work applying to.

"Webster College," said Debbie, looking over the scattered haul on the coffee table. "The one in Massachusetts?"

I shrugged. "They just send me stuff. I don't know why."

"I know why," mom said to her sister. "Her PSATs were almost as good as Harrison's."

Harrison's, naturally, had been perfect. Harrison's entire academic career, from PSAT to Roarke to Harvard to the largesse of the late Cecil B. Rhodes, had been paved with gold.

"More likely I'm just on a big long list somebody sold to somebody else."

"You know where you're applying yet, hon?" said Debbie. Her own sons had gone to Wharton and were doing various sketchy things on Wall Street.

I made a face. I knew how bad it was. To be a senior at a place like Walden and not know where you were applying to college? Luckily, my mother answered for me.

"Cornell, probably. I mean, that just makes sense. And anywhere else she wants."

"I'm going to make some tea," I said. I gathered up all the mail and brought it with me into the kitchen, where I filled up the kettle and set it on one of the burners. (The range was a Viking no member of our family had ever deserved, at least in terms of our culinary skills.) While I was waiting I opened a letter from a college in Wisconsin I'd never heard of (*Dear Miss Oppenheimer*... it began. The "Miss" itself was disqualifying) and another from NYU, extolling the value of its international campuses. The Webster booklet I put aside for later. The last one was a standard envelope in standard fawn, and I was halfway through the first paragraph before I realized that it wasn't from a college at all. Also, it wasn't for me.

Dear Mrs. Oppenheimer,

(The letter read.)

As you are aware, the curatorial staff of the American Folk Art Museum hopes to mount a major exhibition in conjunction with the upcoming PBS documentary *Celestial Visions* by S. S. Western, concerning the life and work of the American Outsider Artist Achilles G.

Rizzoli, which is currently scheduled to air in the fall of 2018. As the owner of nearly all of Rizzoli's known works, we are reaching out to you once again in hopes that you might reconsider allowing the works to be exhibited at the museum. Obviously, the museum considers your collection of Rizzoli's work to be of crucial value and importance to our understanding of this great, albeit neglected, artist and our exhibition can only enhance the significance and value of that collection. Our curatorial staff would be delighted to meet with you or your representatives to reassure you that your Rizzolis will be professionally handled and highly secure during the entirety of the exhibition process.

We hope very much that you will agree to discuss the matter with us.

With all best wishes,
Denise Kelly
Director, American Folk Art Museum

The kettle whistled. I set the page down and turned off the flame, then I made a pot of PG Tips, the only tea I drink. I was also hungry, as I usually was after practice, but there was, as usual, no sign of dinner in the "gourmet" kitchen, food prep having ceased to be a major activity in the house when Gloria, our housekeeper, retired four years ago. Mom might have hired somebody else, but by then culinary Brooklyn had flowered all around us, and the delivery app had been born. Our evening meals, in other words, tended to come after a perfunctory exchange—likely by text—about what to order, and the two of us would eat separately, without further contact.

The letter, to be honest, didn't make much of an impression on me that first time through. I folded it and slid it back into the envelope, then I turned it over to examine the olive rectangle of the American Folk Art Museum's logo. I was familiar with the museum, of course—it had been a destination for class trips at Walden Lower, and it was right there across from Lincoln Center, and next to the New York Temple of The Church of Jesus Christ of Latter-day Saints (a place I'd long been aware of, thanks to what Harrison referred to as our brother Lewyn's "pioneer debacle"). But then again, the American Folk Art Museum does not occupy the same psychic real estate as the Museum of Natural History does in the minds of every young New Yorker. I'd never been to it outside of those class trips, or ever heard Johanna mention the place.

Still, this letter was obviously neither random nor impersonal; it was specific in its intent and "reaching out to you again" definitely implied that this was not the first communication. I wasn't familiar with the artist called Achilles G. Rizzoli, which was itself almost a parody of an artist's name, with its mash-up of Greek mythology and fabled Italian art publisher (I knew about that from Lewyn). Also, though I was hardly well-informed about any art, "Outsider" or otherwise, I *was* well aware that our father had collected works by twentieth-century painters, most of which were now fabulously valuable. They were stored in a warehouse in Red Hook, but sometimes went out on loan to museums around the world. My grandparents, Hermann and Selda Oppenheimer, who died before I was born, had also collected paintings, but they were Old Masters, and all of those had been sold or donated after their deaths, so no crossover there, either. All in all, it struck me as the height of improbability that any Oppenheimer of either generation might ever have purchased even a single work by a so-called Outsider Artist, let alone such a person's entire oeuvre. And the only work of art my mom herself had ever purchased was a portrait of me by a Walden art teacher, at the annual fundraising auction. And it was horrible.

When I passed through the living room again, holding my mug in one hand and the heavy backpack with the other, the two of them stopped talking. They had their heads close, a posture I couldn't help noticing because while those two had always performed a kind of pantomime of sisterliness, I had never believed that they were really intimate. And yet there was a definite cessation of the conversation when I passed through the room, and then a definite recurrence when I departed. That *was* interesting. I took my mug and my backpack to the foot of the staircase and began to ascend.

"But she knows all that," I heard my aunt Debbie say, and I stopped right there on the step, breathing.

"Well, sure. She even met the woman once. A few years ago. Her first trip to New York City, ever in her life, can you imagine? I took her out to dinner at some steakhouse somewhere, before she went to see *Wicked,* and Phoebe was there for that. Unbelievably awkward. I mean, what do you talk about with somebody from the Florida panhandle? Yes, the buildings are tall. Yes, there are a lot of people, and they all walk very fast. And a twelve-year-old! Not such great conversationalists, either."

"It's like a *New Yorker* story," Aunt Debbie laughed.

No, I thought, frozen on the third step. *It's just not.*

"There wasn't any other way. We had to be realistic. I was forty-seven that year. It was too much of a risk. I was nervous enough entrusting it to a twenty-three-year-old from Pensacola who'd already had two kids! We had only one, you know."

My aunt laughed her snorting laugh. I thought: *Wait, one what?*

"I think we were both getting a little weepy about the thought of the older kids leaving. And you know, there it was, and we could afford it. So we said, you know, *Why not? We might as well.* And that was it."

After which my aunt said something I couldn't make out. And then nobody said anything, and after a moment I went on up the stairs with my cooling tea and my heavy backpack and my purloined letter from the American Folk Art Museum, past the birthday photos of my sister and brothers on the back porch in Chilmark, growing up through the years before I was born—the years before, apparently, *Why not? We might as well*—feeling exactly what any sentient person would be feeling, under the circumstances—in other words, very fucking confused.

Chapter Twenty-Seven

Maybe a Connection After All

In which Lewyn Oppenheimer reveals the family configuration to be not fated, not natural, and also not fair

Later that night, I brought the letter to my brother Lewyn, who lived in the basement of our house.

Lewyn, who was sadly the only one of my siblings I spoke with on anything like a regular basis, had returned to Brooklyn Heights when I was seven and installed himself across the landing in his old room. He was a total stranger, a depressed twenty-four-year-old who, for a long while, seldom left the house, and I tiptoed around him like my own private Boo Radley. Eventually, though, he emerged from his eddy and moved all the way down to the miniwarren of rooms in the basement, with its own small kitchen and separate entrance.

One thing that didn't escape me, even when I was really young, was the fact that none of my triplet siblings seemed to enjoy the company (let alone value the counsel) of any of the others. Lewyn, for example, could barely tolerate being in the same room as Sally, and he actively loathed Harrison (who was, to be fair, not all that difficult to loathe). Harrison treated Lewyn with disdain and seemed to have forgotten Sally's existence. Sally had taken herself away from all of us, and only appeared for family events of unassailable gravity—the funerals, mainly, of significant Hirsches and Oppenheimers. Obviously, I still lived with our mother, but apart from me only Harrison intentionally spent time with her. Once, I knew, there had been a semimandate that all three should gather on their birthday, but Johanna seemed less and less committed to enforcing this as the years passed and the three of them declined to soften toward one another in the slightest. Every time I climbed the staircase I had to watch the three of them grow up in those annual birthday photographs, but then the photographs ran out and that version of our family—Oppenheimer 1.0, I'd privately named it—had run out, too. Oppenheimer 2.0 consisted of me and our widowed mom in a huge empty house, those others far apart from one another in fixed orbits. Harrison lived on the Upper East Side but traveled constantly on his noxious mission to make the world awful. Sally was far away in Ithaca and Lewyn was downstairs. Of the three of them, only Lewyn seemed to regard me as an actual sister rather than, say, the subject of a documentary they had each happened to watch. It was all very regrettable and unfortunate, but weirdly I also understood that it had little if anything to do with me, personally. Like everything else of any note in our family, these rifts and obstructions seemed to have predated my arrival.

Lewyn wasn't handy, but he did design the basement space himself, out of a big room that had once, apparently, been a play area for my older siblings. There was a work space and a long living room and then, behind the galley kitchen, a bedroom that opened onto the Esplanade-side garden. He'd maintained, since his return from Utah a decade earlier, some form of facial hair, and if his biweekly appointment at the old barber shop behind Borough Hall represented the extent of his grooming and self-care routines, it was a vast improvement on the brother who moved back in when I was seven. Now, at thirty-five, Lewyn was generally fit, generally upbeat, and finally single again after an aimless couple of years with a woman he'd met in his master's program, about which I could not help but feel some relief. He didn't seem all that unhappy about it, either.

He opened the door with a phone at his ear and beckoned me inside with his other hand.

"Yes, I know," my brother was in the middle of saying. "No, Hans, I'm not telling you no. I'm telling you we'd need to take more care this time. A lot more care."

He listened. He looked at me and gave a flicker of a smile.

"No, I understand that you want it. I understand it's central to what you're doing. That's why I'm not saying no. But what I am saying is that you're going to need to put a better handling protocol in place this time." He listened again. Then he walked to his desk, jotted something on a Post-it, and held it up for me to read:

Moron.

I smiled.

"Hans. A hole. There was a hole in that Diebenkorn, do you recall? Perfectly round, like from a pin. Surely you can understand why I'd be reluctant to send you the Marden or anything else without a very strong commitment to its transport and care. In writing."

I sat in one of the chairs and picked up a Sotheby's catalog on the table beside it, waiting for him to get rid of Hans in the other room. When he finally did, he picked up his laptop and typed a note.

"Wallraf-Richartz Museum in Cologne," Lewyn announced, when he was done. "Great museum, but the last time they requested a painting, it came back damaged."

"From a pin?" I asked. "What were they doing, playing pin the tail on the Diebenkorn?"

"Oh, who knows. I try not to get paranoid about these things. I actually didn't end up restoring it, but I made them pay for all the consulting. He never admitted responsibility, though. Which I don't appreciate."

"Hans," I said.

"Yes. Hans."

"The moron."

"Well, not really. You down here to vent?"

I laughed. "Not this time."

Venting was our typical thing. It was good to be able to talk about our mother, her many vicissitudes and shortcomings. Here, it was a low-stakes topic, and often highly enjoyable.

"School okay?"

"Except for bio, yeah." The truth was, I had done badly on that quiz, and it mattered. Walden had somehow persuaded the admissions officers at the nation's best colleges that it was special enough to forgo the usual grading and ranking of its students, but the elaborate academic profiles it provided in lieu of a transcript might just mention that I was struggling this fall. Of course, if I got in Early Decision somewhere it wouldn't matter much, but that was obviously not going to happen if I didn't actually apply anywhere.

"Well. Bio. I don't think you're headed for STEM. Do you?"

"No. No STEM. Strictly a humanities girl."

"How's Mom?"

Well. Mom. Mom was Our Lady of Perpetual Entertainment, usually. I ought to have come down with a tidbit already at hand, but that hadn't been on today's agenda. I had to think for a moment.

"She said this weird thing, earlier. Not to me. To Aunt Debbie, but I overheard. She said they had me because they thought, *We might as well.* I mean, holy shit, right?"

"Seriously?" said Lewyn.

"My entire existence. *We might as well!* What does that even mean?"

He looked at me. Then he said, "Wait, are you really asking that? Because we could talk about it. If you want."

I felt a little chill then. It hadn't been a real question when I'd come down to Lewyn's apartment. It wasn't what I was here to talk about, except that now, apparently, it was. "What don't I know? I mean, I had a surrogate, because Mom was too old. I know that. I met her a few years ago. Tammy something."

"But the rest of it. Mom never said?"

I crossed my arms. "Lewyn, Jesus, just spit it out. I know I'm not adopted. I look just like her." I did, too, far more than Sally, for example. I couldn't remember our father, of course, but there were plenty of photographs in the house. I didn't look like him at all.

"Okay. I can't believe I'm the one telling you this, Pheeb, but you're, like, completely our sister."

I burst out laughing, but noted, even as I did, a strong surge of unease.

"Duh. Well, I would hope."

"By which I mean, the exact same age as the rest of us. Just born later."

"Sure," I said. But it still wasn't getting through, clearly. Then I said: "What the fuck?" It was a phrase that seemed to fit so many occasions.

Lewyn sighed. "I'm going to have a glass of wine. Would you like one?"

He went to the kitchen and I heard him open the fridge and take out the bottle. Clink and clink as the two glasses hit the countertop. Squeak as the cork was wiggled loose. He returned and handed a glass to me. Then he sat down beside me on the couch.

"I could kill Mom," was the first thing he said. "I mean, this should be coming from her. I speak with no authority about anything. I was your age at the time, and not paying much attention to either of them. All three of us were applying to college, and working through the leaving home stuff, which I think in retrospect had to be a big part of why they did it."

"Did *what?*" I said. "I mean, could you be any more annoying right now?"

"Well, they sat us down one day. Senior spring. And said, basically: *Yay! Your baby sister is on the way.* You were being born in Florida somewhere, in the summer. We were all in shock, obviously. I can't speak for Sally and Harrison, but I can tell you I assumed it was an adoption. So I said, 'You're adopting a baby?' and Mom said, no. There'd been four of us, at the beginning. Four . . . I guess, embryos. But you didn't put four embryos into a uterus at the same time. It was too dangerous. So the doctor had one frozen and the other three . . . well, were us."

I stared at him. I couldn't form words, and even if I'd been able to, what was there to say? The revulsion of having to think about our mother's uterus was bad enough, but imagining yourself in a freezer, *for years,* was otherworldly.

"You had no idea," Lewyn observed.

I shook my head.

Until that moment, the great, impenetrable drama of my life had been those planes, hurtling into conflagration, rendering our father only a tiny part of so much sudden nothingness, but also, appallingly, in the same abhorrent instant, somehow a party to the mass murder of others. The unspeakable act, or series of acts, had transformed us, the four Oppenheimer children—but especially my infant self—into human repositories of this great American tragedy, and tragedy had accompanied all four of us from that day forward. It was obvious to me already that I'd missed the best time of our family. I'd missed the young parents, the parents energetic enough and interested enough in young children to get down on the ground with them and shake maracas in Music Together class, or cheer from the sidelines of some game in the park. I'd missed the full house on the Esplanade, its rooms lively with arguing or laughing kids and grown-ups. I'd missed the full dinner table (and the actual food cooked for it), and the paternal grandparents with their massive Manhattan apartment. I'd missed a dachshund called Jürgen and the end-of-summer birthday celebrations on Martha's Vineyard, in a house likewise full of kids and food and noise and summer books and summer board games, at least as our mother described it. What I got instead of all that was a widowed mom, so much older than the mothers of my friends, bowed down by understandable grief and not remotely capable of solo parenting a toddler, child, or teenager. I also got a single living grandparent in New Jersey who never looked at me (or even at our mother, her own daughter) with recognition, a large empty house with myself and my mom in separate rooms on separate floors, and meals that arrived in plastic containers packed in plastic bags and hung from bicycle handlebars. And naturally, not a single actual memory of our father, Salo Oppenheimer. It wasn't fair.

It also, apparently, wasn't fated, not if I was understanding my brother correctly. I'd always accepted that I wasn't a spontaneous (if late) flowering of our parents' love, or even an "accident" (as the term was generally understood) because the surrogacy quashed that notion even if Johanna's advanced age at the time did not. But I'd always assumed that I'd at least been, well, *made* at the general time of my birth. Not—

Oh.

It was, just . . .

"You had no idea," my brother said again.

"No. Shit. What did they do, pick out the three best-looking blastocysts? And throw the dud in the freezer?"

"No clue," said Lewyn, "but I'm impressed by your use of the word 'blastocyst.' Are you sure you're not STEM?"

"Or maybe they just did *eenie meenie mynie mo*?"

Lewyn signed. "I wasn't there. Or I was, but I was just a—"

"*Blastocyst.* Yeah. Fuck."

"I'm sorry, Pheebs. If it's any comfort, I always thought the whole thing was completely awkward and horrible, but on the other hand, not personal, either. It was only about the best chance for the best outcome. And the outcome was good, at least in the sense that they got three healthy babies, and childbirth didn't kill the mother."

"That's a low bar," I said, but I also knew it wasn't.

"Drink your wine," he said, and I did. In the receding shock, it went down well.

"So it could have been me and you and Sally, with Harrison in the freezer."

"And I would have had a much nicer childhood, yes."

"Or me and Harrison and Sally, and you'd be a senior in high school now."

He nodded. "Yes."

"*We might as well.* Like, it's on ice. We can get a surrogate. Why not?"

He shrugged. "As I say, I wasn't present, and I wasn't consulted. If you really want to go there, you're going to have to ask Mom."

"I can't," I said, my voice flat. "Because I hate her."

We sat together in silence. Finally, Lewyn said, "You don't really. I don't, either. We're not the hating type."

I nodded, reluctantly. I actually loved that my brother could say this and apparently believe it was true. I wasn't at all sure that could be said of the others: Sally, who had quite pointedly exiled herself, and Harrison, a self-styled oracle of intelligentsia to people in MAGA hats all over the country. They represented the opposite of Lewyn, who had not only come back home but hadn't left again.

"Actually," I said, remembering, "this is not what I came to talk about. So maybe we'll put a pin—you should pardon the expression—in this topic—"

"Ouch," he said, but he was also obviously relieved to move on.

"And you can tell me what you make of this."

I handed him the letter from the American Folk Art Museum. Lewyn took it from its envelope and read, frowning.

"What does it mean?" I asked, impatient.

"I'm not sure. This was addressed to Mom?" He checked the envelope and frowned again. It was clearly established that he, Lewyn Oppenheimer, oversaw the Oppenheimer Collection. This had been a consequence of his temperament and affinity, and also of the fact that he was an accredited curator. This was also clearly stated on the collection website and in all publications. Scholars, dealers, and fellow curators at museums all over the world had always dealt with him directly on matters involving the nearly two hundred works assembled by Salo Oppenheimer.

"Apparently not the first time they've tried to contact her," I said.

"About somebody named Achilles Rizzoli. And we supposedly own nearly all of his paintings. Which is very strange, since I've never heard of him."

"I googled him. He died in the 1970s. He's an 'Outsider Artist.' I googled that, too."

Lewyn got up from the couch and retrieved his laptop. "Well, I'm quite sure they're mistaken. We don't own a single piece of Outsider Art. He came close to buying a Warhol once, but he decided against it. He didn't want to open the door to Pop Art, I think. He was such a purist."

"Too bad," I said. I wouldn't have minded owning a Warhol. Who didn't like Warhol?

"Oh, this is interesting," my brother said. He had the laptop open on his kitchen counter. "There are a couple of Achilles Rizzoli works in the Bay Area, one in a private collection and one at the De Young. Nothing else has been seen since the first Outsider Art Fair in 1993. A lost collection!"

"Very dramatic," I said. But the truth was that I wasn't all that into art, any art, not even Warhol. "Are you going to say something to Mom?"

But he didn't answer. He was looking at the letter again.

"Lewyn?"

"Oh," said Lewyn, looking up. "I just saw . . . I think, maybe there's a connection after all, but I still don't . . ." He returned to the letter from the museum and stopped talking.

"Lewyn! What?"

"It's just . . . this documentary filmmaker. Give me a second," he said.

I watched him lean closer to his laptop. This was obviously going to be very annoying, waiting for him to spit it out. I walked across to his desk and picked up the letter myself.

"S. S. Western," I read. "Never heard of him."

"Her," said Lewyn, but he didn't look away from the screen.

"Okay. Never heard of her."

"I have. Or at least, I saw her name once, on a letter. In a lawyer's office. S. S. Western."

"What lawyer?"

"Mom's. You were there, too. Just a baby."

"So Mom knows this woman?"

My brother shrugged and read aloud from the Wikipedia page. S. S. Western's film about three generations of an Oakland family had been broadcast on PBS. Her film about a lesbian/separatist record company had been shown at Sundance. And her portrait of a Nebraska Klansman who converted to Judaism had won a human rights award.

"Is there a picture?" I asked, and he nodded. I got up and stood behind him. The photo was of a slender African American woman posing before a backdrop that read *Visions du Réel.* She had gray dreadlocks to her chin and a broad smile and a bright pink scar below her neck.

"Have you ever seen her before?" I asked, and he said he hadn't. I hadn't either, so that was everything we knew, which in this case was pretty much the same as nothing at all.

Chapter Twenty-Eight

Existentially Defrauded

In which Sally Oppenheimer achieves one of her therapy goals

My first sit-down with one of Walden's cadre of tenacious (yet principled!) college counselors had taken place the winter of my junior year, and it featured a glossary of admissions-speak that included the words "holistic," "fit," "range," and that perennial favorite, "outside the box." The gist of it all, and this was of primary importance to students and parents alike, was that you couldn't just walk into the Ivy League today, no matter who you were, or where your parents went to college, or how many AP classes you'd taken (a moot issue at Walden, where AP classes weren't offered because every class was considered AP-equivalent). It was different now.

Unlike many of my classmates, who continued to hope (despite the aforementioned reality check) that Legacy status would carry them over the line to Mom's or Dad's alma mater, I discovered early on that I was unable to "see myself" at either of the relevant institutions: Skidmore, where my mother had gone, and Cornell, attended by my late father (as well as my brother and sister, though it had taken Sally some extra years to graduate and Lewyn had transferred out). I'd been to Ithaca a couple of times over the years, but I couldn't remember ever having set foot on the campus itself. And I'd never been to Skidmore. I wasn't even sure where it was.

Did I "see myself" at a city school or a country school? my college counselor, Shura, wanted to know. She had a shaved head and a silver bar through her earlobe.

I couldn't answer.

Did I "see myself" at a large school or a small school?

Same answer, or nonanswer. The truth was that I just didn't particularly "see myself" anywhere at all.

What were my primary interests? the counselor asked, trying a different tack.

I didn't think I had any primary interests. I wasn't sure I had any interests at all, let alone enough to divide them into primary or secondary.

"Well, do you want to stay East? I went on a tour of small liberal arts colleges in the Midwest last summer. I am completely in love with Grinnell."

"Oh?" I said. "I've never heard of it. Where is it?"

"Iowa."

I just looked at her. I was lifelong New Yorker. I didn't know from Iowa.

"Or what about the South? Vanderbilt's very hard now, and Duke's impossible. But I love Davidson, especially for creative people."

Which is . . . me? I thought, with growing agitation. I hadn't done one thing that could possibly be interpreted as "creative."

"And where is Davidson?"

"North Carolina."

"So what you're saying is, I shouldn't apply to Cornell?" I asked, finally getting with the program.

"No, no, I wouldn't say that. On the contrary, if you're interested in Cornell I think you should apply, and I think you should apply early. But I'm not getting that sense from you. Are you feeling family pressure to apply to Cornell?"

Family pressure? I was fighting an urge to roll my eyes. For a moment I imagined them—Lewyn and Sally and Harrison and Johanna—lined up on a long sofa and browbeating me: *Apply to Cornell! Apply to Cornell!* This would require the four of them to be in the same place at the same time. No, I was not experiencing *family pressure.*

That was pretty much the end of my first sit-down with the college counselor. I left with a long list of schools to investigate, and the name of a book I was supposed to read, called *Colleges That Change Lives,* but I did no investigation and I never got the book, and months went by without my ever once "seeing myself" anywhere.

A few days after I intercepted that letter from the American Folk Art Museum, I was scheduled for another sit-down with Shura, and this time my mother was present and very much accounted for. Johanna hadn't forgotten the three-part assault of the triplets' senior year, or the rounds of meetings with that earlier squadron of Walden counselors (who, back in the year 1999, had not yet been forced to contend with "holistic," "range of options," "fit," or thinking "outside the box," because back in 1999 over half of Walden's graduating class had merely walked into the Ivy League, with the rest heading in droves to Wesleyan, Oberlin, and for extreme outliers, Hampshire). In the fall of 1999, Harrison's academic star had been so bright that Walden, with its bizarre nongrading policies, had only served to dull its light. Sally and Lewyn had been middling students, utterly without distinction, but Cornell had welcomed them, nonetheless. The process, in the end, hadn't exactly been pleasant, but it was generally straightforward.

"Did you have a think about the colleges on your list?" Shura asked me.

Of course I hadn't. I'd spent the summer working at a Children's Aid Society day camp, and coming home every night so blinded by exhaustion that my only off-time activity had been watching old movies with Lewyn, down in his apartment.

"Well, a bit," I said. "But I still don't *see myself* anywhere in particular."

"I'd like Phoebe to apply to Cornell," said my mother, stunned that she needed to point out the obvious. "You know, her father went there, and her older siblings. Also there was a very substantial donation of art, back in the early seventies."

"Oh?" said Shura, trying to look interested. Her silver rod was gone today. Instead, a little coil wound in and out of three holes in her left lobe. "Have you been thinking about Cornell, Phoebe?"

"I'm . . . thinking about thinking about it," I said, improvising. Then I said: "My sister lives in Ithaca. I'm planning to go up and visit."

"Really," Johanna said. "When is that happening?"

"We're working it out," I bluffed.

We left with another list of fourteen schools to investigate, and another suggestion that I read *Colleges That Change Lives.*

The following week, Walden furloughed the seniors for a couple of days so we could more "holistically" consider a "range of options" "outside the box," and I caught a ride to Ithaca with a classmate named Jack Neubauer and his dad, a theater director of such prodigious enthusiasms and ranging preoccupations that he barely stopped talking, querying, opining, and wondering aloud for the entire five-hour ride. It was a head-spinning tear through theater and politics and Walden and more theater and still more politics, and after I finally exited the car in front of my sister's house on East Seneca Street, I just stood there for a moment in the cool afternoon air, breathing the wondrous quiet.

My sister's house was old, about as old as our house on the Esplanade. This made sense, I supposed, given the work Sally did, work that our mother preferred to speak of as "antiques dealer," though that (as I suspected Johanna knew perfectly well) was only a part of it, and very much the lesser part. In fact Sally cleaned out houses—filthy, packed, and often septic houses—ostensibly in search of objects of value and obviously for money but also, I had come to understand, for some unfathomable satisfaction she derived from it. Apart from mandated holidays and the first preconscious part of my own life, I had never lived with Sally, but I had always lived in Sally's room, and that room still retained a lingering imprint of its former occupant. I had no detectable style of my own, either domestic or, if I was honest with myself, sartorial, and I had simply moved into the space, inheriting the shade of blue Sally had chosen in 1997, and a rug she had also apparently chosen at ABC Carpet. If Sally had left behind items of clothing, I might have found myself wearing those, as well.

No one came to the door when I knocked, but it swung inward when I tried it, onto dark wooden floors so brightly polished I thought for a moment they might be wet. I stepped inside, noting first the smell of chicken roasting and then the familiar chords of the *All Things Considered* introduction. Four o'clock already; that was a long day in the car. A thin black cat came loping in from the living room and immediately began coiling between my legs.

"Hello," I said. "Who are you?"

"Hello?" Sally called from the kitchen. "Phoebe?"

"Yep. It's me."

"Oh, I didn't hear the door." She came out, one hand still in an oven mitt, and gave me an awkward hug. "Wow, you're big."

"Uh-huh."

It was usually like this with Sally: ever so slightly brittle, if generally affectionate. In fact, I wasn't any taller than I'd been the last time we were together, or any broader if it came to that. It was more likely that Sally still had a sense of me as short and soft at around the age of twelve, and hadn't felt the need to update it.

"You look great," I said, because Sally really did. She had let her hair grow past the crew cut for the first time I could remember, and it brushed her shoulders, dark as root beer but now run with silvery strands as well. Sally would not be the sort to color her hair.

"How was the drive?"

"Exhausting. But interesting. I came up with a boy in my class, and his dad."

"Also looking at Cornell?"

I nodded. "But heading to Hamilton tomorrow, and then Dartmouth."

"And where else are you looking? C'mon back, I was just putting the vegetables in."

I followed, but didn't answer. I wasn't looking anywhere else. Actually, I still wasn't sure I was even looking at Cornell. All those hours in the car and I'd barely given a thought to the place, or to college in general; I'd just been trying to follow Jack's father through his various discourses on communism in the American Midwest, and the new crop of playwrights he was nurturing, and the destabilization of the two-party system, and the founding philosophy of his theater. Jack himself, I couldn't help noticing, plowed through at least half of the book he was reading during the same period. I wished I'd brought a book.

"I'd rather not think about any of it, if you want to know the truth," I said. I pulled out one of the chairs at the kitchen table. "Maybe I don't want to go at all, or not yet. Maybe I should take time off, but even if I did that, they still want you to get your shit together enough to apply, then defer, and I'm, like, if I'm organized enough to apply, why am I not organized enough to actually go?"

"I agree," Sally said, coming to sit at the table with me. "It's like this big conveyor belt to get you out the door of your parents' house, that's all it is. More people should take time off. If they don't, they get here and just get overwhelmed. Why not go work for a couple of years? You can work for me."

I looked at her in shock. "Really?"

"Why not? Not everyone likes the work, it's only fair to say. And I can be a little bitchy as a boss."

"I had a bitchy boss last summer. At the day camp. I can handle that."

This had been an unpleasant woman from Queens who seemed to hate children, but the other counselors, a mix of high school and college students, were friendly and fun to hang out with, and as a group we had reached an early and silent accord: *we tolerate the boss, we focus on the kids, we hang together on the weekends.* There was one boy I'd loved in particular: a Yale student, African American, crazy smart, and also from Brooklyn. He could quiet the kids with a few wiggles of his fingers. He'd promised to stay in touch, but hadn't.

The room was bright and warm and immaculate. The dark wooden countertops and gleaming white sink, at least four feet wide, looked as if they got wiped down any time a speck of salt or a drop of water marred their surfaces, and the table, which I remembered from my last visit, was long and wide and each leg looked a little like a thick double helix of solid wood. "I always liked this table," I said.

"Yes, me too. It belonged to the woman who used to own this house. Actually it was her family's dining table. She called it 'brown furniture.'"

"Is that a technical term?"

"Sort of. Technical for 'completely out of fashion.' Today, anything not made from the 1940s to the 1970s is out of fashion. But that's okay. It'll come back, and meanwhile I have a nice table." She went back to the stove, opened the oven door, and dribbled olive oil over a pan of carrots and parsnips, then she slid it back into the oven with a thunk, and as she did the room filled with a deep and peppery waft of roasting chicken.

"Oh my God, that smells so good," I said. We hadn't stopped for lunch, only bathroom breaks. "Thank God somebody in our family can cook."

"Can't you?" said Sally, getting a bottle of beer from the fridge.

"No. I have no domestic skills. I could never do this," I said, waving at the kitchen. "It's so pretty here. I mean, I completely understand why you wanted this and not, you know, Brooklyn."

"Well!" Sally smiled. "Those weren't the only two options, you know. To be honest I never made this big decision: *I. Like. Ithaca. I'm. Going. To Stay. In. Ithaca.* I just . . . kind of got comfortable. So I stayed. And I like my house, and I like my job. I like my cat. And also, I've met someone."

I looked at her. Was this going to be it? The big declaration? Obviously anticlimactic, but kind of awesome, too? *See under Dyke,* I remembered thinking, years ago, when I was twelve and Sally came down to the Vineyard for a couple of days. Of course they'd been throwing Gender and Sexuality in Society down our throats since third grade at the Walden School, and at least half the faculty and staff brought their same-sex partners to Founder's Day, the annual school celebration, but I had also been taught not to make assumptions based on how a person looked, spoke, gestured, dressed, or wore their hair, which was confusing since it was ridiculous not to note the correlations. My own lesbian classmates at Walden had no discernible markers; they looked like everyone else and dressed like everyone else and in fact widely preferred newer terms like "pansexual" to the old-fashioned "gay" or even "bi." But the lesbian teachers, mainly my siblings' age, were all powerful women with short hair in button-down shirts and sometimes a tie, and they looked you in the eye and told you—silently!—that they'd taken far too much shit for far too long to tolerate your acting in any way like a dick about any aspect of who they were, so if you were not completely chill on the subject it was time to reconsider your decision to be a middle school student at the Walden School. Any questions?

I had no questions. I had ascertained, early on, that my own gender identity and sexuality were generally white-bread cis-hetero, and that was fine, but anything else would have been fine, too. And Sally was fine. I had never, for what it was worth, seen my sister in makeup, and only once—at our grandmother's funeral in New Jersey—in a dress (and looking none too happy about it, either). I had also never, until now, seen Sally's hair extend past her jawline. And I had never heard Sally so much as mention a companion of either (any) gender.

"Do tell," I said simply. So Sally did.

Her name was Paula. She'd come to Ithaca for the vet school (large animal, Sally clarified) but turned out to hate the crack-of-dawn hours and the muck, so she'd gone into research. Now she taught at the vet school. "That's her cat, actually," said Sally, who seemed, for the first time, ever so slightly embarrassed.

"Nice cat."

"Yes. His name is Pyewacket."

"Well, that's . . . unusual."

"After the familiar in *Bell, Book and Candle*. You know that movie?"

I did. I had watched it with Lewyn one night the previous summer, after a long day of camp counseling. "You know," I said, "I'm not really here to go on a tour of Cornell. I mean, I'll do it, but it's not why I'm here."

"Okay," said Sally, with caution.

"I want to talk about some things. I'm tired of us all being so . . . you know, nobody connected. I don't know you enough. I don't know Harrison at all."

Sally smiled. "That might not be such a loss. I hate what he's doing. Actually I hate everything he's done since he left for college. Maybe we don't all get an opportunity to make the world better, but can we at least not fuck it up more?"

"I don't disagree," I told her. "But he's my brother, just as much as you're my sister. I know we didn't grow up together, but I'm an adult now. I'd kind of like us not to be this broken. I mean, if it can be helped. Maybe there's something I'm not understanding."

Sally was quiet. After a moment she got up and fetched the dishes from one of the cupboards and set the table. "Want to wash up before dinner?" she said.

I took my bag upstairs. I remembered the room, on the third floor, which had a massive four-poster bed (this had also, apparently, come with the house; I could hardly imagine getting it in or out!), and I dropped my things on it and went into the bathroom. The view from the window stretched down the slope of East Seneca Street, toward the main part of town. I felt something warm against my ankle and looked down to see the cat, Pyewacket, looking up at me. "Pye, Pye, Pye," I said, remembering how Kim Novak had said something similar in the film, and reaching down to stroke the black cat's ears. When I left to go back downstairs, Pyewacket was getting comfortable on the four-poster.

Sally had set everything out on the kitchen table: the chicken on an old ironstone platter, the vegetables still in the pan. There was a salad, too, and a jar of pickled green beans from, Sally said, the farmer's market. I was so hungry I genuinely forgot what I'd wanted to talk about. My sister hadn't, though.

"Here's what I want to say," she told me, cutting into the crisp chicken skin. "I'm not very . . . emotional, you know. Or maybe you don't. But I've never been the person running toward the big, deep discussions. It's done me a lot of damage, I'm aware. And that's totally self-inflicted, but it's also what comes naturally to me. As far as what you said, before, about our being broken, you're absolutely right. And you are absolutely entitled to have any conversation with me you want to have. But I have to tell you, I'm going to hate every minute of it."

"Sorry," I said, and I meant it. I'd been eating throughout this speech. I couldn't even slow down, the food was too good.

"And at the same time I'm kind of so proud of you for putting me on the spot like this. You absolutely are a grown-up. To me you're always that baby, you know?"

"So much younger, you mean."

"Right."

"And yet, exactly the same age as the rest of you."

Sally stopped cutting her food. "Well, well," she said. "I see somebody's had *that* conversation with you. Mom?"

"As if," I told her. "And it's a big deal, too. I mean, what if it was you, left behind like that? How would you feel?"

Sally considered. "Existentially defrauded. Since you asked."

"Well, there you have it. I feel existentially defrauded. I missed everything because of a random decision some doctor probably made while he was eating his lunch. I missed everything good."

"Oh, I wouldn't say that. You missed a ton of crap."

"I missed having siblings. You know, around me."

"Not such a great experience, actually."

"I missed Dad."

Sally held her bottle between her palms and picked at the label. She was wearing a denim shirt, open at the neck, the sleeves rolled up nearly to her bony elbows.

"Yeah," she said. "That isn't fair. The dad part."

We ate in silence for a moment.

"Do you know an artist named Achilles Rizzoli?" I asked her.

She shook her head. "One of Dad's?"

"It's up for debate," I said. "Lewyn's never heard of him, but a major museum seems to feel we're hiding most of his life's work."

She shrugged. "Not my field. I was more than happy to hand that stuff off to Lewyn."

"What about someone named S. S. Western?" I asked her.

Even if she'd tried to say no, I'd have known she was lying. But she didn't say no. She didn't say anything for a long moment. Then she nodded. "I suppose you have a reason for bringing her up."

"I do," I said, and I told her about the letter from the museum. Then I took another piece of chicken off the platter, and waited.

"Fine. But first, I really need to ask you if this is what you want. Existentially defrauded, we said. Right?"

I nodded.

"Because this is actually a burden. If you're asking me to share it with you, I'm willing to do it, but there are very good reasons not to want this."

The crazy thing was that I all of a sudden *didn't* want this. Whatever it was I'd suddenly crashed up against, it had to be bad, a game-changer, and did I really want a game-changer right now, in horrifying close-up? Was it too late to go back to the big house in Brooklyn, with the closed-off mom upstairs and the closed-off brother in the basement? Because how was any of it my responsibility? I'd hardly been an active participant.

But of course I said yes. I had come all this way in order to say yes. So Sally told me.

S. S. Western was a person named Stella, Sally explained, and Stella had been our father's lover.

I stared at her. "How do you know that?"

"I saw them together. There's no doubt in my mind. I don't know when it started, but I am absolutely certain it never stopped. Or not till he died. They were together."

I just looked at her. I couldn't get the words to line up correctly.

"But . . . what do you mean, together?"

"I mean they had a place somewhere, I don't know where. In Brooklyn, probably. Ever since I can remember, he said he was going out to the warehouse, where the paintings were, spending hours there almost every evening. It was normal for him not to be home with us in the evening. But after I saw them together, I started paying closer attention. Sometimes he came home late. Sometimes he came home in the morning. I could see him, from my window. Your window," she added. Our window overlooked the Montague Terrace door.

"You're telling me," I said, "that he was going back and forth between our family and this . . . person? And you don't even know for how long?"

"Yes." Sally nodded. "And no, I don't know for how long."

"But you . . . you saw them. Where? When was that?"

Sally calculated. "I was in eighth grade, so I guess . . . 1995? I followed him to an art show, and I saw them together. And I mean together. And . . . well, this is embarrassing. I'm not trying to put myself in the narrative here, but I think it's relevant to say that I had kind of an instant crush on her, too. She was very beautiful. It was kind of a shock to me as a closeted little middle schooler," she said, after a moment. "Well, there you go. There goes that perfect dad you never got to know. You can thank me now."

"Do you think Mom knew?" I asked her.

Sally shrugged. "I was hardly going to be the one to tell her, and she was hardly going to confide in me. And obviously our father's love affair was never a topic of open conversation, chez Oppenheimer. Can you imagine? But eventually, I think she knew. I think she found out, and I think . . . well, if I'm being completely honest, and I think that's what you're asking me to be, I've always wondered if maybe her finding out made her desperate enough to do something she probably shouldn't have done. Like bring a baby into that kind of a mess. Of course, now, I'm glad she did it. Because it's you," Sally finished, lamely.

I just looked at her. "I'm not sure I'm understanding," I said, but even as I said it I did begin to understand. I understood it just fine. How distant from *We might as well* that decision had been, really.

I looked down at the ruin of my plate. I couldn't remember eating it all. I couldn't remember being hungry.

"I was an unpleasant little teenager," my sister said. "I just thought about myself. But now I think about Mom, and what that must have been like for her. Three adolescents dying to leave and a husband who'd already checked out? Gruesome. But I was too angry at him to think about her. I was angry at him till the day he died. In fact, I told him . . ."

Her throat caught. She spread her hand out on the table: white fingers, dark brown wood.

"What?" I said.

"The night before he died, I told him I knew. I said I'd known for years.

I was very not nice about it, either. I said he was a terrible father. And that's the last thing I ever said to him. How lovely is that?"

"Sally. You didn't know it was the last thing you'd ever say to him."

"No. But I've known every day since. It's been a bit of an issue for me, in therapy. Years with one of Ithaca's finest!" She smiled.

"Well. Okay. I'm glad you have that."

We sat together in silence. I got up to take my plate to the sink.

"I named you," Sally said. "Did anyone ever tell you that? She wanted a *P* name, for her father, because he'd died the winter of that year. I suggested the name Phoebe. I was thinking: *Phoebe, phoenix.* Maybe I was more hopeful than I remember being. Maybe I thought: Okay! This baby could be like a phoenix, rising out of the wreckage of our very fucked-up family. That didn't happen, but it wasn't your fault. You were our sister, and we all treated you like you were nothing to us. We just packed up and left you there, in all of that crazy. I feel terrible about it. I've felt terrible for years."

She certainly looked as if she felt terrible. She was hunched forward, hands around her bottle, avoiding my eyes. "Well, you can stop," I said. "I'd probably have done the same if I'd . . ." I searched for the words. "Been born in the first round."

"Okay. Thanks." Then Sally shook her head. "Well, good. That was another of my therapy goals. Forgiveness for abandoning you."

"Fine. Now you can stop going, I guess."

"Better not. I've still got a long list of shit to get through."

The cat came trotting down the stairs and into the kitchen. Outside, now, it was fully dark.

"Did you ever wonder where he was going that day?"

I looked at her. I wasn't at all sure I was ready, not for *this*.

"I was told," I said carefully, "a business trip. To Los Angeles."

"Okay."

"But . . . what are you saying?"

"I'm saying . . . I think he might have been on his way to Stella. It's just an idea I've always had, that she was out there and he was going to her, and it meant he was finally leaving. Not me and the boys, we were already gone.

But Mom. And, I guess, you." She looked at me. "I can hate him for you, if you want. You got so little of him, it doesn't seem fair. I had enough, and some good things to remember. Let me hate him for you."

I nodded, but not because I agreed, necessarily. I just had no words left.

Chapter Twenty-Nine

A Bit of Liberation

In which Sally Oppenheimer admits to having done a highly crappy thing

Jack Neubauer and his father, on an accelerated schedule and likely already en route to Hamilton, were not at my 11:00 A.M. information session at the Welcome Center, nor on the tour that followed, a New Yorker–worthy speed-walk through the endless campus. I wasn't prepared for how much colder it was up here, only a few hours north of the city, but my sister had given me a parka to wear. I kept my hands deep in its pockets as I chased after the guide, a chirpy, backward-walking rugby player named Celeste, trying to imagine the various members of my family as students here and attempting, unsuccessfully, to "see myself" at Cornell. When Celeste bade us all farewell at Ho Plaza, I headed north on Central Avenue to the Johnson Museum, where Sally had arranged to meet me, and where, against all odds, a small selection of our grandparents' art collection was on display.

"This really is a nice coincidence," Sally said, when she puffed in a few minutes later. "They've only been up a couple of times since I've been living here. Once there was a big exhibit of the whole collection, and occasionally individual paintings get included here or there if they fit with other shows.

Religious art, Venetian painters, depictions of the afterlife, that kind of thing. You've never seen any of this stuff, have you?"

No, I hadn't. It's a truth universally acknowledged (at least within our family) that I have zero feelings about art, despite Lewyn's occasional efforts to enlighten and entice me. I followed Sally up the stairs, not exactly unhappy to be here but still braced for a less than pleasurable activity. The paintings were part of a large exhibition called, quite simply, "Gifted to Cornell," a hodgepodge of everything from primitive objects to a shiny blue Koons balloon dog, big as a garden shed. The only common denominator was that they'd been donated by grateful alumni (or perhaps, like Hermann and Selda Oppenheimer, in anticipation of future alumni). Sally found the relevant canvases in an alcove off one of the larger rooms, with a dedicatory plaque of its own:

From the Oppenheimer collection,
gifted to Cornell in 1970 by Selda and Hermann Oppenheimer
with additional gifts in 1999 by Solomon Oppenheimer '75
(P: Lewyn Oppenheimer '04, P: Sally Oppenheimer '04)

The collection comprised thirty-one paintings by Old Masters from
northern Europe, fourteenth through nineteenth centuries.
Artists included Joos van Cleve, Hans Burgkmair, Lucas van Leyden,
Rogier van der Weyden, and Hans Baldung Grien.

"I guess they don't care that Lewyn didn't graduate from Cornell," Sally observed. She was inclining toward a painting whose label read: Bartholomeus van der Helst, *Boy with a Spoon,* 1643. "I suppose it doesn't matter, from a development perspective."

"No," I said. "I guess not. Is your class still considered 2004?"

Mom and I had driven up in 2012 to watch Sally get her degree.

"Apparently so. I can't say I'm all that involved with either class."

We spent a couple of minutes looking at the four paintings. As usual, when faced with art—presented, usually, by Lewyn, but also on class trips to museums—I had no idea what I was supposed to be looking at. These paintings were "good," obviously, or they wouldn't be in a museum; beyond that I was clueless.

"It's very . . . dark," I said, in conclusion.

Sally laughed. "Phoebe, I feel exactly the same. C'mon, I want to show you some stuff."

Outside, my sister pointed out the pillared, classical pile across the quad. "I spent a lot of time there, after I reenrolled. I still had no big academic interest in anything particular, but there was this professor there, in women's studies, who urged me to be part of that program, so that's where I ended up. I had the business by then, and I was working all the time, but they were very accommodating. It was a good department for someone without a vocation," she said thoughtfully. "I mean, I had a vocation. I have a vocation. But academically, no. Not like Harrison, or, I guess, Lewyn. Eventually." She looked again at Goldwin Smith Hall. "MJ Loftig, her name was. I think she's at Columbia now."

"How come you dropped out?" I asked. "Or . . . took a leave, or whatever?"

"Oh, well, I was living in the house on East Seneca, with the woman whose business I took over. Her name was Harriet Greene. I was working for her and getting to know the business, and it was just so much more interesting than anything I was studying here. And also she wasn't very well, and didn't have any family."

"So she was like your mentor."

"Kind of. She was a very crotchety person, but fond of me. I think she saw me as a fellow traveler. There aren't that many people who do what we do, and actually like it."

We started to walk north, to Thurston Avenue.

"You mean buy and sell antiques?"

"No," Sally laughed. "I mean clear out putrid old houses. For Harriet the clean-outs were what she had to do, sometimes, to get to the furniture, or whatever else of value might be in there. For me, I think it's kind of the opposite. I love old things, and I definitely love finding something great that I can sell or find a good home for, but sometimes I feel like they're my excuse to go in there and empty out the houses. The first time I did it, it just made total sense to me, and I never cared that people found it strange, or thought it wasn't a real job. I don't even mind that the clients think it's crazy, somebody making a career out of clearing away their mess. Harriet taught me how to talk to people about what we could do for them, and the psychology of it, and then also how to make money from what we found. She taught me everything I needed to know."

I walked with my hands clenched in my pockets. "So this woman, Harriet, did she die?"

"Uh-huh. About three years after I moved in. By that time I was running things by myself, pretty much. I never formally bought the business or anything, I just took over her contacts, and she had one employee I kept on. He still works for me. And her name, I made part of the new business name, Greene House Services. Sort of a tribute, I guess."

"Oh!" I looked at her. "I always thought it was 'green,' like environmentally green. I didn't realize it was someone's name."

"It's both. There's absolutely an environmental element. Some houses get toxic. They're full of plastic and waste. They're a pollution in itself. Getting them clean, recycling what can be recycled, making a space habitable for human beings, all good for the planet as far as I'm concerned. Actually," she said, "Harriet's own house wasn't in the best of shape when I moved in. She was clean, but she had the space packed out with furniture. It needed a bit of liberation, too."

This was hard to envision. Both times I'd visited before this one, the East Seneca Street house had enjoyed Sally's signature order, not to speak of her passionate cleanliness.

"So she left the house to you then?"

"Oh, no," Sally said, smiling. "We never discussed it, and she died without a will. But after the executor came in, I told him I'd buy it at fair market value, with the furniture, and he agreed. Nothing in the house was updated, so it wasn't going to be an easy sell. But I loved it. I still love it."

"What happened to all that furniture?"

"Sold some. Kept some. Here's the bridge."

At the Thurston Avenue Bridge, I looked down into my very first Ithaca gorge, now outfitted with a suicide net but still spectacular. We stood as long as we could bear the chill, staring at Triphammer Falls, then walked the rest of the way across, bending forward into the wind. Sally led me into a gray stone courtyard, where she stopped. "Lewyn lived there, freshman year," she said, pointing. Then she gestured at the building right in front of us. "I was here."

"So close! You must have seen each other all the time."

Sally smiled. "We might have *seen* each other, occasionally. But we stayed out of each other's lives, completely. Almost as if we'd talked about it beforehand, which we didn't. I never told anyone I had a brother at Cornell. I'm pretty sure he didn't tell anyone he had a sister, either."

"But didn't people know?" I asked. "I mean, you had the same name."

"It wasn't like now," said Sally, "with everything online. There wasn't an 'online,' really, except for chat groups and stuff on AOL. There was some kind of university database, but only computer students did anything with it, and you couldn't just google someone, or try to find out about them on social media. There wasn't any social media, not even MySpace."

I didn't know what MySpace was.

"I also know for a fact that he told at least one person Oppenheimer was a common name, so another Cornell student named Oppenheimer wasn't anything to him."

"Like Simon Peter," I laughed. "He denied you."

"Well, we denied each other. We just didn't want to know each other here."

"I think that's sad," I told her. "Where are we going now?"

We were going to a place called Carol's Café, a location all but unchanged from Sally's student days, apparently. Inside, out of the cold, we brought our coffee to a table. "I asked Paula if she could join us for lunch, at Moosewood," she said, stirring sugar into hers. "I honestly don't care if you go to Cornell or not, but you have to experience Moosewood."

Paula had made her appearance late the night before, when both of us had run out of steam and were sitting side by side on the Victorian couch in the formal living room, watching Stephen Colbert on television. She was a tall woman, still broad shouldered and strong from the rowing she had done in college. She'd blown through cheerily that morning on her way out to the Ag Quad, leaving a kiss on Sally's cheek that was far more sensual than I had ever witnessed a kiss on a cheek to be.

"She'd like to get to know you better," said Sally.

"Okay," I said. "But I'm a carnivore. And isn't Moosewood all the way on the other side of campus? Why did we come all the way up here?"

"Well," Sally was stirring her coffee, "I was thinking, last night, that there was something else I wanted to talk to you about. And I wanted to show you the dorms, because you're right, it's sad what happened with Lewyn and me in college. I still think about it."

"Another therapy goal?" I smiled.

"I'm afraid so. And the fact is, I did something really crappy to Lewyn back then. And he still hasn't forgiven me. And he's been absolutely right not to."

"Oh. Well, it couldn't have been that bad," I said warily.

But it was. It was so bad that Sally actually began to falter as she told this story, which was all about a person named Rochelle Steiner who had been her freshman-year roommate, and her friend, and . . . well, this was actually a big part of the problem. "You can't imagine," Sally said, "how deep in denial I was. It was a catastrophe that I thought I might be gay. Obviously, people were, and they were out. Plenty of gay women here at Cornell, and Walden was totally ahead of the curve, a very gay-friendly place. And it's not like I grew up in some Born Again home in Indiana. The world really *was* okay in 2000, or at least the part of it I was living in. But to me it wasn't okay, and it wouldn't be for a long time after that. So all during my freshman year I was sharing a tiny little room with this woman, and falling in love with her, and the effort it took to not let that out, or not even let it get through to myself, was just overwhelming. And then this incredibly unlikely thing happened. She met Lewyn and the two of them fell in love."

I stared at her. "That's . . . wow," was all I could think of to say. "Inconvenient. Awful, actually."

Lewyn had never mentioned a person named Rochelle Steiner. He had never mentioned any woman at all, not in a romantic sense, except the one from his master's program.

"Rochelle Steiner," I said aloud, hearing the name in my own voice.

"He lied to her, of course. Like I said. That was his contribution. But by the time he did that, I'd already been lying to her for months. I said I had a twin brother, and he went to college in New Hampshire. I don't even know why I told her that. I was so angry at him. And her. All I could think of was how to punish them. So I brought her up to the Vineyard with me, and sprung her on him. On all of us, I guess. That was the same night, the night I told Dad what a horrible person he was."

"And this was the crappy thing."

"Yes. Highly crappy."

"You must have been very unhappy," I said, whereupon Sally burst into tears.

I sat, watching her, my hand on her wrist. There were others in the café, scattered about at the tables, mainly with open books. A few looked over, but saw that the weeping woman with her face in her hands wasn't alone, and went back to whatever they were doing.

"We all had an awful fight. Lewyn, apparently, had told Harrison I was a lesbian, and Harrison just announced it to everyone."

"Bastard!" I said, horrified. "Both of them."

"Yes. And then Dad actually told me it was okay, but I was so furious at everyone, and so embarrassed. That's when I told him I knew about Stella. It was the last night of his life, and I basically left him with: *you're a terrible father*. And that was our nineteenth birthday, all of us screaming and stomping off. You were crying, too," she recalled. "For what it's worth."

"Well, at least I got to participate in one important family event."

Sally sighed. "And that was that. Because the next day, as we all know, Dad got on a plane and died, and we were all, just, frozen right where we were. Where we still are, I guess."

I took my sister's hand, and thought: *Yes. But not for much longer.*

Chapter Thirty

A Bit of a Bastard

In which Harrison Oppenheimer explains what negotiation is for

I want it on record that I declined my brother's invitation to join him inside the Fox News affiliate on Forty-Eighth Street. I found Harrison's car and driver parked outside and got into the back to wait for him there, but then, succumbing to temptation (and the luxury of the limo's waiting television), I tuned in to watch him do his thing.

The topic at hand was a class-action lawsuit alleging discrimination by college admissions officers, specifically at Harvard. The effort, mounted by Asian applicants, had been predictably co-opted by groups far more concerned with keeping Black and brown people out than with letting Asian people (one member of the panel actually used the word "Oriental") in, and the only other person of color at the table—apart from Harrison's eternally present friend, Eli Absalom Stone—could do little more than beat back increasingly personal assaults. Harrison himself asked an attorney named Shaunta Owens whether she was aware that the average SAT score of accepted African American applicants in her own UPenn class (1983) had been a full hundred points lower than that of white applicants, and when she answered yes he plowed on unforgivingly. "And are you not deeply chagrined by this fact? How do you expect your own accomplishments to be fairly viewed through the scrim of obvious pandering to political correctness? When somebody looks at you and sees entitlement on the basis of ethnicity—"

"Someone like yourself," interjected Shaunta Owens, whom Fox was identifying as "Commentator."

"Someone like any person capable of understanding that when you let a person of statistical inferiority in over a person of statistical superiority you are *insulting* them, *insulting* the person who has been declined in their favor, and *insulting* the integrity of the entire process. I feel insulted on your behalf, and I'm amazed you do not."

"I'm certainly insulted by your tone," said Shaunta Owens. She looked, to me, as if she was ready to overturn the table.

"If I may," said Eli Absalom Stone, who was seated between my brother and this person, Shaunta Owens. "Throughout my life as a scholar and writer, I have considered myself to be far more burdened by the perception of unearned advantages given to me because of my ethnicity than by my ethnicity itself. Before I applied for anything—college admission, or a scholarship, or a job—I went to some lengths to avoid any personal uncertainty about my accomplishments by ensuring that my credentials were not only on par with the statistical averages of their successful applicants, but actually with their upper strata."

Here, Fox helpfully flashed the pertinent facts below Eli Absalom Stone's navy-blue bow tie: "Graduate of Harvard University and Rhodes Scholar."

"If they hadn't been, I would not have applied. End of story. I was not willing to trade my own integrity for a leg up I in no way deserved. And it gives me a great deal of distress, Ms. Owens, to think that *so many of us* seem willing to *trade their integrity* for what I can only see as a form of *Jim Crow treatment.* However it may present itself."

"I'm very comfortable with my accomplishments, thank you, Mr. Stone," said a barely-keeping-it-together Shaunta Owens.

None of this was surprising, by any means. I was about to switch it off when my brother spoke again.

"Justice Thomas has written that these 'special consideration' programs brand minorities with a badge of inferiority and may give them cause to feel that they are entitled to preferences in all corners of society. Any institutional preference is also, de facto, institutional discrimination inspired by prejudice, and that is unacceptable in whatever form it appears. I'm sure you can agree with that, Ms. Owens."

"And besides!" said the Fox News host, a woman of extreme blondness with a Borax smile. "You'd have to be crazy to think there's anti-Asian discrimination at any of these top-tier places. I took my twins on a college tour last spring break, I'm telling you, every other person we saw was Asian. I mean, everywhere!"

Jesus Christ, I thought.

"I'm sorry, miss?" said the driver, through the intercom.

"Oh, I'm sorry. I didn't realize I said it aloud."

I did turn off the television after that.

It had always been like this. Every time I got it into my head to spend time with Harrison, to get to know him a little bit better and be, perhaps, a little bit better known by him, I had run into the very same obstacle: Harrison. More specifically, the noxious, unbearable opinions and associations of Harrison, ostensibly the family star, certainly its most visible member. Harrison, as current president of Wurttemberg Holdings, was also the one responsible for maintaining and extending our individual and collective wealth, and I supposed that was a good thing (I personally had no intention of declining the security and advantages that came with that wealth), but his extracurricular activities as toady to the current president and inhabitant of that vile gray zone between fiscal conservative and Tiki Torchbearer made him less and less palatable every time I resolved to try again.

After returning from Ithaca the week before, and in an ongoing effort to avoid the now-looming task of applying to college, I'd emailed my brother and suggested we talk. In person.

Arranging this turned into an ordeal of its own.

Oppenheimer_H@WurttembergHoldings.com

October 17, 2017. 10:21 A.M.

Yes, lovely to hear from you. Certainly we can meet. Why not come to office next Tues 11:15 am.

Cc'ing Flora who will confirm.

H. Oppenheimer

P.Oppenheimer@WaldenSchool.com

October 17, 2017. 10:40 A.M.

Harrison, I am a high school student. At 11:15 next Tuesday I will be in Latin class.

Hi Flora.

Phoebe

Oppenheimer_H@WurttembergHoldings.com

October 17, 2017, 12:10 P.M.

Delighted to hear that Walden is finally offering Latin.

Begged and pleaded, to no avail.

Tuesday at 4 pm office.

Cc'ing Flora who will confirm.

H. Oppenheimer

P.Oppenheimer@WaldenSchool.com

October 17, 2017, 12:31 P.M.

Sorry, track practice. Can I just come visit on the weekend?

Phoebe

Oppenheimer_H@WurttembergHoldings.com

October 18, 2017, 9:33 A.M.

Will be at board retreat in Virginia. Suggest 10/28 6:30 Harvard Club.

Cc'ing Flora who will confirm.

H.

And on like this for another half dozen go-rounds, with his proposed dates stretching into November. At last he suggested I meet him at Fox News the following Saturday, then come back to his apartment. Whether or not he'd finally sensed there was something of possible consequence I wanted to talk about I wasn't sure, but naturally I accepted. Not the Fox News part, though. Waiting for him in a limo in front of the studio was about as close as I could bear to get to Fox News.

After Ithaca I'd taken a few days to think through Sally's various revelations; they were intense, intermittently distressing, and, in complete contrast, somehow also a great relief, as the previously invisible pegs of my own secret history began to drop into their appointed holes. I'd also decided to stop wondering why this was apparently my job, this reweaving of the shredded fabric of our family, the figuring out what was owed to whom by whom and how we were all supposed to become unstuck with one another. Maybe I just wanted it more than any of the others did, or was better able to understand that I wanted it, or to say that I wanted it, or all of that at once. But the bald fact was that there wasn't anybody else volunteering to make it happen. Our father was dead. Our mother was basically estranged from Lewyn—despite his physical proximity—and Sally, and not terribly interested in me (except, at the moment, in where I was going to college and how far behind I was on my applications). Sally and her brothers did not speak, Harrison and Lewyn were locked in mutual disdain. I had a real sense that if things didn't improve by the time I graduated Walden and (presumably) left home, the center—whatever center remained in our family—would not hold, not for one moment longer.

If not me, in other words, who?

If not now, in other words, when?

"I hear you're going to see Harrison appear on Fox News tomorrow," our mother announced on Friday afternoon, as I made my post-practice tea.

"Well, yes and no. Yes to Harrison, no to Fox News. I cannot deal. How do you stand it?"

"He's entitled to his opinions. You can't say he isn't well-informed."

I could if I wanted to, I thought. Instead, I hedged. "I doubt they're very proud of him at Walden these days. He's like a one-man repudiation of everything they hold dear."

"I sent my children to Walden to be educated. Not indoctrinated."

"Fair point."

"And one thing I have always admired about Harrison is his self-awareness, and his drive."

That's two things, I thought, but I didn't interrupt.

"He knew from an early age what he wanted, and he worked very hard for it. I wish Sally and Lewyn had had a bit more of that."

I got a spoon from the drawer and lifted my tea bag out of the mug, depositing it in the trash. There was no point in noting that Sally, too, had chosen an occupation at a relatively early age, or that she ran a hale little business which more than supported her and more than fulfilled her. Or that Lewyn, after some undeniable wandering, had found work commensurate with his talents and interests.

"Drive is fine. But not everyone knows what they want as early as Harrison did. I don't know what I want, for example."

I don't even know where to apply to college, I almost said. I didn't. It didn't matter.

"Have you decided where you're applying to college?" she said, meeting my expectations.

"I'm narrowing it down," I said. An utter fiction.

I waited in the limo for another half an hour after switching off Harrison's panel, time I passed in monitoring its lively Twitter response. This debate ranged in substance from deeply unpleasant comments about Shaunta Owens's "Black accent" to the usual praise for Eli Absalom Stone and his great, self-reliant rise. Regarding Harrison himself, the predominant words were: "blowhard" and "dickwad," with an opposing cluster of "sensible" and "hypocritical libtards!" but none of this struck me as at all remarkable. I put my phone away when he finally turned up.

"Hello there," my brother said, climbing in beside me. He gave me a perfunctory kiss on the cheek, then another on the other cheek. (It was one of the habits—some might call them affectations—he had picked up during his Rhodes years.) "Eli's here. We're dropping him at his apartment."

Eli had been waylaid on the sidewalk. He was signing a book for a man and his teenaged son.

"Okay," I said.

I had met Eli before, of course. It was hard not to meet Eli when seeing Harrison. Eli lived a few blocks from my brother, in another elegant Sutton Place building, and though his primary affiliation was with a policy and education think tank based in DC, the two of them were mainly engaged in the common pursuit of writing books and "instigating change" together. Not the kind of change my own classmates were always going on about, either.

"Hello, Eli," I said when he joined us.

"Little Phoebe! My word. How old are you now?"

I told him. Seventeen. "And please don't ask me where I'm going to college. It's all anyone wants to know."

"It's a glorious time! Don't suffer. Delight in your choices and opportunities."

"By which you mean," I said, "my privilege?"

"There is nothing wrong with privilege. The suffering of others is no reason not to make the most of your own life. Should you stay home and rend your garments because somebody in Calcutta can't take the SAT?"

I glanced at Harrison. He was smiling, looking out at Sixth Avenue as it passed.

"Go to college, become educated, and create opportunities for people in Calcutta. This is called progress."

"Oh," I said with what I hoped was evident sarcasm.

"Your generation has become so marinated in self-loathing. They talk about the phones and the internet as great afflictions. These are not afflictions. The utterly pointless whining about collective guilt—this is the affliction. Let me ask you something. Have you ever enslaved another human being?"

I sighed. "Directly? No, of course not."

"Bashed a little puppy's head in?"

"Not that I can recall."

"Called someone . . ." He made quote marks with his fingers. "The N-word?"

I looked, involuntarily, at the driver, who was Black.

"No. Please."

"I'm happy to hear it. Great job! Now as a person"—again with the quote marks—"*of color,* I wave my magic wand and absolve you of all crimes real and imaginary. You may go, secure in the knowledge that the best thing that can be done for so-called minorities is to stop trying to help them *because* they are minorities. People can rise on their own. If it isn't on their own it doesn't last and it doesn't count."

"Like you," I said. "On your own."

"Entirely. Albeit with the great assistance of Plato, Sophocles, Mark Twain, Homer, Shakespeare, Donne."

I could almost hear the happy chorale that seemed to accompany Eli Absalom Stone wherever he referenced his story, though these days he did so less and less, mainly because he needed to less and less. The advent of Eli Absalom Stone, orphaned Black boy from the Appalachian mountain shack, bound for Harvard, Oxford, and the kind of cultural influence usually attached to people of entirely different antecedents, had saturated the populace.

We let him off at his apartment building and he leaned back in to say something to Harrison about dinner that night, with Roger, at Per Se, and it was arranged that they would meet for a cab at seven. Then I was given another double kiss, in which I felt the sharp edge of Eli's bow tie against first one cheek and then the other, and he exited the limo. I felt better when he was no longer there. I always felt better when he was no longer there.

"You haven't seen Eli since when?" said Harrison, holding the door for me a moment later.

"I don't know. Couple of years?"

"Before he spoke at the Republican Convention."

Yes, I thought. Very much so. "He's looking well."

"He should. He's had dinner at the White House twice this month."

This struck me as a dubious claim to health.

"And you, Harrison?"

"Once. In early August, before he left for vacation."

"Steak and apple pie, with an extra scoop of vanilla ice cream for the commander in chief?"

"You needn't be snide, Phoebe. Not everyone can win a presidential election."

I said nothing. It would be such a waste to lose my cool now.

Harrison's apartment actually comprised two apartments, purchased simultaneously and knocked together. It had also been "gut" renovated, then decorated with remorseless modern furniture. While this was not the tragedy it might have been to our sister Sally, it struck me as regrettable. The place did have a truly impressive view of the East River. Then again, I had never felt the East River to be all that attractive.

"What can I get you?" said Harrison. "I'm having a juice my doctor sends over. It's repulsive, but supposedly good for me. I'd offer you one, but I need them all, apparently. It's very strict."

I asked for tea. He didn't have real tea, just chamomile.

"Can you see our house from here?" I asked him. I was standing at one of the windows when he brought me the mug.

"I never looked. Maybe. You could fall out trying, though. It doesn't seem worth it."

"I study in your room, you know. I sleep in Sally's, but I study in yours. I love looking out on the harbor."

"Mm-hm," he nodded. He had brought himself a glass bottle of bright green juice, and had set his phone on the coffee table. It was abuzz with social media mentions, from his Fox panel. Harrison was trying not to look at it. "Well, why not? You have the whole house to yourself. Almost the whole house."

"If you're referring to Lewyn, he never comes upstairs. He's pretty much only in his apartment."

"By which you mean: in the basement."

"Yes, in the basement."

"Classic," Harrison said, drinking his juice. He had taken off his jacket in the kitchen and loosened his crimson tie (worn, I supposed, in support of his alma mater, currently under assault by all those rejected "complainants").

"You know, Harrison, it's a completely separate apartment. He could live anywhere. He chose to live there."

"If he could live anywhere, why would he choose to live there? He's afraid to leave home, obviously. It is truly pathetic."

"Actually, I've always assumed that he didn't want to leave me."

I heard myself say this, and it came as something of a surprise: another thing I hadn't quite put together. Like so many things these days.

"Don't be silly. You don't need looking after. You have a mother. You have an excellent mother."

I shook my head. "I have a once-excellent mother who is not all that interested in being a mother right now. Which is completely understandable given that she has been raising children for thirty-four years. I'm not sure how into it I'd be, on the second go-round."

"She is devoted to all of us. Equally."

"Oh, Harrison," I laughed. "Don't even."

"You're mistaken," he insisted, but he was good enough to leave it there. For a moment neither of us spoke. And then he asked me what it was I wanted to talk about.

"Stella Western, mainly," I said, without further preamble.

He crossed his arms. "Aha," he said.

"This is a name you are familiar with."

"Very familiar, yes. Stella Western is someone who has caused us all a good deal of grief."

I smiled. "Well, not me. She's caused me no grief at all, that I know of. Exactly what grief has she caused you?"

I watched him. He was regarding his juice bottle with outright hostility, as if it, too, had offended him. His jaw was set and his eyes were nearly closed. He was looking just a little bit . . . old, I realized. Or was it only the hairline, beginning to alter? And the lines running across his forehead, deep now as he glared, a spattering of makeup still along his forehead, which was just like the forehead of our father, in photographs. I could see him working through the options: *truth and consequences* versus *pride and consequences.*

"Phoebe," he said, turning to me, and this time, for the first time, without any of his prior condescension. "It's very difficult to know when to share information like this. It might change the way you feel about things. I'm not cavalier about it. I care about you. You are my little sister."

"No," I said. "I'm not, really. You should try thinking of me as your own age. I mean, exactly your own age. Like, down to the minute. See if that changes things."

He frowned at me. "All right," he said, after a minute. "I wasn't aware you knew about that."

"Well, now you are. So can we move this along? What grief has Stella Western caused our family?"

Harrison sighed. "There were some legal issues. Mom needed help. She confided in me. This was . . . well, a long time ago. Just after Dad passed away."

I had never had much love for this term, at least under the relevant circumstances. There was not one thing in the violent, deliberate, murderous collision of Salo Oppenheimer and his fellow passengers and their airplane with the South Tower of the World Trade Center that earned the ethereal, dreamy "pass away." But I let it go.

"What kind of legal troubles?"

Harrison shrugged. "Just . . . nothing to concern yourself with."

"Jesus, Harrison. I know they were involved. Stella Western and Dad."

Now he was staring at me. For a moment he was truly speechless. "And you learned about all of this how?" he finally said.

"Do you mean, which of our naughty siblings decided to enlighten *the baby*?"

"Actually, that is not what I mean. As far as I'm aware, I'm the only one of the *siblings* who knows anything about this."

I laughed at him. I had to. And besides, it felt ridiculously good.

"Who?" Harrison demanded. "Not Lewyn."

I shrugged.

"So. Sally. And how does Sally know? I highly doubt Mom shared any of this with *Sally*."

He said our sister's name with such profound disapproval. Of the three of them, he was the most intractable. He was unbearable, too.

"Sally has known since she was thirteen. Since all of you were thirteen. She saw them together, Harrison, if you must know. And she didn't tell anyone else—not Mom and certainly not you. Did you know that our father had a habit of staying out all night and coming home at dawn?"

After a moment, he said: "No. Actually."

"She could see him from her window. My window."

Harrison didn't answer.

"So would you please tell me about the legal troubles, Harrison?"

He sighed. "Stella Western wanted things from us. She wanted things she had no right to ask for, let alone assume she'd receive."

"What kind of things?"

"Property," he said shortly. "It was craven and it was disgusting."

I just gaped at him.

"Oh, don't look at me like that. *Privileged white family oppresses poor artiste. Of color!* Call the Walden morality force!" Harrison leaned back and crossed his legs. "It was a negotiation. It's how grown-ups settle their differences in a civilized world. And we settled them. In any case, I don't understand why this is something you need to burden yourself with. As you pointed out in your email, you are a high school student. Your concerns are—or should be—Latin and track. And yes, applying to college."

"Fuck applying to college!" I shouted. "Fuck this ridiculous, pathetic, thoroughly manufactured 'rite of passage' that's supposed to tell you if you're qualified to make money in America, and reassure your parents they did a good job raising you. It's the most asinine thing! I don't care about any of it. I don't want to rank my extracurriculars or freak out about ten points on the SAT I didn't get. I don't want to apply to Cornell because I have a thirty-five percent higher chance of getting in there, just because my father, whom I don't even remember, went there. And I don't want to end up crying because some school *I can see myself at* decides it's *unable to offer me admission at this time.* All I want is to go somewhere interesting and read some good books, and learn from people who know more than I do, and maybe talk about the world with people my own age."

"There's nothing wrong with making money, Phoebe. And I'm happy to say, in this country at least, you don't need formal qualifications to do it, just an idea and a work ethic."

"Says the man with degrees from Harvard and Oxford, and an almost two-hundred-year-old company that was handed to him to run."

"It was handed to me," he said, placidly, "first and foremost because I was the only one of us who had the first idea of how to run it, but also because I was the only one of us who seemed to care about acquiring wealth."

I glared at him. This was not untrue, at least, for Lewyn and Sally. For myself, I wasn't sure.

"I told the board, and Mom, when I came home from England, that I would take over, and I like running the company, but I also made it clear that I'd be structuring things so I'd have time to do my other work. Because while I am extremely serious about financial security for myself, and for Mom and incidentally for you, Phoebe, I do have additional interests and projects, unrelated to the company."

"Your additional interests and projects," I said, "have been noted. And for the record I have no personal objection to making money. I might not go in for the baubles, but I'd probably miss the infrastructure if it suddenly disappeared. I'm especially fond of our house, for example. And I appreciate the education."

"I'm happy to hear it. I've long since given up on my other siblings."

"But please don't misunderstand me. Building a border wall. Gutting healthcare. Criminalizing abortion. Keeping down the shithole countries. Very much not okay with me, so if you're going to do it, do it for yourself. Don't delude yourself that it's on my behalf, or anyone's behalf but your own. You really are a bit of a bastard, Harrison, you know."

He shrugged. He downed the last of his juice. "There are worse things to be."

"And possibly a bit of a racist."

"Now that," he turned to me, "is completely untrue. I'm race-blind. My best friend—"

"Is African American. I know. Blah, blah."

"No," Harrison said shortly. "He is not. Eli is American, full stop. Are we German American?"

I smiled. I was actually sort of enjoying this, I realized.

"The real racism is the assumption that some ethnicities need a leg up."

"Or a handout."

"Or a handout. Precisely. It's what Eli has been saying since he was seventeen."

"And what Eli says . . ." I left him hanging. Then I sat back against the couch, arms folded tightly and looking for all the world like the petulant child he apparently thought I was. When I finally looked at him, he was actually smiling at me.

"You've got a respectable brain there, Phoebe. What are you planning to do with it?"

"*Help people and make the world a better place.* It's what I'm planning to say in my application essay, anyway. What are you planning to do with yours?"

"Show people how not to be such pathetic idiots."

"Awesome."

Harrison said nothing for a moment. Then he said, thoughtfully: "How do you feel about chickens?"

"How do I . . . what?"

"Tell me, what are the college advisors advising you to do?"

"Oh, they keep giving me lists of places to research and telling me to read this book called *Colleges That Change Lives.*"

Harrison smiled. "And have you?"

"What? No. Of course not."

"Phoebe. You are an idiot."

He got up abruptly, leaving me to stare after him as he padded away, across the off-white carpeting, in his socks. A moment later he was back with a blue paperback in his hand. He tossed it into my lap. "My own copy. Take it. It's yours."

Colleges That Change Lives: 40 Schools You Should Know About Even if You're Not a

Straight-A Student. There was a boy on the cover, looking into a reflecting pool. A graduate in cap and gown looked back.

"What makes you think I'm not a straight-A student?" was all I could think of to say.

"No grades at Walden. Doesn't matter. There happens to be a chapter about Roarke."

I opened the paperback at random to a description of Grinnell's educational philosophy. Shura was "completely in love" with Grinnell, I recalled.

"I didn't even read it back when I was applying to college. I read it when I found out I was going to Roarke and someone told me it had a chapter. Besides, I didn't think Mom brought this home with me in mind. I think she figured Lewyn and Sally might need some off-brand place to go."

I nodded. I was still turning the pages. "Pretty ironic," I said.

"What is?"

"That you ended up at a college in the off-brand book, and they ended up at an Ivy League school."

When he didn't respond, I looked up from the book. He seemed to be dealing with a completely new idea, and not at all happy about it.

"Well, in due course I did as well," he finally said.

I smiled. "Of course you did. Anyway, thanks." I closed the book and set it down on the couch beside me. "I hope it's been updated since the year you applied to college."

"I'm sure it has. Roarke has been updated, too, you know. The board voted last spring to admit women. I disagreed, but it's been settled. You should think about applying. It changed my life, just like the title says."

It was the most intimate thing he had ever said to me.

"All right," I told him. "I will read it." Then, grudgingly: "Thank you."

I lifted the mug of chilly tea to my lips. It was as bad cold as it had been warm.

"You're wrong about Lewyn, you know," I told him. "At the very least you have to see he's done an excellent job with the art. He's published exhibition introductions, and articles in art journals. Not to mention a book about the collection as a whole."

"Self-published," said Harrison, with deep scorn.

"No, Harrison. Not self-published. A very good academic publisher." I shook my head. "For some reason I don't understand, you have made up your mind that he's some kind of incompetent buffoon. Maybe he was, once. I wasn't here. But he isn't today and he hasn't been for many years. He's the only brother you'll ever have, and you're missing your chance to know him as he actually is. Right now."

"Thank you, Phoebe. Very heartfelt."

"And Sally, too. Sally is a wonderful person. And an entrepreneur."

"Sally cleans houses. Lewyn went off to be a Mormon, like somebody joining a cult."

"Well, so what? So he went walkabout for a year or two. He had to figure things out, and he did. So did Sally. Just because you already knew everything, that doesn't mean . . . I don't know. That you win."

"The person who knows the most wins. Not necessarily the smartest. The one who knows the most."

"Oh my God, Harrison. You are absolutely pathetic."

The two of us sat in silence for a while.

"Here's something else I'd like to know," I said, opening up my backpack and removing the letter from the American Folk Art Museum. "What about this Achilles Rizzoli? Subject of a documentary by Stella Western. Apparently we're hiding his entire life's work somewhere. What do you know about it?"

He was scanning the letter. He did not look pleased.

"I see you've opened your mother's mail. Is this a habit for you?"

"I opened it by accident," I said. "I'm getting so much mail from colleges right now. Please answer my question."

He said nothing.

"Did you know there was an earlier request about these paintings?"

"Drawings. Not paintings. I can't say."

"So you did know."

"That's a possibility."

"And you won't tell me."

"I'm not at liberty to do so. Not at the present time." He crossed his arms like a petulant toddler.

"Jesus, Harrison."

"Hard no."

"I thought negotiation was how grown-ups settle their differences in a civilized world."

"There's nothing to negotiate," he said. "You don't have anything I want."

I came very close to smacking him, my seventeen-years-older brother.

Then something occurred to me.

"What did you want from Stella Western? In the negotiation. You said she wanted property—what did you want?"

Harrison seemed to consider this. It was not brief.

"We wanted her to promise never to contact us again. This letter is a breach of that promise."

"This letter is from a museum, not from her."

"Debatable."

"And what did she get for the devastating punishment of never contacting us again?"

My brother set his jaw. "A house," he said, finally. "She'd been living there for years. She was living there when Dad died, and she wanted to stay."

Harrison turned to me.

"She had a kid. I mean, she and our father had a kid. And I suppose she wanted to stay in the home her kid knew. So I guess it was worth it to her. I can't say we had a heart-to-heart about it. We could have kicked her out," he said, a little defensively. "We didn't. But that was the agreement. She got the deed; she agreed never to contact any of us again. Obviously," he said, "I'll need to involve our attorney."

I gaped at him. For a long time I couldn't manage to say anything, and when I finally did, all I could come up with was: "You're kidding."

"I wish I were kidding, but there you are. Yes, Phoebe, our father got this person pregnant, and now she apparently considers it her prerogative to fuck with us forever. Have you ever considered what it was like for our mother? After he died? And so suddenly, in such a horrible, public way? And then to be alone, with you to raise? Only not as alone as she'd have liked, because suddenly here was this woman with a very personal story to tell about her late husband, not to mention assorted claims about what she'd supposedly been promised, or already given. A valuable house. A room full of art works. Not so nice, is it? So yes, there was a negotiation. There was an agreement, which is clearly not being upheld. And now that you know all this, maybe you can find it in your big bleeding Walden heart to be just a little bit more sympathetic. Think of it as a way to *help people and make the world a better place.*"

I couldn't stop staring at him. It was still coming across, like wave after wave on the beach behind the Vineyard house, relentless and without conclusion. My mouth felt dry and my hands clenched around nothing.

"I'm . . . You just . . ."

But then I had to stop again.

"Have you met . . . him, or her?" I finally said.

"Him," said Harrison. "And no. Never met him. Don't want to meet him. Why would I? And don't ask me how old he is. Well, older than you. It's obvious he was conceived while the three of us were still living at home, which is absolutely appalling. I refuse to think about him. I absolutely refuse to care about him. Why are you looking at me like that? I don't even know his name."

Chapter Thirty-One

The Love and the Passion

In which Lewyn Oppenheimer encounters his late father, and recounts his own wanderings in the wilderness

I didn't talk to Lewyn about what Sally had told me, and I didn't talk to him about what Harrison had told me. For a week I didn't talk to anyone except my school friends and my teachers, but not, of course, about the only thing I was able to think about. Everything else was just horrible stasis and churning distress.

Well, except I did read *Colleges That Change Lives*. There was that.

The following Sunday Lewyn and I went to Red Hook together, and together we went through the warehouse, checking every corner, storage area, and crawl space of the building for something that might have been overlooked. There was nothing: not a single work of Outsider Art by a person named Achilles Rizzoli, let alone an entire trove comprising most of the artist's life's work.

Even without success, it was lovely to see Lewyn at the warehouse, watching him go through the paintings, canvas by canvas and frame by frame. Each work was stored in low light, braced and padded, dehumidified and recorded, with physical files of supporting materials and Lewyn's reference library. He spent a couple of days each week out here, sometimes opening the collection to scholars or curators and doing administrative work related to the loan requests that came in constantly. Over the years he'd found, in addition to his own general interest in the selections our father had made, a specific interest of his own in what he called "abstract depictions of tension around the expression of religious faith," which sounded very much like the kind of thing you'd read about in the art journals he contributed to, if you could actually comprehend that stuff. It was a topic he said he'd first encountered in Utah, during the period even he now referred to, with no small degree of sarcasm, as "my wandering in the wilderness." Abandoning our search after every conceivable part of the building had been checked, we went to pick up Italian sandwiches at F & M and returned, unwrapping them on the warehouse steps to take advantage of the late-afternoon sun. There was a steady stream of dogs, pulling their owners along toward the park and pier at the end of Coffey Street.

Neither of us had experienced Red Hook in its prior incarnations, so the proliferation of art galleries and whiskey bars along its side streets, the very hip young moms and cunningly attired children, and the more than locally famous lobster pound and key lime pie shop—not to mention the Fairway—had never struck us as out of step for the Brooklyn we had always lived in. With its cobblestones underfoot and the beautiful harbor at the bottom of the street, our father's indefensible purchase in the early 1980s now appeared every bit as shrewd as certain of his earliest purchases of art had been. The houses on either side of the warehouse had all been sold in the years after his death, and in the warehouse itself Lewyn had upgraded the systems, bringing the technology of preservation and security into line for the twenty-first century, and carving out an office for himself in one corner of the cavernous first floor. Otherwise he had left the building pretty much alone.

"Did you ever come out here when you were a kid?" I asked, unwrapping my sandwich.

"No. He never took me. Though, to be fair, I don't think I ever asked to come. I had no special feeling for art back then. Pretty ironic that I had all of this in my own family and I still had to find it through an art history survey in college, just like anyone else."

"But you knew about it?" I said. "You knew he was buying paintings and keeping them here?"

"Oh, sure. But it was more in a negative context—this was the place he went to not be with us. It represented his absence, not anything good. I don't know how the others felt, but it's been pretty painful for me."

"What do you mean?" I was trying to get my mouth around my sandwich.

"Well, just the lost opportunity, for the two of us. This was something we might have been able to do together. But it was a hidden thing, and I had no idea. Not just what was in the warehouse. What was in him. Do you understand?"

I wasn't sure I did, but I nodded.

"Okay. So after Dad died I don't think Mom came out here right away, she just kept up the security and the bills and that was it. Then, maybe a year or two later, she came with an appraiser so he could make an inventory. Then, after I was back from Utah, I came by myself. I had the inventory, but I don't think I really believed it until I actually saw the paintings. The first time, I just sat on the floor and cried. I mean, for hours."

I looked at him. "But why?"

He smiled, but sadly. "It was the passion. The love and the passion, all over the walls out here. This was what he'd given it to. Not to me, certainly. I don't think to Sally and Harrison, either. I don't think to Mom, which in a way was worst of all. I didn't need the appraiser to tell me what he'd done. This," he pointed back over his own shoulder, at the front door, "is a world-class collection, assembled without any oversight or guidance, and as far as I can tell, without any interest in artist reputation, or likelihood of appreciation. He completely ignored abstract expressionism, which was all anyone was trying to acquire in the 1970s. He bought the paintings he responded to, personally, and so many of the purchases were just astonishingly prescient. A Twombly blackboard painting! That was the first piece he bought, and it was a very intentional purchase. No internet back then, and he didn't just stroll into some gallery off the street, either. He had to have actually seen it somewhere, or at least a picture of it, but I have no idea where. It was with a dealer in Turin. I don't think it had ever left Europe. Having it shipped over, not to mention the purchase, itself—that would have involved many letters, bank transactions, trans-Atlantic phone calls. Probably took months, or even years. Today the paintings in that series are at MOMA, the Tate, the Whitney, the Menil. And a warehouse in Red Hook. It blows my mind, actually. He bought these California painters no one was paying attention to then, like Diebenkorn. There are two Ocean Park paintings in there! He went to an auction in London and came back with a Francis Bacon triptych. There's a Hockney sprinkler painting and a slab painting by Hans Hoffman! And two Ruschas. Jesus." He shook his head.

I was getting the gist of this, though most of the details escaped me. I didn't say anything, and in a moment he continued.

"And you could say, well, okay, Bacon and Hockney. Twombly—you didn't have to be a genius to see what was going to happen with them. And even a couple of years ago there were paintings in the collection that had been pretty but not worth very much back when he bought them and they were still pretty but not worth very much—just pictures he'd loved and wanted to own, by artists who never really broke through. But I'm telling you, the world's caught up to a lot of those painters, too. Agnes Martin, for example. No idea where he even came across her in the late seventies, but there she is. Alma Thomas. Okay, she had a show at the Whitney in '72, but nobody bought her work for another generation. And some of the Italian artists—Piero Manzoni and Lucio Fontana. *Arte povera.* Dirt cheap when he bought them. Not today. This is a treasure house. I can't believe I get to work here."

"Almost makes up for what you didn't get from him," I said carefully. "When he was alive."

My brother sighed. "Yeah. Almost." He took another bite of his sandwich.

I wrapped the rest of my sandwich back up in the butcher paper it had come in. I'd managed to get through less than half of it.

"Lewyn," I said, "can I ask you something?"

He turned to me. "If you have to ask permission to ask me a question, it's probably not about the weather."

It wasn't about the weather.

"Would you tell me what happened out in Utah? I mean, I don't actually know. I've never asked."

"No one in this family has ever asked," said Lewyn. "Isn't that interesting?"

"Well, I was so young when you came back."

"Yes. You're excused."

"But I'm not so young anymore. So would you?"

Lewyn seemed to consider. He was halfway through his own sandwich, but he was slowing down.

"My freshman-year roommate at Cornell was Mormon," Lewyn said. "He was from Utah. He was at the vet school."

Like Paula, I nearly said. I hadn't mentioned Paula to Lewyn. Or to our mother.

"So he told you all about it?"

"He told me a bit, yes. And the next summer I went to Palmyra, to watch him perform at Hill Cumorah."

He said this as if I knew what it meant. I didn't, so he had to explain.

"Then, after Dad died, I was very, I guess, lost in a lot of ways. We had to go through all that gruesome stuff together, and we were all barely speaking to one another. Also there was somebody I'd been in love with. She wasn't speaking to me, either." He looked glumly down at his sandwich.

"Rochelle Steiner?" I said.

Lewyn turned to me, plainly stunned.

"Sally told me. Sally also has a lot of regret about Rochelle Steiner."

"Well, she should," he said tightly. Then he clammed up again.

"Maybe it's something the two of you should talk about."

Lewyn shook his head. "I'm more likely to go out for a beer with Harrison."

I opted not to say that a beer with Harrison was equally in the realm of the possible, and very much my personal intention where my brothers were concerned.

"So it was a bad time, that year."

He nodded. "And there was this moment, I remember thinking, I'm just going to reach out for anything that makes me feel better." He stopped. "I've always thought, good thing it wasn't drugs. I'd be dead."

"Well, religion is the opiate of the masses, I've heard."

"Something to that."

"So," I said, nudging him, "you went to the local Mormon church and said: *Here I am! Convert me!*"

"No, no. First of all, temples, not churches, and you can't enter the temple until you already are a member of the church. But it didn't happen like that, either. I got this insane idea to go and be in the pageant, myself. I'd seen it performed. I saw these hundreds of people, working on it together. And their faith together. And I thought, well, I'll fill out an application and mail it in and see what happens. I told myself it would be an interesting experience, not necessarily a religious one. And I said I was a church member already, which was wrong of me."

"They couldn't check? I mean, wasn't it all on some database?"

"Probably. Or maybe they couldn't imagine a non-Mormon taking the trouble to apply, and lying about it. I got a letter instructing me when to turn up in Palmyra, and so I went. And I get to this community college, Finger Lakes Community College, where everyone was staying, and I'm completely terrified they're going to find out I'm not one of them. But they kept us so busy, right from the get-go, and no one was lurking around questioning anyone else's bona fides. Everything was superorganized, very structured, and crazy accelerated. You audition, like, on the first day, then you get put into a cast team, and bang, you're running around from breakfast to bedtime, not just rehearsal but workshops and service assignments. I was cast as a Lamanite."

"A what?" I said.

"Generic bad guy. Mainly I shook a spear in the air."

A pair of Dalmatians with a short woman attached came by, slowed, and then veered hopefully toward the sandwiches. They were pulled away.

"You know what's interesting, they actually recognized me as Jewish, they just assumed I was a convert. They all wanted me to know how much they loved and supported Israel. I probably did more thinking about the Bible in those two weeks than I ever had before. And by then I'd read the Book of Mormon. Or skimmed it."

I didn't want to say anything. I wanted him to keep going.

"And then, I started to get this feeling around it, not just all the moving parts of putting on this big show, but the presence of history, and the story of Joseph Smith and the early church, unfolding on the exact spot where it happened—just the meaning of the place, and the undertaking. And there are so many families doing this together, and the feeling of community was really overwhelming." He paused. "Do you believe in anything?"

"Anything? What do you mean?"

"Any story. Do you believe that Moses led the Israelites out of Egypt?"

I just looked at him. I'd never really thought about whether I *believed* it. "I guess it probably happened," I said. "I mean, some version of that." But the two things, I realized, were hardly the same.

"The thing is, we're only two centuries out from Joseph Smith, and we have actual artifacts. His stuff, and contemporary accounts. I mean, you can't visit Moses's actual tent in the desert and see the exact chair he sat in, and we don't have a testament from his right-hand man, but it doesn't matter, because it's not really about the evidence. At some point it becomes real to you in spite of evidence. You just . . . stake your life to one particular story."

"Lewyn, you are making this sound very culty. You realize that."

"Am I?" He seemed surprised. He took another bite of his sandwich. Then he wrapped up the rest. After a moment he said, "These people, they were so unbelievably kind. Even after they figured it out, they were very decent to me. They called me into the director's office and they asked me, point-blank, was I a member of the church? I felt terrible. It was the worst

I'd felt all that year, which was saying something. And they asked me why I was there and I honestly couldn't say why. And they asked if I wanted to join the church, was that why, and I didn't know that, either. And I ended up telling them about Dad, and how he died, and after that they couldn't do enough for me, so I felt awful about that, in addition to everything else. I was a mess, basically."

"*Were* you thinking of converting?" I asked. "I mean, at that point?"

Lewyn sighed. "I'm not sure. I was trying to be open to the possibility. Anyway, I had to drop out of the pageant, but they didn't make me leave. They kept setting me up with people to talk to, and I spent the next couple of weeks up there, going to the historical sites and doing more reading. Do you know what the Sacred Grove is?"

I laughed. "Lewyn, do I look like a person who knows what a 'Sacred Grove' is?"

He smiled, but faintly. "The Sacred Grove is behind Joseph Smith's house in Palmyra. It's where he went to pray. It's where he saw angels. It's the most beautiful place I've ever been. The first time I went there I got lost in it, actually. I was looking for it, and I didn't realize I was already in it. Very *meta*. Harrison would have found it hilarious."

He was right about that, I thought.

"I'd never considered myself remotely spiritual, you know? But when I was in the Sacred Grove, I felt something. I did. I couldn't have said, *Wow, these supernatural things happened here, just as I'm being told.* But there was *something.* Maybe it was just the stillness and the beauty, and that horrible year. I just kept going back to the Grove, and watching the pageant at night. And I met this family from Provo, and they were driving back home and planning to stop in Missouri and Illinois on their way back. You know, to places from Mormon history. And they invited me to go with them. So I did. I left New York with the Kimballs, and I went west."

"Guess you didn't miss your little sister."

"I barely thought of my little sister. I barely thought of any of you. Something was working its way through me. I kept trying to bring my old identity together with whatever that was, but I could never get it to happen."

A Black woman with a bulldog and a little boy came past, headed for the park and the pier at the bottom of Coffey Street. The boy turned back to stare at us as he walked.

"We stopped in Nauvoo on the way west. Nauvoo is where the Mormons were settled when Joseph Smith died. After that it was where the community set off to Zion, which eventually became Utah. We saw all the historical sites, like the jail where Smith died, and his house, and his grave, and that was all fine. You know, interesting, but not special. But then that evening, I took a walk down to the river. The Mississippi, by myself. And I was looking west into the sunset, and I just felt that same thing I'd felt in the Grove. I didn't think *This is God,* or even *The testimony is true.* I didn't know what it was. But the peace of it. I just wanted it all the time."

Opiate of the masses, I thought. But I didn't say it out loud.

"So I just kept going west with the Kimballs, and they kept talking to me about what they believed. When we reached Provo, I looked around a little bit and then I got a job for a while, at a bookstore. And eventually I rented an apartment, and that became my life for the next year. All very normal. No cult indoctrination, just a lot of reading and conversation. And the next fall I formally transferred to Brigham Young, and I was majoring in art history and making friends. I even started dating a cousin of the Kimballs I met at one of their firesides, though, to be honest, I think she was even more interested in leaving the church than I was in joining it. And I was talking to missionaries all this time, and the Kimballs introduced me to their bishop and he was just this wonderful guy. Everyone was very respectful of my Jewishness, and about Dad. And I did keep moving toward it—I mean, baptism and confirmation. I think I wanted it, some part of me, just never all of me. I think I told myself, you don't have to rush this."

"Just out of interest, where did Mom think you were all this time?"

"Ithaca, at first. There wasn't a lot of communication going on, like I said. Also, by then we all had cell phones. Flip phones, not smartphones, but you could text on them. So she'd check in with me. *Are you ok?* And I'd text back, *I'm ok.* That was the extent of it for a while. Then I called in November or December and told her I'd taken a leave from Cornell, and she wanted to come rushing out to Utah to rescue me, probably with a deprogrammer or something, but I promised her I was fine, because I actually was fine. I went home on the anniversary for the next couple of years. Well, anniversary and our birthday. Very much an ordeal. But I wouldn't stay. It was painful seeing any of them. Any of you."

Lewyn had zipped up his jacket, to the chin, and now sat with his hands in his jeans pockets. It was starting to get cold and starting to get dark.

"Should we go?" he asked.

"Just tell me the rest, okay?"

"What rest? I came home. Obviously."

"Come on, Lewyn. Something must have happened. Unless . . . you didn't actually get baptized, did you?"

He shrugged. "Not quite. I did write an undergraduate thesis on four Mormon artists. I think that's actually what ended it for me."

"Mormon art? Made you not want to be a Mormon?"

He seemed to consider. "Actually, I would say yes. That was a big part of why. I'd always been curious about what divides 'fine' art from 'commercial' art. I think a lot of people are. Especially with an image that explores some aspect of religious faith, there's an element of conveying or, to be crude, 'selling' the idea of a specific belief, presumably the artist's own specific belief. But we'd put an Old Master annunciation in a very different category than a depiction of Joseph Smith visited by angels, painted in the 1960s. That might actually have been my topic if I'd stayed for my PhD, but it didn't come to that. At BYU I got interested in these four artists. Friberg, Anderson, Lovell, and Riley. Between them they created the visual iconography of the modern LDS church. Their paintings illustrate the scriptures; they're in every Mormon home, they're on the walls of every visitors' center at every Mormon site. I saw them for the first time in Palmyra, and then I saw them virtually every day for the next four years. They're undeniably powerful, but when I started to study the work, and the artists, I learned that only one of the four was actually a member of the church. The other three were professional illustrators, for magazines and advertising, and the covers for pulp novels. When the companies they'd been working for started to replace illustrations with photographs, their work dried up and they all needed money, so one of them accepted a commission from the church, and then they kept handing the job off to one another when they could afford to stop doing it. But it was never even personal for any of those three, let alone spiritual. In fact, they were so uncomfortable with it that I started to think of the images as a form of dishonesty. And then it all began to feel dishonest."

I nodded. "Okay. That makes sense."

"And the bishop, like I said, was a very kind person, and he tried to bring me back, but I started to think I just wasn't going to get there. And then one day I was sitting in a Starbucks in Provo, and these two missionaries came up to me, and I invited them to sit down. And they got out their pamphlets and the pamphlets had the Tom Lovell painting of *Moroni Burying the Plates* on the second page. Moroni's on the Hill Cumorah, but it's hundreds and hundreds of years ago, so the hill is covered with trees, and it's winter and he's dug this hole in the ground and he's praying before he buries the plates, because he knows he's about to die and he's the last descendant, and this is the record of his people and how Jesus appeared to the Nephites, but it's all going to be okay because someday God will send the right person to dig right here and that person will find the plates and translate them, and the Aaronic Priesthood will be restored and everything else."

I made myself not say any of what I was thinking.

"And these two missionaries are getting to the point where they're telling me *I know this testimony is true*, and *You can know it too if you ask God sincerely*, and I'd been hearing those exact phrases and looking at that exact same painting for four years by then, and I knew it wasn't true. I knew it had never been true. And these poor guys are just staring at me because I've started to cry and laugh at the same time, right there in the middle of Starbucks with everyone looking at us, and I'm just crying and laughing and saying, *I can't, I can't, I can't*. And they actually ended up calling an ambulance for me because they were so worried about me, and I got myself hospitalized for a couple of days, which was not something I would have asked for but frankly it was the right thing to happen, because I was a complete mess and very much not capable of handling what was happening to me. And after a few days, when I went back to my apartment, I realized there wasn't a single thing from there that I wanted. So I went to the airport and I came home."

He stopped. He looked past me, up toward the top of the street, where someone else was now heading in our direction. Someone without a dog.

"And that's it. That's all she wrote."

"Oh my God. Lewyn. I'm so sorry."

"For what?" He sounded surprised. "I had to find out what I believed. People need to. I learned that I cared more about art than anything else. And I met some truly good people. And I got my degree, only a couple of years behind schedule. I have no complaints."

"I'm so glad you came home," I told Lewyn. "I wouldn't have made it without you."

"My pleasure."

The someone on the street was closer. I could hear the footsteps, and I turned to see. He was young, Black, carrying a Fairway bag. He was whistling. He was also, I realized, familiar.

"You know him?" Lewyn asked me. I had already gotten to my feet. I was already waving.

But he didn't see me, not yet. He wore a blue parka over a blue shirt. The shirt had a ceremonial crest: yellow acorns on a shield of red and white. When he got closer I could read what it said underneath: Silliman College.

"Hi! Ephraim!"

Then he stopped. He pulled at one of his earbuds, then the other. He held out his arms. "Phoebe. Wow." He scooped me up, somehow without letting go of his groceries.

"What are you doing here?"

"I live here." He pointed to a house down the street from the warehouse, on the corner. "I live there."

"That's incredible! We own this building. I mean, warehouse. Neighbors!"

The young man, Ephraim, said: "Ah."

"This is my brother Lewyn."

"Hello," said Lewyn, holding out his hand. They shook.

"Ephraim was a counselor for Children's Aid last summer," I told Lewyn. "He goes to Yale. What are you doing home?"

"Fall break," said Ephraim simply. "I have a project I needed to work on, and my suitemates decided to spend the break watching every episode of *Stargate* in our living room. Besides, I wanted to see my mom."

"That's so sweet!" I said. "This is amazing! I thought you were going to keep in touch."

He looked, I saw, abruptly uncomfortable. I wished I hadn't said it. But we had been friends. And united in disdain for our boss, that awful woman who hated kids.

"Would you like to join us?" said Ephraim. "I'm making dinner."

I declined, automatically. "No, no, that's okay."

"We can't," Lewyn said at the same time.

"Actually, we just ate," I added.

"But just come in and say hello," he insisted. "It's time you met my mom."

My brother and I exchanged a glance, and then, an instant later, a nod. Neither of us, we would later admit, had any idea that "It's time you met my mom" was anything but a pleasantry, nor the slightest sense that some momentous thing might be about to happen. But we followed him anyway.

Chapter Thirty-Two

Everything Is Important

In which Lewyn Oppenheimer needs to sit down

Later, each of us would say that it was the scar we noticed first, that jolt of pink incongruity at her clavicle, and then the other features, so familiar from the Wikipedia page we'd stared at, only a couple of weeks earlier: those gray dreadlocks, that small person radiating importance, though whether in the world or merely to ourselves, we couldn't have said. I was in front of Lewyn as we entered the room, so I never saw his face as he looked at her, and he never saw mine. I reached back for him, but it was Ephraim who took my arm.

"Oh," somebody said, and I thought for a moment it might have come from me, but it wasn't me. It was Stella Western, standing in the doorway of her own kitchen, watching the three of us walk into her home: three of Salo Oppenheimer's five children, in the same place, at the same time, for the first time. "Oh boy," she said, a moment later. "Well."

"Are you her?" Lewyn said, which did sound stupid, but I knew exactly what he meant, and I supposed she did, too.

"I'm Stella," said Stella. "And I think you're Lewyn."

"You live here?" my brother said. "This is your son?" He turned to

Ephraim. He was trying to remember Ephraim's name, I knew. I didn't blame him. It seemed to be hitting him in pieces.

"Honey." Stella came across to us. "Phoebe? Is that right?"

"Yes," I nodded. Then I hugged her. I had no idea why. I just wanted to.

"Lewyn. Can I hug you, too?" Already, her eyes were streaming.

Lewyn let her, but his face was full of dismay.

"Now I know all of you," Stella said. "I met Sally once. I didn't know it was her, but I liked her. I met your brother. Harrison. That wasn't so nice, but he was taking care of his mama. Your mama," said Stella. "And I respected that. Do you want to sit down?" she asked Lewyn. "I think maybe you should."

I dragged my eyes away from her and looked at Lewyn. He really did not look all right.

"Lewyn, sit down," I said, and he did, on a sofa. And I understood that he knew only what I had known a few weeks ago, before Harrison, before Sally. Which was nothing. So I took his hand.

"Lewyn," I said carefully, "this is our brother. Ephraim is our brother."

"Well," said Ephraim, nodding, "half, anyway. Half brother."

Lewyn stared.

We were in a dark living room, lined with horizontal boards painted blue, two leather sofas facing each other in front of a fireplace. There was a framed poster on the wall above the mantelpiece, from Stella's documentary about the Klansman-turned-Jew, and another next to the kitchen door, "Oakland 3-Gen," the bottom of the poster lined with laurel-wreath award logos. I wanted to look at everything, but mainly at Stella. Then at Ephraim. Then at Stella again. I was overwhelmed.

"I didn't even know you existed till a couple of weeks ago," I finally said to Ephraim. "I mean, I knew that you existed, just not that our father had a child. I mean, another child. I mean, former child," I amended. "I'm sorry." I said this to Lewyn, who was still gaping at both of them. Then I turned back to Stella. "My sister told me about you and . . . our father. Harrison told me you'd had a son." I put my hand on Lewyn's shoulder. "I was getting around to it, I promise. It's a lot, you know."

Lewyn said nothing.

"Lewyn," Stella said, "you need a drink?"

To my surprise, he nodded.

"Okay. Hold tight." She disappeared into the kitchen and came back with a bottle of wine. "You probably shouldn't," she said to me. "I don't want to get in trouble."

"Oh, fuck that," I said. I was feeling distinctly light. I looked again at Ephraim, and then at Lewyn, and I knew I wasn't imagining it. The shape of their jaws. The cheekbones. The wide shoulders. The long legs. They were like a positive and negative photograph of the same person. My heart was pounding. I held out my hand to Stella, and Stella put a glass of white wine in it. "To the Oppenheimers," I said, with a not altogether unpleasant surge of mania. "God bless us, every one."

Lewyn nodded. But then he set his glass down on a table. He turned to Ephraim. "When were you . . . how old are you?"

"Born in '97. I'm twenty. And a half."

He was doing the math, we all saw. "Jesus," he said. He said: "I'm an idiot."

"You're certainly not," Stella said. "Great pains were taken to hide this from you. I signed an agreement saying I would never try to contact you or interact with you in any way, which was pretty challenging when you started coming out here to work in the warehouse, Lewyn, but I did my best. Then Ephraim comes home last summer and tells me Phoebe Oppenheimer is working with him as a camp counselor."

"You knew who I was?" I asked him. "Last summer?"

"I've always known," Ephraim nodded. "She told me everything, as soon as I could take it all in. I knew all your names. Sally I read about on the website for her business. I've seen Harrison on television, and I read his book. One of his books." He made a face. "Not a fan of that book." He turned to Lewyn. "I did like your book, though. About the Oppenheimer Collection."

"Oh, so you bought that copy," Lewyn said. He was trying for sarcasm, but failing.

"I wanted him to know his father," Stella said. "I prefer not to lie, as a rule, but especially not to the most important person in my life. Harrison was involved in our negotiations, but I didn't know about you, Lewyn. What you knew. If you knew anything."

Lewyn was shaking his head. "Nothing," he said. "We were told nothing."

I went and sat beside my brother on the couch. I took his hand.

"Sally knew," I said. "She saw them together, at some art show." I looked at Stella. "Did you know that? That she saw you?"

After a moment she nodded. "It was many years ago, in the bathroom at the folk art museum. She said something that made me wonder if she could be Salo's daughter. But she didn't tell me her name, and it just seemed so unlikely. What would she be doing there? I didn't tell him about it. I didn't see the point in worrying him." She looked at me, and then at Lewyn. "I want you to know, I have always cared about you. All of you. Even Harrison, though I can't say it's the same. Because you're Salo's children. You're the parts of him that are still here. I don't think Ephraim remembers him, which makes me very sad."

Ephraim shrugged. It was clear that he was sad about it, too.

"I don't remember him, either," I heard myself say.

"No. I'm sorry." She sighed. "I suppose I'll be getting a letter from Burke Goldman Finn and Emerson now. Reading me the riot act, because we've met."

"You won't," Lewyn said. "Because we won't be telling her."

"Besides," I said, "you might even call it fate."

"Fate might have moved things along a little bit faster," Lewyn said. "You're sharing a street here, with my . . . *our* . . . our father's art collection."

Stella nodded. "At one point your father owned most of the street, the buildings on both sides of the warehouse. They were sold off, after his death. Except for this one. I had to fight for this one. But I didn't see any other way. Too many changes, too quickly. Of course, I was terribly worried about money. And I knew it wasn't what Salo would have wanted for us. Mostly I couldn't face moving Ephraim on top of everything. He spent his whole life here, till he left for college."

Lewyn was shaking his head. "I just . . . this is incredible. And I am furious."

"You don't look furious," I observed.

"This is what furious looks like. How could she hide this from us? What was she thinking?"

Stella sighed. "She was thinking she had lost her husband. And I'm sure she was in great pain, because I was, also. And she wanted to be able to control what she could and protect her kids the way she thought they needed protecting, and I completely understand that, even if I disagreed with her idea of how to do it. I told her, at the time. I said, they're going to need to know who Salo really was, and what made him that way. The accident, for example. I know why he couldn't bring himself to talk about it, but after he was gone, I thought it was important. I told Ephraim, anyway. It might have been the most important thing I told him. Was it?" she asked her son.

"It was all important," he shrugged. "Everything is important, since I can't remember him on my own."

"Wait," said Lewyn. He seemed to have come fully awake now. "What accident?"

Stella said nothing. Ephraim said nothing.

"What accident?" Lewyn said again. And then I said it, too.

I could tell we were both afraid of the answer. But Ephraim was right: everything was important, and where our father was concerned, this turned out to be the most important thing of all.

We stayed for hours. We stayed long enough that we were hungry again, and Stella cooked dinner for all of us, and I went with Ephraim upstairs to his childhood bedroom. There was a desk at the window, which overlooked the roofs of three houses. Beyond them was the brick wall of the warehouse. "You kept an eye on things," I noted.

"I did. I saw your brother occasionally, especially in the last few years, before I left for school. Never you or the others."

"Lewyn took up the mantle," I said. "I've only been out here a couple of times before today. Was it fun to grow up in Red Hook?"

"Except for the skateboarding, a blast. The cobblestones," he clarified. "But I jest. My mom is extremely protective. She didn't want me skateboarding anywhere. *The Stuyvesant Spectator*, that was my sport."

I looked at him.

"Student paper. "The Pulse of the Stuyvesant Student Body." No knee-pads necessary."

"Stuyvesant! That's some commute from Red Hook."

"It was a bitch. A girl in my class made a database of commute times for our grade. I was in the ninety-first percentile with one hour twenty-eight minutes average, via two buses and a subway. But there were worse. Kids from Rockaway or parts of Queens. It's a great school, though. I was very prepared for Yale."

The desk was covered with files and notebooks, and a laptop. "Your project?" I asked.

He nodded.

I picked up one of the books: *We Wear the Mask: 15 True Stories of Passing in America.*

"I'm . . . writing about white-to-nonwhite ethnic self-reassignment."

"What does that mean?"

"Well, there have always been Black people passing as white. If they were light-skinned enough, it could be a very attractive opportunity for all kinds of reasons, chiefly economic. But it also happens in the other direction. Much less common. But not unknown. And," he added, "ongoing."

"Like that woman, a couple years ago."

"Rachel Dolezal. Yes."

"So these are people voluntarily declining ethnic privilege?"

"Essentially. But of course it's complicated. Anyway, this," he tapped his desk, "is about someone . . . in the public eye. I've been working on it for nearly a year, with a research team at *Yale Daily News.* I need to be very, very thorough, not just for myself, though I certainly wouldn't want to start my career in journalism by making a mistake of this magnitude. I know it's going to be absolutely cataclysmic for the person I'm writing about. And their reputation. And . . ." he said carefully, "for everyone who's trusted them, or worked with them. So I'm here, going back over all the sources, just interrogating every bit of information. I'm nearly ready to publish."

"I can't believe you're my brother," I told him suddenly. "I'm so happy."

He smiled, but he was holding back. "I'm happy, too. It was hard not to say anything, last summer. I'm sorry. I promised my mom. She was very distressed about the whole thing. Not just because of the contract. She respects your mother. Salo respected your mother, and she honors that."

I hugged him. After a moment, he hugged me, too.

When we went back downstairs, Lewyn and Stella were still at the dining table, the open bottle of wine between them. "You should hear this, too, Phoebe," said Lewyn.

"What?"

"I'm telling Lewyn about the Rizzoli drawings," Stella said. "Not just a film subject."

"Oh no?" I said.

"They met because of the Rizzolis," said Ephraim. "At the Outsider Art Fair."

"Re-met," his mother corrected. "I'd already begun working on Rizzoli, though there wasn't much to film. I'd found a couple of people who'd known him, but there wasn't a lot of expertise around. Even as a concept, Outsider Art was brand-new, and frankly, at that time, there was only room for one artist."

"Henry Darger?" Lewyn asked.

Stella sighed.

"Who's Henry Darger?" I said.

"The Pelé of Outsider Art," Lewyn said. When I looked blank he added: "The soccer player everyone's heard of even if they don't know anything else about soccer."

"Oh. Well, I've never heard of him. Either of them."

"I loved that your father bought the Rizzolis from the dealer. Certainly there wasn't any financial upside, absolutely no prospects at all for Rizzoli back then. When I saw the rest of the art he'd collected I really understood what an outlier Rizzoli was, for him. I know he did that for me, so I'd have access to the pictures. And because they were right here, right up the street, I was able to film every piece in detail, which has really been a godsend since I haven't laid eyes on them since 2001." She paused. "I asked her for them.

Your mother. While we were working on our agreement. Actually, I begged her for them. Not just because of my film. They were a part of my story with your father. Finally, she said she didn't have them and didn't know where they were, and if I brought them up again she would terminate our negotiations and I could move out of the house. I didn't believe her, of course. That she didn't know. But I had to let it go. I'd already spent a year with a lawyer I couldn't afford, and I was exhausted and in debt. I loved the Rizzolis, but I didn't need to own them. I needed to own this house." Ephraim put his hand over hers. Stella nodded. "I don't know if your mother understood what those pictures represented to me, or if it was simply because I was asking for them. But I do know that it became something really painful for her, and I felt terrible about that. We were both grieving, and we were both angry. But when Salo was alive, those pictures were in the warehouse, and after I asked for them they apparently were not. Or so I was told."

"They're not there," Lewyn interjected. "We looked, just this morning. And in all the years I've worked in that building, I've never seen a single piece that matches the pictures I saw online, let alone an entire collection. I would absolutely give them to you if I could. But I don't know where they are."

"Harrison does," I said.

All of them looked at me.

"He does. He wouldn't tell me. But he does. Mom does, too. I mean, if Harrison knows, Mom knows."

"Well," Stella said, after a moment, "after the film airs on PBS, a lot of people will want to see those pictures. Maybe they'll be more willing to comply with the museum's request than they were to mine."

"I don't think they'll be willing," I said. "I think it will take something more. I think we'll need to come up with something else."

And we began to work out what that something else might be.

Chapter Thirty-Three

Tabula Rasa

In which it is established, once and for all, that Oppenheimer is not a particularly common name

I dressed up a bit for my appointment at Rochelle Steiner's law firm, which was on Madison Avenue and Forty-Fourth Street, right around the corner from the Cornell Club, where she had once climbed onto a chartered bus, chosen a seat next to the toilet, and set a number of complicated, long-ranging things into motion. It was a general law firm, and it looked to be evenly balanced in terms of women and men, which might have been one of the reasons Rochelle picked it (and after Harvard Law, a clerkship for a New York State Supreme Court judge, and the obvious fact that she was ridiculously good at practicing law, she probably had her pick of attractive options). A woman showed me into the office one afternoon a couple of weeks later, and from the beginning it didn't go as I'd planned. Which is not to say that it went badly. Just . . . not as planned.

"Phoebe Oppenheimer," said Rochelle Steiner. She got up from behind her desk. "Well."

I'd been doing pretty much everything I could do to seem older than seventeen, from the go-to-work skirt I'd bought for an internship at Wurttemberg the summer before junior year to the mascara swipe, and I was instantly thrown, but I did my best to crawl back into the saddle. "Hi, my name is Phoebe."

"Yes. Phoebe Oppenheimer. Like it says here on your file. Which my assistant prepared for me when you made your appointment." Rochelle held it up: a generic red folder, with a name on the label: *Oppenheimer, Phoebe.* "You'll recall that you gave my assistant your name."

I nodded. Exactly thirty seconds in and I was bested. No longer trying to seem older than seventeen, now I was trying to seem older than ten.

"Yes."

I took the seat Rochelle Steiner was pointing at. The desk between us was wide and covered with an old-fashioned blotter, which made no sense given the oversized iMac desktop weighing it down. The walls were not crowded, the better to focus on her college and law school diplomas in oversized frames, and a photograph of a very young Rochelle, standing beside a woman in a sleeveless yellow dress.

"I used to know a couple of people named Oppenheimer," Rochelle was saying.

"Oh? Well, it's a common name."

Rochelle threw her head back and howled with laughter. It was so surprising I could only stare at her.

"I'm certainly not falling for that one again," she said, after a moment. "Phoebe Oppenheimer. Sister of Sally and Lewyn, I presume. And that other one, from Fox News. What a *shanda*."

I could not disagree, so I said nothing.

"The last time I saw you was on a beach on Martha's Vineyard. September 10, 2001. A hard date to forget."

"I'm afraid *I've* forgotten it. Given I was in diapers at the time."

"I'm sorry. And your father. I'm so sorry about that. I shouldn't be cavalier. Even before what happened the next day it was already awful and surreal. In fact, you might have been the only member of your family I didn't loathe when I left your house that night." She stopped. She looked intently at me. "Wait. Do you even know what I'm talking about?"

"I know enough," I said. "There's been a lot of *Come-to-Jesus* in my family over the past month or so. Oppenheimers, as I think you might know, are not natural sharers of information. I figure I've got a few more months to get them sorted out before I take off."

Rochelle raised her eyebrows. "Where are you going?"

"Oh God." I shook my head. "Not you, too! We just met!"

"I meant . . . well I guess you're going to college. I wasn't asking where."

"Sorry," I told her. "Little sensitive."

Then, without any forethought, at least on my part, the two of us smiled at each other.

I hadn't been shown a college-era photograph of the woman on the other side of the desk, so I would not be in a position to appreciate the transformation until later, but it was impressive. Rochelle Steiner was still short and still thin, but she no longer looked like a middle schooler trying to pass for a grown-up. The wavy hair she had once braided into submission now landed where it fell, mainly in curls, and the complexion that had stubbornly clung to adolescence had at last moved on. Rochelle wore a simple wool dress and not a single piece of jewelry or lick of makeup. She looked as if it took her about four minutes to get herself dressed in the morning.

"So. Phoebe Oppenheimer. How may I help you today? I doubt you are having an intellectual property issue, and I certainly hope you're not filing for divorce. Which leaves me with what you told my assistant when you set up the appointment." Rochelle held up the folder again, then opened it. A single blank sheet of paper was clipped inside. "Tabula rasa."

I sat forward in my chair. "We're having—my brother and I are having—a family issue."

"Which brother? You have two, I seem to recall. One of them lied to me from the moment we met, the other, as I said, I barely knew, but I still want to smack him."

"You and me both," I agreed. "Actually, I have three brothers, not two. Which may or may not be relevant. I brought you this."

I reached into my bag and handed Rochelle Steiner a copy of the letter from the American Folk Art Museum. (The original I had finally delivered to our mother the day after I'd seen Harrison. I had to, since he was obviously going to tell her about it.) When the lawyer finished reading it, she said: "Yes?"

"These artworks were once a part of our father's collection. They were kept in a warehouse in Brooklyn which my father purchased in the early 1980s. The rest of his art collection is still there, but these particular works have disappeared. Lewyn and I believe that our mother removed them, sometime around 2002, 2003."

"Well, that's certainly her right. Unless your father specified otherwise, his surviving spouse is the default heir to his estate. Is that the case?"

I nodded.

"Then they're her property. She can move them, store them, throw them in the Hudson River if she wants. I hope she hasn't, it sounds like they're important, and probably valuable. But there's no legal issue."

"We also believe that our father intended them not to be included in his collection. We think he meant them to go to someone else. A woman he was involved with."

Rochelle raised her eyebrows. "Well, I'm sorry to hear that. Sudden deaths often create this kind of difficulty. Things that don't get settled while the person is alive, or they're kept secret and have to come out eventually. Learning about the deceased person this way, it's got to be very painful for you. And . . ." she added, "your brother."

"Well, it's been a process. What would you advise us to do?"

"Do?" Rochelle sat up. "I'd advise you to talk to your mother. It's the only thing you *can* do."

"But I have," I said. "Weeks ago. She insisted she knew nothing about it. Refused to discuss it further."

"Well, I'm no therapist, and I don't even know you, but I have to say, I'm surprised you'd take that without a fight. Talk to her again. Tell her you won't let her off until you understand what it means. Tell her if she's trying to protect you, she can stop. Tell her that if she's trying to be vindictive, she should stop for her own sake. You could tell her you love her, too. That might accomplish more than anything else, since you're the youngest and, as you put it, about to 'take off.' You'd be amazed. A lot of intractable issues suddenly become very pliable when people start telling other people they love them. Assuming it's true, of course."

I thought about it. It was true. Of course it was true. Only just at the moment it had gotten lost behind a couple of other truths. After a moment I said: "Can I ask you something?"

"Keep it short," Rochelle smiled.

"Are you married?"

Rochelle didn't say anything right away. I could tell that she was weighing a kaleidoscope of potential implications as they slipped in and out of position. "I was," Rochelle finally said. "I'm not. Now."

"Huh."

We sat in less than comfortable silence.

"It's a personal question," Rochelle Steiner said.

"Yes, and I appreciate your answering it. Why did you, by the way? Answer it. If I may ask another personal question."

Rochelle went silent again. It was interesting, I thought. I resolved to be more like this, myself: not to speak until I was ready. Obviously, people waited for you.

"My mother died," Rochelle said. "About four months ago."

"Oh, I'm sorry."

"You asked why. I think that's why. I'm not at my usual strength. I'm wobbling a bit."

"You were close to your mother?"

"Very close. But she wasn't a well woman. She needed a lot of care." She shook her head. "Now we're really off the tracks."

I nodded. "It's okay. I mean, it's okay with me. Did she have . . . cancer? Or something like that?"

"No. Well, yes, at the end, but she'd been ill for many years. Since I was a child. And I was responsible for her. Now I'm not, so it should all feel easier, but somehow it doesn't. Also, I'm her executor, which ought to be very straightforward since there's not much money involved, but I can't seem to close out the estate. My mother filled up her house with absolute junk, for years. Just packed it in. And every time I go out there, to make a start on it,

I end up opening the front door and just looking at it, for hours, and then closing the door and leaving. Okay!" she said brightly. "That's enough. Let's get back to your problem."

"But you solved my problem. At least, you gave me something to try. Actually, I'd like to return the favor. Help you solve yours."

"Well, thanks," Rochelle said, getting to her feet. "But I prefer the usual formal invoice for services rendered, which comes to zero in your case, since we're calling this a pre-hire consultation. Besides, as I said, my mother's gone. And her illness, unfortunately, couldn't be fixed with declarations of love. I can attest to that."

I got to my feet, too.

"I wasn't thinking of that part," I told Rochelle Steiner. "I was thinking about the house. I mean, if it's all right with you, I know a person who could help with that."

Chapter Thirty-Four

Excavation

In which Sally Oppenheimer describes the refraction of pain, and Phoebe Oppenheimer gets hired

On the Monday of Thanksgiving week, Sally's employee Drew backed the Greene House Services truck into Lorelei Circle in the Hamlet of Ellesmere, Long Island, where I waited with her former roommate, Rochelle Steiner, each of us with a large Dunkin Donuts cup in one hand and a chocolate cruller in the other. Neighbors in the cul-de-sac, forewarned about the coming of the truck, had offered no resistance to this inconvenience, relieved that the injured house was finally being dealt with. A few of them had even turned up to help, which I thought was nice but which only seemed to cause Rochelle additional discomfort. She was *very* discomforted, this much was obvious, even to me, and I'd only met her once in person and spoken to her on the phone a few more times. Now, with the truck easing backward and the neighbors watching, I think I finally understood the magnitude of what Rochelle was dealing with. The professional, accomplished, and clearly brilliant woman beside me was quietly losing her shit.

It wasn't the reunion that I'd imagined. When Sally emerged, she hugged me but shook hands with Rochelle from as far away as she seemed able to stand and still execute the gesture. Then she said something respectful about Rochelle's mother, and how sorry she was to have been called under such circumstances.

"I haven't even started," Rochelle told her. "And it's been months."

"That's completely normal," said Sally. "And you have started. If you hadn't, I wouldn't be here."

I started to think it might be all right after all.

My sister and Rochelle went inside, and I helped the man named Drew to set up a tent just off the porch, and a line of tables under that. He didn't say much. When I asked if he'd been working with Sally for a long time, he only grunted, though not unkindly. But when one of the neighbors offered him a coffee I saw him hesitate, then accept. He took a donut, too.

When they emerged, Sally brought Drew inside, and Rochelle came and stood beside me. "Apparently this isn't the worst she's seen," said Rochelle. "That's pretty sobering. But maybe she's just being polite."

"Oh no, I'm sure not," I said.

"It's nice of you to come out for this. Don't you have school?"

I did have school. I also had school tomorrow, and a half day on Wednesday, but I'd decided to miss all three. I was a senior, after all, and I had college applications to work on, or at least that was what I'd told my homeroom teacher, who signed the formal excuse for my absence. It wasn't true. I had already completed the only application I intended to submit. And I'd also submitted it.

"I wanted to be here," I told Rochelle. "Not just to help out. The thing is, I've never seen Sally work. I know she's good at what she does, but I've never had an opportunity to watch her. I hope you don't mind."

"Of course not," Rochelle said. "That's really nice. It must be nice to have a sister."

I smiled. "It is. And brothers. I love my brothers, too."

Rochelle nodded. We weren't going there, apparently. Yet.

Lewyn had wanted to come out. He had asked me more than once, and even called Sally to talk it over. Both of us told him no, but for different reasons. Sally was nervous enough about seeing Rochelle again, and didn't need the additional stress of Lewyn's obvious emotions, so I sat him down and laid it out for him. *It isn't your time. This is about Sally.*

He understood, or said he did. That morning he had seen me off to the Barclays Center where I'd caught a train to Ellesmere. Probably, now, he was working at the warehouse and pretending he didn't care that both his sisters and the only woman he had ever loved were all together, and up to their elbows in trash.

It was that bad and worse, I discovered, when Sally allowed me inside. By then I had on a disposable white suit over my clothes, rubber gloves, and a dust mask over my nose and mouth, but I still couldn't escape the feeling that I was wading in bioactive muck. The house was dense with broken-down matter, papers and plastics, abandoned food and piles of clothing, much of it still on store hangers. Little could be salvaged, but Sally was a maniac for recycling, and bin after bin filled up under the tent. Rochelle seemed to hold it together fairly well, until, at around noon, she unearthed the first relic: a debating trophy, behind piles of crumbling newspapers in a downstairs cupboard. "Let's go out for a bit," I heard my sister say.

I kept on with what I was doing. I was feeling the rhythm of it, the weird mindlessness of reaching and picking and sorting and, above all, expelling matter. Space began to open in the rooms, and filthy air to expand around the objects. It was glorious to see the floor, or at least the destroyed carpet (once . . . brown?) that covered the floor, and then to see that small, open area widen and grow. It was thrilling to find some article that might conceivably be personal. When I did—a pocketbook, a silver chain, a photograph—I carried it reverently outside and placed it on the designated table.

"You're hired," Sally told me when I came out carrying a recipe card file.

"You already hired me. Remember?"

"Yes, but I was just being nice. Now I'm serious. You're a good worker."

"It's very . . . satisfying, isn't it?"

"It can be. I find it satisfying. It's not everybody's cup of tea. Obviously."

Rochelle came over and took the recipe file from my hands. "I remember this," she said. "When my dad was alive, my mother was such a great cook."

She had opened the box and pulled out a card marked *Eve's mother's chicken Florentine.* "Eve was my friend in grade school. Her mother made this dish, which I loved, so Mom started making it, too. But really it was veal at my friend's house, and my mother objected to veal, so she made it with chicken." She stopped. "I'm sorry. You don't want to hear about my friend's mother's recipes."

"No, it's good," Sally told her. "It's good for you to have these memories. You're excavating them. Literally. And they belong to you. You'll probably have a lot more before this is over. And a house you can say good-bye to."

Rochelle nodded, but glumly. She put the box on the sorting table and went back inside.

"Jeez," I said, "were you always so . . . insightful?"

Sally burst out laughing. "Me? Absolutely not. But you can't help picking it up. Years of watching people go through this process. They're everything: furious, relieved, bitter, grasping, unbelievably generous. But that's just the pain, refracting all over the place. The pain's the only thing they all have in common."

We went back to work. There wasn't a lot of talking. It took four hours for Drew and me and a couple of the neighbors to finish the living room, after which we moved on to the kitchen. Sally was working in the garage and Rochelle went upstairs to go through the bedrooms before the heavy lifting moved up there. When I went outside for a rest and something to eat, I found my sister and Rochelle on the oddly immaculate front porch, each in a chair, deep in conversation. I took my sandwich and some coffee around to the backyard.

It took most of three days, in the end. I stayed with Sally in a motel, so wrecked each night that I fell asleep in the bathtub, then again, in bed, during Rachel Maddow. Rochelle had wept over a desiccated stuffed dog, unearthed from beneath her mother's bed, and a camp autograph book, circa 1991, and on the third day, in an airtight Tupperware tub in what had been Rochelle's mother's bedroom closet, a satin wedding dress. Each afternoon we sent a couple of trucks to the dump and another to the town recycling. Windows were opened. A shockingly pristine dining set of vintage chrome-and-green kitchen chairs and a matching table were carried out of the basement, and everyone stared at them.

"Ever seen these before?" said Sally.

Rochelle shook her head. "No. Never."

"They're beautiful."

"Yes."

No one spoke for another minute.

"Actually," said Rochelle at last, "I think I love these. I think I would like to bring these to my apartment. I am going to throw out my table from Ikea, which I hate, which I have always hated. Why did I buy a table I hated?"

"It's a mystery," said Sally.

"And I am going to make this my kitchen table and chairs."

"Bravo!" said Sally.

"Can I come visit this table and chairs?" I said.

Rochelle looked surprised. But she rallied. "Of course you can."

And when everyone else had gone back to work, I stayed where I was, and asked something else.

"Can I bring my brother? Because he would really like to see you again."

Rochelle must have been expecting it, if not at this exact moment, then at some point, ever since I'd loped into her office weeks earlier in my I'm-not-a-teenager getup. Possibly she had made up her mind about it then, and the door had been ajar ever since, waiting for the next thing to happen, which now it finally had. And she also had a nearly empty house, a filthy nearly empty house, and an industrial cleaning company booked for the week after the holiday, and a Realtor set to come in after that, and a brand-new (old) kitchen table and set of matching chairs, and also Sally Oppenheimer, who had once been her friend and who was still Sally Oppenheimer, but a stronger, more thoughtful version of Sally Oppenheimer, as she herself was a stronger, more thoughtful version of Rochelle Steiner, who had made some bad mistakes of her own.

But those were only some of the reasons she told me yes.

Chapter Thirty-Five

True Stories of Passing in America

In which assorted Oppenheimer siblings consider veritas in multiple contexts

On December 15, two events of some significance to our family took place, almost simultaneously.

The first—my admission to Roarke's first coeducational class—would make my brother Harrison very happy and even, it would not be excessive to say, proud.

The second, not so much.

On the eighteenth, an unprecedented gathering of the Oppenheimer brothers—*all* of the Oppenheimer brothers—and myself, was convened at the Harvard Club, in a private room upstairs.

The choice of this location, like many things Harrison concerned himself with, had been settled after several rounds of negotiation, which was how grown-ups settled their differences in the civilized world. While everyone agreed a private home was vastly preferable to a public space, Harrison refused to go to Stella Western's home, and Ephraim would not enter the house on the Esplanade without an invitation from Johanna, which was very much not forthcoming. For reasons that had grown only more volatile throughout that day and the two preceding days, no one wanted Ephraim to be seen entering Harrison Oppenheimer's apartment building on Sutton Place. All of Sutton Place, indeed, had been inundated with press, and while most of it was concentrated on the building one block to the north of Harrison's, that was not far enough away.

And so, the Harvard Club. In itself an ironic choice.

Eight days earlier the *Yale Daily News* had printed the story Ephraim had been working on for nearly a year. Within twelve hours the story was surging on Twitter, then AP picked it up and someone from Jake Tapper's office called early the following morning. Ephraim was ready. His mother, too nervous to watch, decided it might be a good time to visit her brother in Los Angeles. For everyone else, the thing unraveled in an alternating stupor of revelation and disbelief, absolutely hilarious to many people, but also—even to some of those same people—deeply infuriating and inescapably sad.

"At what point did you decide that there was something worth investigating here?" Jake Tapper had asked Ephraim Western, who was speaking from the Yale Broadcast Studio.

"I actually had a very strong reaction the first time I saw him in person," Ephraim said, looking nervously into the camera. "That was five years ago. He came to my high school, to speak about affirmative action, which as you know he strongly opposes. I remember looking at him and thinking, 'That man is not Black.' It was visceral, and it never left me, but of course subjective reaction is not fact and it's not a valid basis of responsible journalism. I realized, in reviewing his published work and interviews, that his identity as African American was an intrinsic part of the dialogue *around* him and his ideas, but that he himself had never explicitly *self-identified* as Black in public or in print. I mean: *ever*."

Tapper said, "He published a book when he was very young, still a teenager. And he famously opted not to include an author photo for that book. Why was that if the point was to create an assumption about his ethnicity?"

"Well, first," said Ephraim, "it's true that he was young when he wrote *Against Youth*, though as our research has established, not quite as young as he said he was. I think deflecting interest in his racial identity was a strategic decision to emphasize his ethnicity even as it made the point, publicly, that ethnicity was irrelevant. We were meant to see him as an intelligent person with a work ethic and a passionate belief in pure meritocracy. But we were also meant to be inspired by his story: a poor boy of color who grows up in a shack, in an underserved southern, rural community, who is orphaned as a teenager, who never goes to school, who self-educates, and who goes on to Harvard and a Rhodes Scholarship and becomes a respected author and conservative figure and informal advisor to the president. All without accepting any form of what he considers unearned preferential treatment. That's a brutal repudiation of identity politics."

"But of course it wasn't based on fact," said Jake Tapper.

"No. None of it was fact."

Eli Absalom Stone had indeed been born in West Virginia (not, as Harrison had once insisted to his brother Lewyn, western Virginia), but the only shack in his early life had been the one his father kept the lawnmowers and Weedwackers in. The family had not been wealthy, except, perhaps, by West Virginia standards; Eli's father was a contractor working mainly in St. Albans, a suburb of Charleston, and his mother had been a homemaker. She'd died in 2006, while Eli was at Oxford, but he hadn't seen her since the day he left home, years before that. Neither had he seen his father, who was alive and unwell and still in St. Albans, and who wouldn't have recognized his son if the two of them passed on the street. Or his older sister, who might have, if—big if—she'd ever felt it necessary to look twice at a Black person.

Also, his name wasn't Eli Absalom Stone.

His name was Rowan Lavery, and a perfect Scotch-Irish reflection of his genetic, philosophical, temperamental (and, incidentally, dermatological presentation) that was, too. Lavery had been educated in St. Albans public schools which were entirely inadequate to his needs, at least as far as he, himself, was concerned. He was too smart for his classmates, his childhood friends, his teachers, his parents, and his older sister (who was still in St. Albans, caring for their father), and much, much too smart for his pastor at the Lutheran church his family attended, who once told him that, with a great mind like his, he ought to consider becoming a high school teacher.

But he was not too smart for Oren Gregories.

The summer before his final year of high school, Lavery had driven to UVA and presented himself to Professor Gregories, a person whose book on cultural identity and cultural displacement he had very much admired. He went back a couple of times that fall. Then he stopped going home.

There had once been an actual person named Eli A. Stone: an African American boy whose very short life had begun and ended in Elkins, West Virginia, two years after Rowan Lavery's own birth. The Absalom got added later: maybe a biblical allusion, maybe a nod to Faulkner. (Maybe it just sounded so good.) Eli, who was brilliant and also a good writer—two things that did not always go together—would spend that year at work on *Against Youth,* and yes it was every bit as eloquent and persuasive as Harrison Oppenheimer would discover in due course. But while the freshly minted Eli Absalom Stone was certainly capable of writing the book on his own, he did have a very involved mentor in Dr. Gregories, and a bit of assistance in finding a publisher. By the time the book came out, pointedly without an author photograph, he would also have been physically unrecognizable to anyone who'd known him before.

Ephraim had found Rowan Lavery's high school history teacher, and his poor pastor at St. Alban's Lutheran. He'd found a former editorial assistant at Eli's publisher who recalled the arrival of the manuscript of *Against Youth,* and the discussions around it, and also the UVA professor who had sent it. He'd even tracked down the author of an old Facebook post proclaiming Stone a fraud and found a very irascible person in Deerfield, Virginia. Deerfield, Virginia, being not so highly populated—143 people had been living there in 1999—it was far from likely that a definitely not local young man living alone in a cabin off Guy Hollow Road would be either unnoticed or forgotten. And so he was not. The irascible person owned the only grocery store within twelve miles, and that year he had watched this definitely not local young man change color and change—as far as he was concerned—race. Being an informed libertarian, this man had read *Against Youth* when it was published that year, and in fact had recommended it to many friends, but the book had no photograph of the author, so he didn't connect the name Eli Absalom Stone with the changing face of the definitely not local young man; that would have to wait for the rise of Fox News, and even then the libertarian—being a libertarian—believed it was none of his business. He said what he had to say on the Coalition of Libertarian Thinkers Facebook page and he went along his way, and that was it for the only known witness to the physiological transformation of the person formerly known as Rowan Lavery. Until Ephraim Western turned up in his email in-box.

Ephraim had also found every publicly available bit of information about the Hayek Institute of Monticello, Virginia, whose membership had long included the wunderkind Eli Absalom Stone along with his mentor, Professor Oren Gregories, and Roger Fount, who was one of those people the president liked to phone late at night. Among the other members, it took him no time at all to discover, was his own half brother, Harrison Oppenheimer.

On CNN and MSNBC, and in the remaining vessels of high-standard print journalism, people wanted to talk about why, but on Twitter and Facebook all anybody seemed to care about was *how*. The world had watched Michael Jackson's skin tone lighten for years, but moving in the other direction seemed to defy understanding. Ephraim had no definitive answer of his own, but it hardly mattered; the topic was quickly handed off to dermatologists and pharmacologists who hashed it out on everyone's behalf, and consensus began to center around *Ammi majus*, or bishop's weed, a psoralen-containing annual plant (possibly in conjunction with ultraviolet light). Don Lemon fielded a panel of experts in facial comparison, and sat them before a split screen of Rowan Lavery's high school graduation photo and a photo of Eli Absalom Stone at CPAC. Nobody dissented. And Alice Lavery, Rowan's sister, came tearing out of West Virginia, screaming bloody murder on CNN. "I know who you are!" she said, pointing menacingly into the camera. "I see you." She wanted a DNA test and she wanted her brother to come back to St. Albans, not just because she intended to beat him to a pulp, but because their father didn't have much time left. (Seeing his only son in permanent blackface would not be conducive to his health, either.)

Fox, which for years had delighted in Eli's quiet and incisive analysis, dealt with the revelations by reasserting the cultural significance of *Against Youth* and bemoaning the ways in which the Black community targeted its own role models.

"You have to hand it to this guy," said Rachel Maddow to Ephraim Western on the eighth day of his media phalanx. (Ephraim was notably more relaxed on camera than he'd been when the story broke. He wore a *Yale Daily News* T-shirt and looked as if he'd just rolled out of bed.) "I mean, the commitment! To make a decision like that, that you'll have to live with, your whole life."

"I don't disagree," Ephraim told her. "I'm only a couple of years older than he was then, and I can't see staking my whole life on a single decision right now. He must have felt it was worth it."

"At least until last week," Rachel Maddow said.

"And," said Ephraim, "we should also recognize, with race and self-identification, the picture gets less and less precise all the time. Thirty-five percent of African American men today have a white ancestor, and thirty percent of white Americans have a Black ancestor. I absolutely believe there's a role for self-identification, but do we want to walk around with a menu of our genetic components? I myself have a white father and a Black mother, but my Black mother's DNA is eight percent white, so does that make me fifty-four percent white and forty-five percent Black? I mean, life's too short! *I'm Ephraim. I identify as Black.* Okay?"

"But isn't that what Eli Absalom Stone did? *I'm Eli, I identify as Black.*"

"He never did, though. Not once, at least not on the record. He darkened his skin permanently so *you* identified him, then he castigated you for making assumptions about his race and his accomplishments. He built a post-racial platform on a racist lie. It was all a con. A very long and very sustained con. And who knows how long it would have continued?"

Eli Absalom Stone's publisher (still the same one, all the way back to *Against Youth*) had stopped shipment of his books (though whatever was already on the bookstore shelves sold out quickly), and his upcoming appearances at CPAC and the Conservative Partnership Institute were canceled. King's College, a Christian college in Manhattan, withdrew its offer of an honorary degree, and Harvard, initially befuddled, canceled Eli's Phi Beta Kappa speech, which was to have taken place the following June (though it took no action on his Harvard degree—how could it?). Even those who held fast to the embattled figure seemed unsure of what they were holding on to. When the Hayek Institute, in a rare public statement, insisted that its longtime member was a writer and thinker of rare gifts, who had lifted issues of race and philosophy to a new level of discourse in America, they were ridiculed, even by other conservative groups.

No response of any kind had come from Eli Absalom Stone himself. He had not been seen in public, according to the scrum around his Sutton Place apartment building. No one had seen him privately, either, except, possibly, for his great friend and coauthor, Harrison Oppenheimer, who lived close by. But he wasn't talking to the press, either.

By the time Ephraim completed his round-robin of media appearances he was seriously behind on his schoolwork in two classes and had lost five pounds from sheer adrenaline, but he'd also received offers to intern at the *Washington Post* and *Slate,* and he was ecstatic. (He had also received four death threats; that wasn't so good.) Stella, returning home from Los Angeles, found a nice potted geranium from one of her neighbors on Coffey Street, its accompanying note congratulating her on having such a remarkable son.

I could not have agreed more. I was ridiculously proud of Ephraim.

On the morning of our Harvard Club meeting, he picked me and Lewyn up in an Uber and we went in together, not saying much on the way. Lewyn, by then, was preoccupied by a number of things, but chiefly by the astonishing return of Rochelle Steiner to his life, sixteen years on and each of them now adult enough to at least recognize when they were behaving like idiots. A week earlier, seated at her brand-new (old) bright-green-and-chrome kitchen table, they had reached a fully mature decision to take things slowly, which meant that he would be waiting another month before moving into her apartment in Murray Hill and possibly two before proposing to endow her with all his worldly goods and otherworldly love. In the meantime, they'd been spending the weekends out in Ellesmere, reckoning with the flotsam and jetsam of Rochelle's excavated childhood. When that was over, and the cleaners were through with their work, and the painters with theirs, and even, at the advice of the Realtor, the stagers with theirs, Rochelle's childhood home would look like a house some other family might imagine as their own: a pretty place on a leafy cul-de-sac in a suburb with a good school district. It sold on the day of its open house.

Neither Lewyn nor I had ever entered the Harvard Club—technically, he had never even entered the Cornell Club, since the purpose of his sole visit, many years earlier, had been to board a bus parked outside—but Ephraim had indeed passed this way before, and he entertained us with an account of his Harvard interview on this very august site as we entered the lobby. He was talking a lot, we both noticed. He was nervous, obviously. In fact, he seemed far more nervous about meeting Harrison than any of his other siblings. And I suppose he had good reason for that.

Upstairs, we found our brother in a paneled conference room. Harrison said that he had ordered coffee before he said hello.

"Harrison," Lewyn responded, "this is our brother, Ephraim."

"Yes," said Harrison.

"I'm very happy to meet you," Ephraim said. He extended his hand. After a pause slightly too long to go unnoticed, Harrison shook it.

"Yes," he said again.

"Actually, I had my Harvard interview in this exact room," Ephraim tried again, clearly grasping.

"I certainly hope it doesn't hold a lingering unhappiness for you."

"What? Oh. No! I mean, I got into Harvard."

Harrison's mouth tightened. Lewyn and I, on the other hand, were trying not to laugh out loud.

"Okay, Harrison," said Lewyn, "you finally got a smart brother. Be happy."

"I never said you weren't smart," Harrison said to Lewyn.

"Oh no, just every day in every way. C'mon, we're not here to talk about that."

There was a knock on the door, and a waiter in a crimson uniform entered with the coffee.

"Well, you've been busy," Harrison said once he had left.

He meant Ephraim, obviously.

"Yes, but I'm going back to school this afternoon. I think it's over, at least until your friend decides to come out of hiding. I wonder if he will."

"It's up to him." Harrison stirred his coffee but showed no sign of actually drinking it.

"Certainly," Ephraim said.

"He doesn't owe anything to anyone."

"You think?" I said, with a laugh. I had to admit, I was completely loving this.

"I'm not sure any of our lives could withstand the kind of attention you've brought to bear on Eli."

"May I ask you something?" said Ephraim. "I'm sincerely interested. Fascinated, actually. What is it about him that earns your loyalty?"

Harrison glared at Ephraim. He glared at Lewyn, then at me. Then he seemed to recall that we were there to attempt some sort of progress.

"Eli is brilliant. An autodidact. A prodigy. And an original and important writer. He has been brave enough to take on some very difficult and complex issues. He personally represents a repudiation of ideas that are currently popular. He has also been immensely supportive of me since we were eighteen years old."

Ephraim was nodding. "All right. First, as I think you may have already accepted, or you're at least considering, his name is not Eli. He is not an autodidact. There may be bravery involved in what he's done; I'm open to that argument. But he can't personally be representing anything because his identity is a construct built on falsehoods. He's lied to every person who read his books, every person who has interviewed him, honored him, bought a ticket to one of his talks. And you. It may also be true that he's supported you as a friend. I can't speak to that. But if he was my friend, I'd be deeply discouraged and confused to find that I'd been lied to about so many things for such a long time."

Harrison shook his head. "Self-invention is a thoroughly American virtue. It always has been. We're a country of fabulists and seekers."

"Fabulists and seekers!" said Lewyn. "Why don't you just say fakes and charlatans? It's nothing to be proud of. Look," he attempted a conciliatory tone, "I can imagine you find this humiliating."

"I would *imagine* no such thing," Harrison snapped. "And let me clarify that just now I'm not thinking about myself at all. I'm thinking about my friend."

All four of us were quiet. Harrison aggressively stirred his coffee.

"Did you ever have any doubts?" said Ephraim.

Harrison sighed.

After a moment he said, "You intend to be a journalist, is that correct?"

Ephraim, surprised, said: "That's correct."

"Then you will understand what's meant by 'off the record.'"

"Certainly." He looked across the table at Lewyn and me. But we had no idea what Harrison was going to tell us, either.

"I had a call last night, from someone I haven't seen for years. To be honest, I haven't thought about him for years, either. He was a classmate of mine. And Eli's."

"At Harvard?"

"No. At Roarke. He and Eli had a . . . well, we can call it a conflict. And he left school, in the middle of the term. In the middle of the night, actually, as I recall. His name is Carlos. He's a professor of political science at the University of Chicago."

"Okay." Ephraim was doing his best not to show any excitement.

"He wanted to know if I believed him now."

"About what?" Lewyn said.

"Eli accused him of stealing something. Plagiarizing something of his. It was very serious. It was his word against Carlos's. It was very stressful for the community. I guess Carlos just . . . blinked first, and he withdrew from Roarke. At the time, I interpreted that to mean that he had actually done what Eli accused him of doing. He left and, I assumed, went on with his life somewhere else. Eli and I became good friends around that time. He invited me to come down to Hayek with him." He looked at Ephraim. "Obviously you are well-informed about Hayek. You've created an unprecedented crisis there."

"I have created nothing," Ephraim said defensively. "I have exposed something that already existed."

"Fine. Well. Carlos reminded me that he had been reading Eli's book, just before this happened. Reading it, and talking about it with some of the others. He told me last night that he'd never suspected anything. He thought the book was amazing and Eli was a genius. He was a fan. And then he was a pariah in our school. It affected him for many years, apparently. He said he was unable to reenter university. He had to give up his place at Princeton. He was hospitalized, he said, for depression. Eventually he managed to get back on track. I found it very awkward that he still wanted to reassure me he hadn't stolen from Eli. And, as I said, he asked if I believed him now."

"And what did you say?" Lewyn asked.

"I said I did. I felt I had to say that. But it might also be true." He looked at Ephraim again. "I reiterate. Off the record."

Ephraim nodded. "Understood."

"I think," said Harrison, "what happened was that I had made a choice. I had no reason not to believe that it was the correct choice. I still want it to have been the correct choice. Everything that came after that . . ." He stopped without ending.

We waited.

"Well, I think that's what I can say."

Lewyn and I looked at each other. It was as near to an admission of weakness as we had ever heard from Harrison. It was seismic.

"Harrison," Lewyn said. "I may never have understood the . . . appeal of this friend. Eli. I thought his ideas about people were rigid and punitive. And I sometimes . . . often . . . had a sense that he was, on some level, insincere, though obviously not to this extent. I don't think I'm especially insightful about people. I'm as shocked as anyone else by what Ephraim discovered. But I never once questioned the affection and the loyalty between the two of you."

After a moment, Harrison nodded.

"And, I want you to know, I respect those things. You and I have never been close, unfortunately, but you're still my brother. As far as I'm concerned, you're entitled to hold on to this relationship, if you want to. You don't owe anyone an explanation. You certainly don't owe me one. Of course, I'm always here if you, you know, want to talk."

Harrison was staring at him. After a while he managed a curt nod. "Okay," he said. He was trying to sound gruff. But he didn't look gruff.

"Me, too," said Ephraim suddenly.

"I just met you," Harrison said. "I don't know the first thing about you."

For a moment, Ephraim did not respond. Then he sat up very straight in his chair and placed his hands on the long wooden table before him. "My name is Ephraim Solomon Western. I am the son of Stella Western and Salo Oppenheimer. On one side, I'm descended from Joseph Süss Oppenheimer, who was a court Jew in Stuttgart, Germany, in the 1730s. On the other side, I'm descended from a man whose name I don't know, but I know what he cost in 1792, in South Carolina. I'd like us to be brothers. Well, we are brothers. But I'd like to know you as a brother."

"We're not starting off on the best of terms," said Harrison, locating, again, some of his essential rancor. "What happened between our father and your mother caused great unhappiness in our family. It affected all of us. The marriage never recovered. Our mother never recovered. She fixed on this idea about having another child, which was a crazy thing to do. Crazy and desperate. Do you remember how disgusted we were?" he asked Lewyn. "And Sally, too—it was one of the very few times we were all in agreement about something. Not that we ever talked about it. We should have talked about it."

"You're right about that," said Lewyn.

"I'm sorry, Phoebe," said Harrison. "I wouldn't want you to leave here associating the words 'crazy' and 'desperate' with your birth. But it was so unfair to you, bringing you into that."

"No worries," I shrugged. "Went right over my head at the time."

"I'm sorry, too," said Ephraim, as if he bore responsibility for any of it.

"Oh, I can get past it, I think," said Harrison. "It's not the biggest problem."

Ephraim sighed. "Okay. What else?"

"You were admitted to Harvard and chose to go to Yale. It's insupportable."

For a long moment no one made a sound, and then Lewyn, of all people, started to laugh. He laughed at his brother Harrison, and then his brother Ephraim joined him and they were both laughing. Finally, even Harrison broke, that infamous Fox News sneer faltering into some weird approximation of a smile.

I looked at the three of them, absurdly different in spite of their common denominator, laughing, trying to laugh, finally together.

Chapter Thirty-Six

The Big Reveal

In which the 10th of September is observed, and also the 11th, and the last of the Oppenheimers leaves home

Nine months later, in early September, the following people made their way to Martha's Vineyard: three about-to-be-thirty-six-year-old triplets and their eighteen-year-old college-bound sister (who was the exact same age as her siblings), as well as an additional brother who hadn't grown up with any of the others, and also Rochelle Steiner, who was about to get married on the same stretch of Chilmark beachfront she had once angrily vacated, promising herself that she would never, never, never associate herself with another person named Oppenheimer, no matter how common the name was.

Our mother did not make an easy adjustment to several of the ongoing developments in our growing, changing family, but at least she had a good long run at it. It took most of the spring to get her in the same room as Ephraim Western, the son of her late husband, but this was finally managed with my help and Lewyn's, not to speak of an excellent bottle of Merlot. (Our mother would never forgive Stella Western, which was deeply connected to the fact that she would never forgive our father, who, sadly, in any case, was no longer alive to be never forgiven, so that was one reconciliation nobody was agitating for.) But above all other things, what Johanna wanted today was what she had always wanted, and that was the company and love of her children, and for the first time since the birth of her triplets thirty-six years before, those three, and the later fourth, had formed and seemed to be sustaining bonds that looked, to her, very much like love. To us, they felt like love. Also, to be blunt about it, we were all hanging out without her. All of us. Even the ones who had reliably disliked one another since birth.

We made her join us. And once she did, we made her let go of many things.

One of the first things our mother gave up was the Rizzolis. There was no great drama about their "disappearance" in her own view, mainly because, to her, they had never "disappeared" in the first place. Leaving her for Stella Western had literally cost Salo his life, and yet only a year afterward Johanna was locked in deeply upsetting negotiations with this person. One day in the midst of all that, she'd been driven out to Red Hook with Mr. Evan Rosen of the law firm Burke Goldman Finn & Emerson, and the appraiser. The appraiser had been dumbstruck, it was fair to say, and she had left him to his professional duties and private excitement and walked around the warehouse on her own, reacquainting herself with a few of the works she remembered: the orange scribbled one, the mustard-colored one with the green stripe, the bad-fairy triptych that had overseen her unwieldy pregnancy. This visit to Red Hook, our mother's first ever, was also notable for a number of things completely unrelated to art, however. First, she finally understood that Salo's warehouse was not located anywhere near Coney Island, and second, she had the indelible experience of actually seeing, from one of the warehouse's upper windows, the small house at the end of the street where her late husband had lived his other life. In its backyard, a woman in long dreadlocks was throwing a ball to a five- or six-year-old boy. A couple of years had passed since Johanna had last seen them at the bookstore on Court Street, and the boy was obviously bigger. He still looked like Lewyn, though.

She was reeling, then, a few minutes later, when the appraiser called her attention to this distinct collection of pictures in a room of their own. To him, they were not very important (in fact, they might well belong to the genre now being referred to as "Outsider") and, compared to the treasures downstairs (Bacon! Twombly! Marden!), they were a bit of an incongruity. Did she know anything about them?

She did. She knew immediately that they were by the artist who turned people into buildings, the one her late husband's mistress had described over dinner, many years before. And she also knew they were important to that woman, because the query sent from Stella Western's attorney to hers had laid it all out: an entire collection of drawings which Stella Western said should belong to her, because Salo had given them to her, or bought them for her, or intended them for her, or some such devastating thing. They caused our mother pain, those pictures. A great deal of pain. And so she had sent them away. It was not a devious or even a complicated gesture. It was not strategic. It was not even particularly rational. She wanted them out, and she wanted them out immediately.

A mover was called on the spot. Hours later the nearly entire catalog of works by Achilles Rizzoli was safe in its new home, a very ordinary storage locker in Queens, indistinguishable from the many thousands of equally ordinary storage lockers in Queens in which spatially challenged New Yorkers stashed the things they didn't want to think about. And Johanna didn't think about the drawings again, not for many years. Not until that first letter from the American Folk Art Museum arrived.

Lewyn and I went with Stella to the facility in Woodside, and we tried to stay back as she was reunited with the pictures, one by one, after so long, but she kept calling us to look: *The Kathredal, The Sayanpeau, The Mother Tower of Jewels.* Technically it all belonged to Stella—our mother, having forced herself to confront this particular difficulty, had given it all away and this time she *truly* did not want to think of it again. Stella had everything moved to the American Folk Art Museum to be assessed and fawned over in advance of the exhibition that fall, but she also wanted each of Salo's kids to have a picture of their own. Harrison declined, but Lewyn requested *The Kathredal* to remain in the Oppenheimer Collection. Ephraim chose one of the schematics for Rizzoli's imagined city, *Yield to Total Elation,* and I asked for the sign Rizzoli had hand-lettered for his yearly exhibition.

ACHILLES TECTONIC EXHIBIT
ADMISSION .10c

I'm not sure why. I guess it just spoke to me.

Sally, graciously, turned down the offer. She said she had never gotten over her first encounter with Outsider Art.

Stella was deeply fond of Lewyn, and she thought Rochelle was a wondrous firecracker, small like herself but coiled to spring. She thanked them for their wedding invitation but she wanted Johanna to be able to enjoy the day completely (having Ephraim there was going to be challenging enough). Still, everyone got invited to a screening of her Rizzoli film that June, and Harrison actually did go to that. Harrison would never be easy with Stella, but he drew upon his native dignity and considerable charm to make their points of contact as tolerable as they could conceivably be. On the other hand, he did come to greatly respect his brother Ephraim. The departure of Eli Absalom Stone from his life (from everyone's life, in fact) had left a void that was obvious even to him; in Ephraim, who started at the *Times* after graduation, he at least found a person he considered capable of engaging with him on intellectual matters. The two of them fell into the routine of a weekly breakfast, alternating (for the sake of principle) between the Harvard and Yale clubs, and no one was more surprised by that than, actually, both of them.

The business with Sally wasn't particularly straightforward, either, but we all got there eventually. Sally, still in dogged pursuit of her therapy goals, was doing a lot of internal excavating of her own, and with just about every member of her family. She cried a lot with me when we worked together in Ithaca that summer, and she cried with our mother when Johanna came up to visit us in late July. She cried when Stella forgave her for following Salo to Henry Darger's opening-night party at the museum (though Stella kept insisting there was nothing to forgive), and she cried each time she introduced another member of her family to her partner, Paula, a woman who (like Lewyn's former roommate, the first Mormon he'd ever met) had come from far away to Ithaca, New York, in order to become a vet (large animal).

Ironically, to me at least, she never cried on the job, not even when a house we were working on was itself choked with sadness. I learned pretty quickly that I didn't share my sister's remarkable ability to wade into muck, to shovel years of layers of unspeakable detritus into plastic bags, nor to deal calmly and professionally with the embittered families that always seemed to surround (and sometimes, unfathomably, live in) these houses. I spent most of that summer becoming acquainted with a broad range of filth (and taking long showers at night, as hot as I could stand, to wash it away), and getting to know Paula, and working my way through the reading list Roarke had sent (to redress some of the lacunae it had identified in my Walden education). At the beginning of September, I flew to the Vineyard to help our mother get things ready.

The woman I found when I got to the cottage was a person I had not yet had the pleasure of meeting: her hair was longer, her clothes were looser, and there was an utterly unfamiliar look of calm on her face. The hug she gave me when I got out of the taxi was entirely without agenda, as far as I could tell. Somewhat to my own surprise, I hugged her back.

"Are you thirsty?" Johanna said. "I made some iced tea this morning. With PG Tips."

"Wow," I said. "Thank you."

There was a pile of yarn in a basket on the floor beside the staircase that looked as if it wanted very much to be a sweater of some kind. "Is that . . ." I said, gobsmacked.

"I'm taking a knitting class in Edgartown," Johanna said, picking it up. "This sweater was going to be for me, but something's gone wrong, and it's going to end up tiny. I'd better give it to Rochelle."

I could only gape at her. "Well . . . that's . . ."

"Oh I know, I know," my mother laughed. "Don't worry, I'm fully aware. It's just fun. 'Stitch and Bitch,' they call it. And the group's only about half summer people."

She said "summer people" as if she weren't one, herself.

"That's cool, Mom. I think Rochelle will be really touched."

"And then I'll make one for you! You're going to need something warm in that ridiculous place, while you're milking the goats."

She had not lost her disdain for Roarke, she'd been very clear about that. "Great," I said.

I took my things upstairs. My room was the one at the end of the corridor, the one our father had once used as an office. There was still a desk from Salo's time, but Johanna had cleared everything else out one July when I was away at camp, and I'd returned to the current arrangement of yellow calico bedspread and a pair of squat pink armchairs. It wasn't attractive, necessarily, but it was summer.

"Phoebe," Johanna called, "I'm out on the back porch."

"Okay," I yelled back.

It was around three in the afternoon. From my window I could see a mother and a little kid far down the beach, both of them slathered with white sunblock, standing about ten feet above the waterline. Every time a wave came in the two of them went bouncing down to touch it, then turned and ran back to the same spot. The wind and the water took away the sound of their laughter, but I watched them do it again and again, the activity somehow every bit as entertaining the tenth time as the first. Then I finished stacking my books on the bedside table and stowed my bag in the closet and went downstairs.

My mother had the tea out, a pitcher and a glass of ice. She had the book section of the *Times* open on her lap, and was on her phone, typing with her thumbs. "It's sweetened, just a little," she said.

"Thank you," I said, surprised that she remembered not just what tea I liked, but how I liked it. I poured myself a glass and sat in one of the old Adirondack chairs. The chairs had always been there, in exactly the same spot. They were as hard and unpleasant to sit on as ever.

"Sorry, just need a sec," Johanna said, without looking up. "The florist wants to know how we feel about black-eyed Susans."

"Oh. Well, how do we feel?"

"I think we feel okay. The only thing Rochelle asked me was nothing red.

She doesn't like red. Well, I don't like red, myself. Okay." She finished and set down her phone. "I think we got lucky with the flowers. The florist is the sister-in-law of the woman who runs the knitting shop."

"Oh," I said. "Well, that's good. Rochelle must have a lot of faith in you."

"I think it's more likely she doesn't much care about wedding minutiae in general. She's not doing a lot of overthinking. She's wearing her mother's wedding dress, you know."

I nodded. I'd personally seen Rochelle's mother's wedding dress come out of a Tupperware container last fall. That it was wearable might say a great deal about the enduring genius of Tupperware, or it might say something else about the value of a good dry cleaner. But mostly it said something about Rochelle.

"Would you like to stay in for dinner?" Johanna asked. "I have some salmon and some corn. Or we could go out."

"Oh. Either," I said. I couldn't remember the last time my mother had cooked for the two of us. This seemed so noteworthy that I decided to say it aloud.

"When's the last time you cooked for the two of us?"

Johanna frowned. "A long time, I suppose."

"Like, a really long time. Did you cook when the triplets were growing up?"

"Well, some," Johanna said. "We had Gloria full-time then, and she cooked. She made wonderful lasagna. I know you think you missed out on a lot of important stuff, but don't worry, you didn't miss much with my cooking."

I smiled. I could feel the late sun on my legs. A not-unpleasant moment passed that way. Then I heard her say: "Did you ever wonder why it took us so long to have you? You never asked about it."

Well. I took a breath. It occurred to me that I ought to be paying very close attention now. This remarkable opportunity—already I understood that it was an opportunity, and it was remarkable—might not come around again.

"Was I supposed to ask? Or were you just supposed to, you know, tell me?"

My mother didn't respond right away. She was holding up her misshapen knitting project, examining some dropped stitch or knot in the wrong place.

"Look," I finally said, "if this is it, if this is going to be the big reveal, you can spare yourself. I know it already. There were four of us. Dr. Lorenz Pritchard, of sainted memory, randomly picked the others to get born and me to go into the freezer. Seventeen years in liquid nitrogen. I guess I ought to thank you for remembering me."

My mother was staring at me. "Which one of your siblings told you that?"

I shrugged. "It was kind of a joint effort. And in case you're wondering, I know why, too. I'm pretty sure I know everything. And it wasn't *We might as well,* either."

"'We might as well'?" Johanna said, mystified.

"I heard you say that, to Aunt Debbie. You were in the living room together. I think you'd had a root canal or something. *We had the embryo, we could afford it, why not?* Frankly, Mom, and I wanted to say this to you at the time, *We might as well* is not a good enough reason to bring a child into the world. But of course, as I eventually discovered, it happened to be completely untrue. So we never had that particular talk."

Johanna, maddeningly, did not respond.

"I heard you say it. Not making it up."

"Oh, I believe you," my mother sighed. "People say things. It doesn't make them true. And there are plenty of things I haven't seen fit to confide in my sister. We were never close, you know. And I was never close to my brother, either. They both saw me as utterly irrelevant to their lives, which wasn't a great start." She thought for a moment. Then she said, "I just realized, that doesn't even hurt anymore. I seem to have gotten past it. I wonder when that happened."

I just looked at her.

"I've tried to understand it all. Not a job for the faint of heart, I can tell you."

Then I understood. "You've been seeing a therapist."

"I have. Since last spring. Sally's idea. She thought I needed to look at some of the stuff I've been very deliberately *not* looking at, for a very long time. A tendency she shares, by the way. Sally is much more like me than you or the boys, I'm sorry to say. She spent years determined not to know that she was gay, and then more years determined not to accept it. I think Paula's the first person she's really been able to love. I don't know how much of that I'm responsible for. I hope not all of it."

"Oh, I'm sure not," I said. I was really looking at Johanna now. This was a different Johanna.

"I started with someone in Brooklyn, last April, but I just hated it. I would come home afterward and get into bed for hours. But I decided to try again when I got to the island in June. I found a wonderful woman out near Menemsha. So yes. A bit overdue, I would say, but yes."

I wasn't sure what form of acknowledgment was appropriate for this kind of revelation. Finally, I settled on: "Good for you."

"Yes. Good for me. Hopefully not too late for me to enjoy my life and my children."

"Oh no, I don't think so!" I paused. "Haven't you?"

"What?"

"Enjoyed your life," I said. "And your children."

"Well, I certainly intended to. I certainly worked hard at it. Things took an unexpected turn, and you know, after that I didn't think too much about enjoyment."

"You're referring to the fact that Dad's plane crashed into a building?"

"Well, no," Joanna said. "If I'm being completely honest, I'm referring to the fact that he got on that plane in the first place. The night before he left, he told me he was ending our marriage. The kids were all in pieces. We'd just had a terrible scene down on the beach. Maybe Sally or one of the boys has filled you in on that. Or Rochelle, for that matter. I don't think any of them really spoke for years afterward, beyond the absolutely necessary. You know what?" she said, suddenly. "I'm going to get rid of these chairs. I hate these chairs. They are so uncomfortable. I want to sit out here and read and look at the beach, and I want nice chairs to sit in."

I couldn't think what to say. I certainly agreed about the chairs.

"I know I'm supposed to tell you that he wasn't leaving you, he was leaving me, but in this case I don't think that's actually true. He was leaving both of us. He'd have been leaving all of us if your sister and brothers weren't technically already gone. The truth is he hadn't wanted another child. Or at least, another child with me. I'm not sure he'd wanted any children with me. I basically told him, with the older ones: *We're doing this,* and he went along. And then with you I did the same thing again. I'd just found out about Stella. I'd just found out they had a child together. I might not have been in my right mind at that particular moment. I'm sorry, I know that's hardly going to make you feel better about the circumstance of your birth."

"Oh, Mom," I managed to say.

"Well, here's the thing. I don't think your father was a bad guy. I think, in his own mind, he wasn't programmed for happiness, so he didn't look for it and he didn't expect it. And then he suddenly *was* happy, and when that happened it had absolutely nothing to do with me or any of our children. Well," she shook her head, "*there's* a revelation to take the wind out of your sails."

It had taken something to get this said, I realized. A massive something. I tried to feel resentful on my own behalf, that my father hadn't wanted either to have me or to stay with me, but I finally just couldn't. This wasn't new information, what my mother had just said. Not really. But getting it into words and out into the world—that was new.

"We know about the accident," I told her, and she said nothing. In fact, she barely moved. "We know about Stella being there, in the car with him. I can understand why he never told Sally and the boys, but I can't understand why *you* didn't tell them. Or me. It might have helped us understand, you know, who he was and why he made the choices he made. I feel as if my first clear picture of him was after I found out. He must have been in so much pain, and felt so guilty."

"I hope you're not implying I was unsympathetic to that," Johanna said sharply.

"No," I said, slightly taken aback. "I don't think that at all."

"Because I spent years of my life obsessing about your father's pain and his guilt, and everything I was powerless to alleviate for him."

"Okay," I said, carefully.

"And I might not have done that if I'd known about Stella. Everything about Stella. I had no idea. I just thought she was some struggling filmmaker who'd gotten her hooks into him, and destroyed our family. I even talked to our attorney about protecting us, financially, but he advised me not to do anything. After your father died, of course, we had to make a settlement with her, but now I can see how much better it would have been if I'd known from the beginning who she was in his life and what she meant, but he only told me that last night, before he died." She shook her head. "He should have told me everything when he met her again. Certainly before we brought you into it."

"What?" I said, catching up.

"But then you wouldn't have been born. So I can't be sorry, because we had you. And I loved you. I'm sorry you never got the functioning, happy family. You should have had that. To be honest, I'm not sure the others got it either, and they deserved it just as much. And I'm also sorry you ever felt you were born too late, but I think you were wrong about that. I think you were born at the exact right time, and I have a feeling your sister and brothers would agree. You're not some random person we were all saddled with, you know. You were their missing piece, and they owe you a lot. All of them. All of *us*."

I drank the rest of my tea. I could not think of one more thing I didn't know that I wanted to know. That was an unprecedented and extraordinary feeling.

"Thanks," I finally said.

"You're welcome," my mother said. Then, a moment later, she said: "Something else I want to get off my chest."

Well shit, I thought. *So close.* I had no idea what might be coming now.

"I threw my wedding dress away. I've been thinking about it ever since

Rochelle told me she was wearing her mother's dress. I got rid of a lot of things like that. Photographs, some of your father's belongings. I did get very angry at one point, and also, that was around the same time I was probably thinking Sally would never need a wedding dress of any kind."

I smiled with relief. "Actually, I think you might get the whole shooting match with Sally. Wedding, babies, everything. But I don't see her in a wedding dress, you're right."

"I should have been thinking about you, though. I apologize. Actually, why don't you do me a favor and take a single apology for everything at once, spare me having to give you an itemized list. I stipulate to everything."

I shook my head. "I've hardly led a deprived life, Mom."

"In most ways, no. But I could have done better. And not just with you. Which is ironic, since making my family happy is pretty much all I've thought about for the past four decades. There's a lesson there, probably."

"Is there? What is it? Secure your own oxygen mask first?"

Johanna considered. "Maybe. Yes." She picked up her proto-sweater again and looked at it. Then she put it to the side.

"I think we should stay in tonight," she said. "Plenty of excitement when people start arriving the next couple days. Let's just take it easy."

I nodded. "Let's. Good."

From across the dune, we heard a dog barking, one of the neighbor's schnauzers.

"I'm thinking about staying on for the fall," my mother said suddenly. "Maybe longer. Apart from the years before you entered preschool, it'll be the first September since 1986 that I won't have a child at Walden. Maybe it's time to see what autumn looks like somewhere else. Why not here?"

I looked at her. "What about the house?"

"I thought I might offer it to Lewyn and Rochelle. Her place is fine for a single person who works all the time, but it reminds me of the apartment your father and I lived in when we were married, on Third Avenue. They should have something beautiful to start their lives together. And if they have children they're going to need the room. I can use the basement apartment if I come back for something, or just to visit. I don't think Harrison would ever want to live in that house, and I don't think Sally's leaving Ithaca. But would it be all right with you? It's your home, after all."

"It's *our* home." I smiled at her. "So yes. So long as they let me stay when I come back for vacations."

"That school of yours hardly takes vacations, if I'm remembering," my mother said. "I can't believe I'm losing another of my children to a flock of chickens."

I chose to leave this comment alone.

The others began to drift in over the following days, by which time most of the details had been settled: black-eyed Susans, and the wine, and beds for every one of Salo's children and—where pertinent—their partners, and a Klezmer band from Woods Hole. I finished the last of my Roarke reading list. Lewyn and Harrison took their brother for a walk through the Camp Meeting Grounds in Oak Bluffs and an impromptu ride on the Flying Horses (where Ephraim managed to grab one more brass ring than Harrison). Johanna hired Lobster Tales to come and cater the rehearsal dinner on the tenth, which was also the triplets' birthday, though she did acknowledge certain humiliating associations with this plan. (In fact, the proprietors of Lobster Tales had not forgotten the family debacle of seventeen years earlier. But they were professionals. And besides, they did the best clambakes on the island—that was just a fact.) The following morning, Lewyn and Rochelle were married near the still-warm ashes by a rabbi from the Hebrew Center of Vineyard Haven, and the anniversary of Salo's death became, as well, the anniversary of his son Lewyn's great ongoing happiness. So life goes.

Some of them left quickly after that. Paula had classes starting at Cornell, and Rochelle had a trial beginning later in the week, and Ephraim, new in his job and frantic to maintain a good impression, rushed back to the *Times*. The rest of us—all three of the Oppenheimer triplets, and our mother, and myself, of course—remained. There was another dinner on the back porch—too many leftover lobsters, too many ears of corn—and a day in Edgartown, laying in a year's supply of PG Tips and procuring a pair of heavy work boots, which Harrison insisted I would need. The next morning, still together, we departed: to the ferry, and the mainland, and north to the parking lot of an old diner in Concord, New Hampshire, where the last of the Oppenheimers met her bus and held her family—most of her family—close, and then let them go.

Acknowledgments

I'm grateful to Professor Yair Mintzk, author of *The Many Deaths of Jew Süss,* for speaking to me about Joseph Oppenheimer, who was quite real and the subject of the also quite real (unfortunately) Goebbels-instigated propaganda film, *Jud Süss.* Joseph Oppenheimer did have one daughter who died in infancy, but there were no living descendants. Achilles Rizzoli was also quite real, and, while he certainly languished in the Outsider Art shadow of Henry Darger (who didn't?), he was the subject of a book (*A. G. Rizzoli: Architect of Magnificent Visions* by Jo Farb Hernandez), a documentary (*Yield to Total Elation: The Life and Art of Achilles Rizzoli* by Pat Ferrero), and a major 1998 exhibition at New York's Museum of American Folk Art. (I have played with the date of that exhibition, as I have with the museum's landmark Henry Darger exhibition.) Rizzoli's great champion has always been Bonnie Grossman of the former Ames Gallery in Berkeley, California.

Thank you to Avi Steinberg, author of *The Lost Book of Mormon: A Quest for the Book That Just Might Be the Great American Novel,* required reading for Jews with LDS fixations (we know who we are). I merely went to see the Hill Cumorah pageant five times, but he . . . well, you'll have to read his book to find out what he did. Thank you to Steve Martin for helping create Salo Oppenheimer's fantasy art collection, to Tina Fallon for being my Red Hook guide, to Lynn Novick for answering my documentary film questions, and to Akash Mehta for talking to me about Deep Springs (which did not inspire Roarke, obviously). Other thanks to Princeton professors Eric Griffith and Gideon Rosen for helping me sound smarter than I am, to Donna Seftel for sharing her Cornell memories, and to Dr. Jessica R. Brown, for reproductive endocrinological expertise. (Readers familiar with the history of assisted fertility may have noted that the first successful gestational surrogacies took place in 1985, three years after Dr. Lorenz Pritchard suggested the procedure to the Oppenheimers.)

Thanks, as always and forever, to my brilliant friend Deborah Michel; to Helen Eisenbach; to Suzanne Gluck, Andrea Blatt, Nina Iandolo, Tracy Fisher, Anna DeRoy and everyone at WME; to Deb Futter, Jamie Raab, Randi Kramer, Rachel Chou, Anna Belle Hindenlang, Jennifer Jackson, Christine Mykityshyn, Jaime Noven, and Anne Twomey at Celadon; and to my ridiculously supportive family and friends.

This novel is dedicated to Leslie Vought Kuenne, who loved her own complicated family and always planted more daffodils. I miss her every day.

Founded in 2017, Celadon Books, a division of Macmillan Publishers, publishes a highly curated list of twenty to twenty-five new titles a year. The list of both fiction and nonfiction is eclectic and focuses on publishing commercial and literary books and discovering and nurturing talent.